PERSIAN
HORSE

PERSIAN HORSE

MARC IVERSON

ORION BOOKS / NEW YORK

This is a work of fiction. Nothing is intended or should be interpreted as expressing or representing the views of the United States Navy or any other department or agency of any governing body.

Published by Orion Books, a division of Crown Publishers, Inc., 201 East 50th Street, New York, New York 10022. Member of the Crown Publishing Group.

ORION and colophon are trademarks of Crown Publishers, Inc.

Manufactured in the United States of America

Library of Congress Cataloging-in-Publication Data
Iverson, Marc.
Persian horse : a novel / by Marc Iverson. —1st ed.
p. cm.
I. Title.
PS3559.V433P47 1991
813'.54—dc20   90-22051
CIP
ISBN 0-517-58310-0

1 3 5 7 9 10 8 6 4 2

First Edition

FOR DELORES,

Whose patience, love, and skill
made this a better book,
and me a better writer.

ACKNOWLEDGMENTS

I would like to express my sincere gratitude to several very special individuals for their help on *Persian Horse*.

For his counsel in all matters relating to the U.S. Navy and the nature of command of a ship in wartime in the Persian Gulf, I would like to thank Captain James A. Hooper, IV, USN. I am also indebted to the officers and men who served in USS *Rentz* (FFG-46) from 1987 to 1988: they were the inspiration for this novel.

To my agents, George and Olga Wieser, thank you for your confidence in me and for placing my book in such capable hands.

For my editors, James O'Shea Wade and Stephen Topping, a special thanks for their incisive analysis and recommendations, and for showing a rookie the ropes.

Thanks to my brother, Andrew, a writer who taught me a great deal about the essence of drama and the nature of character.

To my parents, Jack and Shirley Iverson, thank you for giving me the love of books and writing, and for your tremendous support throughout the writing process.

Lastly a salute to Master Chief Gunner's Mate (SW) David A. Baker, USN, a shipmate who saw the danger.

PERSIAN
HORSE

Prologue

USS BULKELEY
THE PERSIAN GULF

"General Quarters! General Quarters! All hands man your battle stations—this is not a drill!" The urgent call of the Bosun's Mate echoed throughout the steel-hulled frigate, accompanied by a rhythmic metallic gong.

The *Bulkeley*'s Captain entered the ship's Combat Information Center on the run. He crossed the rapidly filling CIC with a few quick strides to stand beside his tactical action officer.

"What have you got, Weps?" The Captain was puffing heavily from his race up the three decks from an engineering space, but his voice held a reassuring tone of professional calm.

John Stewart, the *Bulkeley*'s tactical action officer, replied without lifting his eyes from the large data console before him. "Three Bogies inbound from Bandar Abbas at . . ."—he paused to depress a button on the console; the range of the inbound aircraft appeared immediately on an information window above the screen—"forty-two miles. Speed four-fifty, altitude angels ten."

"Sqwawk?" the Captain asked quickly, referring to the IFF, Identification Friend or Foe, signal transmitted by all aircraft when interrogated by equipment on board the *Bulkeley*.

"One of them appeared to show a COMAIR sqwawk just after they lifted off, but they were mixed in with the regular commercial traffic out of Bandar. None of them are responding to interrogation now. They started off in the COMAIR corridor to Dubai and then turned due west toward us."

The Captain studied Stewart's console to verify for himself that the delta formation of aircraft was indeed clear of the commercial air corridor electronically marked on the display.

"They've refused to acknowledge our warnings all the way, Captain," Stewart said, sensing the Captain's thoughts. "We're continuing to transmit them on international and military air distress." He switched the communications toggle on his console to reply to a call from another station in the Combat Information Center. "TAO, aye . . . stand by." For the first time, Stewart shifted his attention from his console and turned to face the Captain. "We have fire control lock-on at thirty-four miles."

The Captain nodded without answering Stewart, his gaze remaining fixed on the amber images of the approaching aircraft.

"Captain; XO. Zebra set throughout the ship," came a metallic voice from the intercom over Stewart's console.

The Captain reached up and toggled the intercom. "Captain, aye."

"Still no response to warnings, Captain," Stewart said, "and they should have detected our fire control by now. The leader is at twenty-six miles."

"Light 'em up," the Captain said harshly.

"Weapons Control; TAO. Illuminate the leader," Stewart quickly ordered.

The continuous wave illuminator of the *Bulkeley*'s long-range fire control radar crackled into electronic life and focused an intense beam of energy on the lead aircraft of the oncoming formation. The powerful illuminator would be used to guide the *Bulkeley*'s Standard missiles to their target, acting like an awesomely powerful flashlight, whose energy reflecting off the aircraft would serve as a homing beacon.

"CWI illuminated, Captain. But they're still coming." Stewart and the Captain watched as the range of the aircraft ominously continued to drop. "There's no way the leader is not seeing the CWI," Stewart said with certainty.

"White Bird on the rail," the Captain ordered, a note of tension creeping into his voice for the first time. At his words, all conversation in the CIC ceased, leaving the space silent but for the hum of electronics. Every man in the Combat Information Center realized that this was it; they were going to shoot.

On the *Bulkeley*'s fo'c'sle the machinery of the missile launcher rumbled into operation. The hatch below the single massive rail of the launcher ratcheted open with a mechanical clank, and a lone white missile raced up the rail from the magazine below. With equal speed, all ten tons of the launcher pirouetted to the right, the missile rail swinging from its vertical stowed position to an angle roughly forty-five degrees off the deck. Once in position, the launcher continued to make minor adjustments to its posture to maintain track on the incoming aircraft.

"Missile on the rail and tuned, Captain," Stewart called out. "Target range, twenty-two miles."

"Stand by for batteries released," the Captain said, his low voice loud in the nearly silent Combat Information Center.

"I have the starboard trailing aircraft in a turn!" an air tracker called out excitedly from across the CIC.

Stewart and the Captain leaned forward over the TAO console, scrutinizing the small amber symbols for any confirmation of the operator's report. And there it was: first the starboard trailing aircraft, then the leader, and finally the port trailing aircraft began a slow turn to starboard.

"Turned north," the Captain said with a matter-of-factness he did not feel. "Probably a raid on the Iraqi coast trying to come in from an unexpected direction."

"The bastards certainly waited long enough," Stewart said. "They were just outside twenty miles when they turned."

"They were just outside hell when they turned," the Captain said gruffly, returning to his command voice. "Reload the bird in the magazine, but keep those assholes locked up until they fly out of range." Without waiting for Stewart's response he turned from the console and stalked out of the Combat Information Center.

1

ABU MUSA ISLAND
THE EASTERN PERSIAN GULF

Aziz stared out into the summer sandstorm that enveloped the Gulf in a choking shroud of grit. The storm filtered the sun's rays into a hazy, white glare that was mirrored by the water's surface, and low, poorly defined waves gave the Gulf the static look of a broad inland lake. Aziz knew that while deceptively inviting in appearance, the waters of the Gulf averaged one hundred degrees Fahrenheit at this time of year and would provide no relief from the steaming oven above.

The gently sloping beach and white-blue water on the eastern coast of the island could have passed for the Mexican Riviera or the shores of the Gulf of Thailand. Anywhere else in the world this beach would be speckled with overcooked, overfed tourists, Aziz thought to himself. He allowed himself an all but imperceptible smile at the contrast between that image and the current occupiers of the beach.

Sipping a cup of strong tea from the thermos at his feet, he watched his men silently go about their work. They had driven the two large Mercedes trucks to the water's edge an hour ago, and the unloading was progressing smoothly. There were many new faces among the group. Perhaps too many for a mission such as this, he thought. But he had either trained the new ones himself or trusted the men who had. No, he realized, what bothered him about the new men was the memory of those they had replaced. The lucky ones were in hospitals, the less fortunate in shallow graves along the border with Iraq.

Major Barzin Aziz appeared younger than his thirty-five years. The ten years of combat service had been kind to him in that regard, if in no other. He was a compact man of medium height with a muscled neck and broad shoulders that his baggy black uniform did not disguise. The close-cropped ebony beard that framed his face highlighted the sharply etched features of his Indo-European ancestry, and the light dusting of gray in the beard was his only concession to age. Although Aziz's face appeared free from concern, the intense black eyes that dominated it missed nothing.

He swung his gaze to the low hill on the beach's southern flank. After a moment, he was able to pick out the marine in camouflage uniform, whom he had placed on the hill to keep watch on the fishing village that lay beyond the rise. That sentry was the only member of Aziz's party in traditional military attire; the Major and the twelve men unloading the trucks were all clad from boot to throat in loose black cotton fatigues. Any weapons they possessed were not visible.

The growl of a diesel engine announced the arrival of another truck from the direction of the permanent Iranian Navy base on Abu Musa.

Aziz poured his remaining tea into the sand, resealed the thermos, and steeled himself to greet the arriving party. The ancient diesel truck drove onto the beach and slid its way toward him, geysers of sand erupting from its tires. Even as the truck was braking to stop, a number of its occupants were leaping off in macho display. The new arrivals were dressed in a hodgepodge of civilian trousers, boots, and military blouses, no two alike. The ragtag force was heavily armed, with M-16s and MP5 carbines much in evidence. Aziz's men ignored the noisy arrival.

"Allahu Akbar, Major!" A tall, heavily bearded man had separated from the group and was striding toward Aziz. The man moved with the assurance of one used to command, and his pounding gait seemed to attack the sand under his feet. He was broad of frame, with the heavy look of an athlete who has let his muscles begin to fade. The man's coal black beard flowed from a face that appeared to be set in a permanent, humorless smile. As the newcomer came to a halt in front of Aziz, the Major's eyes were drawn to the white turban that crowned the man's head. The white turban was usually reserved for the mullahs.

"Allahu Akbar, Zade Kalil." Aziz smoothly shifted his focus from the man's headgear back to his face. His tone was distinctly neutral.

"It is *Colonel* Kalil, Major. You do not remember from the briefing?"

Slight intended, slight taken, Aziz thought. "It was my understanding that the Guards had forsworn officers. Do they not look to their local mullahs as their commanders?" Aziz asked mildly.

Kalil colored visibly, a darkness replacing his previous smile. "There are no mullahs here, Major. The Revolutionary Guards Command has assigned me the rank of Colonel for this operation. You will remember that."

Aziz turned to face the sea. This was going to be even worse than he had anticipated. "And *I* am in tactical command of this operation, *Colonel*," he said. "You will remember that."

The Revolutionary Guards commander seemed momentarily uncertain how to respond. He gestured threateningly towards Aziz, starting to protest. "But I—"

"Have your men report to my Sergeant Major to receive proper uniform. I rely on you to control them and ensure they execute their portion of the plan."

"You have no need of concern there, Major. They . . ." But Aziz had turned and was walking away, headed down the superheated sand toward the trucks.

The insolence of the man! Kalil thought. His eyes narrowed as he watched the retreating back of the marine officer. Reflexively, his hand went to his belt to draw the pistol that was usually there. He had set it aside when he observed at the briefing that he was the only "senior" officer who was armed.

Well, that was all to the good, he thought, as he forced himself to cool his rage. Killing the military team leader at this stage would hardly be prudent, no matter how justified.

The Supreme Guards Command had been wise to see that Revolutionary Guards participation in this mission was essential, both to ensure that the Islamic Republic's interests were best served and to receive proper credit when the operation was a success.

Ordinarily, Kalil would not have personally headed up the Guards component in such an operation; he viewed freedom from exposure to the actual dangers of combat as one of the privileges of his rank. There were plenty of Guards anxious to reap the rewards of the martyred warrior, and he was only too pleased to give them the opportunity. He had not survived the length of this on-again, off-again war and risen as high as he had by taking dangerous risks. But a man who aspired to the Supreme Guards Command had to take on the occasional high-profile assignment. Kalil had recognized this mission as the achievement that would catapult him into the ranks of the Supreme Command. If he had to tolerate a certain element of physical danger, as well as the presence of the hated marines, it was a small price to pay.

Kalil longed to have the "professional" military removed from his southern Gulf area of jurisdiction. Let these marines join their brothers in pursuit of holy martyrdom along the five-hundred-mile northern front with Iraq, he thought, and leave missions such as this to the Guards. The Iranian Navy had never truly recovered from its earlier engagements with the Americans during the Tanker War, and now his gunboats were proving every bit as effective in the attacks against the tankers as the larger ships of the navy.

I will tolerate this only as long as necessary, he decided. When we complete this venture it will be a Guards triumph, and the marines need not be there to share in the glory.

Satisfied with his decision, Kalil strode down the beach to join the others.

USS BULKELEY

The dense curtain of billowing sand veiled the Gulf in an oppressive fog. Fishermen at work in small, open boats in the eastern Gulf cursed the sandstorm as they cast their ancient nets. The poor visibility made their work, already difficult in the heavily trafficked Gulf, far more dangerous. They knew that at any time the giant form of a ship might take shape out of the sandstorm, close aboard to their craft. The monster bulk of a supertanker would appear where a moment before there had been nothing, and in another moment it would be swallowed back up by the storm. Many fishing dhows had been lost in this fashion, smashed to kindling by the giant ships, which seldom even knew they had run over the smaller craft. The merchant ships had radar to find each other in the sandstorm and avoid collisions, but those radars seldom detected the wooden dhows. The fishermen took the threat of collision seriously, and each worked with one eye constantly scanning the wall of wind-borne sand around them.

At midafternoon another ship in the seemingly endless stream plying the Gulf emerged from the stinging sand clouds near the fishing dhows. The fishermen froze in their actions as the ship became visible less than one hundred yards away. With hearts pounding, they watched the ship's rapid approach until it was apparent the vessel would pass clear of them. Once the danger was past, the fishermen cautiously returned to their work. They had no greater interest in this ship than in any of the others that made their trade so difficult and dangerous, but the hard angular lines and low profile of this ship proclaimed it as different from the others. The ghostly gray vessel was a warship.

At four thousand tons, the Perry-class frigate *Bulkeley* was dwarfed by the seagoing skyscrapers that bore the vital petroleum products into and out of the Gulf. The ship was just over one and a half times the length of a football field, but it appeared as a toy beside the elephantine bulk of the supertankers. Size and power were relative, however, for the *Bulkeley* held enough firepower in her missile and gun magazines to reduce any of the massive tankers to a burning hulk.

Lieutenant Commander John Stewart was losing the battle to keep the free-flowing perspiration out of his eyes long enough to complete a sweep of the horizon. His six-foot frame had the long, angular lines of a swimmer, and in his widespread stance against the life rail he took up half the available space on the *Bulkeley's* port bridgewing. Reradiated heat coming off the surrounding metal raised the temperature on the wing several degrees. Stewart had trimmed back his already short black hair prior to entering the Gulf, but that concession to the heat was having little cooling effect. His lack of any tan showed that he was a stranger to the long hours in the sun that were the fate of topside watch standers.

Slowly, with methodical precision, he twisted his upper body in a forty-five-degree arc, binoculars pressed close against his face. Stewart longed to return to the air-conditioned confines of the frigate's bridge and Combat Information Center, but the superior visibility afforded on the exposed wing drew him out there at least once on each of his watches. He had the bridgewing speaker turned up full blast so he would miss nothing that was happening in the CIC below. The tankers he was able to briefly glimpse as they emerged from the storm were given an unreal appearance by the glassy reflectivity of the flat seas.

The sound of the watertight door opening behind him diverted Stewart from his search of the surrounding waters. Looking over his shoulder, he saw Scott Septenano, the young lieutenant, junior grade, who was the current officer of the deck, step through the door onto the wing.

"Another day in paradise," Stewart said ironically. He returned his attention to his search of the surrounding water.

"Yes sir." Septenano smiled, following Stewart's gaze out across the Gulf. "And think how lucky we are to be here before Robin Leach discovers it."

Septenano was used to having Stewart step up to the bridge unexpectedly from the Combat Information Center during their watches. The other tactical action officers preferred to remain in CIC for their entire watch, not wanting to miss a single detail presented on the data display consoles or a single word uttered over the radios. But Stewart took a different tack. He said a TAO needed the taste and the feel of the watch that he could only get from the bridge.

"Are you sure you wouldn't be more comfortable *inside* the bridge, boss?" Septenano asked, his lack of enthusiasm for the extreme heat apparent in his tone.

Stewart replied without lowering his binoculars. "Radar conditions can go to hell at any time, especially in these sandstorms." He dropped the glasses, letting them ride against his chest, and turned to look at Septenano. The stocky young officer was watching him intently, a glimmer of perspiration forming where his high forehead met his crew-cut chestnut hair. "When that happens CIC is blind, and you OODs and your lookouts are the only reliable eyes the ship has. You've got to have the best picture you can, even if that means spending half your time out on the bridge-wing. If we get jumped, you may be the first one to realize it."

Septenano understood Stewart's words precisely. With the *Bulkeley* in her assigned patrol station, monitoring activity in the southeastern Persian Gulf, they were only sixty miles off the coast of Iran, or ten minutes by air for Iranian F-4 or F-14 aircraft.

Satisfied that no new contacts were preparing to run down the *Bulkeley*, Septenano turned to go back into the bridge. He saw that Stewart, his khaki shirt already beginning to darken with perspiration, was looking aft toward the *Bulkeley*'s 76-millimeter gun mount. As gunnery officer, the 76-millimeter was Septenano's responsibility. He smiled approvingly at the devoted efforts of his senior chief gunner's mate and gunners, who were diligently performing maintenance on the critical weapon without regard for the blazing sun.

"Don't let them overdo it," Stewart said without shifting his gaze from the gun mount. "A four-oh gun won't do us any good if the gunners get flattened by the heat."

Septenano nodded. Stewart was a demanding officer, both as a TAO and as a department head, but there was no one with whom Septenano would rather stand watch. He followed Stewart back into the bridge, sealing the watertight door behind him. Stewart crossed to the chart table, where the junior officer of the deck, a veteran chief electronics technician, was reviewing the *Bulkeley*'s track.

Chief Marquez was roughly twice Septenano's age, but he was appreciative of the young officer's ability as an officer of the deck. The chief's job was to be Septenano's right-hand man, and Stewart knew it was no coincidence that the Captain had paired his most junior OOD with his most experienced and trusted enlisted watch stander. They made a fine team, their relationship forged through mutual respect.

The chief looked at Stewart's sweat-dampened khaki shirt and smiled. Chief Marquez, along with several of the bridge watch standers, was wearing a pair of the lightweight coveralls the Captain had authorized for wear in the Gulf. The chief was Stewart's equal in height and had the trim build of an eighteen-year-old. With his square, chiseled features, deep-set eyes, and weather-lined face he looked like he belonged in a Navy recruiting poster.

"You should switch to coveralls, Mr. Stewart. They're a lot cooler."

Stewart gave the weathered chief an answering smile. "I haven't spent ten years in the Navy to dress like a garbageman, Chief," he said with mock seriousness.

With Marquez's chuckles in his ears, Stewart bent to study the chart on the table at the back of the bridge. After a fast review of the chart he turned to Septenano.

"Flight quarters will go at fifteen thirty."

Septenano smiled ruefully. "How convenient. Right at relieve the watch, eh, Chief?"

Chief Marquez looked up from the chart and returned Septenano's smile with a resigned shake of his head.

"Had to happen, sir. It's pizza night in the mess, so I knew we were in for something."

Both men recognized the news about flight quarters as a reconfirmation of the oldest law of the sea: all complex evolutions, minor crises, and major disasters take place just prior to the arrival of the next watch team, thus ensuring a lengthy turnover and missed meals and sleep. Flight quarters, the launch or recovery of one of the *Bulkeley*'s two helicopters, was a controlled nightmare in this part of the Gulf. It required the bridge team to maintain a steady course into the wind, which frequently meant running against the traffic flow of commercial shipping. With war having re-ignited between Iran and Iraq, the huge tankers wanted to make maximum speed into and out of the Gulf. They were not about to slow that pace to accommodate U.S. Navy flight operations.

Stewart gave the two men a sympathetic smile and then turned and headed for the rear of the bridge and the ladder down to the Combat Information Center. He was a third of the way down the ladder, his head and shoulders still visible above the trunk on the bridge, when he stopped and turned back towards Septenano and the Chief.

"One other thing that might interest you," he said. "There's going to be a woman in that bunch coming in on the helo."

SEALORD 25

Above the sandstorm, the air was clear and the sky searingly blue. The Seahawk helicopter cut a path through the sky hundreds of feet above the towering storm clouds. The pale bluish-gray paint scheme of the aircraft made the Seahawk difficult to detect against the background of sky and clouds.

Kim Mitchell was tightly belted in on the bench seat beside the sensor operator, known as the SENSO. By looking past him to her left, she could view the roiling, dirty white clouds below through a Perspex observation window. She split her attention between the view outside the helicopter and a pile of three-by-five index cards held tightly in her lap, on which she was busily jotting notes.

The aircraft commander's voice echoed through her flight helmet above the roar of the Seahawk's two powerful engines.

"We're level at five thousand. We'll stay up here through the transit to keep above the storm. Not much to look at for you and your friends I'm afraid, Miss Mitchell." Both Kim and the SENSO were plugged into the aircraft's internal communication system.

Her concentration on her notes broken by the pilot's voice, Kim turned to look back into the interior of the aircraft, where the other reporters were buckled in.

Quick introductions at the airport had provided her with their names and organizations, but she knew little else of the three men beyond their professional reputations. She could see that Neil Perren, the AP man, was asleep, mouth open wide, his snores dueling with the noise of the engines. Hunched beside him on the bench seat, the CNN cameraman, Mack, had assumed the closest thing to a fetal position that his restraining harness would allow. His eyes were locked on the deck as he appeared to try to control his fear. Lastly, she glanced at the senior CNN correspondent,

Bob Bosca, who looked up from his paperback long enough to flash her a fatherly smile along with a thumb's-up. He absently chewed a piece of gum as he turned again to his book.

Kim returned to her notes, wondering what criteria had been used in selecting the members of the press pool. The three men were veterans of covering the Middle East, but she was based out of Rome, and her primary beat was southern Europe and the Mediterranean. Shuffling through her pile of note cards she found the folded-up fax from her assignment editor at World Network News.

Selected to participate in Department of Defense Press Pool covering Gulf war. Have booked you on next flight departing for Bahrain. Contact Navy Public Affairs at Unified Command Rome for details. Congratulations.

Going had meant dropping a complex story she had almost completed on the future of NATO and canceling several interviews, but that was a small price to pay. The chance to cover a war from a Navy ship, and to be one of the first women to do so, was too extraordinary an opportunity to pass up. Kim had arrived in the tiny Gulf state of Bahrain two days after receiving the fax, her visa and entry requirements finessed by the Department of Defense.

Remembering her brief underway stints on ships of the Sixth Fleet out of Naples, she had dressed for the environment. The tough cotton pants, long-sleeved shirt, and running shoes she wore would serve her well in the often harsh conditions of a ship at sea. Kim had forgone both jewelry and makeup; with her fine ivory complexion, she scarcely needed the latter in any case. Pulling back her thick auburn hair had further emphasized the deep, bottle-green eyes that could be disturbing in their intensity. The effect, if a bit severe, had not deterred the Navy public affairs officer from giving her an appreciative once-over at the military air terminal at Dubai.

They had been briefed that the flight out to the *Bulkeley* would take just over an hour. The *Bulkeley*. She had been visibly shaken when the young lieutenant had told her which ship they would be visiting first. The officer had detected her surprise, and Kim had quickly covered by saying she knew some of the crew of the

Bulkeley and had not realized the ship was deployed to the Gulf. That was certainly true enough, but it was only one member of the crew that concerned her.

Sliding the fax to the bottom of her stack of note cards, Kim resumed her writing, oblivious to the noise and vibration around her.

THE BULKELEY

"Read back the passenger manifest again for me, Goldman."

Stewart was hunched over the seated air controller in the *Bulkeley*'s darkened Combat Information Center. All around him, operations specialists were intently monitoring activity on radar and tactical data consoles similar to the one before him. The ATACO, the air tactical control operator, responded to Stewart's question, repeating the names he had grease-penciled on his console's CRT. "Neil Perren, AP; Robert Bosca and Tim Mack, CNN; Kim Mitchell, WNN. That's all of 'em, sir."

"Christ," Stewart swore under his breath. "Okay, Goldman, let me know when they're thirty minutes out."

Straightening up, Stewart returned to his preferred watch-standing position in the center of the CIC. He donned the radio headset at the large data console reserved for his use as tactical action officer. Although his mind was working at flank speed as he tried to evaluate the implications of what he had just heard, Stewart forced himself to focus on his responsibilities as TAO. He keyed the deck-mounted switch for his headset, designed to allow hands-free operation of the radio, and heard the distinctive warbling of the outgoing satellite transmission. He waited until the warbling ceased and then spoke.

"COM JTF, this is *Bulkeley*, over."

There was a ten-second pause.

"*Bulkeley*, this is COM JTF; roger, over," the voice, representing Commander Joint Task Force Middle East, responded from two hundred fifty miles away.

"This is *Bulkeley*. Sealord Two-Five is airborne out of Dubai with press pool on board. Estimate Sealord return to home plate at one-five-four-five local, over."

This time the delay on the other end lasted almost a minute.

"*Bulkeley*, this is COM JTF, copy all. Report when press pool embarked, over."

"This is *Bulkeley*, roger, out."

His report complete, Stewart doffed the headset and scrutinized the large tactical display console in front of him. Video symbols on the CRT marked the positions and identities of all the air and surface contacts that *Bulkeley*'s radars and other sensors were tracking. The local "tracks" were augmented by contacts received by radio data link from other navy ships and the AWACS surveillance aircraft on station over the Gulf.

A rapid scan of the current tracks showed the normal high volume of merchant shipping and COMAIR, commercial airliners, crisscrossing the Gulf. Stewart zeroed in on the potential threats. An Iranian Saam-class frigate, the *Abaland*, was operating north of the Straits of Hormuz, approximately twenty miles to the east of *Bulkeley*. In the aftermath of Operation Desert Storm, following the departure of the bulk of Allied forces, few had been surprised when Iran struck at its weakened neighbor. The Iranians had resumed their attacks on Iraqi shipping in the Straits, and the Iraqis had reciprocated by attempting to sink all vessels going to and from Iran's Gulf ports. The war-weary U.S. was running periodic convoys of American-flag ships to Bahrain, Saudi Arabia, and the Gulf Emirates, trying to maintain the vital flow of oil from the Gulf. The Iranians and Iraqis had thus far steered clear of those convoys, preferring to strike at each other's unescorted shipping. Stewart knew the *Abaland* could be waiting to carry out just such an attack. Although current U.S. policy excluded intervention in Iranian attacks on unescorted merchants, Stewart would nonetheless keep a close watch on the Iranian frigate.

To the north, the scope showed limited military air activity over land. There was a small Iraqi raid under way and a desultory response by Iranian fighters. The Iranian pilots were apparently not particularly interested in engaging the larger Iraqi raiding party. Stewart took note of the raid and evaluated the aircraft as a nonthreat to *Bulkeley* and her sister ships in the Gulf. Even as he was studying the raid, he heard the cool, professional voice of his track supervisor going out over the radio with a report to COM JTF on the Iraqi raid.

The joint military and civilian air complex at Bandar Abbas was Stewart's real concern. The high volume of military transports and COMAIR using the airport made it relatively easy for Iranian attack aircraft to take off undetected. They could then mimic their commercial counterparts until they achieved an attack position on ships in the southeastern Gulf. This morning's near engagement with the flight of three Iranian aircraft had only been the latest in a series of increasingly provocative flights out of Bandar.

At the commanding officer's direction, on each watch an air-search radar operator was always assigned to track and identify all aircraft going in and out of Bandar Abbas. It was intense work, and the operator burnout rate was high. The TAOs on watch directed their respective CIC watch officers to ensure the "Bandar controller" position was rotated at least every two hours.

A sudden curse from behind him diverted Stewart's concentration from the tactical picture. Turning, he saw two operations specialists struggling to remove a cheesecloth filter from one of the CIC's ventilation diffusers. As the cloth gave way and the two men lowered it to the waste can below the diffuser, Stewart could see what looked like a pound of fine brown sand cradled in the cloth. The *Bulkeley*'s normal ventilation and air-conditioning filters were no match for the superfine sand of the Gulf. As additional layers of defense, the crew had installed sheets of air-porous foam over all the ship's external intakes, and cheesecloth filters over all the ventilation diffusers. Ordinarily the cheesecloth was emptied twice a week, but with the severity of the current sandstorm, they were forced to change the filters on a daily basis.

Thinking of the massive storm took Stewart's thoughts back to the inbound helicopter making its way through the curtain of sand. Kim Mitchell. That was the last thing he needed to deal with now. Just the idea of including a woman reporter in the DOD press pool had seemed ludicrous to him and his fellow officers. The U.S. was not actually at war with Iran or Iraq, but that did not make the danger any less real. Only ten days before, *Bulkeley*'s sister ship, the *Manchester*, had engaged in a running gun battle with Iranian speedboats during a night transit of the Straits. Six of her crew had been wounded, and the resultant uproar in America had included calls for both retaliation and for a U.S. pullout from the Gulf.

At that moment, Stewart was very glad for the defused blue lighting in the CIC. It served to enhance the images on the consoles, while also concealing a troubled expression he would have been hard-pressed to explain to his watch team.

USS PASCAGOULA

The massive white bulk of the *Pascagoula* was the dominant presence in Bahrain's Sitrah Anchorage. The "White Ghost of the Arabian Coast" had been painted a stark, flat white, in contrast to standard Navy haze gray. This was due to the heat-defusing properties of the lighter color, and also in acknowledgment of *Pascagoula*'s all but permanent assignment to the inferno of the Gulf. Although the flagship rocked peacefully at anchor, close examination of her open decks and superstructure revealed dozens of armed sentries manning self-defense weaponry ranging from automatic grenade launchers to Stinger missiles. Of equally low profile were the Spectre and SeaFox patrol boats that periodically traversed the harbor, searching for anything that might present a possible threat to the *Pascagoula*.

The flagship for the Commander Joint Task Force Middle East spent much of its time in Sitrah Anchorage, located in Bahrain Harbor, or pierside in the port proper. Through both the Gulf war and the renewed Iran-Iraq war, one dependable constant had been the steadfast support of the emir of Bahrain for the United States, and his willingness to let his country's principal port serve as a base of operations for U.S. ships in the Gulf. Given the dispersed nature of the ships assigned to COM JTF, scattered as they were on various missions throughout the Gulf, the flagship could perform its mission of command and control almost equally well whether in port or at sea. Rear Admiral Boone, Commander Joint Task Force Middle East, or COM JTF, maintained a staff of more than forty officers and enlisted men on board the *Pascagoula*. Both the Rear Admiral and his Chief of Staff were senior to the ship's commanding officer, but they were scrupulous in observing his authority to run his own ship. The flagship was the epicenter of tactical and operational control for United States military forces in the Persian Gulf.

Lieutenant Commander Jim Garmisch took another sip from his rapidly cooling mug of coffee and scrutinized the tactical plot. Deep in the interior of *Pascagoula*, a converted ready room served as the Tactical Decision Center for COM JTF. Garmisch shifted uncomfortably in one of the old leather ready-room chairs, not liking what the tactical plot showed. Taking up one whole bulkhead of the TDC, the plot was a massive map of the Persian Gulf showing the current positions of all U.S. and allied units, and the known positions of Iranian and Iraqi forces. The plot was continuously updated by petty officers who gathered fresh information from incoming data-link and voice-radio communications.

The current U.S. force disposition was spread desperately thin, Garmisch thought. Two ships were down in the Gulf of Oman, below the Straits, forming up a convoy of U.S. flagged ships. Further south, an older Knox-class frigate was alongside a destroyer tender in Oman, undergoing a ten-day repair availability. The *Manchester* was pierside in Bahrain, taking *Pascagoula*'s usual spot, with her crew working around the clock to patch up the damage done to the frigate in her recent engagement.

That left Garmisch, as staff watch officer, only two healthy and fully operational units in the Gulf itself. In the northern Gulf, off the coast of Kuwait, a Spruance-class destroyer maintained a radar watch on the escalating air war between Iran and Iraq.

To the east, there was *Bulkeley*, patrolling between Abu Musa Island and the Iranian coast. Her position concerned Garmisch the most. Activity by RevGuard gunboats, operating out of both the Iranian mainland and Abu Musa Island, was way up since the attack on the *Manchester*. That ran contrary to the established pattern, Garmisch knew, especially since *Manchester* reported having sunk two of the heavily armed speedboats. Since the Iran-Iraq war had flared up again, the Iranians had always backed off to a much lower presence after any interaction with U.S. forces. That wasn't happening this time, and Garmisch was worried by the implications.

After a long look at the tactical plot, he made up his mind.

"Fisher," he said to a youthful junior petty officer who was updating information on the plot. "When you finish that, how 'bout swinging by officers' country and picking up a refill for us— my special blend." Garmisch held up the nearly empty coffee pot.

Operations Specialist Third Class Fisher picked up the pot and headed for the door out of the TDC.

"Oh, and Fish," Garmisch added in seeming afterthought, "see if you can locate Captain Lacey while you're up there and ask him to please contact me as soon as he can."

Fisher nodded and, sensing something was up, took off at a quick pace to locate the Chief of Staff.

THE BULKELEY

Lieutenant Commander Dave Lawrence, executive officer of USS *Bulkeley*, peered out through the small viewport of the blast door on the ship's port helo hangar. He could see that, if anything, the visibility had gotten worse. The sandstorm was actually closer to a stinging, grit-filled fog than a true storm, and it had closed the visibility around the ship down to less than half a mile.

There was no sign yet of the *Bulkeley*'s SH-60B Seahawk helicopter, call sign Sealord 25, although he knew from Stewart in the Combat Information Center that the helo was overhead and descending. The ship had been at flight quarters for fifteen minutes, and the members of the Blue flight quarters team were all on station.

As executive officer, one of Lawrence's duties was to meet arriving passengers brought in by helo. He provided the welcome and then oriented them to the ship. Captain Donelli was always on the bridge during flight ops, particularly amid the K Mart parking lot that was shipping traffic in the Gulf.

There they were.

The snout of the SH-60B had just pierced the haze at a range of one thousand yards and an altitude of five hundred feet. Within seconds Lawrence lost sight of the helicopter as the storm closed in around it once more. Knowing the Seahawk was out there but not being able to see it left him with a slight sense of unease. He was used to sailing in fog, but fog seldom persisted throughout an entire day. This sandstorm had blown up yesterday and seemed to be growing worse by the hour.

They would be working this as a low-visibility approach, Lawrence thought, the ATACO in CIC combining his skills and sensors

with those of the pilots in the aircraft. After a long moment Lawrence saw the helo reappear, one hundred yards out on final
approach to the ship. He breathed a little easier as he stepped
away from the door to allow the other members of the flight deck
team access to the deck. The hangar was filled with the muffled
roar of the aircraft's engines as the Seahawk touched down. Lawrence waited in the forward end of the hangar for the passengers
to disembark. Within minutes, the press pool was led inside by a
flight deck Bosun's Mate. Lawrence observed that they all kept
their cranial helmets and life vests in place, a sure sign of inexpe-
rienced helicopter passengers.

Lawrence waved the small group to his side and signaled them,
over the noise of the aircraft still turning on deck, that it was safe
to remove their helmets and vests.

"Welcome on board *Bulkeley*," he shouted over the now diminishing rotor noise. "I'm Dave Lawrence, the executive officer. I'll
be looking after you during your stay here. We'll try to make this
a useful and informative visit for you."

The senior reporter of the group, Bob Bosca, introduced himself
and all the others to Lawrence, who stepped forward and shook
hands with each of them in turn. When he reached Kim she had
just managed to untangle herself from the awkward cranial helmet. She smiled at him through her jumble of scattered hair, making little effort to straighten it, and Lawrence was surprised by
the understated beauty that her baggy, functional clothing and
disheveled hair could not conceal. He was still disturbed and
mildly amused that they had sent a woman reporter to overnight
on a ship in a war zone, but her warm handshake and relaxed
smile eased his concerns a bit. The other three reporters were
more what he had expected, although the young cameraman,
Mack, seemed barely to have survived the flight in.

As Sealord 25's engines shut down, the hangar became relatively quiet, and they were able to lower their voices to a normal
level.

". . . anyway, Commander, we know we're one more burden
you probably don't need right now," Bosca was saying for all of
them, "and we'll try to make this visit as nondisruptive as possible."

The others nodded in agreement, Tim Mack a bit unsteadily and Perren with a bored smile.

"I'm sure you'd all like to clean up and settle in," Lawrence said. "Dinner will be in the wardroom in one hour, at seventeen hundred. If you follow me, I'll show you to your quarters and give you a feel for where things are."

After a cursory tour of the ship, Lawrence placed each of his guests in a stateroom. Bosca was put in with the chief engineer, a Mustang who was almost the older reporter's age. Mack joined two of the pilots in one of the three-man rooms, and Neil Perren was doubled with Scott Septenano.

Having made the three male reporters at home, Lawrence led Kim up one more deck and showed her into a small one-man stateroom, approximately the size of the double staterooms below.

"This baby's all yours, Miss Mitchell," he said in a friendly way. "I've moved my personal gear out, although I can't promise that you won't be awakened in the middle of the night by a couple of phone calls intended for me." Lawrence glanced down at his nearly empty desk and noticed his small lock-back knife resting in his in-basket. Almost as an afterthought he pocketed the knife.

"I didn't intend to displace you, XO. I'm sorry."

Lawrence smiled, impressed by her use of the shipboard short-hand for his executive officer's title. "Not to worry," he said, and crossed the room to open a narrow door, revealing a small water closet with an adjoining shower. "This XO's perk is why we've placed you here."

Kim blushed slightly, remembering what the public affairs office had said: separate head and shower facilities were mandatory if a woman was to spend a night on board ship. Navy regulations.

"Well, nonetheless, I'm sorry about the inconvenience."

"No problem. It's my pleasure." Lawrence moved to leave. As he was closing the stateroom door, Kim called to him.

"XO?"

"Ma'am?"

"Can you tell me . . . is there still a Lieutenant Commander Stewart assigned to this ship?"

Great, Lawrence thought. Time to call off any bogus ideas of high-seas romance. Oh well. He smiled artificially. "There certainly is. He's combat systems officer, has been for almost two years." He saw a strange look of resignation cross her face. "Do you know John, Miss Mitchell?"

"Yes. From some time ago. Although I'm not sure he'll be very happy to see me." She paused in thought, leaving Lawrence to ponder her cryptic remark. "Will he be at dinner, do you suppose?"

Now Lawrence heard more anticipation than resignation in her voice. "Should be. He gets relieved as TAO right before chow. But," he added with a hint of satisfaction, "he goes back on watch from midnight to four."

She turned away. "Thank you, XO. I'll see you at dinner."

Lawrence closed the door and headed forward in the direction of the CIC and the bridge. Terrific, he thought. Do I fill the old man in on that little historical footnote or not? He was on his way to brief the Captain on the arrival of the press pool. Well, I can give him a heads-up or wait until it comes out at dinner. Either way he's not going to be thrilled.

Donelli had opposed embarking the press pool from the outset. He considered the idea both an unnecessary risk and an unwanted distraction. When COM JTF informed him there was going to be a woman in the party as well, his displeasure had flared into anger. Ironically, it was Stewart who kept Donelli off the Command Net when he was fully enraged and ready to incinerate the unlucky staff watch officer who had delivered the news.

Well, the XO thought as he headed forward, this will make the CO's day and should make for sparkling dinner conversation.

IRN ABALAND

The Iranian frigate cruised at low speed through the waters of the eastern Gulf, its movement barely leaving a wake in the tepid seas. Topside lookouts kept watch in the steaming heat of late afternoon, but the impenetrable wall of the sandstorm made them all but ornamental.

Captain Ajami hurried impatiently up the bridge ladder. He had been summoned to the *Abaland*'s bridge when the *Bulkeley*'s helicopter had been detected on radar. The Americans flew a host of different military helicopters, some deadlier than others, and Ajami had left standing orders with his officers to alert him whenever one was detected.

The *Abaland* was one of two remaining Saam-class frigates in the Iranian Navy; the others had been lost in action against the United States. She was roughly three quarters the size of the *Bulkeley*, with a larger cannon than the American frigate but much less effective missiles. She was well maintained, and her crew was made up of combat veterans.

Ajami grunted as he hoisted his compact frame into the captain's chair. "Where are they, Lieutenant?"

The officer of the deck spoke without lowering his Zeiss glasses, keeping them fixed on a point forty-five degrees off the bow of the Iranian warship. "We have seen the helicopter on radar only, my Captain." He turned from the binoculars to look at Ajami. "The *Bulkeley* is visible occasionally, when the storm briefly opens."

The Captain nodded his acknowledgment. A check of the radar in the CIC on his way to the bridge had shown the American ship at eleven miles. That would be just at the edge of visual range on a good day.

"The radar returns have merged," the chief manning the bridge radar called out.

Excellent, Ajami thought, the aircraft will most likely remain on deck until its evening patrol. So far the consistencies outnumbered the surprises. He settled back into his chair for what he thought would be a long night.

"Continue as before, Lieutenant. No closer than eight miles, no farther than fifteen." He looked across his bridge to where the marines had installed the special radio. "And raise Abu Musa Base on that thing. Tell them the target remains in the gunsight."

2

THE BULKELEY

S tewart splashed cold water on his face at the small sink in his stateroom. Ten years of service in the Navy had exacted their toll on the face that echoed back at him from the mirror. His once-full, black hair was markedly thinner, with ribbons of gray marching north from his sideburns. The puffiness around his eyes showed the result of port-and-starboard TAO watches for a sixth straight day. The watch rotation meant he was on watch for four to six hours and then off for a similar period of time, averaging twelve hours of watch in twenty-four. But what with his regular work as department head, General Quarters, and special evolutions that required his presence in the CIC or on the bridge, he could spare little time for sleep when he was off watch.

His reflection also showed him that his trip from the relative coolness of the Combat Information Center to the heat of the bridge had dampened his shirt with sweat. In areas of the Gulf where the threat was relatively low, the Captain allowed his crew to adopt "Persian Gulf yachting attire," a simplified uniform consisting of T-shirts, shorts made from uniform trousers, and tennis shoes. This made the crew feel a bit cooler, as much psychologically as physically, in the intense heat of the summer Gulf. In periods of higher danger, such as when transiting the Straits or patrolling near Iran or Iraq, they reverted to the combat uniform of steel-toed shoes, long pants, and long-sleeved shirts.

Crossing to his locker, Stewart extracted a clean khaki shirt to replace his sweat-stained one. He removed the first shirt, dropping it onto the lone steel chair in the stateroom, and quickly changed his T-shirt. He grabbed the old khaki shirt and searched for his insignia to transfer it to the fresh shirt. Stewart carefully positioned the gold oak leaves and surface warfare pin, ensuring their angles were precisely correct. He pulled the shirt on and stepped back to the mirror. For the first time he noticed the dark bristle on his cheeks and chin. It would be nice to shave, he thought, but there isn't any time. He knew the old man would rather have him punctual than immaculate, especially with unwanted guests. God only knew how the Captain would react to Kim.

Wishing he had more time to think it all through, he checked his appearance in the mirror one last time and headed for the wardroom.

THE PASCAGOULA

The sun was low in the sky to the west of Bahrain Harbor. The backlighting it provided gave the white-painted flagship silhouetted against the reddening sky an unreal appearance.

Garmisch sat facing the COM JTF Chief of Staff across the low "mock wood" coffee table in Lacey's relatively large stateroom.

Lacey had been in with Rear Admiral Boone when Fisher had gone looking for him, so Garmisch had waited until the end of his watch to seek him out. The Chief of Staff leaned back in a relaxed pose, one arm resting on the back of the couch, a half finished paperback on the cushion beside him.

"So what's up, Jim?" he asked casually.

Garmisch leaned forward, choosing his words carefully. "Captain, I have some concerns about the *Bulkeley*'s patrol area and the level of IRN and RevGuard activity out there." He paused, looking for a reaction from Lacey. The Chief of Staff's expression remained the same, determinedly bland. Garmisch continued. "I wanted to talk to you before going to the Admiral"—that drew an increase in interest from Lacey—"and see if you agree that my concern might be valid . . . or am I just getting a little paranoid?"

Lacey smiled. "You're paid to be paranoid, Jim. What are the specifics?"

Better make this good, Garmisch thought as he steeled himself to present his suspicions. He had only been assigned to the COM JTF staff for three months and standing staff watch officer for less than two. Not exactly extensive credentials, in comparison with Lacey's. The Chief of Staff had been CO of a ship assigned to the Gulf during the war with Iraq. Lacey had worked for Admiral Boone in his current job for more than a year, and he probably understood the Gulf as well as anyone who didn't speak Farsi or Arabic.

"Something has changed in the Iranians' pattern of operation," Garmisch began. "Following that attack on *Manchester*, they should have scaled down operations to wait for our counterpunch. They always have in the past."

"That's assuming we hit back," Lacey said. He was referring to the ongoing Cabinet-level discussions over how to respond to the attack.

"Yes, sir. But the Iranians have to assume that we will. They should be in a defensive posture. Instead, we're seeing stepped-up attacks on shipping by RevGuard boats, both in the Straits and south of Abu Musa. Stranger still, they're keeping that Saam frigate, the *Abaland*, literally on station in *Bulkeley*'s patrol box."

Lacey remained placid, showing neither encouragement nor doubt.

"*Abaland* is sitting there like a sacrificial lamb for our retaliatory strike," Garmisch said with conviction. "Not only that, since she's been operating near *Bulkeley*, she hasn't challenged a single merchant." It was an established Iranian tactic to have the Saam frigates "challenge" or identify merchant ships transiting the southeastern Gulf. Once they determined the vessels' destination and cargo, the Iranian warships would pass that information to the RevGuards to help them select their targets.

"All of which says what to you?"

From Lacey's tone, Garmisch knew he was running out of time to make his point. "It tells me that *Abaland* is bird-dogging *Bulkeley* for some kind of Iranian strike." Sink or swim, Garmisch thought, as he relaxed back in his chair.

"And what's your read on the increased RevGuard attacks in *Bulkeley*'s area?" Lacey asked.

"My hunch is they're giving her a lot of action to monitor, a lot to look at and keep track of."

Lacey rose, stretching stiffly, and moved to his desk. He picked up a message board fat with recent traffic. "Our intel gurus don't seem to agree with you," he said, flipping through several messages until he located the one he sought. "Quote, 'Sources close to the Iranian Supreme Defense Council indicate that attack on *Manchester* was a renegade action by RevGuard units and was not sanctioned by Tehran. Direct confrontation with U.S. forces is not sought by Iranians at this time,' unquote." Lacey looked up. "We've had other traffic showing them diverting their southern-based attack aircraft to the front with Iraq up north. With *Abaland*'s sister ship in dry dock, that doesn't leave them a whole lot to attack *Bulkeley* with, does it?"

Garmisch lowered his eyes. He had seen all the same messages while on watch, but something still didn't add up.

Taking a deep breath, he met Lacey's steady gaze. "It may seem improbable, Captain, but whether it's *Abaland* herself, RevGuard speedboats, or whatever, I'm convinced *Bulkeley* is going to get hit."

Lacey looked at his watch. "Chow time," he said quietly. The Chief of Staff carefully straightened his immaculate uniform and then crossed to his stateroom sink to wash up.

Sensing his audience was at an end, Garmisch rose to leave.

"There's enough smoke here to talk to the Admiral," Lacey said as he dried his hands, his eyes on them rather than on Garmisch. "Get the details down on paper—how long *Abaland* has been operating near *Bulkeley* and so forth—and bring them up to the Admiral's cabin." He looked over at Garmisch. "Don't worry about disturbing us at dinner."

THE BULKELEY

The wardroom of the USS *Bulkeley* was a triumph of function over form.

The fifteen-by-twenty-foot space held two small dining tables, seating for fourteen officers and guests, as well as a tiny lounge used for reading or watching the ship's closed-circuit TV. The decor was spartan yet eclectic; a framed reproduction of a Turner oil of a seventeenth-century man-of-war hung on the bulkhead nearest the captain's table, while a large framed photo of John Wayne in the role of a naval officer dominated the opposite wall.

As he entered the wardroom, Stewart immediately picked out Kim, clustered with her fellow reporters near the captain's table. The executive officer was holding forth to the group on some vital detail about the *Bulkeley*. At the sight of Kim, Stewart felt a sudden charge of excitement course through his body. It was a feeling he'd been certain he had lost.

Before her eyes could meet his, Stewart turned to the three junior officers in the lounge. Troubled by his reaction to seeing Kim, he was still determined to show her that he saw her presence on board as no exceptional event. The young officers were watching an episode of *Magnum P.I.* with varying degrees of interest.

"Has our boy saved Honolulu from Communism and Japanese tourists yet?" he asked them. Stewart's voice had an easygoing tone that did not reflect his feelings. This was going to be tougher than he anticipated.

Scott Septenano looked up, his eyes alight with irony. "No, but he has decided to go back to school and get a college education." Scott's companions, Naval Academy graduates both, pointedly ignored the shot fired at their fictional classmate.

Stewart gave Scott a little smile. Ordinarily he would have engaged the younger officer in a good-natured exchange of insults directed at their respective alma maters. But his thoughts were elsewhere. Turning, he crossed the wardroom to join the press group.

"Hello, Kim. How are you?" After all the months of forcing her image from his mind, Stewart was riveted by her actual physical presence. Those deep green eyes and the sensual curve of her mouth brought memories of intense pleasure flooding back to him. But the eyes that could bewitch were now cool and without passion.

"John, it's good to see you." The toneless nature of her greeting seemed to contradict the warmth of the words. Stewart could read very little in her expression or her demeanor towards him. Her smile was polite, but she held her body stiffly.

An uncomfortable pause followed. Dave Lawrence sensed the tension in the group but was unsure of its source. He broke the silence, gesturing to Stewart.

"I see Kim and our weapons officer have already met," he said. "Gentlemen, this is Lieutenant Commander John Stewart, the head of our combat systems department."

The reporters introduced themselves one at a time. Stewart observed that the one named Perren met his gaze for barely a second as they shook hands. The man appeared more interested in the program on the TV behind Stewart than in the introduction.

"So, Commander," Bosca began, "your XO tells us this is your second tour in the Gulf. How do you find it different this time from the last?"

"The Iranians and the Iraqis have better weapons now," Stewart responded coolly. "Otherwise, it's the same garden spot it was before."

Bosca continued to question Stewart, with Perren occasionally contributing, as Kim listened in silence. After a few minutes, Bosca noticed that Stewart was distracted and giving only polite, cursory answers to his questions about the ship's weapons systems and conditions in the Gulf. He glanced briefly at Kim and noted the intensity with which she followed Stewart's perfunctory responses. Bosca sensed there was some hidden tension between the two, something they were both striving to keep submerged. Extinguishing the cigarette with which he had quickly replaced his gum upon their departure from the helicopter, the older man put his hand on Lawrence's shoulder.

"Excuse me, XO, isn't the ship's galley hereabouts somewhere? Could we have a look at that before the Captain gets here?"

Lawrence looked nervously at his watch. Ten minutes to go. "Sure, if we hurry a bit. It's one deck below," he said. The XO headed for the wardroom door.

"Come along, Neil," Bosca called out merrily.

"I'm sure this is going to be riveting," Perren said under his breath as Bosca herded him and Tim Mack toward the exit. The older reporter looked over his shoulder at Kim, now standing alone with Stewart near the head table.

"You and the Commander can catch up on old times. We'll provide you with any heart-stopping details we encounter on sea-going food preparation." Bosca winked mischievously as he closed the door behind him.

Kim turned to Stewart, keeping her voice low so that it would not be heard over the TV. But a strong hint of annoyance came through. "He doesn't know anything about us," she said, answering Stewart's unspoken question. "I only met the three of them for the first time six hours ago."

"Just good reporter's intuition, I guess." Stewart rested his hip against the table, folding his arms with what he hoped passed for nonchalance.

Kim forced herself to turn away from him, gliding her hand across the surface of the Turner painting on the adjacent bulkhead.

"I thought you'd be in a new assignment by now, John."

He followed the smooth action of her hand as she traced the outline of the ship in the painting. "By rights I should be, but my relief's wife got real sick just before he was supposed to fly out and meet the ship. Bad break. Anyway, the CO didn't want to gap my billet, especially with us going to the Gulf. I agreed to stay until we outchop from this nuthouse." Stewart looked casually over his shoulder at the cluster of junior officers in the TV lounge; they remained intent on their program. Turning back to her, he lowered his voice. "Now how in the hell did they talk you into coming out here?"

Her eyes shifted from the painting to lock on his. "This was too good an opportunity to miss"—there was a flash of anger there— "and I didn't know the ship would be the *Bulkeley*, or that you would still be here."

"You'll be sorry to hear this captain isn't a drunk," Stewart said, his voice hardening but maintained at a level just above the background noise of the TV. "I don't know what you'll write about."

Kim seemed to pale momentarily, but then she spoke with acid in her voice. "I didn't go looking for that story! He shouldn't have been in command long enough for me or any other journalist to hear about it!"

Her angry tone drew the attention of the junior officers sitting in the lounge across the wardroom. Kim looked from them back to Stewart.

"If you all hadn't covered up for him, protected him, there wouldn't have been any story!"

As Stewart was about to respond, their attention was diverted to the wardroom door, which burst open with a crash.

Commander Vincent Donelli, USN, entered the mess at full tilt. His displeasure was apparent in his clouded face, as well as in the tense way he held his stocky, bull-like body. The junior officers by the TV leapt to their feet and quickly shut off the set.

Kim looked from the Captain back to Stewart. She was not sure whether the man's arrival was a blessing or a curse.

"Evening, Captain." Stewart's relaxed greeting to his CO bore no evidence of the brief confrontation with Kim and convinced her that the Captain's intimidating manner was not unexpected but rather part of his personal style.

Ignoring the greeting and oblivious to everything but his own thoughts, Donelli stalked over to the table. Stopping at the foot, he appeared to notice Kim for the first time. He briefly looked her up and down.

"Well, Weps?" he said to Stewart. The words were more of an order than a question.

"Captain Donelli, this is Kim Mitchell of World Network News." Stewart turned to Kim with a cool smile that she found difficult to read. "Her companions are touring the galley with the XO."

Donelli did not offer his hand to Kim but shifted his frown briefly, in what she thought he imagined to be a polite smile.

"Glad to have you on board, Miss Mitchell," he rumbled, a slight edge of sarcasm in his voice. He was not prepared to disguise his displeasure at having the distraction of a woman on board his ship in a war zone.

Without waiting for a response from Kim, the Captain moved to the head of the table. "Your friends may find my manners wanting, but we'll have to start without them." He gestured Kim to a seat on his left. "I try to minimize the time I'm away from the bridge and CIC. I'm sure you understand."

Kim nodded, her composure almost restored. "It's not our intention to disrupt your ship's routine, Captain."

As he sat down, Donelli automatically glanced to his left at the ships heading indicator that he had had installed on the wardroom bulkhead. The indicator gave a readout of the *Bulkeley*'s current course. The Captain trusted his OODs to inform him of course changes, but he knew that things had a way of developing rapidly and unpredictably in the Gulf, and the indicator made him feel a little more at ease when he was away from the bridge.

Kim followed the Captain's example and took her seat. Looking across the wardroom, she noticed that the junior officers had automatically taken seats at the smaller table, although five open chairs remained at the captain's table. Food appeared at her elbow almost immediately. She helped herself sparingly from a serving bowl of garden salad in which several of the vegetables showed their age.

Stewart, seated beside her, noticed her small sampling of salad. "Last loadout of fruit and veggies was two and a half weeks ago," he said. "Some of this stuff is collecting social security."

She offered him a small smile and returned her attention to the Captain.

Captain Donelli spoke without looking up from his food. "So, Miss Mitchell, my XO tells me you and Stewart here know each other. From where?"

Kim was taken aback by the bluntness of Donelli's question. She looked briefly at Stewart for some sign of how she should handle it, but he was working on his food as if oblivious to the situation. Damn him, she thought, if he doesn't care about what I tell his captain, then I'm not going to worry about it.

"We met a couple of years ago, Captain," she began, choosing her words carefully. "I was working at our bureau in D.C. and they sent me down to Norfolk to interview the commander of the Second Fleet about Navy drug interdiction efforts."

"Must have been when he was Admiral Jarvis's fruit loop," Donelli interrupted, glancing at Stewart.

"Fruit loop, Captain?" Kim asked, confused by the unfamiliar term.

"His aide," Stewart said, looking up from his plate. "Remember the blue and gold aiguillette I wore in that job? The fruit loop."

"Oh yes, now I recall. Well anyway, Captain, John helped me out in setting up that interview with Admiral Jarvis, and then we worked together a few other times while he was stationed at Norfolk."

"Personally or professionally?" Donelli asked, his expression giving no sign that the question was intended to be clever. He fixed his eyes on Kim, waiting for a response.

"Well, Captain," Kim began, sensing Stewart's eyes on her and realizing she had no idea what she was going to say. Before she could complete her sentence, the door of the wardroom opened and Lawrence hurried in, followed by the three male reporters. Kim tried not to let her relief at the welcome distraction show.

"Fascinating setup, XO; a far cry from the army field kitchens I've gotten used to over here." Bosca beamed in mock interest. Perren and Mack appeared terminally bored.

"Sorry we're late, Captain," Lawrence said nervously. He moved cautiously to take his place at the Captain's right hand. Relieved at the absence of the explosion he had anticipated, the XO gestured magnanimously to the reporters. "Gentlemen, please have a seat."

As Lawrence was about to introduce the three reporters, Donelli cut him off. "Two-Six is down," he said, looking from Lawrence to Stewart.

"Damn," Stewart cursed. He kept his voice low, but the intensity of his tone conveyed more than mere professional interest. "How bad, Captain?"

"Possible rotary coupling failure. Hammond has one in the pack-up kit, but he's talking thirty-six hours to change it out."

Although the terminology was unfamiliar, Kim deduced that they were talking about a helicopter. "Captain, is that the aircraft we flew in on that you're referring to?" she asked.

Donelli shifted his gaze to her, and this time he did manage a bit of a smile. "Not the same one, ma'am. You came in on Two-Five. No, I'm only out half my air force."

The Captain was about to fulminate on the unreliability of all things mechanical in the conditions of the Gulf, when Bob Bosca suddenly spoke up. "Captain, I'm Robert Bosca of CNN. My associate Mr. Mack and I would like to shoot an interview with you." He paused. "At your convenience, of course."

Donelli grimaced. Having these people crawling all over his ship in a war zone was bad enough, but the prospect of being ambushed on camera by some clever reporter was even worse. Still, COM JTF had advised him of what was probably coming when they had set up the visit. Full cooperation and accessibility, those were his marching orders from Admiral Boone. All part of a captain's job, he told himself.

"Well, since you fly off tomorrow, my convenience had better be pretty damn soon, hadn't it?" the Captain asked rhetorically. Stewart brought his napkin to his lips to conceal his smile at Donelli's obvious discomfort.

"We would all appreciate an on-the-record interview, Captain," Kim added. "The XO made it clear that you don't want us talking to men on watch, and we'll respect that."

"I also told them that your instructions to the crew are to speak freely when they're not on watch," Lawrence cut in to clarify, "as long as they avoid classified topics."

"And we appreciate that, XO," Kim said as she turned again to Donelli. "What would be a good time for you, Captain?" She flashed him a beguiling smile.

No way out of this one, Donelli thought. He set his napkin on his plate.

"I'm going back to the hangar to look in on their progress with Two-Six," he said. "After that I'll be on the bridge or in my cabin. You're welcome to come up and we'll talk. But I can't promise I'll stay put in one place for long."

The reporters voiced their thanks as the Captain rose to leave.

"Now if you'll excuse me," Donelli said, "I'll leave you in the capable hands of Lieutenant Commander Lawrence." This time his smile appeared to be genuine.

The assembled group watched the wardroom door close behind the fast-moving Captain. Neil Perren sagged back in his chair, exhaling as if he had been holding his breath. "Not exactly Mister Congeniality, is he?" he said to no one in particular. Turning, Perren looked over his glasses at Kim. "He is going to be a real handful."

Before she could respond, Stewart cut in. "If you were expecting some public relations wizard, I'm afraid you're out of luck." Stewart could not keep a mild edge of anger out of his voice. He knew it was partly his own exhaustion talking, but he continued anyway. "Captain Donelli's a hardcase, but he knows his business and he knows this ship. Listen to what he has to say and you'll learn more about the Iran-Iraq war than you could from all the rest of us combined."

Perren sat up indignantly and was about to respond when the wardroom was invaded by the blare of the 1MC.

"Captain to the bridge! Captain to the bridge!" The speaker's tone was urgent.

Stewart and the XO leapt to their feet as one and charged out of the wardroom.

The two officers reached the bridge in a matter of seconds and found that the CO had beaten them there. He was on the starboard bridgewing with the OOD and JOOD; all of them looking fixedly through binoculars at something off the ship's beam. As he crossed the bridge, Stewart could see that the OOD was barking directions into the sound-powered phone handset used to control *Bulkeley*'s topside weapons stations. Scooping up a pair of glasses himself, Stewart joined the party on the bridgewing.

"Gun One track the leader. Gun Three stay on the trail boat," the OOD directed, his voice filled with tension.

Stewart picked out the indistinct, high-speed contacts silhouetted against the sand-masked light of the setting sun. He locked on to them with the powerful binoculars and the details were immediately clear.

Boghammers.

The sleek modern speedboats were headed south at high speed, and from their course it was clear they would cross the bow of the *Bulkeley* at close range. Both boats mounted heavy-caliber machine guns aft, but Stewart wasn't able to make out any other weapons or determine the number of crew on board. Stewart recognized the Boghammers as the same type of gunboats that had attacked the *Manchester*, and he knew that the Swedish-built craft were a favorite of the Revolutionary Guards. He estimated their range at approximately two thousand yards.

"General Quarters, Captain?" the XO asked. He was standing beside Donelli, straining to make out the small boats through the sandstorm.

"No. We'll watch them a bit," Donelli answered. He bent down and spoke into a battle intercom. "TAO; Captain. Have you got them locked up, yet?"

A metallic voice quickly responded. "No firm lock-on, Captain. Four and Five are having trouble tracking them."

Stewart immediately suspected that the small radar cross section of the boats, combined with the poor atmospherics, was making it difficult for the ship's fire control radars to lock on to the Boghammers. He turned to Donelli, who was studying the gunboats intently.

"Pass the targets to the TDTs, Captain?" Stewart asked. His tone was part question and part suggestion.

"Concur," Donelli responded forcefully. Keeping his eyes fixed on the Boghammers, the Captain bent to the intercom. "TAO; Captain. Pass control of the gun to the starboard TDT."

As Donelli was speaking, Stewart noticed that the reporters had found their way up to the bridge. They were clustered around the open door leading to the bridgewing, Kim in front. Stewart fixed his eyes on hers.

"If you want something interesting to write about, follow me!"

And then Stewart was moving, not waiting for her response, heading aft toward the ladder that led to the deck above the bridge. The sound of her hurried footsteps on the steel deck behind him told Stewart that she had taken up his challenge.

He went up the ten-foot vertical ladder in three vaulting strides and then headed forward to the target designation tracker, or TDT, located above the starboard bridgewing. The TDT was an optical tracker mounted on a T-shaped pillar rising from the deck. The fire controlman manning the device was hunched forward, his arms spread across the broad yoke of steel.

As Stewart reached the starboard TDT, he saw the operator training his binocular-aided tracker on the lead boat. There was a whine of drive motors as the operator was given control of the gun, and the 76-millimeter turret amidships slewed to point at the lead Boghammer. As the operator moved his TDT, the gun mount followed its movements.

"How's she tracking, Landis?" Stewart's voice was cool and professional. He heard Kim come up behind him as the operator replied.

"His ass is mine, Mr. Stewart," the operator said without turning from his optical sight. "All I need is the Captain's go-ahead and that baby's history."

Stewart turned to Kim and pointed to the pistol-grip control the TDT operator clutched in his right hand.

"See that trigger? One order from the CO and we can start putting high-explosive holes in those boats as fast as he can squeeze the trigger."

Kim watched in fascination, alternating her attention between the gun mount, the TDT, and the Boghammers—now at a thousand yards and still moving toward the frigate.

"Will he give the order to fire?"

"I don't think so," Stewart observed. "Look there."

Kim looked from Stewart back toward the speedboats in time to see the Boghammers altering course to parallel the *Bulkeley's* track. As the two of them watched, the speedboats continued on at high speed, gradually moving forward of *Bulkeley's* beam and opening in range.

"Was that an aborted attack on us, John?" she asked.

Stewart spoke without shifting his attention from the Iranians. "Not likely. Appears our friends are on their way to hit some poor sucker in the tanker lanes down south." Stewart paused to watch the TDT operator edge the tracker gently to his left to follow the lead boat. "Part of our job here is to monitor the attacks they launch out of Abu Musa Island," he continued. "They've got a regular navy base there, but also Revolutionary Guard gunboats."

As the speedboats faded from view, Stewart headed for the life rail and looked down on the crowded starboard wing. The voice of the TAO, going out on the Command Net to report the Boghammers' current position, course, and speed to COM JTF, echoed up to him from the bridgewing speaker. He saw Captain Donelli nod, as if satisfied with the report and the departure of the gunboats, and gesture to the reporters to reenter the bridge. Before following them he looked up toward Stewart.

"Weps, drop down to CIC and tell them to retake control of the gun." Donelli's tone darkened. "And I want some answers on why we couldn't lock those clowns up."

"Aye, Captain." Stewart gave Kim a cryptic smile before heading for the ladder to the bridge. She watched his retreating form for several seconds before following him.

As Stewart and Kim reentered the bridge, Neil Perren was stepping forward to ask the CO a question. Perren took a half step back in surprise as Donelli vaulted into his elevated captain's chair with a grace that his stocky physique would not have indicated. He pulled a well-chewed cigar from his pocket and bit down on it, showing no interest in lighting up, and spun in his traversable chair to address the journalists.

"With those unpredictable RevGuard bastards out tonight, I think I'll stay on the bridge awhile. Two-Six can wait." The Captain looked from the male reporters to Kim.

"Now, Miss Mitchell, Gentlemen; what about that interview?"

ABU MUSA ISLAND

The setting sun, filtered through a mask of airborne grit, bathed the beach in a dying, smoky light. The temperature would start downward now, but even at its coolest, an hour before dawn, it would remain in the high nineties.

Major Aziz was satisfied with the progress of his preparations. The black Zodiacs were inflated and nestled at the water's edge, each equipped with a specially silenced outboard motor. The equipment was carefully distributed among the boats, according to his instructions. Only the cargo raft showed any exposed objects above its gunwales, and they extended less than a foot.

With the light failing, and the outfitting of the boats complete, he had directed Sergeant Major Rafsani to assemble the men for one final briefing.

"They are ready, Major," came a low, controlled voice from behind Aziz.

Turning, he saw the massive figure of his old comrade-in-arms. The man's silhouette was little softened by the deepening twilight. The two men had trained together under the Royal Marine instructors at the Special Boat Squadron School in Dorset many years ago. Only the two of them left out of the thirty who had started there, Aziz thought. And much of their survival could be attributed to the fact that they had managed to serve together for most of the twelve years of nearly constant war with Iraq.

"What does your gut tell you, Hadi," the Major asked, "about the chances for success?"

The big man's face was cocooned in an enormous night-black beard; only his eyes were readily seen. When he spoke the beard seemed to open, reluctantly, to allow the passage of his words.

"It is a good plan. Our men are the best. My only concern is with the Guards."

Aziz gave an almost imperceptible nod of acknowledgment. He had fought the inclusion of the Revolutionary Guard unit from the outset. They had little discipline, were not well trained, and their contempt for the professional military made them suspect on any joint operation. The Southern Command had backed him on this against the Regional Guards Commander, but then word had come from Tehran: the Guards were to be included. There would be no further discussion.

"The tasks we have assigned them are relatively simple, old friend," the Major said. "But if they fail in those tasks—or endanger the mission—you and I will solve the Guards problem."

"As God wills." There was a hint of a smile through the larger man's beard.

"Let us join the men," Aziz said. The Sergeant Major strode off in front of the Major, as was proper.

The force of nineteen men sat cross-legged on the crest of a small bluff overlooking the Zodiac boats. The Guards had donned the black clothing, but they were still distinct, sitting in their own group a few yards to the right of the marines. Not a good sign, Aziz thought as he mounted the bluff. He positioned himself in front of the two groups of silent men; Sergeant Major Rafsani was behind him and to his right. Kalil rose from his place at the head of the Guards and joined Aziz before the men. Aziz was relieved to see that the Guards Commander had foregone his white turban and was now bareheaded along with the rest of the men. Kalil folded his arms sullenly and gave the Major a curt nod, as if signaling him to proceed.

Aziz restrained his first impulse, which was to tell Kalil to sit back down and listen as if his life depended on doing so—for it would. Instead, he raised his hand, palm outward, to the group. "God is great," he said in a voice just loud enough for the farthest man to hear.

"God is great," the assembled men echoed back, the Guards twice as loudly as the marines.

"A great enterprise awaits us," the Major said as he scanned the group slowly. "Our success will bring glory to God and our Islamic Republic."

The Guards gave a brief cheer with shouts of "Allahu Akbar!" Kalil and Aziz's marines remained silent.

"Each of you was assigned his mission at the operational briefing. If you have any final questions, ask them now." There were no gestures or voices from the seated men.

Aziz addressed the Guards directly. "So there can be no chance of misunderstanding, remember that this is a military operation" —he glanced at Kalil—"and I am the Commander of that operation. Colonel Kalil will assist me in this—but there can be only one leader."

"There will be no misunderstanding, Major," Kalil said, speaking slowly. The anger in his face was obvious to Aziz, but not to the men seated in the gathering darkness.

"Sleep if you can," the Major said to the assembled group. "We leave when the moon is down."

THE <u>BULKELEY</u>

"The only thing worse than flying in one of these fucking sandstorms is doing it at night," Lee Hammond said, as much to himself as to the others who crowded around the CIC chart table with him. Stewart stood beside the pilot, along with the current TAO, Lieutenant Jack Nelson, and the ATACO. Donelli required Stewart, as the senior tactical action officer, to conduct the mission briefs for all nighttime helicopter patrols. It meant that Stewart lost a little more sleep, but the Captain could rest easier.

"That's why you guys pick up all of that fabulous flight pay, Lee," Stewart said. He shared a stateroom with Hammond, and they got along exceptionally well for an "Airdale" and a "Black-shoe."

After six days operating in the same patrol box, the chart of the area was boringly familiar to Hammond. His copilot, "Mad Max" Rogers, was up on the bridge, verifying the visibility, wind speed, and barometric pressure. The Weatherfax had already confirmed there was no sign of the storm abating.

Hammond gave the chart a quick scan and looked up at the air controller. "Looks like low vis all night, Goldman. We're going to have to get right on top of 'em for IDs, even with the infrared."

OS1 Goldman nodded in agreement. His job became even more important under these conditions. It was his responsibility to keep Sealord clear of other air traffic, steer her away from Iranian warships and oil platforms, and keep the helo from violating the airspace claimed by half a dozen Gulf states. The three men moved to Goldman's ATACO display console, where the current surface and air picture had been selected.

"Our boy is still hanging in there about twelve miles to the east," Stewart said, pointing to the video symbol that represented the Saam frigate *Abaland*.

"Maybe he's assigned to the same box as us," Nelson joked.

"Could be, Jack. Either way, you and Goldman just keep us away from our Iranian friend," Hammond said. He patted the .357 Magnum holstered under his left armpit. "They tend to get a bit edgy around helos, and Sealord already has all the holes she needs in her by design." He turned to Stewart. "Any other activity?"

"You know about the two Boghammers we saw headed south about two hours ago," Stewart said. "No sign of them since, and no distress calls on bridge-to-bridge to indicate they've zapped anyone." Every ship in the Gulf, merchant or military, carried a VHF radio on its bridge. The radios were all tuned to channel 16, the so-called Gulf Common, which allowed the ships to talk to each other. With the strange atmospherics of the region, VHF radio ranges as short as five miles or as great as two hundred were not unusual. "If we get a sniff on them we'll let you know."

"Okay," Hammond said. "Looks pretty standard except for the visibility. We'll be back on deck at midnight for gas, and at zero four hundred for a crew swap."

As the pilot headed for the door out of the Combat Information Center he was cut off by Nelson. "Met the press people yet, Lee?" Nelson grinned conspiratorially, looking over Hammond's shoulder to verify that Stewart was still on the other side of the CIC.

"No. I was in my pit when they got here. I heard the woman's a real looker."

"That's a fact. *However* . . ." Nelson strung it out. "She and Stewart apparently have the hots for each other from way back."

"Damn the bad luck," Hammond boomed with feigned disappointment. "Guess I'm stuck with you as my date for the senior prom."

Hammond elbowed Jack Nelson aside and headed aft through the darkened passageways to the flight deck.

Kim listened carefully to Captain Donelli's responses as the small recorder she had set on his desk silently recorded the interview. They had moved to the Captain's cabin when it had grown too dark on the bridge to continue there. Donelli's sea cabin was located at the base of an inclined ladder that led to the bridge. The Combat Information Center was directly across from his door. By design, he was only seconds removed from either critical location.

The Captain had proved to be surprisingly forthcoming in the aftermath of the brief encounter with the Iranian speedboats. He almost seemed to relish the threat of confrontation that the boats had posed.

"That's business as usual," he had said. "We're not at war with Iran, so they have to pose a direct threat to us, or show 'hostile intent,' before I can act."

Bosca had jumped on that, and he and Perren had been trying unsuccessfully for the last fifteen minutes to get Donelli to give his opinion on the policy. Kim grudgingly admired the flinty Captain's ability to turn away the question, never answering directly. At one point she interjected a question about the stress on the crew from operating continuously in a lethal war zone. Bob Bosca gave her an irritated look for having changed the subject, but Donelli welcomed the opportunity to move onto less treacherous ground.

"That's a vital issue which people still don't understand very well," Donelli began. "These kids have been just magnificent so far, but the unrelieved tension of sailing in the Gulf is bound to take its toll." He unwrapped a fresh cigar and inserted it, once again unlit, into his mouth. "Hell, even in World War Two, ships would spend only thirty or sixty days in a high-threat zone and then pull back to some safer spot so their crews could recharge their batteries. Here it's three or four months straight, and we have to maintain maximum readiness, whether in port or at sea."

Kim nodded and took a few notes, as the Captain expounded on a question he clearly relished answering.

"How do you feel about playing policeman out here in a war we're not directly a party to?" Neil Perren interjected.

"I can deal with it. Being perceived as a potential threat by both sides has its disadvantages," he added, shifting his attention from Perren to the other reporters, "but it's not that much different from what you people do."

"How do you mean, Captain?" Kim asked.

"You're supposed to walk the tightrope too, correct? To not take sides, to remain . . . *objective*?" Donelli spoke the last word with a trace of disgust. "Let's just say I have no illusions that your coverage of me will be any different from what you'd give the Iranian CO sitting on that frigate that's dogging us." He sat back in his chair and studied Kim.

"If you mean that we wouldn't paint a falsely positive picture of you or your ship out of some sort of idealistic patriotism, you're right, Captain," Kim responded, trying to suppress the beginnings of anger. "We're here to report on the war in the Gulf, not to cheerlead."

Donelli flashed a cold, dangerous smile. "No need to tell me that. I'm quite familiar with what happened to Bill Wallach when you were on board his ship." Kim froze for a moment, her cheeks reddening slightly. Before she could respond, Donelli continued. "Don't misunderstand me, Miss Mitchell. If what you reported was true, I think you performed a service for the Navy. The man shouldn't have remained in command."

"Some of your officers don't agree with you." Kim regretted the words before she had finished speaking them. Bosca looked over at her nervously, unsure of where all this was heading.

"Stewart, you mean? Well, men develop loyalties to their captains, Miss Mitchell; that's the way the system is supposed to work. Stewart's my top department head—one of the best I've ever worked with, in fact—and he'll make a helluva captain someday. He succeeds because he puts the interest of the crew and the ship ahead of his own. A lot of officers never grasp the concept that loyalty has to travel in both directions; Stewart has. The only problem with an officer like him is that once he gives his loyalty to a ship—or a man—he has trouble seeing their weaknesses." Donelli paused, fixing his eyes on Kim's. "I don't think you understand what it means to a man like that to think he has contributed to his captain's downfall."

"Oh, I think I do understand, Captain." Kim had listened to Donelli in silence, and she spoke now with the mechanical precision of someone exercising great control. "But apparently this loyalty you're talking about . . . only extends to the Navy."

Suddenly the conversation was interrupted by the growling tone of the sound-powered phone at Donelli's desk. The Captain answered the phone, listened for a moment, and then started to speak animatedly.

Bosca saw Donelli's sudden distraction as an opportunity to head off trouble. "Thank you, Captain," he said, rising from his chair. "We've taken up enough of your time." But Donelli was already hotly chastising some unfortunate caller. He waved to them with a slight smile and continued his conversation without breaking stride.

"Come on, Kim," Bosca said, gesturing to the door. As she walked past Bosca to the door, Perren assisted Mack in disassembling his videocam tripod.

In the darkened passageway outside Donelli's stateroom, Kim turned to Bosca. "*Damn* it. I'm sorry, Bob. That sort of thing is not supposed to happen." She sighed. "I'm sure I confirmed any misgivings he had about having reporters aboard."

Bosca chuckled softly, his face barely visible in the glow of the red night-lighting. "On first impressions I'd wager our Captain is a little more broad-minded than that." He paused thoughtfully. "However, if you're going to make the most of this trip, you better resolve whatever's wrong between you and Lieutenant Commander Stewart."

"You're right—of course. I wonder if I can find him, talk this out."

Bosca held his wrist up to his face and read the illuminated dial of his aging Rolex. "Eight thirty. I'd be surprised if he wasn't already in one of those shoe boxes they call a bed. He did mention at dinner that he was going back on watch at midnight."

THE PASCAGOULA

The only illumination visible on USS *Pascagoula* was the dim glow of her two yellow anchor lights, one at the bow and one at the stern. Her tall, boxy silhouette was all that distinguished her from the tankers and cargo ships sharing the anchorage at Sitrah. Topside on the dark ship, heavily armed security forces kept a continuous silent watch. The harbor appeared innocent of trouble, but any watercraft that drew too near the *Pascagoula* was immediately intercepted and escorted clear by the high-speed SeaFox patrol boats that quietly criscrossed the flagship's anchorage.

Garmisch reached the Admiral's quarters at 2000, just as eight bells sounded throughout the flagship. Knocking on the door and then entering the flag mess, Garmisch saw that Rear Admiral Boone and the Chief of Staff were at the large dining table in the center of the mess, having their after-dinner coffee. The lack of any greeting from the senior officers told him that this was going to be a hard sell.

"Good evening Admiral, Captain."

"All right, Jim." Boone skipped the formalities, setting a tone that was not encouraging. "Captain Lacey has given me the outline of your theory. What have you got to support this?"

The fact that Garmisch was not asked to sit down was an even worse indicator of the Admiral's disposition. He pressed on anyway, carefully laying out his supporting data, which showed almost a 50-percent increase in RevGuard activity since the attack on *Manchester*. Then he handed Boone and Lacey a marked-up chart showing the respective positions of the *Bulkeley* and the *Abaland* over the last six days. From the chart it was apparent that the two ships had routinely operated within ten to fifteen miles of each other. Lastly, Garmisch described how *Abaland* was not following any normal mission pattern, was in fact doing nothing except patrolling in close proximity to *Bulkeley*.

Boone heard him out, carefully reviewing the information Garmisch had assembled. At the conclusion of Garmisch's presentation, the Admiral remained rigid, looking at him impassively through a full thirty seconds of silence.

"This is all fairly interesting, Lieutenant Commander Garmisch," Boone said. "But you hardly have sufficient indicators here to prove that an attack on *Bulkeley* is imminent, or even planned."

"A lot of it is circumstantial, Admiral," Jim admitted, feeling his chance to convince the old man slipping away. "But coming on the heels of the unprovoked attack on *Manchester*, this unusual activity is a bad sign. Something is wrong out there."

Boone gave him a flat, humorless smile. "You've been on board what, two months, Jim?"

"Almost three now, sir."

"And your background is primarily engineering, as I recall?"

Garmisch knew where this was going. He unconsciously glanced down at the impressive row of combat decorations below the pilot's wings on Boone's military-creased shirt before catching himself and meeting the older man's gaze.

"Yes sir. Two chief engineer tours before coming here. But I was the lead tactical action officer on my last ship. I spent almost as much time in CIC as with the plant."

Boone smiled at that. "I'm not questioning your background, Jim. I only do this to illustrate a point." The Admiral leaned back in the plush leather chair. "That point being that analysis of indicators and prediction is difficult enough even for the professional

intel guys—those same spooks, by the way, who don't see anything abnormal about the current level of activity in the eastern
Gulf."

That's it, finito, Garmisch thought. But Boone continued.

"I do think there's enough anomalous behavior here on the part
of our Iranian friends to request a special intelligence estimate
from CENTCOM. I'm not prepared to pull *Bulkeley* back, however;
you don't have enough to go on, and our presence in that part of
the Gulf is vital."

Garmisch nodded his understanding. The request to CENTCOM,
the U.S. Central Command located at MacDill Air Force Base in
Florida, for the special intel evaluation would help, but it would
take at least twenty-four hours to get a response. Meanwhile *Bulkeley* would continue to be bird-dogged by *Abaland*, and the attack
that Garmisch felt was imminent would draw closer.

"In the aftermath of the *Manchester* attack, those bastards would
love to intimidate us away from the Straits and Abu Musa," Admiral Boone said with finality. "But that's exactly what we will not
let them do." He turned to Lacey. "Let's get this message out
tonight, Captain."

"Will do, Admiral." The Chief of Staff looked from Boone back
to Garmisch. "Meet me in the TDC in fifteen minutes and we'll
put the message together."

"Aye, Captain. Thank you, Admiral." Garmisch turned and
headed out of the room, feeling the two men's eyes on his back.
As he closed the door behind him, he felt his body relax almost
involuntarily.

Heading forward through the darkened passageways toward
the Tactical Decision Center, Garmisch spoke his thoughts aloud:
"I would be thrilled to be wrong on this one."

3

THE <u>BULKELEY</u>

S tewart moved steadily aft through a succession of red-lit passageways. He balanced a steaming cup of coffee in his hand
as he navigated the familiar obstacles of the darkened frigate.
It was 2330, half an hour to midnight, and he had less than fifteen
minutes before he was due in the CIC to relieve as tactical action
officer.

He recognized the first pain of a headache beginning at the back
of his neck; one more sign of how poorly he had slept. The coffee
would not help the headache, he knew, but remaining alert was
more important than being comfortable. Stewart came to the end
of the long passageway between the two hangars, which led to
the flight deck, and shifted the plastic cup to his other hand as he
reached for the watertight door. Pushing the door open, he was
immediately struck by the wave of heat from the dark flight deck.
Stewart stepped out onto the deck, closing the watertight door
and sealing the ship's air-conditioning in behind him.

The moon was low, he saw, and when it went it would take
what little visibility there was with it. Looking down the flight
deck to the stern of the ship, he could make out the shadowy
figures of four men. Stewart knew from the hour that the four
men must be turning over the after .50-caliber-machine-gun
watch. There would be two gunners coming on and two going off
for a few hours of sleep. He stayed in the shadow of the hangars
and did not disturb their watch turnover. The scene was being

repeated in numerous watch stations throughout the ship, with dozens of men shifting the watch and entrusting their reliefs with keeping the ship safe while they slept. Ultimately they were trusting him, Stewart realized. As tactical action officer, Stewart acted for the Captain in his absence. That responsibility weighed heavily on him, but it also served to reaffirm his desire to achieve a command of his own one day. One man, a ship's captain, responsible for the lives of more than two hundred others: it was at once a frightening and an exhilarating thought to him.

Stewart took a sip of coffee and tasted the grit of sand that had already settled on the cup's rim. He tossed the tainted coffee over the side and wished again that he had skipped the few hours of restless sleep. Stewart knew he had hit the rack as much to avoid Kim as to benefit from any sleep.

The scene in the wardroom had not been pleasant. In only minutes of conversation they had returned to the issue that had finished off their relationship. You brought it up, too, he reminded himself. Seeing Kim again and feeling the magnetic pull of her eyes had brought back memories of the passion and excitement of his time with her. But the recollection of what had happened to Captain Wallach would not stay buried in his mind.

Things had been going so well for them then, too. Kim had been unlike any woman he had ever encountered. When he first met her in Norfolk, she charmed Admiral Jarvis into giving a far more honest interview than he had intended to, and Stewart had marveled at her skill. He had loved her directness and admired the way she moved so smoothly between the different worlds of Washington politics and the Navy. He soon understood that her disarmingly pleasant style served a dogged determination to get at the truth.

Although not a classic beauty, Kim conveyed a suppressed sensuality that attracted him from the beginning. One casual dinner had confirmed that the attraction he felt to her was not one-sided, and the next weekend found him bending the speed limit in his haste to join her for the two days in D.C. As their relationship grew, the intensity of the romance exceeded anything in Stewart's experience. Although his demanding job as an Admiral's aide kept him on the road a great deal and away from Kim, their reunions were explosive expressions of physical and emotional affection. Their romance even survived his return to sea duty—or at least, it had seemed to initially.

His new assignment was to a Norfolk-based Perry-class frigate, the *Fraser*, and during Stewart's first six months on board, the ship was under way almost continuously, and Kim was frequently gone on assignment. Their opportunities to be with each other were few, but they continued to make the most of them. Although he hated being away from Kim, Stewart found his new job to be the most rewarding of his career. It was made so by his relationship with his commanding officer, Captain Wallach. Wallach was a superb CO who took a particular liking to Stewart and taught him a great deal. In half a year working for Wallach, Stewart learned more about seamanship, tactics, and leadership than he had the whole prior part of his career. Their mentor-pupil relationship was marred only by Stewart's suspicion, based on close observation of his captain, that Wallach took an occasional drink while under way. He never saw any evidence that it impaired Wallach's judgment or professional performance, but it bothered Stewart nonetheless.

At the conclusion of one particularly grueling exercise, Wallach had declared that he was throwing a party to celebrate the ship's success. The captain had insisted on Stewart bringing the attractive journalist, whom the whole wardroom knew he was seeing. Wallach had already been fairly drunk when Stewart and Kim had appeared at the party, drunk enough to invite her to go to sea with them the next week on a day cruise to get a look at the "real Navy." Sensing trouble, Stewart had tried without success to turn the whole thing off.

He never knew what made Wallach go off the deep end that day at sea with a woman on board, and a woman reporter at that. The half-drunken interview the captain had given Kim in his cabin had been the point of no return—both for Wallach and for Stewart's relationship with Kim. Asking her to suppress the story had been one of the most difficult and painful things that Stewart had ever had to do. When he found that she could not, or would not, kill the story, his pain had turned to anger. Kim simply could not understand why he would want to leave Wallach in command of a Navy ship, why he wanted to protect the man. It was then that Stewart realized that despite all their closeness and passion, she really did not know him, did not understand that personal loyalty was of paramount importance to him. In the aftermath of Wallach's relief, Stewart asked for and received a transfer to a new ship. His new orders brought him to the *Bulkeley*.

The electronic beeper on his watch roused Stewart from his brief reverie; only five minutes until he had to be in the CIC to relieve as TAO. Recalling that he wanted to stop by Radio Central and pick up his message traffic before going on watch, Stewart turned and headed back toward the superstructure.

As he secured the door behind him, Stewart reflected that avoiding Kim was not the answer. He determined to find her in the morning and talk it out, no matter how painful it might be.

The *Bulkeley* moved at an almost stately pace down the western leg of her patrol track. Ships in constricted patrol boxes such as the *Bulkeley* operated at low speeds, especially after nightfall. Visibility worsened dramatically at night, particularly in the summer sandstorms common to the Gulf, and the low speeds were intended to give the officer of the deck time to respond in the event of a late detection of a threatening object.

The ship's surface search radar gave a clear picture of merchant and military shipping, as well as the ubiquitous oil rigs, but many of the myriad small craft that plied the Gulf would not appear on the radar at all. Wooden dhows were used by fishermen, smugglers, and other seafarers. The dhows, resembling a stylized version of a viking longship with their high prows and sterns and single great sail, were modeled on a design unchanged since before the time of Christ. Neither the dhows nor the modern fiberglass boats, also widely in use, provided a significant radar reflection. As had been reality since time immemorial, the true eyes of the ship were her lookouts and bridge watch team. Avoiding a collision or surprise attack was a central responsibility of these men, but there was one even greater concern to them in these waters.

Mines.

The threat of mines was foremost in Scott Septenano's mind as he relieved the bridge watch that night. It was shortly before midnight when he spoke the traditional words, "I relieve you, sir," and assumed the deck. A quick reading of the Captain's night order book had confirmed the worst: moonset was only half an hour into his watch. The already poor visibility would deteriorate further with the loss of that source of light. He walked forward to the bridge windows and looked down to the fo'c'sle. Septenano had waited to relieve as OOD until his night vision was sound, and with his darkness-adapted eyes, he could clearly make out the figures of the mine watch. They were stationed as far forward on the bow as possible. He could see the two sailors alertly scanning the waters ahead of *Bulkeley*, one using binoculars, the other his unaided vision.

Without taking his eyes off the men, Septenano called out to the Bosun's Mate of the watch, "Boats, I want you to make a circuit of each of the lookout stations once an hour. Pour coffee into 'em, talk to them—do whatever you have to, but keep 'em awake and alert."

"Aye-aye, Mr. Septenano," a salty basso voice came back from the darkness.

Mosopu was his Bosun. That's a plus, Septenano thought to himself. The big Samoan was a pure professional who had learned his craft at Noah's knee. He would not have to provide any further direction; Mosopu would anticipate everything and make the watch run smoothly.

En route to the bridge, Septenano had stopped off in the CIC to get a feel for the larger picture and determine when flight quarters would go next. Jack Nelson had been in the process of turning over TAO with Stewart, and he had reviewed the surface picture for them both. Merchant traffic to the south of *Bulkeley* was running heavy, as it always did after dark. The supertankers and cargo ships headed for the Straits were willing to run the greater risk of collision at night in order to reduce their chance of being attacked. The limited visibility was a double-edged sword, hampering both hunter and prey. Nelson had pointed out that their shadow, the *Abaland*, was still loitering at a distance of roughly ten miles. Just stay away from us on my watch, Septenano had thought.

"Contact twenty degrees to port!"

The young OOD darted across to the port side of the bridge in response to the urgent shout from Chief Marquez. Bringing his binoculars up and looking through them in the general direction of Marquez's report, Septenano immediately saw the dim white light. It was practically on top of them!

"Right full rudder!" he ordered. Captain Donelli had insisted his OODs maintain the conn during nighttime steaming.

Every eye on the bridge stayed on the faint light as the *Bulkeley* slowly swung around to starboard. There had been no time to increase speed to help the turn come around. Septenano estimated the distance at five hundred feet, and whatever it was had drawn within ten degrees of his bow.

"Fishing float, Mr. Septenano," Mosopu called from the port bridgewing. Spinning to his left and looking out the wing window, Septenano saw Mosopu pointing to the object. He focused hard through his binoculars and at last could make out the kerosene lantern on a pole made fast to a small raft. The sharp seaman's eyes of the Bosun's Mate had made out the float unaided by binoculars.

"Jesus," Septenano said under his breath. "Left standard rudder, steady two-five-zero."

"Left standard rudder, steady two-five-zero, aye sir," the helmsman responded.

As the *Bulkeley* gracefully arched back to her original heading, Mosopu joined Septenano and Chief Marquez in a quiet huddle near the captain's chair.

"Good job spotting that thing, Chief," Septenano said. His relief was palpable. "You too, Mosi; good eyes." He looked away from the men and back out ahead of *Bulkeley*. "Tonight's going to be a real son of a bitch," he said softly. "Especially when the moon goes."

SEALORD 25

Hammond shifted his eyes from the instruments to the view offered through his cockpit windscreen. Once again he cursed the Iranians, the Iraqis, and anyone else who was responsible for his having to fly in this mess. With no visible horizon and little to use as a reference, he was flying on instruments and instinct. The ceiling—if you could call it that—of the sandstorm was barely one hundred feet off the deck. They were at five hundred feet, descending to get a closer look at a contact that *Bulkeley*'s TAO, via OS1 Goldman, had asked them to investigate. Both the *Bulkeley*'s AN/SLQ-32 electronic warfare system and the airborne counterpart on Hammond's helo had detected a surface-search radar that corresponded to those used on Iranian La Combattante patrol boats. Triangulation of the two ESM lines had pointed right to the ship they were now on top of.

The contact was some twenty miles south of *Bulkeley*, steaming in the shipping lanes. Unfortunately, as Hammond was only too well aware, some merchant ships carried the same radar as the Iranian gunboats. Leveling off at three hundred, Hammond could just begin to discern the outline of their quarry.

"I've got him, Goldman," the pilot said into his voice-activated helmet mike. Communications between Sealord and *Bulkeley* were via a secure-voice and data link of exceptional clarity.

"Roger, Sealord. Turn left to one-five-zero to remain clear."

"Copy," Hammond responded, putting the aircraft into a slow bank to the left. The maneuver would keep Sealord from closing within three miles of the contact. Hammond would go in closer for the ID, if necessary, but three miles was the prescribed "keep-out zone" established by COM JTF. Not coincidentally, three miles was the edge of the effective-range envelope for Iranian antiaircraft guns and shoulder-held SAMs.

"She's warmed up, boss. Let's see what we've got." Max Rogers's voice echoed in Hammond's helmet. Lee quickly glanced to his right and saw that his copilot had finished the warm-up on the infrared night vision device and was moving it into place. When Hammond looked outside again, he saw the dark silhouette of the contact fade from view as the sand closed in around it. Even at three and a half miles, the storm effectively concealed the ship.

"He's not a bad guy," Max said, somewhat disappointedly. The whirling sand and water vapor were not sufficient to obscure the heat sources and "hot-spot" outline of the contact. The cloudy, spectral outline visible through the NVD was readily identifiable as that of a merchant ship.

"Definite tanker," Max said. "He's a big dog, but I can't tell much more than that, unless you want to close him."

In silent response, Hammond started a slow climb to five hundred feet, banking back toward the north.

"Okay, ATACO," he addressed the *Bulkeley's* airborne tactical control operator, "we've got a positive ID on that guy as a large tanker. Who would you like to look at next?" Hammond eased a bit in his harness as he leveled off at the higher altitude. Stewart was right about us earning our flight pay tonight, he thought.

THE ZODIACS

The rubber boats, moving through the water with their silenced electric motors, were as quiet as Aziz had remembered. He had worked with these boats before, in an operation on the Iraqi side of the Shatt-al-Arab waterway. Then as now, the boats gave little warning of their approach.

Looking aft from his lead boat, the Major could make out the dim outline of the Zodiac following in his wake. The Sergeant Major controlled that craft, which was arguably the most important to their mission. Aziz would have preferred to space the boats farther apart, but the poor visibility did not allow it. It was more important that they not lose contact with each other, and he had expressly ordered each boat commander never to lose sight of the boat ahead. Without seeing it, he knew that ten feet astern of Rafsani's boat lay the cargo raft, under tow. Farther back would be the other two rubber boats that made up the remainder of his small flotilla.

As he returned his attention to the water ahead of the lead boat, Aziz's glance passed across the form of Kalil, seated amidships in the center of the Zodiac. Major Aziz had divided the RevGuards among the four manned boats, and if Kalil objected, he had not said so. Prior experience had convinced Aziz that the Guards were considerably less combative when they did not have a mob of their peers from which to draw courage. He wondered briefly if

Kalil's surly compliance presaged something more dangerous than his direct opposition. Well, it was too late to look back now. Dividing the Guards would prove useful in other ways if there was trouble from that quarter.

The only conversation on board any of the Zodiacs was between the coxswain of Aziz's boat and another marine, who sat just forward of the boat's stern. This marine sat low in the bottom of the boat, his seat on the athwartship strake given up to a breadbox-size electronic device. The marine wore a headset, which was plugged into the device; whatever display the equipment generated was covered with a black plastic shroud. The marine kept his head under this shroud, wearing it like a hood. Periodically he would call out a bearing, and the coxswain would check his small compass and adjust the boat's rudder to conform to the direction given.

Aziz was not pleased that his fate and the fate of his mission rested with that black box. He trusted the man who operated it, however, and he trusted in God. He did not understand the workings of the direction finder, as he thought of it, but he did know that the machine was dependent on the Americans continuing to transmit their radars. There had been much discussion of this at the briefing. What would happen if the Americans simply secured their radars for maintenance? What if the radars broke down, or the direction finder failed? But ultimately there was no alternative; the position provided by the *Abaland* could only get them headed in the right general direction, and active search transmissions from the Zodiacs, even if possible, would prove suicidal.

Inshallah, Aziz thought: as God wills. We have done all we can to prepare; now the time to act is upon us. He had lost count of the number of his combat missions since the war had begun. Each flowed into the other in his memory, the only distinction being the remembrance of one or more of his men who had died in the course of an operation. This was to be his last mission, Aziz had decided. Whether it ended in success or failure, he was going to put the fighting behind him. He would return to his home in the Zagros Mountains. They could come after him if they chose, but he had had enough of the killing.

Even as he reflected on his decision, Aziz felt the growing tension of the men in the Zodiac with him. The adrenaline punch of approaching combat was an old friend Aziz knew well. His men, even the ones new to the team, were veterans of fierce fighting and would be experiencing similar sensations. He could not be so certain of what the Guards might be feeling. He had been promised that they all had combat experience, but that was not altogether reassuring. To the Guards, combat experience could well mean rocketing an unarmed merchant ship, or battling among themselves in one of their interminable power struggles. He had directed that all weapons have their safeties on while the force was embarked in the boats. It was an unnecessary order for his marines, but it might prevent a nervous Guard from getting them all killed.

Aziz had a good idea of what would befall his force if they were detected before reaching their objective. He had seen the effects of high-rate-of-fire cannon and heavy machine guns on landing parties in rubber rafts. The one rocket-propelled grenade launcher they carried in Rafsani's boat was hardly an equalizer. No, stealth was everything. The same darkness and wind-borne sand that might keep them from locating their target provided their only chance of reaching it alive.

The Major peered out over the night-black water, trying to find something to focus on.

In the darkness, he heard the unmistakable rotor sound of a large helicopter approaching from out of the south.

Aziz shot his clenched fist over his head and waved it back and forth in a slow arc. Sergeant Major Rafsani saw the signal to halt just as the sound of the helicopter reached his ears. He relayed it in turn to the other Zodiacs.

Aziz was thankful for the suddenness with which the Zodiacs lost speed once their engines were cut. Regardless of the awful visibility, the Major did not want to show a wake or present a more easily detectable moving target to the helicopter's computer-aided radar. He had studied the Seahawk's known capabilities carefully, and he felt that with the low reflectivity of the Zodiac's neoprene skin, radar detection was unlikely. His greatest concern was infrared detection. The Iranian Navy intelligence officer at the briefing had been uncertain what type of night vision device the Seahawk carried or how good it was.

At Aziz's signal to halt, the coxswains had immediately secured their Zodiacs' electric motors: that eliminated one heat source. Also, as prearranged, his men dropped below the gunwales of their respective boats to reduce their chance of visual or IR detection.

As he listened to the pounding sound of the fast-approaching aircraft, Aziz thought he could feel the vibration of the helicopter's rotors through the skin of the Zodiac. The aircraft was almost upon them.

THE BULKELEY

0145. A quick glance at his watch showed Stewart that his tactical action officer watch was almost half over. So far it had been a relatively normal night.

They had copied one report of an attack over Gulf Common at the outset of the watch. A voice with a heavy German accent had barked over the bridge-to-bridge radio circuit that his ship was under attack by speedboats at the western exit from the Straits. A cool, controlled British voice had swiftly responded, identified itself as the Omani Navy, and asked the German for his precise location. The German, presumably the stricken ship's master, could be heard yelling curses at his attackers before he answered with his position. He identified his ship as the Panamanian-flag *Andes Commerce* and stated that the speedboats had raked his ship with machine-gun fire, then broken off their attack. There was little damage to his ship, he said, and he was continuing on to his destination in Saudi Arabia.

Stewart had called COM JTF and reported the attack, including in the report his suspicion that the speedboats were the Boghammers that the *Bulkeley* had earlier encountered. Tape units in the *Bulkeley*'s CIC had recorded the tanker's distress call, and Stewart's CIC watch officer drafted a complete transcript of the radio conversation and transmitted that to COM JTF as well.

The rest of the watch had been devoted to using Sealord to identify all surface traffic out to a twenty-mile radius from the *Bulkeley*. Once a vessel was identified by the helo, its location and nature were then transmitted through the *Bulkeley*'s data link to other Navy units in the Gulf.

"Sealord has ID'd Alfa India as a large dhow, Mr. Stewart," the ATACO called out from his console. Stewart had directed Goldman to vector the helo to the northwest of *Bulkeley's* position to identify each of a large number of small contacts between Abu Musa Island and the ship. The vessel designated Alfa India was the fourth of the contacts that the helo had positively identified and, thus far, all of them had proven to be fishing boats or smugglers making the run between Iran and the United Arab Emirates.

Better safe than sorry, Stewart told himself. With the amount of RevGuard activity emanating from Abu Musa, it was always prudent to identify contacts near the island.

Suddenly, the relative silence of the CIC was broken by an urgent voice from the speaker tuned to Gulf Common.

"Mayday! Mayday! This is *Andes Commerce*. I have an out-of-control fire started by those bastards' gunfire!" Stewart crossed the CIC to stand directly under the speaker. He recognized the German master's voice, now far more excited than before.

"*Andes Commerce*, this is Omani Navy. Pass us your current position and we will head fireboats out to you. Do you have any casualties? Over." The same British voice had promptly responded to the new distress call.

"One casualty—our cook; he could be hurt pretty bad. We are twenty miles northeast of Abu Dhabi port," the German answered impatiently.

"Roger, *Andes Commerce*. Help will be on the way shortly." The Navy of the Sultan of Oman had both active duty and former Royal Navy officers in command of its very modern missile patrol boats. The Omanis viewed the Straits of Hormuz as their charge, and they acted aggressively and efficiently to police them.

Stewart called out to the ATACO as he picked up the "growler" to the captain's cabin.

"Goldman, get Sealord headed south and see if you can pick out which of those contacts might be this damaged merchie." The rough position *Andes Commerce* had given was only twenty-five miles southwest of *Bulkeley's* location. After two "growls" on the sound-powered phone, Stewart succeeded in waking the sleeping captain. He quickly filled Donelli in on the situation.

"I've got the picture, John," Donelli said, his voice still clotted with sleep. "When Sealord reaches her, have Hammond raise

them directly on Gulf Common and offer to take their man off."
The helicopters embarked on U.S. Navy ships in the Gulf had
been equipped with VHF radios against the possibility of just such
a need. "You get on bridge-to-bridge now, talk to the master and
the Omanis and offer humanitarian assistance. Then let COM JTF
know what we've heard and that Sealord is en route."

"Aye, Captain. Got it."

As Stewart got his watch team moving and picked up the
bridge-to-bridge radio handset, he reflected that maybe this was
not going to be such a quiet watch after all.

MV <u>ANDES COMMERCE</u>

The flames on the fantail of the *Andes Commerce* loomed large in
the overpowering darkness of the Gulf night.

Captain Rolf Hauser smiled with satisfaction as the radiance of
the fire increased. He stood a good twenty feet back from the
flames, alone on the poop deck of his ship. The three low trays of
oil were burning quite merrily now, and they were not close
enough to any flammable fixture to do any damage. Had this been
an outbound run from the fuel piers in Saudi Arabia, the fire
would have been far more dangerous. But *Andes Commerce* was on
her way into the Gulf, and accordingly she was free of her cargo
of liquified natural gas. In the galley below the poop deck, a
smudge pot was putting out dense clouds of oily smoke, which
were venting out the open portholes in the ship's transom. There
would be major smoke damage in the galley to complement the
authentic bullet holes already there.

Satisfied with his work, the master turned and headed back to
the bridge.

Hauser was a tall, razor-thin man, his balding pate long ago
shaved of any remaining trace of hair. Unlike most of his contem-
poraries, he scorned the usual wide-brimmed captain's cap. He
eschewed the use of any hat in fact, and years of Indian Ocean
steaming had long since browned his scalp to an unnatural oaken
hue.

As he reentered the bridge, all conversation ceased. His first mate, a Saudi and a Shia, newly assigned for this particular transit, moved to his side.

"We were just called by the Americans," the mate said quietly. The Saudi's broad smile was visible even on the darkened bridge. "Their helicopter is on its way to 'assist us.' " He placed a mocking emphasis on the last two words.

"Very good."

Hauser did not care for this man, or for the other two "replacement" officers he had been provided. Although of differing nationalities, they were all Shia Muslims, as was the crew of his ship. The new officers had talked to each member of his crew when they boarded the ship in Singapore. Hauser did not know the nature of their conversations, but he sensed there would be no trouble with crew members compromising the story.

The master verified the speed on the engine order telegraph. Still dead slow. Good. The flames and smoke would appear far more impressive if they were not blown aft by a speed-induced, self-created wind.

"Now we wait," he said.

Turning from the first mate, Hauser left the bridge and headed aft to his sea cabin. He entered the cabin, which was lavish even by the standards of the supertankers that traversed the Gulf, and went to the small bar. He downed the first shot of single-malt scotch in one swig and poured himself a second. Even five years ago this wouldn't have been necessary, he told himself as he emptied his glass again.

No. Five years ago would have been before the start of his numerous runs into the war-torn Gulf. It would have been before the money had become so good and his life-style improved accordingly. When he had started, the premium paid to captains making a round trip run into the Gulf had been twenty thousand dollars; compensation for the risk of having your ship shot up, as his had been on three separate occasions. Now it was up to thirty-five thousand. And he had to keep coming back. Hauser could have supported his more lavish way of life if not for the gambling. The racetrack in Hong Kong had become his narcotic, and even the premiums and his healthy master's pay were not enough.

Four hundred thousand dollars.

That was the figure the man in the casino at Macao had proposed. Not a vast fortune, but enough to let him settle his debts, take his company pension, and live quite comfortably. The man had only smiled and shaken his head at Hauser's halfhearted attempt to push up the amount. They had read him too well.

It occurred to him suddenly that the man in the casino had possessed the same too easy smile as his new first mate. Throwing down one more shot of the comforting liquid, Hauser headed for his cabin door.

Trust was a wonderful thing, he reflected, but it was not to be overvalued.

THE ZODIACS

Aziz looked skyward, barely exposing his eyes above the gunwale of the Zodiac. The distinctive rotor noise seemed to be diminishing to the south, but still he waited, fearing the aircraft might be circling in a wide loop. The sound grew weaker and weaker until it finally faded from earshot.

Standing up in the bow of the Zodiac, Aziz gave the signal to Rafsani and his coxswain. They passed it down the line, and in a moment the five boats were under way once more.

"What was the helicopter doing here?" Kalil's voice hissed in his ear. The Guards leader had silently made his way forward in the boat until he was directly behind Aziz. "What of the diversion? There was supposed to be a diversion!"

Aziz noted the equal parts of fear and anger in the larger man's voice. "So there was," he said. "It may have started late or been done improperly. Either way, the aircraft has departed." The night patrols by the American aircraft had been a given in all of their planning, and the need for an effective diversion had been recognized from the outset.

"Those dogs in intelligence!" Kalil cursed. "I told them to let me have my boats make a real attack near the Americans as a diversion."

"What you proposed would draw the ship itself away," Aziz said. "We only want to divert the helicopter." He resumed his watch ahead of the boat as if to say their discussion was at an end.

The Major heard Kalil curse under his breath and then move noisily aft in the Zodiac.

It was not a good sign that Kalil had been able to come from behind without alerting him. Aziz was forced to admit that he, too, had been shaken by the unexpected presence of the aircraft. Surprise worked both ways, he thought to himself, and the only certainty of battle was chaos.

THE BULKELEY

Damage Controlman Third Class Andy Barron wished for the hundredth time that his watch were at an end. Whenever he stood the mid, he wondered why he had volunteered for this watch station.

Andy looked aft from his position on the *Bulkeley*'s fantail and watched the ship's luminescent wake frothing gently in the dark. He glanced to starboard and saw Steele, the other member of his gun crew, readjusting his sound-powered headset for a more comfortable fit. They had exhausted all their new conversation early in the watch, and Steele had staked out the starboard side as his, leaving Andy to his thoughts. The only sound that broke the monotony was Steele acknowledging Mosopu's periodic calls on the phones to make sure they stayed alert.

As an engineer, Andy would ordinarily be standing watch in the plant, but when the Captain had asked for volunteers to augment the .50-caliber gun crews, he had jumped at the chance. The chief engineer had voiced no objections since the young petty officer had progressed so rapidly in his in-rate professional training.

The gun crew watches had seemed a great opportunity to do something dangerous and exciting; the kind of thing for which he had come into the Navy. No one, least of all his father, had understood when he had passed up the chance to work in the family hardware store, maybe run it someday, in order to enlist in the Navy. Andy was not exactly sure what had driven his decision. He only knew he was not ready for the stationary, predictable life the family business promised.

The reality of the .50-cal watches was not so glamorous, either.

The gun crews were exposed to the Gulf's ferocious combination of heat and sand, which dissipated only slightly after dark. From sunrise to sunset, the heat was so intense and so physically draining that daytime watches were limited to two hours, rather than the normal four or five. And so far the action that Andy sought had failed to materialize. They had trained intensively on the trip over from San Diego, and they continued to train and to test-fire the guns on a daily basis. That was interesting to Andy, but it was not the same as real action. They had come close a couple of times in encounters with Iranian ships and RevGuard speedboats, but they'd never been in an actual fight.

Andy lifted his binoculars and slowly panned the water astern of the ship, as the Bosun's Mates had taught him. The *Bulkeley* frequently encountered dhows, speedboats, and flat-bottomed craft that reminded him of the bass boats at home in Michigan. He and Steele had responsibility for anything approaching from *Bulkeley*'s blind side, the area from amidships aft. There was another gun crew on the deck above the bridge, covering the forward hemisphere of the ship. On the fantail there were two tripod-mounted .50-cals, each equipped with a night vision gunsight. Both of the heavy machine guns were loaded, with plenty of extra ammo standing by.

The powerful .50-cals, with their explosive-tipped ammunition, could shred a Boghammer or any other Iranian gunboat in a matter of seconds. The machine guns' only tactical limitations were their firing cutouts, which limited the train and angle of depression of the guns to prevent the gunners from accidentally hitting their own ship. If an enemy got inside the firing arc of the machine guns, literally alongside the ship, there were two twelve-gauge riot shotguns in an adjacent gun locker. Each of the gunners was supplied with a flak vest, but the bulky vests were usually laid across the tops of the machine gun breechblocks in an effort to shield out the invading sand and donned only when action seemed imminent. The gun crew also had a hands-free night vision sight, which was in its box at Andy's feet. They used the sight to identify contacts spotted with binoculars or the naked eye; the drain on the sight's batteries was too great for it to be in continuous use.

Andy and Steele had not seen a single contact on their watch. The crew they had relieved had told them that the ship had passed through a dense crowd of fishing dhows several hours earlier.

But that had been when the moon was still up.

Hell, Andy thought, given the dhows' tendency to run without lights, they could be passing through the same group right now and he'd never see them. He took a slug of cold water from a nearby ice chest and wiped off the fine layer of sand and grit that had settled on his face.

Steele's voice split the relative stillness.

"Mosi says one more hour till relieve-the-watch."

Kim sat up carefully in the steel-framed bed, still uncertain of what obstructions loomed above her in the dark of the executive officer's stateroom. She had slept fitfully, waking repeatedly as the unfamiliar sounds of the starting and stopping of machinery echoed through the ship. When she had most recently awakened, she realized with a start that she had been dreaming about John. The details would not come back to her, but she felt an afterimage of the press of his body against hers and the warmth of his breath on her neck. For the last half hour she had lain awake in the miniature Murphy bed, trying to return to sleep—but not certain she wanted to return to her dream. But sleep would not come. Only more thoughts of John.

She flipped on the overhead reading light and sat back against the bulkhead. Feeling the coolness in the air, she pulled the bedclothes up around her shoulders. To protect both men and machines, the *Bulkeley*'s three air-conditioning plants were kept in full operation around the clock. The small outside temperature drop following nightfall caused the AC plant to actually make some of the crew spaces uncomfortably cool.

The chill in the air combined with the strange mechanical noises of the *Bulkeley* to send a shiver through her that was not entirely caused by the cold. Shaking off the chill, she smiled inwardly at the unlikely image she would present to her editors if they could see her huddled in this tiny bed, feeling a mild touch of baseless

fear. They had not sent her here to be intimidated by her surroundings.

She could never easily define what had drawn her to journalism
as a career. Coming from a small town, there was a certain glamor
to it, of course, but she had found herself most attracted by the
idea that the job had to do with cutting through lies and vague-
ness and distilling the truth. She had been accepted by Columbia
in her senior year of high school, but the family had had no
money for college. Kim left home and first attended a junior college, working nights and weekends to amass enough money to
pay for Columbia. It took her almost two years, but when she
finally had sufficient funds for her first year, the university again
accepted her. She attacked her studies with a motivation seldom
found except among those who have to work for everything they
have.

From her first job on her high school paper through Columbia
and then on to her initial job at *Newsday*, she had always been the
tough one, the woman reporter who would take the difficult stories, the uncooperative interviews, and the assignments in dangerous locations. Kim had staked out that territory for herself in
journalism school when she observed that many of her female
counterparts were happy taking the more traditional "women's"
stories. Male editors at first found her desire to take on the toughest stories to be cute, but when she performed and came back for
more work of the same type, they became believers. She was
proud that she had received this assignment to cover the *Bulkeley*,
but it had not surprised her. Sailing on this ship in the middle of
a war was no more dangerous than Beirut or El Salvador had
been.

Taking a deep breath, Kim forced the fog of memory from her
mind. The small clock over Lawrence's desk read three A.M. Almost time to get up and dress, she thought. She had tried to locate
John after the interview with the Captain, only to be told that he
had "hit the rack," as the junior officers watching the wardroom
TV had put it. She'd considered waking him but had thought
better of it. He'd looked tired enough at dinner to sleep for twenty
hours, let alone the three available to him. She had seen the strain
of this duty in his face, but also the warmth in the dark eyes she

had once found so attractive. John had still moved with the natural grace she remembered and showed the same quiet strength. When she had returned to her cabin she was struck by a hard-to-define feeling at the knowledge that he was sleeping only a few dozen feet away.

Kim had made up her mind then and set her alarm so she could catch him when he came off watch at four A.M. The hour was strange, perhaps, but at least it would give them privacy. Besides, her time on board the ship was fast running out.

Kim was not quite certain of what she would say to him. She only knew that what she had thought was a closed chapter in her life was proving not to be. She wondered if they could ever get over the Wallach incident. In some ways she still could not believe that whole thing had been so important to him. He had asked her not to print the story, and she had wondered a thousand times in the intervening months if she would have gone ahead with it if she had known fully the wall it would erect between them. Telling herself she had done the professional thing—the right thing—no longer helped.

Kim realized her preoccupation with Stewart was not only troubling her emotionally, it was keeping her from covering the story. Better to talk to him and have it out, she thought. The feelings that seeing him again had raised in her had to be dealt with.

Too restless to sit in bed any longer, Kim got up and went to the mirror to dress and prepare. The background sounds of the *Bulkeley* continued their shifting metallic symphony, but now she did not notice them.

THE ZODIACS

There it was!

The ghostly green silhouette of the *Bulkeley* appeared distinctly in the night vision scope. Major Barzin Aziz, veteran of a hundred battles, silently made his own prayer of thanks to God. Now came the difficult part.

He estimated the ship's range at five hundred yards, but the scope magnified the image somewhat, and he could not be certain. The four-thousand-ton frigate, moving slowly to the west, was still not visible to the unaided eye. Keeping the scope pressed to his face, he gestured with his free arm, pointing the direction for his coxswain to steer. The Zodiacs descended on the *Bulkeley* from the north, coming in from her starboard beam. Aziz directed his boat around to the right until it was roughly paralleling the *Bulkeley*'s course. With the Zodiac and the frigate headed in the same direction, he was able to make a gross calculation of the ship's speed. Five to seven knots, he thought, signaling the coxswain to slow to seven knots.

They had practiced the approach many times in the harbor at Bandar Abbas. Initially, Aziz had had an experienced Iranian Navy officer with him in his Zodiac, helping him to judge the appropriate approach angle. The Major had quickly realized that the approach was really a math problem, and he had excelled at math while in school. Soon there was no need for the navy officer. An Iranian frigate would run a straight-line course through the harbor at speeds between five and ten knots. Aziz would match the ship's speed, resolve the geometry in his head, and select the angle of approach. It was critical to use sufficient speed and lead the target ship enough so that his line of boats would intercept the frigate amidships. Aziz had joked with his men that they were human torpedoes and he was the U-boat captain firing them.

What had worked well so many times in the controlled conditions of the harbor appeared far more difficult in the sand-choked darkness. Aziz forced himself to keep the scope on the amidships area of the *Bulkeley*. He fought the natural urge to train the scope on the bow and bridge. They must intercept her amidships: detailed study of design plans for this class of ship by Iranian naval intelligence had identified the blind spot. A visit by the Iranian trade representative in Brussels to the same type of ship in service with a NATO navy had confirmed it. There was a twenty-foot-long stretch of the open weather deck amidships that could not be viewed from either the bridge or the flight deck–fantail area. That was the key.

Aziz made his decision. He signaled the coxswain to increase speed to twenty knots and then extended his arm to indicate a course forty-five degrees off the Zodiac's port bow. As the lead

Zodiac came up in speed, the other boats followed suit. Aziz knew they were right on the threshold of motor noise, and that the speed would produce a small wake. He had decided, given the unpredictable visibility, that reducing their exposure time was more vital than complete silence. As his boat came around to the left, he adjusted his arm to give the new relative heading he desired.

They were at what Aziz judged to be two to three hundred yards when the darkened shape of the *Bulkeley* became visible through the clouds of sand. The ship appeared immense in the darkness. One of the Guards in the lead Zodiac began a whispered prayer at the sight of the ship, but he was quickly silenced by Kalil. The only illumination on the frigate came from the running lights, visible in the vicinity of her bridge. Aziz lowered the night scope as they drew nearer to the ship and her outline became more distinct.

Two hundred yards. There was no sign of alarm as the *Bulkeley* continued at her ponderous speed. Looking back, Aziz could see that the column of Zodiacs had closed up when the approach signal had been given, just as in their many practice sessions. All five boats were visible to him, little more than five yards separating each from the one ahead of it.

One hundred yards and closing. If we're detected now, Aziz thought, we can still do a great deal of damage, as we'll soon be inside the firing arcs of their guns. But the boats proceeded on unseen.

We've done it, Aziz thought, we're in the blind zone! He allowed himself a small smile of satisfaction. As the lead boat came within twenty yards of the *Bulkeley*, the coxswain expertly took off speed and turned his craft to glide in against the ship's hull. When the rubber boat kissed the steel skin of the ship, two of the marines threw fiberglass grapnels up to the weather deck, where they wrapped around lifeline stanchions. Rafsani's boat, towing the cargo raft, slid in behind the lead boat. The crew of the Sergeant Major's craft moved to secure it against the hull amidships, matching the actions of Aziz's men. The remaining boats maneuvered alongside the first two Zodiacs, and the marines made the boats fast to each other.

At the Major's signal, a small marine from the lead boat went up one of the grapnel lines with acrobatic skill, gaining the weather deck in seconds. He quickly tied off the boats' grapnel mooring lines to secure cleats and stanchions on the deck. Next he made fast a rope ladder and dropped it noiselessly to the boat below.

Without need of a signal, two marines went up the ladder, each with a silenced Sterling submachine gun slung over his back. They quickly took up defensive positions, one covering the large watertight doors amidships and the other watching forward along the open deck. Aziz was on deck next. He pointed to the waiting Sergeant Major, who clambered from his craft to the lead boat, brushing Kalil aside at the base of the ladder. In seconds he had joined Aziz on the ship. The Sterling that Rafsani carried looked like a toy in his hands.

The bearded giant spoke softly. "God has smiled on us, Major."

"He has done his part; now we must do ours. Summon your team, my friend."

4

THE BULKELEY

S tewart sat in the elevated captain's chair in the center of the CIC. From his perch, he had a good view of almost all the CIC watch standers at their various data consoles. The chair placed him just behind and to the left of the ATACO console, and he was watching intently as the video symbol representing Sea- lord slowly tracked toward the contact they had identified as the *Andes Commerce*. Now it was just a matter of waiting. The mer- chant had acknowledged their radioed offer of assistance, and Sealord was almost on top of the tanker's location. From out of the bridge-to-bridge speaker Stewart heard Lee Hammond's voice trying to raise the injured ship.

"*Andes Commerce*, this is U.S. Navy helicopter inbound to your location, over."

There was no response.

Stewart heard Hammond try again without success.

"Tell Sealord we're hearing them go out, Goldman," Stewart directed the ATACO. The helicopter was clearly on the right chan- nel and frequency.

As Hammond continued trying to raise the suddenly unrespon- sive merchantman, Stewart shifted his attention to the rest of the "environment" in the area around the *Bulkeley*. A review of the TAO console showed some C-130 military air transports on their way out of Bandar Abbas and headed north, probably to Shiraz or Bandar Khomeini. There was the usual heavy tanker traffic to the south in the vicinity of the *Andes Commerce*. Stewart noted that their playmate, the *Abaland*, was a little more distant than she had been lately, loitering about fifteen miles to the east. There was little else of interest.

Twenty minutes earlier, the petty officer manning the fire control search radar had reported a few "paints," indications of radar return, on a contact about a mile to the north of the *Bulkeley*. By the time Stewart had gotten over to the man's side to take a look at the contact, there was no longer anything there. He had watched the sweeps of the radar with the fire controlman for several minutes, but the blip had not returned.

"Ghost contacts" were common enough in the Gulf, particularly at night. The radar could have picked up some floating reflective debris that had crested a wave, or it could have seen a reflected image from something much farther away. There were many possibilities. Nevertheless, to be certain, Stewart had called the bridge and had Scott Septenano and his lookouts check out the radar contact visually. They had seen nothing in that direction, as the dense, enveloping dust storm continued to hamper visibility.

At that moment, Stewart was distracted from his review of the tactical picture by a metallic voice originating from the CIC-bridge intercom.

"TAO; bridge. I'm sending Mosopu down to wake up reliefs. Do you want him to get Jack Nelson up?" Septenano was obviously not interested in spending any more time on this watch than was absolutely necessary, Stewart thought. Depressing the intercom toggle switch, Stewart replied in the affirmative. He then returned his attention to the status of Sealord's mission.

"They've got a visual on the merchie, but still no joy on Gulf Common, Mr. Stewart," Goldman said without lifting his eyes from his display screen. "No joy" indicated that Sealord had not been able to raise the tanker.

"These guys better answer up soon, 'cause Sealord's down to one plus zero zero." The ATACO provided Stewart with the aircraft's fuel state: one hour plus zero minutes of gas remaining. That was not a lot of time, Stewart knew, to get into a hover over an unfamiliar ship, hoist up the injured man, and get back to the *Bulkeley*.

"Tell them to keep trying to raise her, make a low pass to show the tanker that they're over them, if Lieutenant Commander Hammond thinks it's safe to do so. We'll give 'em another few minutes to answer up." Stewart lifted a sound-powered growler from its cradle. With a few vigorous cranks of the small handle on the growler's station, he sent the distinctive tone that gave the device its nickname down the line to awaken Donelli. It was time to get the old man directly involved in this one.

Sergeant Major Rafsani moved noiselessly through the darkened passageway. He had studied the *Bulkeley*'s layout for days, as had all the marines, but making one's way through the red-lit steel corridors was not the same as tracing them on a detailed blueprint. Still, the prints had been very accurate, and the ladders and doors he encountered all seemed familiar from his study of the ship.

It was a good plan, he thought. Coming aboard in the latter part of the sailors' midnight watch would ensure that a minimum of them would be up and about. It also guaranteed that those sailors who were on watch would be at their most tired, their readiness and attentiveness dulled by lack of sleep.

As he led the two other marines forward toward their objective, Rafsani allowed a small part of his thoughts to focus on the assignments the others would be fulfilling.

Once the whole assault force had reached the deck of the ship, the Major had directed the team leaders to start the stopwatches they carried. Each team would have three minutes to reach its objective. At Aziz's signal, the teams had silently fanned out to head for their targets. A marine and a Guard were left behind to watch the cargo raft and the Zodiacs, more to prevent anyone who might discover them from sounding an alarm than anything else. Rafsani was confident that the other team leaders were following their briefed instructions precisely. The teams would carefully avoid the communal areas such as the wardroom, chiefs' mess, and mess decks, where there was the possibility of encountering members of the crew. They had reviewed all the known watch stations on the *Bulkeley*, and their knowledge was further augmented by the innocent questions asked by the trade representative during his visit to the NATO ship. Rafsani thought their chances of proceeding without detection were in the acceptable range.

If they did encounter a crewman wandering the darkened passageways, it would be a surprising and short experience for the unfortunate sailor, he thought, somewhat regretfully. The Sergeant Major had no great hatred for the Americans. To him, they were professional military men not unlike himself. He would have far preferred to have been killing Iraqis, the invaders of his homeland and murderers of his people. But they were far from that war now, and he would do what he had to do. As always, once the battle was joined, he would fight first for the Major and his fellow marines—the enemy and the mission placing a distant second in his motivation.

Stepping over a foot-high hatch coaming, Rafsani realized that they had reached their target. He moved a step farther down the passageway to give his men room to access the door. It was of solid aluminum, with both a combination lock and an electronic cipher device affixed to it. There was a small, closed port at head height in the door, with a cage in front of it similar to those used in protecting bank tellers. A plate above the door read COMMUNI-CATIONS CENTER and was emblazoned with two hand-painted lightning bolts.

The Sergeant Major checked the radium-illuminated stopwatch at his wrist.

Thirty seconds to go.

Aziz had waited until the last of his teams had departed before heading forward with his own group. He had done so partly to see the others on their way, and partly because his team was the largest and therefore ran the greatest risk of detection. He had not wanted this group to be so large, but on the spur of the moment he had decided it was wiser to keep Kalil with him. Letting the Guards Commander out of his sight could only bring trouble; if Kalil was going to present a problem, the Major wanted to be close at hand to limit the damage. To Aziz's chagrin, Kalil had insisted on bringing along another Guard, who was purportedly the Colonel's "aide."

With ninety seconds to go, Aziz had led his party of seven men inside the skin of the sleeping ship. They had moved very cautiously past the well-lit but apparently empty wardroom and down the passageway past the officers' staterooms. The noise of the ship was a mixed blessing the Major had not been prepared for. Although most of the machinery sounds were low-frequency hums, they could still mask the approach of a crewman as easily as they concealed the presence of his group.

He led his team quietly up one vertical ladder and brought them to a halt. They were now around a corner from the small corridor which held both the door to the Combat Information Center and a ladder to the bridge. His team waited in the cramped space at the base of yet another vertical ladder. Aziz knew this ladder led to the port bridgewing. They would wait here for the remaining seconds. At his order, this team would split into two smaller ones, each with its own target.

The Major released the safety on his Sterling and noted with approval that the marines, as one, did the same. He observed Kalil and the other Guard fidgeting nervously and shifting their assault rifles from port arms to down at the deck and then back to port arms. He reminded himself to remain well clear of the two of them when the assault began.

To someone unfamiliar with the physical design of a warship, the passageways and ladders would seem an obstacle course of trip hazards, knee knockers, and fittings designed to tear clothing and skin. This perception was magnified once "darken ship" had been set and the various obstacles were hidden in the dim red light.

To Bosun's Mate Second Class Mosopu, these same passageways were more familiar than the home he had grown up in on American Samoa. The big man was at home in the darkness and harbored a secret pride in the knowledge that his night vision and instincts were unmatched by any man among the *Bulkeley*'s crew. In the mornings of his boyhood he had risen several hours before dawn to accompany his father as crew on his uncle's fishing boat. The ability to function at sea in the black of night was crucial to the fisherman's craft. It was an ability that had never left him.

Mosopu had made excellent time, stopping first at officers'

country to wake Lieutenant Nelson and then rousing Chief Marquez's relief from his berth in the CPO quarters. Now he was headed forward with his great loping stride, toward the "coops," the crew compartments. These three large berthing areas were stacked one on top of the other on three successive decks running deep into the hull of the ship. The *Bulkeley*'s entire crew of two hundred, excepting the officers and chiefs, lived in the coops.

Mosopu disliked the midwatch as much as anyone, and he eagerly anticipated waking his own relief, BM1 Solo, and the rest of the oncoming watch team.

As he stepped into the passageway that led to coop one, Mosopu saw a dark figure silhouetted at the entrance to the coop. Great, he thought, one of Solo's guys has got up on his own.

Mosopu opened his mouth to call a greeting to the figure—but what he saw froze the words in his throat. The man had turned toward him, and even in the uncertain light the Bosun's Mate could make out the unfamiliar uniform and the strange weapon the man cradled in his arms.

The marine squinted at the dim silhouette of Mosopu, his vision still not fully adjusted to the hazy red light. The Iranian was not immediately certain whether the approaching figure was his team leader returning from posting a sentry at the other side of the berthing compartment, or someone else.

Mosopu did not hesitate. The Bosun's Mate was not sure who or what the figure represented, but he instantly knew that the stranger was an enemy—on Mosopu's ship. He crossed the ten feet between them with one long stride and leapt toward the armed man. The second the marine had delayed had been too long; he was just bringing his gun down to bear when the massive figure crashed into him, slamming his machine-pistol against his chest. The two men sprawled to the deck, the two-hundred-fifty-pound bulk of the Samoan driving the breath from the far smaller Iranian.

Lying across the stunned and faintly struggling marine, Mosopu wedged his beefy forearm against the man's throat. He shifted his position astride the Iranian, operating on instinct, and bore down with all the weight he could bring to bear. The Iranian's windpipe collapsed under the enormous pressure. Mosopu felt the man's warm breath against his face as the marine exhaled in an almost resigned fashion, his body going limp.

There was still an indication of life in the marine's eyes as the Bosun's Mate pulled away from their pileup on the deck. Mosopu looked down into his stunned opponent's face and shrugged helplessly, as if to say there was nothing he could do.

His focus on the dying man was broken by a whispered voice that came from the ladder well beside them, which went down to coop two.

"Harare?" The low voice was controlled yet urgent. Two brief sentences followed in a language the Bosun's Mate did not recognize.

Mosopu realized his struggle with the strange-looking soldier had been over in seconds. This other intruder must have heard them crash to the deck and was now wondering about his compatriot. Charged with the adrenaline of the fight, all of Mosopu's senses were operating at one thousand percent. He heard the man below quietly place his foot on the first rung and start up the ladder. Moving with uncommon speed for so large a man, Mosopu scooped up the strange gun and headed forward, leaving the coops and the marine's shattered figure behind him. He could not chance going back toward the chiefs' mess, as the ladder the second man was climbing faced dead aft. There was a good chance, he thought, of catching a bullet in the back if he headed that way.

Got to tell the bridge! his mind screamed. Got to get the security force out!

What in the hell was going on? He forced himself to concentrate on where he could go to sound the alarm. He was forward of all the berthing compartments in a part of the ship that was normally unmanned at this time of night. There was no telling how many of those guys were back around the coops. That one he killed looked like an Arab of some sort. Iranians? Iraqis?

Then he remembered: there was a damage control repair locker up forward in this part of the ship. The repair locker had a growler and a sound-powered phone link to the bridge!

■

As the sweep hand on his stopwatch marked three minutes exactly, Sergeant Major Rafsani reached across and depressed the electric buzzer that served as the "doorbell" for Radio Central.

After a twenty-second delay, the port in the door was opened by a sleepy-eyed radioman in his early twenties. Before the young sailor could register what he was seeing and react to it, Rafsani's gloved hand was through the opening underneath the cage, which was used to pass out radio messages. The radioman saw the hand softly toss something—a black soda can?—past him and into the heart of Radio Central. The sailor slammed the port closed, but the hand had already been withdrawn. At that same instant, an earsplitting crack deafened the radioman and a searing white-hot light filled Radio Central. The young sailor collapsed to his knees, clutching his ears in pain. He looked across the space to see if the watch supervisor and the other two radiomen had survived, but his eyes would not function properly. He could see only a few feet in front of him; the distance beyond that was shrouded in a white-yellow corona of light.

To the three marines outside the door, the explosion was little more than a muffled crash. The sealed Radio Central had contained most of the noise of the flash-bang grenade and undoubtedly would amplify its effects, Rafsani thought.

Without need of direction, the marine immediately to the Sergeant Major's right raised his submachine gun and pointed it at the combined lock mechanisms on the door a mere five feet away. Moving the gun's barrel in a small circle he emptied all thirty-four rounds into the locks. The integrated silencer did not dampen all sound, but the noise of the bullets striking was far greater than that made by the Sterling gun. The marine was already slipping a new magazine into his weapon as Rafsani kicked in the shattered door.

Once inside Radio, the Sergeant Major took quick stock of the situation, as his men covered him from behind. The flash-bang had done very little equipment damage, but two of the Americans appeared to have caught the blast head-on. One was on the deck, eyes tightly shut and flash burns on his face, moaning softly. The other serious casualty remained where he had apparently been sitting when the grenade went off. There was blood on his face, and he appeared stunned. The two remaining radiomen, one of whom was the man who'd opened the door, showed the usual effects of the flash-bang. They were disoriented, but even now their blindness and shock were receding.

Rafsani gestured to his men, and they moved quickly to gather up the Americans. The marines carried and pushed the injured men, as their physical conditions required, to the aftermost part of the space, near the access door. There they seated the Americans on the floor against a bulkhead and silently kept their weapons trained upon them.

The Sergeant Major went about his task with equal speed and efficiency. He crossed to the forward bulkhead of Radio Central, pulling a CO_2 fire extinguisher from its bracket as he went. After a moment of searching among the stacks of transmitters and couplers, he found what he was looking for: the primary power panel. He pulled a boxy, fist-size device from a pouch on the heavy equipment vest he wore and attached the device to the top of the power panel. Rafsani carefully set the device's timer for thirty seconds and then moved to join his comrades near the access door.

The three black-garbed marines shielded their eyes as the thermite grenade detonated with a high-pitched *whoosh*. The explosion sent a directional jet of superheated flame into the heart of the panel. In an instant, the multitude of lights on the various pieces of radio gear were extinguished, as were the overhead lights. Strategically placed battle lanterns, hard-wired into a separate power source to serve as emergency lighting, immediately clicked on. They provided sufficient but spectral light in the still-smoky room.

Rafsani crossed the space to the power panel, which was burning and sparking weakly. He emptied the fire extinguisher onto the panel, smothering the small fire.

We cannot have any unnecessary damage, he thought, allowing himself a small smile in the darkness.

Scott Septenano tried to catch himself, but his instinctive reaction to turn toward the bright light had been too fast for him to overcome.

"God damn it! Turn out that light!" He held up his arm to shield his eyes—but it was too late; his night vision was ruined.

The light that shone in through the bridgewing door was blindingly bright, its effect amplified manyfold in the almost total darkness. The bridge watch team was staggered by the intense beam, their night-adjusted eyes wracked with pain as they tried to look away.

"All bridge personnel move to the ship's control console! Do not attempt to give an alarm," Septenano heard a strangely accented voice boom from behind the light. What the hell is this? he thought.

"Who the fuck is that? Turn off that goddamn light, whoever you are! I'll have your ass at captain's mast for this!" Septenano yelled, furious at this dangerous prank played on his watch. He headed across the bridge toward the light, his hand still in front of his face, trying to block the searing brightness.

"This is not a game," the voice said harshly. "We are armed. Move to the console or you and your men will die."

Septenano stopped cold several feet from the powerful light. This wasn't somebody playing around; he did not recognize the voice as that of anyone in the crew.

The light came forward into the bridge, and Septenano heard the sound of more than one set of quiet footsteps accompanying it. As his eyes slowly adjusted, he was able to make out the dim silhouettes of several figures beside the man who held the light.

He could see the guns.

"Mr. Septenano . . . what do we do?" The whispered question came from Brooks, the quartermaster, standing at the chart table behind him. Septenano's mind raced. Brooks at the chart table, the helmsman and lee helmsman already at the ship's control console, Chief Marquez by the captain's chair—there was no one near enough to the 1MC to even try to sound an alarm.

"My patience is at an end. Move to the console now." To emphasize the masked voice's sincerity, one of the other shadowy figures pulled back and released the bolt on his weapon. It was a sound that every man on the bridge recognized.

"We'll do as he says, Brooks," Septenano said, trying to keep the anger out of his voice. "Move over to the helm." He looked across the bridge to his junior officer of the deck. "You too, Chief."

One at a time the sailors crossed over to the ship's control console, which contained both the helm and the engine order controls. Septenano was the closest, and he went slowly to stand behind the seated helmsman, the spotlight beam following him across the bridge. Brooks came next, leaving his work at the chart table and being tracked by the light as he moved across the deck.

As the quartermaster stepped between the large centerline gyrorepeater and the console, he was briefly between the intruders and Chief Marquez. Septenano heard the mechanical *clack* of a latch releasing and instantly knew the sound. Marquez had pulled an M-14 from the rack by the captain's chair! He turned to see the chief, now spotlighted by the intense beam, lifting the rifle to his shoulder and pulling back the operating rod.

Septenano heard the bolt slam home at the same time he saw Chief Marquez lifted off his feet and thrown back against and across the captain's chair; the bridgewing windows shattering behind him. Septenano seemed to hear the low pops of the silenced weapons only after the bullets had found their mark. Along with the other sailors clustered at the console, he stared in horror and disbelief at the broken figure that only seconds before had been their shipmate.

The superbright light quickly moved off the corpse and once again focused on Septenano at the console. The commanding voice was subdued this time.

"That death was not necessary. It is in your hands to prevent many others."

Our reliefs should be up here any time now, Andy thought to himself as he lowered his binoculars after one last sweep of the water aft of the frigate. He looked across the cluttered fantail at Steele, who was sitting on the mechanical capstan. Andy could see that Steele was having a hard time keeping his eyes open. He walked across the warm deck and clapped the other gunner on the shoulder.

"Hang in there, bubba. Help is on the way."

"Yeah, right." Steele yawned, rubbing his eyes.

Andy crossed behind Steele and went to the life rail on the starboard side of the fantail. More from boredom than anything else, he scanned off to starboard with his binoculars.

Nothing.

Then, as he had been doing all night on the port side, he leaned gingerly out over the lifeline and looked forward along the hull.

Jesus Christ—there was something there, wedged in against the hull amidships! The object was indistinct, just a black mass about two feet above the sea. Could it be some floating debris that had gotten pulled against the hull by the suction from one of the sea chests? The underwater sea chests filtered seawater from the Gulf for use in equipment cooling and fire fighting. He ran through the ship's layout in his mind: no, there was no sea chest near there, and yet whatever it was seemed to be riding against the ship as if it was attached.

"Steele!" he called to his fellow watch stander in a low, urgent voice. The seated sailor looked over at him uninterestedly.

"C'mere quick, and bring the nightscope!"

Picking up on Andy's urgency, Steele scooped up the night vision device at his feet and joined him at the rail.

"So, what's up?"

"Take a look at that. What the hell could it be?"

Steele followed the younger sailor's lead and leaned across the rail to look forward.

"Holy *shit*." Steele uttered the words in a hushed tone. Balancing precariously over the lifeline, he brought the scope up to his eyes to try to make out the details of the floating black object. In the green radium field of vision provided by the nightscope, he could make out two rafts or boats of some kind, bobbing gently alongside the hull amidships. "Some kinda little boats," he whispered to Andy. "No sign of anybody in 'em."

As Steele continued to study the boats through the night vision device, Andy darted back to the capstan. Steele had left the sound-powered headset on the capstan when he had come to the rail. Andy quickly donned the earphones, turning away from the starboard side to prevent his voice from carrying forward.

"Bridge; fantail."

There was no response.

"Bridge, this is the fantail. Answer up, Mosi!" Again, the line remained silent. Andy tried three more times to raise the bridge but there was no answer. He felt the first cold toxin of fear rising in his stomach.

Andy rejoined Steele, who was still at the rail scrutinizing the mysterious boats.

"Something real bad's going down, Dale. I can't get anybody to answer up on the bridge."

"Mosi probably just went off the line to go do wake-ups," Steele said, trying to convince himself as much as Andy.

"Yeah. . . . But you know if he did, he would have put the circuit on the speaker and Mr. Septenano or Chief Marquez would answer up, and—"

"Fuck!" Steele cut him off. "There's a guy climbing down into one of the boats—a guy with a gun!" He pulled back from the rail in an effort to remain out of sight.

Without waiting for Steele, Andy raced across the deck and got behind the starboard .50-caliber mount. Yanking the flak vest clear of the top of the gun, he swung the .50-cal around to point forward in one smooth movement, but it was to no avail: the boats were well forward and below the gun's firing arc. He could not even see them from behind the machine gun.

"No way—they're too far forward," Steele said, joining him behind the gun. He reached down and opened the gun locker beside the mount. "We're gonna have to make something happen with these." He handed Andy a twelve-gauge pump shotgun and a sling bag of cartridges.

"Hold it, Dale. Whether it's just that the bridge is off the line or something worse, we've got to sound an alarm, get people moving."

"How do you figure to do that?" Steele whispered hoarsely.

Wordlessly, Andy pushed the puzzled sailor clear of the gun mount and trained it directly out on the frigate's starboard beam. He drew back the powerful bolt, leaned back to steady the gun, and loosed a fiery salvo into the night sky.

■

Simultaneous with the assaults on Radio Central and the bridge, Aziz halted at the closed door with Kalil beside him. This part of the operation should not require any more than the two of them, he knew, but the marine a few yards behind them in the passageway was still a worthwhile precaution. He looked at Kalil and caught the Guards Commander's eyes for a brief moment before turning back to the door. With a practiced application of force he kicked in the lightweight door with his steel-toed boot and charged into the dimly lit space. Aziz came to a halt two steps into the room, his Sterling held waist high. God had indeed smiled on them.

The man Aziz knew must be the Captain of the *Bulkeley* looked across his desk at the Major, his expression quickly shifting from one of surprise to one of raw anger. The Captain was standing behind the desk in a disheveled state that showed he had only recently arisen from his bed. He had been in the act of buttoning his khaki shirt when Aziz had crashed in, but he made no move to continue that action, instead dropping his great meaty hands to his sides.

"Who the fuck are you and what the hell are you doing on my ship?" Aziz was not surprised by the fury etched in the Captain's voice. The American officer ignored Aziz's weapon and kept his eyes riveted on the Major's own. Aziz felt Kalil come up behind him in the cramped stateroom, but he kept his eyes on the Captain.

"Your ship is a prize of war of the Islamic Republic of Iran, Captain." Aziz paused to let the words register. "At this moment your bridge, engineering control station, and radio room are under the control of my men. The sounding of any general alarm will result in many deaths, as my men are covering all the exits from your berthing compartments."

"Son of a bitch," the Captain said softly. His face, at first flushed with outrage, was now drained of all color. "What exactly is it that you—*people* want?" The Captain made no attempt to keep the disgust out of his voice; his baggy, sleep-robbed eyes had narrowed to angry slits.

Before Aziz could respond, he heard Kalil speak up beside him, his voice heavy with insult. "Your vessel has been taken as a prize for Islam and the Revolution! What we choose to do with it is a matter of God's will and does not concern you. Be thankful your lives have been spared thus far! You—"

"Your ship is a prize of war, Captain," the Major repeated calmly, cutting him off. Damn the fanatic idiot! "We are at war, after all, whether formally or not."

The Captain's face remained impassive, but his balled fists and tightly drawn shoulders radiated intensity.

Hoping to forestall the inevitable explosion he anticipated, Aziz kept his own voice low and controlled. "We intend to sail your ship to Iran, where you and your officers and men will be interned until you can be repatriated to your country." The story at least sounded plausible, he thought.

As the Captain was about to reply, the small cabin echoed with the distant sound of heavy-caliber machine-gun fire. Aziz cocked his head to listen. There was not supposed to be any gunfire from the stern! As the gunfire continued, he shifted his attention back to the Captain. The American must have detected Aziz's concern, for the Captain's face bore a grim smile.

"Do not be too quick to smile, Captain," Aziz said as the gunfire died away. "This battle is already decided." As if in punctuation, the Major's last word was followed by an explosive blast from the passageway outside the captain's cabin. Aziz met this occurrence with an expression that indicated the detonation was something he had expected. The smile left the Captain's face.

"Nizarem," Aziz called out loudly, his eyes still on the Captain. In an instant the marine from the passageway was inside the cabin, his gun trained on Donelli.

"This marine will escort you to your bridge," the Major said. "Do not give him any cause to add to the toll of those already dead."

The relative quiet of the Combat Information Center was ruptured first by the metallic pounding of the .50-caliber in the distance, and then by a percussive blast that rocketed the space's door from its hinges. Stewart spun around at his position in the center of the CIC to see a group of heavily armed men leaping through the shattered, still-smoking portal and into the space. As his mind raced to register what was happening, his eyes settled on the operations specialist who had been seated at the console closest to the doorway. The man lay slumped across his console, his back ripped open by the blast.

Stewart grabbed for the intercom toggle to alert the bridge, only to find that the first man into the space was immediately beside him, his weapon leveled at Stewart's head. Stewart held the intercom switch in his hand for a moment as he looked into the hard, emotionless eyes of the man who held the gun. Then he dropped his hand to his side. Whatever was going on, he knew he could serve his ship better alive than by dying in a futile gesture.

Two more intruders, both garbed all in black and armed with automatic weapons, split off to the left and right sides of the CIC. Each stopped at a position where he could cover half the men in the blue-lit space. The Combat Information Center was silent except for the background chatter of radio transmissions on the various circuits. The petty officers manning the consoles had frozen and were watching Stewart for a clue as to how to respond. Stewart was about to address the intruder who still held the gun to his head when another two men entered the CIC.

The first of the two had the look of a leader about him, and he seemed to immediately take in the situation as he rounded the chart table and moved to the center of the CIC. One look at this man told Stewart that he was dealing with professional opposition; these were no wild-eyed terrorists. The second, larger man who followed was more difficult to read. Stewart watched him glance around the CIC with disdain, his broad, densely bearded face carved into a sneer. How many of them? Stewart wondered. And how in hell did they get on board undetected?

The one whom Stewart had identified as the leader came to a halt a step in front of him. He gestured to the first intruder, whose gun was still trained on Stewart's forehead. The man lowered his weapon.

The leader looked Stewart up and down quickly before shifting his gaze to the other men in the CIC. "You are in charge here?" he asked commandingly in clear but accented English.

Before Stewart could decide whether or not to answer, the multitude of radio speakers throughout the CIC suddenly went silent.

Goldman, the ATACO, who had been diverted from his air control assignment by the entry of the Iranians, turned quickly back to check the systems status board above his head. A number of the previously green lights on the board had gone to amber. He flicked several switches on the status board. There was no change in the lights.

"Mr. Stewart, we've lost the link with Sealord," Goldman said, ignoring the presence of the armed intruders. "But I still have their track on the air search."

Stewart, his mind still reeling from the sudden invasion of the CIC and the implications of the attack, focused his attention on the immediate problem. He shifted his gaze from the leader of the intruders to the seated ATACO.

"Switch up land-launch and see if you can raise them. If not, go to MAD," he said, using the acronym for the Military Air Distress circuit.

The leader listened to this exchange without apparent interest. "Your radios will no longer function," he said, addressing Stewart. "That has been seen to. This ship is in our hands." He paused, increasing the volume of his voice so he could be heard throughout the Combat Information Center. "Any attempt to resist on your part will be answered with death."

Stewart listened in silence, thinking frantically all the while of how he could get the ship's security force deployed, or at least get weapons to some of the crew.

"I state again," the leader concluded, "we are in control of your ship. To resist us will bring swift death." He turned to address the black-garbed intruder covering Stewart. "Bring him," he ordered. Ignoring the other occupants of the CIC, the leader turned and headed out.

At the hammering sound of the heavy-caliber gunfire, unmistakable even deep within the skin of the ship, Sergeant Hoveyda and the two Guards accompanying him broke into a run. Racing through the dimly lit and unfamiliar passageways was the last thing Hoveyda wanted to do, but something had gone seriously wrong, and it was his responsibility.

He vaulted another of the seemingly endless hatch coamings

and came to a brief halt to get his bearings. As the heavy-breathing Guards joined him, he registered where they were from the map in his mind and then continued aft down the darkened passageway.

Damn both the Guards and the American engineers to the bowels of hell!

Hoveyda was supposed to have silenced the after machine guns long before this. His mission had been simple enough: secure the engineering control station, then take out the gun crew, which naval intelligence had told them was stationed on the ship's fantail. As with the other teams, his was to strike with the element of surprise and quickly crush any resistance.

Things had gone badly from their arrival at the engineering Main Control station. The automated nature of the *Bulkeley*'s engineering plant was supposed to limit the Main Control personnel to a minimum. At most there should have been two men on watch there, and a few others spread throughout the other engineering spaces. Hoveyda was taken aback when, on entering Main Control, they had found more than half a dozen of the ship's engineers there, apparently conducting some sort of drill.

For his "simple" assignment he had drawn only one other marine, Eslam, and three of the Guards—the idiots! After surprising the Americans in the control station, he had ordered them back from the engineering consoles lest they do something to disable the ship. The Americans, angry and surly after the initial shock, had been slow to move away from the consoles. One of the Guards had screamed impatiently in Farsi at the Americans' apparent leader, an older man in khakis. When the man stared at him uncomprehendingly, the Guard had crossed to the man and knocked him to the ground with the butt of his rifle. Even as the American was falling, a massively built black sailor had grabbed the stunned Guard and begun beating him ruthlessly. Hoveyda had watched in horror as the other two Guards, not wanting to risk shooting their comrade, had joined the fray, lashing out with their rifles. Briefly shocked at how rapidly things had spun out of his control, Hoveyda had recovered and fired a burst from his weapon overhead, directly above the struggling group. Both the Americans and the Guards had frozen.

With his limited English, Hoveyda had yelled at the Americans that he was perfectly prepared to kill them all—which was not quite true but had expedited the untangling of the brawl. The Guards had dragged their idiot fellow who started the whole fracas to one side, while the Americans huddled around their injured officer on the other. Hoveyda had noted with mixed feelings that the Guard was unconscious, but still breathing. The large sailor had beaten him ferociously in the short span of time.

That unnecessary conflict had put him minutes behind the timetable for neutralizing the fantail machine guns. He had left Eslam, the only man in his team he could trust, to hold the Americans at bay and watch the injured Guard. He and the remaining Guards had been headed aft when the distinctive sound of the .50-caliber gunfire had commenced.

Hoveyda had no idea what the American gunners could be shooting at, but it was not a good sign. As his little group rounded a narrow corner, one of the Guards caught his knee on a projecting fire-hose rack and went sprawling to the deck. Hoveyda stopped and waited while the Guard's comrade helped him to his feet.

The sound of the machine gun ceased. Out of ammunition or what? Hoveyda wondered.

More slowly now, he picked his way aft, followed closely by the Guards. They soon found themselves at the base of a ladder leading up to the fantail, a watertight scuttle at the ladder's top.

The Sergeant stopped to consider. The original plan had been to surprise the Americans and try to take them alive, since they could do nothing with the .50-calibers at such close range. But that plan had lost much of its appeal, since the Americans had obviously been alerted.

Now there was little choice; taking prisoners had ceased to be an option.

Hoveyda handed his Sterling to one of the Guards and slowly mounted the ladder. He moved carefully, fearful of making any noise, even with the closed, heavy steel hatch between him and the gun crew on the fantail. He was forced to stoop under the hatch as he reached the top of the ladder. With slow, deliberate moves, Hoveyda detached two grenades from his belt and placed them on the top rung of the ladder.

Stewart stepped out of the ladder trunk and onto the bridge and saw that the red interior lights, normally used only when the ship was sitting at anchor and never at sea, had been turned on. Their illumination cast the scene in an unreal rosy glow. A quick scan of the bridge showed him that the situation was no better here than in the CIC.

Scott Septenano and his watch team were clustered near the ship's control console, and the Iranians were in a group near the port bridgewing door. The leader was directing the others in short clipped sentences in what Stewart took to be Farsi.

As the marine on the steps below him shoved Stewart forward, he almost collided with the broad figure of Captain Donelli. The Captain stood frozen just a few feet forward of the ladder trunk, staring fixedly across at the starboard side of the bridge. Stewart followed Donelli's gaze across to the captain's chair and the broken body of Chief Marquez. He felt briefly nauseous and forced himself to look down, away from the lifeless form. On the blood-spattered deck below the captain's chair he saw the M-14 resting in a pile of shattered glass; it was clear what had happened to Marquez. Stewart looked again at Donelli, but the Captain was no longer staring at Marquez's body. He had fixed his eyes on the Iranian leader. On the red-lit bridge those eyes appeared to Stewart to burn like lasers at the Iranian.

The leader seemed to sense something, for he turned from his discussion with his men and spoke directly to Donelli as if they were the only two men on the bridge. "Apparently we have trouble somewhere on the ship." He gestured to the dead man in the captain's chair. "You see the result of resistance, Captain." It was a statement, not a question.

"I respect the desire of you and your crew to fight for your ship, but my men are professionals." He paused. "And unlike your men, they are professionals at this type of fighting."

Donelli remained silent, his eyes continuing to drill into the Iranian's.

The leader crossed to the 1MC station on the after bulkhead of the bridge.

"With that gunfire, we have lost the element of surprise. At this moment my men are gathering up and isolating your officers in your wardroom. Your chief petty officers have been taken to your berthing compartments, where they will be sealed in with your crew in such a way that escape will be impossible."

He pulled the 1MC microphone from its bracket and gestured to Donelli.

"I can get on this public address system now and tell your crew what has happened. I can tell them, particularly the many sailors in the berthing compartments, to remain where they are and not resist. I can do this—and the anger and frustration will be overwhelming; many will still die trying to fight in a losing cause." The Iranian spoke each word deliberately. "If you will talk to them, tell them this . . . lives will be saved." He held the microphone out to the Captain.

Stewart marveled at the cruel logic of the Iranian's reasoning and the sheer balls of the man. He watched Donelli closely, as did all on the bridge, whether they understood English or not. Donelli's face was as unreadable as a blank tombstone. When the Captain spoke, his voice was barely audible, his lips drawn into a small, humorless smile.

"You can go fuck yourself. I want you and your animals off my ship."

Across the bridge, Stewart heard the large bearded one exclaim angrily in Farsi and saw him raise his weapon at Donelli. The leader gestured to him to lower the gun. The man scowled and kept the MP5 pointed at the Captain, but he made no move to fire.

The leader held the microphone out to Donelli for a moment longer and then pulled it back. His expression showed neither surprise nor anger, only resignation.

"As God wills. I hope the cost of your pride is not too great."

As the Americans and Iranians looked on, the leader turned the toggle switches to send his voice throughout the ship.

■

Kim glanced at her watch and verified that it was almost four o'clock. A helpful young officer had told her that Stewart would most likely have completed his watch turnover by four or a little later. She checked out her appearance one last time in the state-room mirror. Satisfied with how she looked, Kim left the state-room and headed for the ladder that led to the wardroom.

She picked her way carefully down the steeply banked ladder. These things were tough enough to negotiate with all the lights on, she thought, let alone in the weak illumination of the red lighting. Halfway down the ladder she halted, as an unfamiliar sound echoed through the ship from the direction of the flight deck. It sounded almost like a chain saw to her, but she knew it couldn't be, not on a Navy ship. The sound ended abruptly and Kim put it out of her mind. Continuing down to the ladder's base, she went to the wardroom door a scant ten feet away. Her hand was on the doorknob when something made her look through the little eye port in the door before turning the knob. The tiny circu-lar window was only three inches in diameter and was intended to let men coming to the door see who was in the wardroom and avoid interrupting ongoing meetings.

Kim was startled to see that the wardroom was practically full. What could they be doing at this hour? she wondered. Her reluc-tance to intrude, combined with the thought that there might be a story here, kept her from going in. She stepped back from the tiny opening, thinking she might be seen peeking through it. Standing back from the door in the relative darkness, Kim realized that with the lack of light in the passageway, the men in the well-lit wardroom would be unable to see her. Moving carefully, to avoid making any sound, she resumed her position at the small window.

Strange, she thought, the officers clustered around the two din-ing tables were in varying degrees of undress; most in T-shirts and one without any shirt on at all. They looked tired and angry, probably irritated at being awakened at four in the morning for whatever was going on. As she looked around the tables, craning her neck to get a better view of the far one, she recognized some of the junior officers but saw no sign of the Captain or Lawrence, or of John. She shifted her feet, trying to see as far to the right as possible so she could get a look at the others at the far table.

Bob Bosca was there, staring off toward the lounge area at something that she could not see. Perren was sitting next to Bosca, his eyes rigidly locked on the table in front of him. She could not see Tim Mack.

And then she saw Lawrence. The executive officer was almost hidden from her view by his position at the table, but she was able to see his face in profile. Lawrence's face was streaked with blood, and he was holding a handkerchief to the blood-matted hair at his forehead. What on earth was going on? Taking a deep breath, Kim was just about to open the door when an unfamiliar figure appeared from the left. The man had his back to her, but the black jumpsuit he wore was unlike any she had seen worn on board the *Bulkeley*. She could also see that the length of his hair far exceeded the military norm. When he turned to address someone out of her view, she felt her heart leap into her throat. The man was bearded, and clearly of Middle Eastern origin—and he was turning toward the door, toward her!

Instinctively, she dodged to her left, eliminating any small chance that she would be seen through the eye port. She braced herself against the bulkhead across from the wardroom, realizing that she was breathing in gasps. Closing her eyes and concentrating, Kim forced herself to slow her breathing to a normal pace. Her last image of the man as she ducked clear of the tiny window was that he was holding some type of strange weapon.

A terrorist? Iranian or Iraqi military?

Focus, she told herself. *Think*. Got to get away from here first . . . but where to? No one had found her in her stateroom, but that was no guarantee she could return there safely. She searched her memory for a hiding place. She had certainly been around this class of frigate enough, between tours with Stewart many months ago on Wallach's ship, the *Fraser*, and the one with the XO today.

Without knowing quite why, Kim headed aft, walking slowly along the deserted passageway. Then it came to her: Stewart had a small office in the catwalk area above the starboard helo hangar. She remembered it because he had joked that it was so isolated they could make love there for days without being discovered. Kim determined to head for the office, at least initially, and cautiously made her way aft toward the starboard hangar.

After mistakenly going up two ladders which led to other

spaces, she found the correct one and gained the narrow catwalk that ringed the hangar. The open hangar seemed enormous, even with the bulk of the damaged Sealord 26 inside it. She moved forward along the catwalk until she came to the door she remembered as Stewart's office.

God, please don't let it be locked, she thought.

Kim felt a wave of relief as she turned the handle and felt the door open. Once inside the tiny office she turned on the main lighting, and the relative brightness boosted her spirits. There were two steel desks in the space, crowding the small room. She pulled out a chair from one and sank into the hard metal seat, feeling a relief she knew would be short-lived. Her immediate goal of finding a hiding place achieved, she started to think about her predicament and what was happening to the ship.

Before she could concentrate, Kim was jarred from her thoughts by the harsh voice emanating from the office's 1MC speaker.

"American sailors." The voice was commanding, and the volume on the public address system had been turned up so loud that the sound hurt her ears.

There was a pause of twenty seconds.

"American sailors. Listen carefully," the voice echoed through the ship. "This is the voice of Major Barzin Aziz of the Iranian Marines. Both you and your ship have been taken as a prize of war by the Islamic Republic of Iran." There was a ten-second pause. "I repeat so there can be no confusion: your vessel is in the hands of the Iranian Marines. Your Captain is under arrest, and you are all prisoners of war. Your officers and chief petty officers are under guard. Those of you in the berthing spaces will find that the exits have been sealed by my men."

Again there was a pause, for what seemed to Kim an excruciatingly long time.

"The fighting for your ship is at an end. Resistance is at an end. Your Captain is with me, and he asks that you cooperate with us and refrain from further—" Kim heard a clamor of shouting voices in the background, and then the speaker went silent. After a thirty-second delay, the voice resumed; now there was palpable anger in it. "Some of your shipmates—those who chose to resist—have been killed. We do not desire any further death. Remain where you are. Cooperate with the marines guarding you, and your lives will be spared. Your ship is being taken to the Islamic Republic of Iran as a prize of war. Once we reach safe harbor, you will all be repatriated to your country."

After another pause to let the last words sink in to all listeners, the voice, now controlled as at the outset, rumbled through the ship again.

"American sailors, cooperate with us and choose to live. Your ship is going to Iran. It can arrive with its crew well and alive, or it can arrive filled with corpses. The choice is yours. Either way this ship will be delivered to Iran. God is great."

Kim heard the 1MC switch off. Reviewing the remarkable events of the last ten minutes, she tried to focus on the larger picture and grasp what an amazing story she was in on.

But all she could think about was Stewart—who might already be dead.

Andy and Steele were halfway across the flight deck when the first grenade went off.

They had been headed up the flight deck toward a passageway that led amidships, when Steele heard the rasp of the opening hatch. They both turned to look back at their just vacated watch station. Andy saw the low scuttle open about halfway and then the two small objects came lofting out, one to the port and one to the starboard side of the fantail. Steele had been first to recognize what was happening, and he had thrown Andy to the hard non-skidded deck as he himself dived.

As his cheek slammed into the abrasive deck, Andy heard the first detonation; it was more of a pop than the loud explosion he had expected. A fiery wind scorched through his hair, stinging his face, and he heard Steele give a painful grunt beside him. The second explosion came right on the heels of the first, and in this one he could hear shrapnel ricocheting across the open fantail.

Slowly raising his head from the flight deck, Andy looked first at the fantail, which was shrouded in thin gray smoke. The scuttle was closed. He turned to his right and saw Steele's back. The other sailor was on his side, his knees tucked into his chest, moaning softly. Andy got to his knees, wiping the black dust of the grenades clear of his eyes, and bent over his friend. Steele had his eyes clamped shut, his face contorted with pain. He was holding his hands tight against his abdomen, and around the shield made by his hands, his shirt was torn and bloodied.

"Jesus," Andy whispered softly, appalled at the sight. He cursed himself silently for not having insisted that they put on their flak vests before leaving the fantail. In their haste to get inside the ship, they had dragged the vests along with them, planning to don them in the hangar. Now the Kevlar vests were lost somewhere in the darkness of the flight deck.

Before he could offer a word of comfort or encouragement to the stricken man, Andy heard the scraping sound of the scuttle being opened again. He spun to look at the fantail. The scuttle lifted only a few inches and then stopped, as if someone had opened it just enough to be able to see out.

In a panic, Andy realized he no longer had his shotgun. It had gone clattering off into the dark when Steele knocked him to the deck.

With a rasping clang, the scuttle was thrown open. Andy searched frantically for his gun. Finding nothing, he looked around Steele for the wounded man's weapon. Where was it? They both couldn't have lost their guns!

Andy saw the silhouette of a man's head rise just above the coaming of the scuttle.

Knowing he was running out of time, he bent down to Steele's side and put his mouth to the injured man's ear to ask him where his weapon had gone. As he was about to speak, Andy noticed the corner of a wooden stock protruding from underneath Steele's shoulder. He was on top of it!

Andy looked up and saw a weapon appear in the darkness next to the head of the figure in the scuttle. The man was slowly training his weapon across the fantail. In a moment he would turn to look down the flight deck at Andy and Steele. Andy rolled his injured friend to one side as gently as he could. Steele let out a loud moan as his position shifted and his hands were pressed harder against his shrapnel-riddled stomach.

The figure in the scuttle heard the wounded cry and swung rapidly toward the source, firing a burst from his automatic weapon as he turned in the circular trunk. As the figure opened fire, Andy slid the twelve-gauge from under Steele and dived to the deck. The firing stopped, the man in the scuttle seeming uncertain of his target. In the almost absolute darkness, the prone figures of the two sailors forty feet away were all but indistinguishable from the deck they lay on.

Andy could hear Steele's rapid breathing a few feet from him, but the wounded sailor was somehow holding back his cries of pain. Andy slowly, painstakingly brought the shotgun forward and aimed it at the fantail and the scuttle.

The figure in the scuttle sprayed a wide burst of gunfire across the flight deck, the rounds passing one or two feet over Andy's head. He hasn't got a bead on us, Andy thought.

This was a bad situation for a shotgun, he reminded himself—too close to the deck. Half his pattern would ricochet uselessly off the deck, and the target presented by his opponent was small to begin with. He would get one shot only. The blast from the twelve-gauge would answer any questions about where he was, and the automatic weapon would carve a path to him.

Then he remembered what the gunner's mate, Senior Chief Lanier, had taught them when he was training for this watch: If you have to use the riot gun, use it smart, he'd told them. A shotgun is even more devastating on board ship because of the ricochets. Make the ricochets work for you, the chief had said.

The air above Andy and Steele was ripped once more by a knee-high pattern of bullets from the man hidden in the scuttle trunk.

The second the firing ceased, Andy pushed himself hurriedly off the deck and into a kneeling position. He took aim at the open hatch, which projected a full foot behind and above the man in the scuttle and was held open at a ninety-degree angle. With one smooth motion he pumped the shotgun, and even as he fired he could see the man desperately ducking below the rim of the scuttle. The nine 00 buck pellets rocketed toward the exposed hatch, the pattern spreading in flight. Of the seven .32-caliber pellets that struck the hatch, three ricocheted down into the scuttle.

Andy heard the agonized scream from within the scuttle and

was immediately on his feet, charging toward the fantail. When he closed to within fifteen feet of the hatch, he fired another round, this one directly into the scuttle. After the blast from the twelve-gauge died away, there was no further sound from the scuttle. At five feet he fired yet again into the trunk. There was no return fire. Giving the scuttle opening a wide berth, he crossed the fantail to get around behind the hatch.

It was totally silent on the fantail, save for the subdued cries of Steele echoing down from the flight deck. Andy kept the shotgun leveled on the scuttle a full minute before darting forward and slamming the hatch closed from behind. He drove the operating wheel home with a few quick spins and jammed a length of life-line stanchion through the spokes in the wheel to freeze the hatch closed. Only then did he realize he was shaking, his whole body racked by a fearsome tremor. He dropped onto the capstan head to steady himself.

When the wave of shaking passed, Andy pushed three fresh cartridges into the tubular magazine of the twelve-gauge. He rose, shook his shoulders as if to rid himself of a chill, and crossed the empty flight deck to join his wounded shipmate. Andy knelt beside Steele and could tell at once that the wounded man had lost consciousness.

Getting to his feet, Andy hoisted Steele up from the flight deck. He placed the wounded man's left arm around his neck, and, still clasping the shotgun, he put his own right arm around Steele's waist. Struggling with the unfamiliar load, Andy headed forward toward the darkened superstructure.

5

SEALORD 25

Something about this really smells, Lee Hammond thought to himself. He brought Sealord into a tight bank and headed in toward the bridge of the damaged tanker.

"Try 'em again, Max," he said to his copilot.

Mad Max tried once more to raise the *Andes Commerce* on the aircraft's VHF radio. There was only static in response.

"Nada," the younger pilot said. "But they must have seen us by now." This was Sealord's second pass close to the tanker. Hammond brought them in even lower than the first time, so close that Max imagined he could see the figures of men on the dark bridge.

There is no way they didn't see us that time, Hammond thought as he broke off to the right and elevated to two hundred feet. He noted that the fires burning aft in the pilot-house had diminished substantially; when they had first arrived on the scene, the flames had been visible five miles off, even through the sandstorm. Must be getting it under control, he thought.

"American Navy helicopter, this is motor vessel *Andes Commerce*. We have you in sight, over."

Max almost jumped out of his harness as the voice boomed over the VHF in his helmet. He had turned the volume all the way up to avoid missing any transmission.

Hammond decided to take control. They were running out of

on-station time, and although he had a lot of confidence in Max, this was not the time to test him.

"I've got it, Max," he said, switching his helmet mike from interphone to radio.

"*Andes Commerce*, this is U.S. Navy helicopter on your port bow. We are prepared to take off your injured man, Captain."

"Roger, Navy helicopter," the German-accented voice responded, "but that will not be necessary. His injuries are not as serious as first appeared. We have elected to keep him on board. Thank you for your assistance, over."

Son of a bitch! Hammond thought to himself, why didn't you answer up and tell us that before we got all the way out here and had to orbit around for fifteen minutes? Containing his anger, he echoed back the master's statement: "Roger. I copy that you do not, repeat, do not require your man to be med-evacced. Is that correct? Over."

"Affirmative. We appreciate your offer of help. Fires on board are under control and we are en route to Abu Dhabi, over."

Well that's that, Hammond thought. "Roger, *Andes Commerce;* we are returning to base. Out." He started a slow arcing turn to port and commenced the aircraft's climb to transit altitude, leaving the still-burning tanker behind them.

"Max, go ahead and let the ship know what's happened. I want to keep my attention focused on flying while we're in this shit."

"Got it," Max responded.

Leaving behind the glare of the flames on board the *Andes Commerce,* the helicopter returned to the enveloping darkness of night and sand. Hammond remembered the old flight school adage about low-visibility flying, and he told himself to let his stick actions on the cyclic and collective and his use of the rudder pedals become automatic. He needed every bit of his concentration focused on getting back to home plate in one piece.

Hammond took Sealord up to five hundred feet and leveled off. For the short trip back to *Bulkeley*, he decided it was not worth trying to climb to an altitude that would take them out of the storm. He glanced at his TACAN readout, a radio beacon that the ship transmitted to guide them back through just this sort of environment, and verified that they had a good lock on *Bulkeley's* direction.

"We've got a problem, Lee." Max's voice echoed in his helmet. "No joy on the voice link."

That was not good, Hammond thought, but not necessarily a big problem.

"Have Kaufman try a reload of the computer," he said, referring to the sensor operator seated at the tactical console in the compartment behind them. "Meanwhile, you switch up land-launch and raise the ship on that." The land-launch circuit was a fixed clear radio frequency that the ship always monitored while a helo was airborne.

"I already tried that too, Lee." There was a hint of uneasiness in the youthful pilot's voice. "No joy on land-launch. Or on MAD."

Now Hammond was concerned. No comms on three separate circuits? It didn't make sense. He selected MAD, the universally monitored Military Air Distress frequency, and went out with a radio check himself. Within seconds there was a response from the AWACS aircraft on station in the southern Gulf, so his radios appeared to be fine. Another look at the TACAN showed that the signal was still coming in strong. A check of the SH-60B's powerful APS-124 radar showed the Bulkeley's distinct radar blip, and it matched the TACAN bearing. With the ship only twenty-five miles away, fifteen minutes by air, Hammond decided to investigate himself before alerting the AWACS. He had no desire to put the ship on report to the Admiral because of some radioman's screw-up, if that was what it was.

"Keep trying to raise them, Max. Try HF or the bridge-to-bridge if you have to." He was careful to keep any element of worry or concern out of his voice.

As they flew on through the billowing sheets of dust and grit, Hammond silently reviewed the procedures for both a lost-comms low-visibility approach and lost-comms landing.

THE BULKELEY

Stewart stood between the Captain and the Iranians as Donelli tried to regain his wind. When the CO had yelled his protest at Aziz during the Major's remarks on the 1MC, the heavily bearded Iranian who accompanied the leader had smashed the stock of his assault rifle into Donelli's abdomen. Stewart had instinctively grabbed the big man and shoved him away from the Captain before the beating could continue. The Major had interrupted his address to the crew long enough to keep the enraged Iranian from shooting Stewart, but the man kept his weapon trained on the American officer.

Finishing his address to the crew, Aziz replaced the 1MC microphone and turned back to the scene of confrontation on the bridge. "Enough," the Major said forcefully to both Kalil and Stewart. Locking eyes with Kalil, Aziz gestured toward the chart table. "Please join me, Colonel." The larger man crossed reluctantly to the chart table, his still-livid gaze remaining fixed on Stewart. It was only when Aziz spoke to him in low tones in Farsi that Kalil shifted his attention from Stewart to the chart on the table before him.

Stewart took advantage of the Iranians' focus on the charts to comfort Donelli, who was still doubled over with pain. "This won't be as easy as they think, Captain," Stewart whispered, putting his arm around Donelli's broad back and keeping one eye on the Iranians. "There's a lot of water between here and Iran."

"Can't let them take her . . ." Donelli wheezed. He fought against the pain in his gut to try to bring himself upright. "We don't cooperate . . ." the Captain said slowly, "there's no ship." He looked up at Stewart, and Stewart saw the resolve in his face.

"Captain." Aziz's voice from across the bridge conveyed a summons.

Under the watchful eyes of the two marines who stood at either end of the bridge, Donelli moved slowly to the chart table. Stewart followed unbidden a step behind him.

Aziz looked up from the chart, a set of dividers in his hand. The light emanating from a small fluorescent lamp on the table gave his face an unnatural pinkish hue.

"You are no doubt thinking that we"—he gestured to Kalil— "will never bring your ship to harbor without your cooperation." He watched the Captain closely for his reaction. "I accept that in principle. My navigation is good enough to set the course, but your men must steer the ship and keep the engines engaged." Donelli gave no sign of acknowledgment. "Therefore it is imperative that I have your cooperation until we are pierside," Aziz said, setting the dividers down carefully.

"Well, you're in a world of shit then, aren't you?" Donelli said tonelessly.

Aziz smiled in spite of himself at the colorful phrase. The Americans were always busy enriching their language.

"The 'world of shit,' as you put it, is your own." Aziz shifted his gaze from the Captain to Stewart. He glanced quickly down at Stewart's gold oak leaves and then addressed Donelli. "This officer is your second-in-command?"

The Captain, still breathing with difficulty from Kalil's blow, looked at Stewart as he answered. "Yes . . . he's my executive officer." Stewart met Donelli's gaze and fought back his surprise, hoping his face showed no reaction to the unexpected lie. The Captain broke eye contact with Stewart immediately and returned his attention to Aziz. In that instant Donelli's intent was clear to Stewart: the Iranians needed their cooperation, and every bit of information or help withheld from them would be a small victory.

Aziz studied the two Americans carefully for a moment before continuing. When he spoke, his eyes remained on Donelli, but his words were for both of them.

" I will issue courses, speeds, and other orders to your watch. I will hold the Captain responsible for the execution of these orders. Should the Captain or the watch standers prove unwilling to comply, I will order his death." The Major locked eyes with Stewart. "Command will then fall to you. If you do not comply, I will repeat the unpleasant process until I reach an officer who will obey our wishes."

Stewart returned Aziz's gaze and found in the Iranian's eyes a ruthless pragmatism that left no doubt of his sincerity. He looked at the Captain for an indication of how he should respond.

The Captain was staring at Aziz, his expression one more of disgust than outrage. Donelli had been studying the chart while Aziz spoke, and he had noted that the Iranians had not made any marks on it or laid out a track. He presumed their destination must be nearby Bandar Abbas. The key, he determined, was to draw things out and buy time, so that someone somewhere might realize their predicament. The Captain would try to prevent any more loss of life, but beyond all else he would not let them take his ship into an enemy port.

"We will carry out your directions to the helm," Donelli said flatly.

"Very good." Aziz turned and addressed Scott Septenano. "Make your course two-zero-zero degrees."

Septenano looked at the Captain for guidance. Donelli gave him a nod that said make it so.

"Left ten degrees rudder, steady course two-zero-zero," Septenano ordered the helmsman seated in front of him.

"You'll never get this ship into your own waters," Donelli said to Aziz, his voice a low growl. "You'll be cut off by other U.S. ships or aircraft long before we reach your territorial waters."

Aziz gave the Captain a tight-lipped smile. "Perhaps, but perhaps not. Your own forces do not know of your fate. Do they?" he asked rhetorically.

The Major watched Donelli for a long moment, but the Captain did not meet his gaze or speak. Turning toward one of the marines, Aziz issued a brief order in Farsi. As Kalil moved to the far side of the bridge to cover the Americans, the two marines slung their weapons and proceeded to lift Chief Marquez's body from the captain's chair. Moving carefully on the deck, still wet with blood, they carried their lifeless cargo out of the bridgewing and aft of the pilothouse. They returned a moment later.

Standing near the chart table with the Captain, Stewart realized he could be on top of Aziz before the Iranian could react. The Major had returned his attention to the chart before him, and he was less than five feet away from Stewart. Such an attack would probably be suicidal, but at the moment anything seemed better than to stand impotently by while they took the ship. He forced the idea from his thoughts. *Think clearly*—forget the anger and focus on a plan, he told himself.

"Colt Sabre, this is Sealord, over."

All eyes turned to look at the source of the voice: the bridge-to-bridge radio in front of the captain's chair.

■

"Colt Sabre, Colt Sabre, this is Sealord, over." The American offi-cers recognized Max's voice as he gave the *Bulkeley*'s clear-radio-circuit code name.

Aziz turned to Donelli; the Major had known this was coming. His men had left the VHF radio with its separate power supply untouched for just this situation.

"That will be your helicopter returning, Captain," he said to Donelli. Aziz walked to the front of the bridge and stared out the large windows. The first glow of dawn was dimly evident. He turned and faced the Captain.

"I require you to operate that radio and tell them they will not be able to land." He paused, watching Donelli's reaction. "Tell the pilots you have a fire on board . . . a dangerous fire in your Radio Central. Your ship is at General Quarters and it is unsafe to land their aircraft."

"Captain," Stewart broke in, "Sealord can't have more than thirty minutes of gas at the outside. If we don't bring them in they'll have to ditch for sure!"

In the background, the voice on the radio continued to call the *Bulkeley*.

Aziz ignored Stewart and addressed Donelli. "They may reach land, they may not. That is not our concern. You will tell them all your resources are occupied fighting the fire, and they cannot land."

Aziz watched as the Captain came toward him, stopping a pace short.

"You said yourself there has been enough killing." Donelli's voice was arctic, and Aziz was instantly on alert. "I will not send any more of my men to their deaths," the Captain said with chill-ing finality.

Aziz sensed rather than heard Kalil move to his side from across the bridge. The bearded Guards leader had his rifle leveled at the Captain's chest from less than two feet away.

"Enough argument!" Kalil barked. "Talk to the aircraft or die!" He poked the Captain hard in the chest with the barrel of his weapon.

The Major knew he was losing control of the situation; he im-mediately regretted not having sent Kalil below to watch the other

American officers. Aziz recognized what kind of man this Captain was, and he knew before he spoke them that his next words would be wasted.

"Captain," the Major said carefully, "the aircraft will not land here. Their fate is uncertain if you send them away; while your death will be immediate if you do not."

"Get someone else to do your killing, Major." The Captain turned his back on Aziz and Kalil and began to walk away.

"Wait!" the Major screamed at both Kalil and the Captain. Aziz brought up his hand to stop the Guards commander, but he was far too slow. At such close range, the force of the blast from Kalil's assault rifle knocked the Captain to his knees as the rounds slammed into his back. He tottered briefly on his knees, a puzzled expression on his face, and then collapsed forward to the deck.

The echoes of the shots had not had time to die in the pilot-house before Stewart rushed to the Captain's side, ignoring the smoking weapon that was now trained on him. The rest of the crew in the bridge looked on aghast.

"Colt Sabre, Colt Sabre, this is Sealord. Sealord. We have you in sight. If you can hear us, we're going to line up for a lost-comms landing, over." The voice on the radio was the only sound on the silent bridge.

Aziz watched as the American officer sought fruitlessly for any sign of life in his stricken commander. He empathized with the grieving man, but he knew he was running out of time to complete the essential diversion of the aircraft. The Major reached over and placed his hand on the still-hot barrel of Kalil's weapon. The Guards Commander kept the rifle trained on Stewart's head. With his eyes on Kalil's, Aziz slowly depressed the barrel until the gun was pointing at the deck. His intent was clear: no more killing.

"You," Aziz said to Stewart, "are now in command here."

The American looked up at the Major, his face a dark mask of anger and grief.

"Pass the message to the aircraft as I have instructed or we will move down your chain of command until we find someone who will." The Major could see his meaning was immediately clear to the man, but the American remained kneeling on the deck, his arms cradling his dead Captain.

Stewart's face took on an unreadable expression that somehow disturbed Aziz more than the man's earlier look of rage. Slowly, Stewart got to his feet. He took a long look down at the Captain. Without a word, he crossed the hushed bridge to the captain's chair and picked up the VHF microphone.

"Sealord, this is Colt Sabre; we copy your transmission. Negative on lost-comms landing. Red deck. Repeat, Red deck. . . ."

SEALORD 25

Hammond couldn't believe what he was hearing. He understood about the fire in Radio Central, but that was no reason to abandon his aircraft to fend for itself. Hammond had recognized Stewart's voice on the bridge-to-bridge, so he knew he wasn't being jerked around by someone from off the ship with their own radio.

He started Sealord into a slow turn once again to maintain the aircraft's orbit over the *Bulkeley's* position. Visibility had improved enough so that they could circle up to a mile from the ship and still keep her in view.

"Colt Sabre, this is Sealord, copy all—but we have to land. We don't have sufficient fuel to bingo anywhere, over."

"Roger, Sealord. We understand your situation, but we cannot let you land. Situation here is too dangerous. Fire out of control." What was there about Stewart's voice? Hammond wondered to himself. You would expect him to be tense with a major fire on board, but Stewart sounded really shook. Things had to be pretty bad down there.

A fast look at the fuel gauges confirmed Hammond's negative outlook on bingoing to any nearby airstrip. In the copilot's seat, Max was busily computing how far and how long they could go at maximum-range fuel efficiency. An airmap showing the coast of the United Arab Emirates was in his lap. The UAE was to the south; to the north—and closer, Hammond thought for the hundredth time—were the islands and mainland of Iran.

"John," he said urgently, not wanting to waste time on formalities, "let me speak to the Captain. We've got to bring her in or we're headed for the drink."

There was a thirty-second delay in Stewart's response over the radio. It seemed like thirty minutes to Hammond.

"Sorry, Sealord. . . . The CO is . . . back with the fire parties in Radio. I say again: fire is too severe. We can't let you land—or launch Sealord Two-Six."

Well, that was it. They had no choice but to try to make land and be ready to ditch if they didn't make it. But what the hell was Stewart talking about Sealord 26 for? Stewart knew as well as he did that Two-Six was down hard and wouldn't be airworthy for at least another twenty-four hours. Hammond puzzled over his friend's statement for a second before putting it out of his mind. He had far more important things to worry about.

"What have you got, Max?" he asked his copilot.

"About thirty-five miles to the beach at Dubai. That's the beach, not a field. At minimum consumption we'll still be in the water ten miles short of there."

"Great."

"The one other option is Abu Musa, only about twenty miles northwest of us."

"That's not an option," Hammond said, as he nosed the SH-60B over to the south. "Give me a course to intercept the nearest finger of dirt at Dubai." He switched from the interphone back to the VHF.

"John, we're going to bingo for Dubai. If you still have radar, follow our progress so you can mark our splash if we go in. We'll try to let the big boys know about your trouble."

"Roger, Sealord . . ." Stewart's voice faded, although Hammond could hear that the radio was still keyed. "Good luck, Lee."

Hammond noticed the sadness in his friend's voice. "We'll see you at the club. First one there buys." He switched back to the interphone. His attention was now totally focused on getting his aircraft down safely.

"Max, come up on the tower frequency for Dubai International and declare an emergency. Once you raise them, shift to HF and try to get through to COM JTF—clear or secure, whatever works."

Ironic, Hammond thought to himself. Twenty radios on *Bulkeley* and now Sealord was their only way of talking to anyone outside the limited range of VHF. Leaving Max to work the radio side of the problem, Hammond fine-tuned the helo's speed and altitude to work every possible mile of range out of their dwindling fuel supply.

THE BULKELEY

Repair locker two was a damage control equipment storage room with several communications links to the rest of the *Bulkeley*. Within the locker, a latticework of shelves and storage bins held a vast array of fire fighting and counterflooding gear; everything from oxygen breathing equipment and submersible pumps to fire hoses and patch kits. The densely packed space was deserted save for the immense figure of BM2 Mosopu. He sat on a low steel bench in the center of the locker, his head in his hands. Upon entering the repair locker he had tried immediately to contact the bridge via sound-powered phone. After several attempts and no success, he had been about to try to contact Main Control when the strangely accented voice had come over the 1MC. Mosopu had found the words all the more chilling because the speaker had delivered them so matter-of-factly.

So the man he had killed had been an Iranian. If Mosopu had known the full extent of what was happening to his ship, he would have tried to kill the other one, too.

Was he the only one who hadn't been taken prisoner?, he wondered. One man against how many Iranians? Either way, he thought, they would be coming for him soon. He rubbed his close-cropped skull with his hand, trying to force a plan to come to him. He looked down at the strange weapon in his lap. He knew enough about guns from his training on the ship's self-defense force to be able to reason out the mechanics of this one. Pulling back what he determined to be the bolt, he sent one unspent round sailing out the ejection port; releasing the bolt, he chambered another round. It was ready to fire. He debated whether to remove what he figured was the gun's silencer, but closer inspection revealed the silencer was built in and could not be removed.

Mosopu stood up in the darkness of the storage locker and took a deep breath. It was time to move; he had been there too long. He checked out the passageway outside very carefully. He did not have a plan as yet, but he knew he had to have two things if he—and the *Bulkeley*—were to survive: more men and more weapons. At the thought, he turned from the door and went to one of the bins, from which he pulled out a fire axe. The steel axe looked like a hatchet in his massive hands.

Mosopu slipped out of the locker, resealing the door behind him, and started across the red-lit passageway. He was headed for the armory.

It was cooler in the darkened helicopter; much cooler than it had been on the flight deck.

Andy raised Steele as gently as possible and slid the seat cushion he had pulled from the copilot's seat under the injured man's head. Steele had been slipping in and out of consciousness. He was out right now, his breathing labored and broken by occasional coughs. Andy had bandaged Steele's stomach wounds as best he could with the large dressings he found in the hangar first-aid kit. He wished there had been some sort of painkillers in the kit as well, but all the drugs were maintained in sick bay.

After the gun battle, Andy had chosen the starboard hangar as a temporary refuge because he remembered the broken helo was shut away in there. The aircraft filled most of the hangar, and its many tie-downs and pieces of auxiliary equipment obstructed much of the remaining open space. The failed rotary coupling assembly, left out when the crew chief had sent the aviation machinists to bed at 0200, took up half the deck by itself. Andy doubted anyone could get to them here without making an alerting noise as they made their way through all the clutter.

Even with the helicopter's sliding bay door three quarters closed, Andy had been able to hear the voice of the Iranian commander on the 1MC. The volume on the hangar 1MC speakers was turned up so the flight deck crew could hear over the noise of an aircraft on deck. The words had stunned him. The Iranians had somehow taken the ship! How many others besides himself, he wondered, were still outside the net of capture?

Steele moaned softly as he shifted his legs on the smooth, cool deck of Sealord 26. Stay under, Andy willed the wounded man. Please stay under. Steele's moments of consciousness were growing less frequent and seemed to be more painful to him, Andy thought. A glance at the battle dressing showed telltale signs of blood leaking through.

What could he do? He considered surrendering to the Iranian Marines in order to get medical aid for Steele. Doc Culver, *Bulkeley*'s independent duty corpsman, was probably Steele's best hope now, Andy thought. But then his memory returned to the flight deck, and the man he had shot. Andy was sure he had hit the figure in the scuttle, and he suspected the Iranians would not treat Steele or himself too gently if they had found out what had happened to their comrade. After struggling with his conscience over the idea of surrender, he finally came to realize that he, a junior third class petty officer, might be the only one on board not under guard—the only hope for his ship.

His mind made up, Andy added another layer to the battle dressing on Steele's wounds and rose from the deck to crouch in the cramped helicopter.

"I've gotta go, Steele," he said to the unconscious form of his friend. "Maybe I can do something to turn this thing around a little. I'll know soon as I get the lay of the ship. Either way, I'll be back in thirty minutes." There was no acknowledgment from the man on the deck of the helo. Andy knew he was talking as much to raise his own spirits as on the chance that somehow some of it was getting through to Steele.

He checked the twelve-gauge and verified it was fully loaded, with one round in the chamber and five in the magazine. Stepping over his wounded shipmate, Andy slowly opened the bay door. He listened intently for any sound that would indicate another presence in the hangar. When he was satisfied, he stepped down out of the helo, closed the door, and headed forward to the hangar exit door. Cautiously, the shotgun pointed in front of him, he inched around the massive structure of the aircraft. He rounded the helo's nose and saw his path to the door was clear.

"Lower your gun and turn around very slowly."

The muffled whisper came from somewhere behind and above him.

■

Sergeant Major Rafsani pulled back from the base of the ladder and stood in silence as he watched the two American sailors lower the bloodstained body of one of their officers down the ladder. They were exceedingly gentle in their difficult work, he noted, as if they thought the dead man could still feel pain. To Rafsani's professional eye, it was clear from the wounds that the man had been shot in the back. The man's insignia made him a very senior officer, perhaps even the ship's captain. That was bad. There were enough problems developing already.

The Sergeant Major crossed the bridge to the chart table, where the Major appeared to be explaining something to Kalil. Aziz looked up as Rafsani joined them.

"God is great, Sergeant. You have your report?" the Major inquired.

Rafsani sensed there had been trouble between the two men. Aziz was being very formal with him, and he had not seen such strain in the Major's face before.

"God is great," Rafsani responded perfunctorily. "All does not go well throughout the ship. I see there has been trouble here also. We must make adjustments."

"How so?" Kalil broke in angrily. "What problems are there that our guns cannot resolve? Of what adjustments do you speak?" He turned to Aziz. "I think your Sergeant Major presumes far too much!"

Rafsani briefly considered and then discarded the idea of slapping the Guards Commander. He would accept criticism, when merited, from those he respected, but not from this cur! He paused, taking a breath to regain control, and then spoke directly to Aziz. "There has been trouble in the after part of the ship. I heard the firing as I was on my way to verify the security of the berthing areas."

"Yes, we heard it, too," Kalil interjected impatiently.

Rafsani pointedly ignored him and continued. "When I reached the area below the flight deck, I found one of the Guards had been killed and another lightly wounded. Sergeant Hoveyda was up on the deck above, searching for their attacker. I joined him, but we found no one."

"One of my men . . . dead?" Kalil asked, somewhat disbelievingly.

Aziz appeared deep in thought. "So both of the after gunners escaped?" he asked.

"It would appear so. Although we did find quite a bit of blood on the deck, as well as some light body armor and an abandoned shotgun nearby."

"At least one of them is wounded then," the Major said, thinking aloud, "and they have perhaps one weapon between them. A problem, but not insurmountable."

"There is more," Rafsani said quietly. The other men stared at him in surprise.

"I left Hoveyda to continue the search and went forward to the berthing compartments." He paused, looking down at the deck. "Harare was lying on the deck on the port side. He was dead, his throat crushed."

Aziz was stunned. He and the Sergeant Major had served with Harare for over four years. The marines were a very close-knit group. Moreover, they were men who were very tough to kill. The loss of two men and the wounding of an additional Guard reduced the effective number of his force to just eighteen men, and Aziz knew the mission had been planned with few men to spare. He had expected some fatalities, but the loss of Harare visibly disturbed him.

"Any indication of who killed him?" the Major asked tonelessly.

Rafsani looked up. "We are searching the vicinity. Jumblatt, who was on the deck below, heard a loud crash, but by the time he reached Harare, the assailant was gone." He let that sink in before delivering the worst news: "And the killer has Harare's Sterling."

Kalil showed no reaction, but Rafsani could see concern darken the Major's visage. The deaths were bad enough, but now some *Bulkeley* crewman had one of their Sterlings! Aziz was mortified. The specially designed, silenced submachine gun had been one of their greatest assets, and now it could be turned against them.

"I have search teams moving through the likely parts of the ship," Rafsani said, as if reading the minds of Aziz and Kalil. "But we have only skeleton sentry and control forces while the search continues."

"You have done what is proper, my friend," Aziz said. "At this moment those three Americans are the greatest threat to our success."

The Sergeant Major turned and looked directly at Kalil. "I would like to take the one who killed Harare myself. He was killed with extraordinary strength and savagery. The man who did this is very dangerous. The nine-millimeter will not be enough."

"Take charge of the search in the area of the berthing spaces, Sergeant Major," Aziz said. "Hoveyda will find the escaped gunners."

Rafsani gave the Major an acknowledging nod and was gone.

Aziz turned from the chart table and stared out the bridge windows. The blood red horizon visible to the east foretold another day of the sandstorm.

"Do not despair, Major," Kalil said with forced cheerfulness. "We have killed two, and now they have killed two. But we have the men—and the guns."

Aziz turned and looked at Kalil as if he were gazing upon an idiot.

"We can not afford a drawn-out fight, Colonel. This ship is to be a weapon, not a battleground."

6

THE <u>PASCAGOULA</u>

Garmisch awakened slowly. His exhausted body tried to fight his mind for a few more seconds of rest. The urgency of the hushed voice finally overcame his body's resistance and penetrated the fog of sleep.

"Mr. Garmisch, come on. Please wake up!"

The light stung his eyes as he tried to make out who his tormentor was. As his mind cleared he recalled that he had left his bunk light on when he drifted off to sleep. In a moment, Garmisch's eyes adapted to the light, and he was able to make out the face of OS3 Fisher leaning over his rack.

"What's up, Fish?" he asked, his mind now in focus.

"Captain Lacey wants you in the TDC ASAP, Mr. Garmisch." Fisher's urgent tone indicated that ASAP meant right now.

Garmisch struggled to a sitting position in his rack and looked down at his watch: 0445. He rubbed his eyes to banish the last of the sleep. "Tell the Chief of Staff I'm on my way."

Fisher was gone before Garmisch could ask him to make an extra-strong pot of coffee and take it to the TDC. After splashing water on his face and throwing on a uniform, he followed the path of the young petty officer down to the Tactical Decision Center.

As he entered the space, Garmisch was surprised to see Lacey himself talking on the radio. The Chief of Staff stood, microphone in hand, at the bank of radios that lined one bulkhead of the TDC.

Bill Claytor, the staff watch officer who had relieved Garmisch, was listening anxiously at Lacey's side, while a petty officer kept a written log of the ongoing radio conversation.

". . . and we've confirmed Dubai International has its SAR bird en route to you. They've got fire and rescue boats on the way too, in case you have to ditch," Lacey said into the mike. The large international airport at Dubai had a search and rescue helicopter available around the clock because of the airfield's proximity to the Persian Gulf.

"Roger, COM JTF. We're running on fumes now. I don't think we're gonna make the coast."

Garmisch was startled to hear that the conversation between Lacey and what sounded like an aircraft in trouble was taking place over a clear HF circuit. The Chief of Staff's appearance was as impeccable as ever, even after his having been pulled from his bed at that hour of the morning. His voice had a soothing professional calm to it, but when Garmisch got a look at Lacey's face, he could see he was deeply disturbed by whatever was happening.

"We copy, Sealord. Remain up on this circuit as long as you can. If you have to go in, we want as accurate a position on you as possible." Lacey released the key on the microphone and handed the handset to Claytor. "Keep them talking, Bill. The AWACS is tracking them on radar, but I want to retain comms with them and give what help we can."

Gesturing for Garmisch to follow him, Lacey went to the large tactical plot that filled another entire bulkhead of the TDC. As Garmisch watched, Lacey pulled an unused helicopter marker from a wall-mounted tray and placed it halfway between the *Bulkeley*'s marker and the coast of Dubai.

"That's Sealord Two-Five, off of *Bulkeley*. She's ten minutes from the beach at Dubai with about five minutes of gas," Lacy said emotionlessly.

He let the words sink in for a second, watching Jim's reaction. Garmisch was about to pour out the legion of questions in his mind when the Chief of Staff continued. "At about zero three thirty the AWACS lost the link with *Bulkeley*. They tried to raise her on the primary and secondary control circuits without success." Lacey gestured across the TDC to where the staff watch officer was speaking into the radio. "Once Bill got word of that, he started trying to reach them on the Command Net, HF secure, UHF relay—you name it. All no joy. That was when he called me."

"Was she attacked?" Garmisch blurted out. His mind had raced ahead of Lacey's recapping of events to his own nightmare scenario.

Lacey gave him a cool smile that showed Garmisch he did not appreciate having the sequence of the story disrupted. "We considered that. But there was no prior indication of trouble. Bill had a status report from them, just minutes before the circuits went dead, on a med-evac they were running. The ship didn't indicate anything out of the ordinary was going on in their patrol box." Lacey looked over at a nearby data display console; its screen showed numerous contacts. "Same thing with their link input," he said. "AWACS confirmed it didn't show any unusual or threatening tracks before they dropped out." Lacey turned back to the tactical plot and stared at the helo marker. "Their helo provided the answer. We got a distress call from her fifteen minutes ago on Tactical Pri, in the clear. Seems *Bulkeley* contacted them on bridge-to-bridge and waved them off because of a fire in the ship's Radio Central."

Lace paused and watched Garmisch's face for a sign that he understood the connection.

"That would explain the loss of comms," Garmisch said. "But how bad a fire would this have to be, for them to wave off their helo when it didn't have enough gas to reach land safely?"

"Pretty bad," Lacey answered. "I know Vince Donelli from quite a ways back. If he wouldn't recover them, knowing the aircraft's fuel state, then his ship must be in real trouble." Lacey stared hard at the *Bulkeley's* marker, as if it could give him the answer he sought. "I've talked to the Admiral, and he's agreed to hold the next convoy at its start position at Al Fujairah. *Daniels* and *Robinson* are the convoy escorts, and they're the closest units to the *Bulkeley's* position. We're going to detach *Daniels* to head through the Straits at thirty knots to assist *Bulkeley*. We'll leave *Robinson* to nursemaid the tankers until we can get another escort down there." He turned to Garmisch. "I want you to get on the Command Net to *Daniels* and *Robinson* and make it happen."

Garmisch nodded slowly, his mind racing through the implications. "Even at thirty knots, *Daniels* won't get to *Bulkeley's* position for over seven hours," he said.

"I know. That's why I've already ordered the southern AWACS to close *Bulkeley* and try to raise them on short-range VHF," Lacey responded. "That seems to be the only circuit the ship can talk on, and we need to know how bad a shape she's in and if she has any casualties. But *Daniels* is still the closest asset we have that can actually help her." He paused and studied Garmisch carefully. "Any questions? I'm on my way to fill in the Admiral."

"I've got it, Captain."

Lacey went to the door of the Tactical Decision Center, turning to look at Garmisch before he exited. "One other reason I want you up here," Lacey said. "If your earlier hunch is correct and the Iranians have targeted *Bulkeley,* this situation could go from bad to catastrophic real fast. If the AWACS gets even a sniff of anything suspicious in the eastern Gulf, I want TACAIR from the *Roosevelt* on top of it."

"Aye-aye, Captain," Garmisch said. As the door to the TDC closed behind the Chief of Staff, Garmisch was already on the radio to the USS *Daniels.*

THE <u>BULKELEY</u>

Andy remained frozen in his position in the darkness, the shotgun barrel still pointed directly ahead of him. The voice out of the darkness had stunned him, and he was not sure how to react. He was torn over whether to try to fight or surrender. Either choice might result in his death.

"Lower your gun," the whispering voice repeated, "and turn around slowly." Just as Andy decided to take his chances fighting, the voice came again, the whisper more high-pitched. "Damn it, I'm an American! Now turn around!"

He realized that in fact it was an American voice—and also, with some shock, that it sounded as if it might be a woman's. He had heard there was a woman reporter on board, but why would she be here, in the hangar? Cautiously he turned to face the speaker, the twelve-gauge still held at the ready. He could just make out the silhouette of a figure at the base of the ladder that serviced the hangar catwalk. Without a word, the figure walked toward him; stopping in a dim pool of light from the open hangar door. Andy was amazed to see that indeed it was a woman. She was dressed in workclothes, and he could tell she was older than he. He couldn't make out much else.

"You can drop the gun," she said. "I heard you and your friend struggling with the helicopter passenger door when you came in." She looked around the hangar warily. "I would have come down to join you sooner, but I wasn't sure, in this light, whose side you were on."

Andy realized he still had the shotgun trained on her and quickly lowered the barrel. "Sorry," he said. He was glad the poor light concealed his embarrassed blush.

"There's blood on your shirt. Are you injured?" she asked. She moved closer to get a better look.

"No . . . not me, ma'am." Andy looked down at his blood-stained shirt reflexively. "Steele—my friend; he's the one who's hurt."

"Forget the 'ma'am,' okay?" She smiled. "I'm not quite that old. Just call me Kim." She gestured toward the silent helicopter. "Would you like me to look at him? I can't promise much, but I have taken some first-aid courses."

Andy was immensely relieved. Just having someone else to talk to, just knowing there was another free person on the ship raised his spirits.

"Please, if you would," he said, and started to lead her back to the door of Sealord Two-Six.

Kim followed him across the dark hangar, carefully sidestepping the numerous obstacles on the deck. When she reached the aircraft's door, she found he had already opened it and climbed inside. Andy gave her a hand up into the hatchway and guided her around the prone form of Steele. She knelt with him beside the injured man.

"Do you have any kind of light?" she asked.

"Just some matches," he replied. She heard him searching his pockets. "And there ain't a whole lot of 'em left, either."

"Go ahead and light one."

The light from the match was painfully bright after so much darkness, and Kim had to give her eyes a moment to adjust. In the flickering light, she was able to make out the wounded man and the large bandages wrapped above his waist. Blood had soaked through in several spots.

"I've got more battle dressings," she heard the sailor say as the match went out.

"Okay, we'll . . ." She hesitated. "What's your name, anyway?"

"Andy. Andy Barron."

"Okay, Andy," Kim said, trying to sound confident and upbeat, "we'll have to change these dressings, and it's going to cost us a few more matches."

"I changed the bandages about ten minutes ago," he said, his voice sounding hollow.

"Oh," Kim said softly. If the man was bleeding from the abdomen at that rate, there was not much they could do for him. She was thankful he was unconscious, given the nature of his wounds. "Well . . . we'll change the dressing one more time, but we've got to get him real medical help if he's going to have a chance."

"I thought about surrendering," Andy said. "You know, giving up so's I could get Steele to sick bay and Doc Culver."

The thought of surrendering had crossed Kim's mind as well. What could she, or even the two of them, do against the unknown number of Iranian marines on board? Now, with this gravely injured man as their responsibility, it might be the only thing to do.

"I think that maybe that's best, Andy. I'm afraid your friend will die soon if we don't get him to your sick bay."

She saw Andy's head slump to his chest. "You're right, I guess," he said, a mixture of resignation and disappointment in his voice. "I just hate to let the ship down—especially if we're the only ones still free."

For several moments, they sat in the darkened helicopter together, listening to Steele's labored breathing. Then Andy rose in the low crouch the bay would permit, and stepped over Steele to the door.

"Let's go if we're gonna do it," he said. "His breathin's sounding worse."

Kim got up off her knees to follow Andy out. Just as he pulled the bay door open, she heard a strange sputtering sound from outside the helo. Andy leapt clear of the door at the same moment that metal fragments exploded in the passenger bay and wire runs dangling from the aircraft's overhead were severed in a shower of sparks. The Perspex observation window behind her shattered as more of the lethal projectiles careened through the open door.

SEALORD 25

The view out the helicopter's windscreen was reasonably encouraging, Hammond thought. The storm had subsided enough in the last half hour to open the visibility out to about five miles, and the predawn twilight had a softening effect on both the water below and the coast just ahead of them. In the distance he could make out the lights of the central city of Abu Dhabi. He knew the airport was a few miles on the far side of the city. What was most important now was to get over land. He would prefer any kind of "hard" landing to putting the aircraft into the tepid waters of the Gulf.

"We're gonna make it!" Max yelled excitedly. He was maintaining the radio link with COM JTF while Hammond piloted Sealord.

"Could be." Hammond was not nearly so confident. They were cruising at one thousand feet. He would have preferred to be higher, to conserve what fuel they had, but the ceiling was at about twelve hundred feet. If they did run out of gas, the last thing he wanted to do was autorotate through the thousand-foot-deep cloud cover. He had gone down to one engine ten minutes ago and had been on their emergency fuel reserve for three times that long. Hammond did not need to look at the instrument panel to know the fuel status light was flashing red and the gauges showed empty.

Concentrating for all he was worth, Hammond could just begin to make out the outline of the beach in the gathering light. Maybe they would make it after all.

His first thought was surprise at the lack of coughing or sputtering as number two engine shut down. Somehow he had always thought an engine that ran out of fuel would announce itself, rather than simply shutting down as if it had been turned off.

"Restart procedure," he said in the suddenly quiet cockpit. A quick glance at Max showed the younger pilot calling in their position while simultaneously flipping through the procedural checklist. Long before Max had found the restart procedure in the compact checklist, Hammond was coolly going through the steps from memory. As he adjusted the throttles and attempted to fire the engine, Hammond felt the sudden sluggishness of the controls in his hands. They were losing altitude with increasing speed; the water below was now clearly visible. He strained against the leaden collective, trying to arrest the speed of their descent. At five hundred feet Hammond went through the restart procedure one more time. This time the engine coughed briefly but failed to turn over.

"Restart is no go," he said into the interphone. "Max, give COM JTF our position from the Dubai TACAN and then brace for impact. You too, Kaufman." Hammond looked over his shoulder and saw the SENSO was already in the crash position, his control table folded up and his gloved hands on the console's shock handholds.

"Remember the drill," Hammond said, "stay in harness until we turn turtle and then get out fast." He was referring to the known tendency of the SH-60B to roll over and invert when it was set down in the water. It was critical to their survival that they stay in place until the aircraft had stopped rolling and stabilized.

Despite Hammond's efforts to slow their descent, the water was rushing up at them at increasing speed. When he judged they were seconds from impact, he put all his strength into one last effort to bring up the nose of the helo.

"Stand by for impact," he ordered.

THE BULKELEY

Lawrence gingerly eased his blood-soaked handkerchief away from the wound on his forehead. Struggling with the two Iranians who had burst into his stateroom had probably not been the wisest course of action, he knew. He was lucky to be alive. Lawrence found that the bleeding had stopped and the pressure of the cloth was no longer necessary. His head still pounded as if a five-inch shell had detonated inside it, but that pain was as nothing compared to what he felt hearing the Iranian Major's words over the 1MC.

"Feeling any better, Commander?" Bob Bosca asked solicitously from across the table. Lawrence looked over at the nearest of the two Iranians guarding them in the wardroom before answering. The Iranians' lack of interest in earlier conversations among the Americans had seemed to indicate that they did not understand English, but Lawrence could not be completely certain. Lawrence stared at the closest Iranian for a long moment. He finally broke the other man's gaze, and the Iranian looked away uncomfortably. Lawrence returned his attention to Bosca. "I'll live," he said softly.

Sparing one more look for the Iranian sentry, Lawrence leaned forward across the table toward Bosca and Perren. The other officers at the table eased forward to listen. "Look," Lawrence began slowly, his voice just above a whisper, "we're in a bad situation here, but they have problems too. Right as they seized control there was fifty-cal fire from the fantail, and then more gunfire from back there a few minutes later."

"We heard it, too," Bosca confirmed.

"So they've got a problem back aft," Lawrence continued, "and maybe more than one problem." He looked up briefly once more at the nearest Iranian and then continued. "We've seen no sign of Kim—Miss Mitchell—and if they've missed her, they may have missed others in the crew also."

Bosca gave him a weak smile. "There was an English-speaking one down here before they brought you in. He had a lot of questions about the presence of us 'civilians.' " Bosca gestured to Perren and Mack. "I told him there were just the three of us, thinking they might not check your cabin. Since we haven't seen her, and she hasn't been brought here, I'd say there's a good chance she's still free."

Lawrence hoped their suspicions were correct, although he realized Kim might be in more danger wandering the ship with the

Iranians on hair-trigger alert than if she'd been taken prisoner with the rest of them. He looked around the table at Jack Nelson and the other officers. "Every one of us who can get free is a potential problem for them. The more delay and confusion we can orchestrate, the better our chances of getting back control of the ship."

"Well, whatever we do, we better act fast," Nelson said. "I heard the engines coming up to speed before they brought you in here, and we can't be more than three hours max from Bandar Abbas."

"I think we've got more than three hours to play with," Lawrence said cryptically.

Nelson, who was also the ship's navigator, was nonplussed. "How do you figure? When I came off watch we were less than fifty miles from Iranian territorial waters."

In silent answer Lawrence pointed to the spot on the bulkhead beside the captain's chair where the ship's heading indicator was mounted. The repeater indicated the ship's current course was two-five-zero degrees.

"West," Lawrence said quietly. "They've got us pointed west —away from the coast of Iran."

Mosopu lashed out with the fire axe again, and again it ricocheted harmlessly off the lock. The high-security lock on the armory door was maximum-strength steel, over two inches thick. The hasp was only one inch thick, but his early blows against it had proven it to be the toughest part of the lock. Now he was focusing instead on the body of the lock, more in hopes of shattering the internal mechanism than of severing it. He flexed his broad shoulders and brought his massive arms around in another blow; the impact jarred his bones but did little to the lock.

The big Bosun's Mate paused to regain his breath and to mop the rapidly accumulating sweat from his forehead. *Damn* they made these locks tough! He looked to his right at the watertight door he had dogged down that led aft to the coops. He hoped the heavy door would be enough to keep the sound of his blows from traveling back to the berthing areas. The strange machine gun was where he had left it, leaning against a bulkhead forward of the armory.

As his breathing returned to normal, Mosopu searched his mind for another way to get into the armory. There was only this one door in, he knew, and the keys to the lock were held only by the duty gunner's mate, who was trapped in one of the coops, and the Captain. The prospects of reaching either one of them seemed slim. For all his strength and determination, the axe was having little effect on the lock. He rejected the idea of firing the gun into the lock, realizing it would take a .50-cal to affect the extraordinarily strong device. What else was there back in the repair locker? Wooden shoring, oxygen breathing devices, fire hoses; none of them would help in this situation. Then it came to him like a revelation—the exothermic cutter!

Throwing aside the axe, he went forward to retrieve the gun. Yes, he thought, the exothermic cutter would do it. Each ship in the Gulf carried one of the powerful cutting tools. The superhot cutting device far surpassed the heat developed in a welder's arc and could slice through almost any steel on the ship. They had been placed on board ships specifically to cut through decks and bulkheads to free trapped men and gain access to fires. Mosopu's General Quarters station was repair locker five. He had been trained and assigned as a fire hose nozzleman, but he had also received basic instruction on the cutter, as had all the fire team. He hoped he could remember all the operating instructions. The device normally required two men to operate it, but he didn't have that luxury. Now if the engineers just hadn't moved it from the forward repair locker. The cutter was kept there because it was the locker closest to the berthing compartments. In the event a mine or missile hit trapped men in the coops, the cutter would be close at hand.

As he headed for the door leading aft, Mosopu's thoughts were totally focused on getting the exothermic cutter. He almost didn't register that the operating "dogs" on the watertight door were slowly turning as the handle was eased up. He froze in his tracks, temporarily hypnotized by the sight of the slowly opening dogs. Looking about, he realized the only path of escape was forward. He knew he was running out of room to keep retreating toward the bow, but he had no choice: he was cut off from the repair locker. Mosopu turned, scooping up the axe as he went, and vaulted forward past the armory. As he crossed the hatch coaming into the next passageway, he hit the bulkhead-mounted light switch, turning off the lights outside the armory.

He was well forward in the ship when the grenade went off in the dark armory passageway behind him.

The *Bulkeley* rode smoothly through the flat seas at a speed of twenty-five knots. The sight of a warship cruising at high speed was not an unusual one in the Gulf and would excite no untoward interest. Astern of the *Bulkeley* to the east, dawn was breaking over Iran. With the appearance of the sun, the cycle that would send the temperature to searing heights was renewed.

A trio of fishermen working their nets from an aged wooden dhow looked up briefly to watch the American warship pass close aboard their craft. They noticed the ship's high rate of speed but gave it little thought. It was well known to them that the Americans were crazy.

Had they examined the *Bulkeley* more closely and compared her to the others of her type they had seen, they would have noticed differences. There were no longer men acting as a mine watch in the eyes of the ship; the lookouts were gone from the deck above the bridge, as were the machine-gun crews and Stinger missile gunners usually stationed there. Though the ship moved gracefully through the waves, there was no sign of life topside. The *Bulkeley* could have been a ghost ship.

Andy landed hard on the nonskidded deck, his right shoulder absorbing most of the impact. He ignored the sharp shot of pain through his upper body and rolled under the fuselage of Sealord 26. Standing in the helo's open doorway, he had seen the flash of the gun before hearing the curious popping noise it made. He was surprised not to have been hit. The man had only been twenty-five feet distant, standing beside the aircraft's tail rotor and rudder assembly. He heard the strange gunfire cease as he rolled clear of the aircraft on the far side. Andy stayed on his belly, the twelve-gauge trained at the after portion of the helo. The sun was on the horizon outside, but the hangar was still quite dark: the only illumination coming from the open door at the forward bulkhead.

His head close to the deck, Andy listened carefully for any sound that would indicate his attacker was closing in on him and the others. The woman . . . Kim . . . was she hurt?, he wondered. He had not heard her cry out, which he hoped was a good sign. The hangar was deathly silent now.

So much for surrender! he thought. He and Kim would be killed before they could even get the words out of their mouths.

Still there was no sound. He waited, fighting the urge to get up from the deck and seek out his attacker. Then he heard them: footsteps—very quiet and far apart. The sound was not loud enough for him to target; he could only be sure that it came from the general direction of the rear of the helo. One man or two? There was no way to tell; the soft footfalls were spaced several seconds apart. He sensed rather than saw that the feet were moving slowly down the opposite side of the aircraft—toward the helo's open door. He tracked the path of the sound with the shotgun as best he could.

Without warning, the sputtering noise of the strange gun began again. He heard bullets rip through the skin of the aircraft in the passenger bay. In the dark hangar, the flash suppressor on the silenced gun was not completely effective: Andy caught a brief glimpse of the shooter's black combat boots in the flare from the firing gun. The Iranian was only a dozen feet away on the opposite side of Sealord. Andy reacted without having time to think about it: he fired the chambered round from the twelve-gauge directly at the boots. The man's screams were drowned out by the blast of the shotgun reverberating in the closed hangar. Andy was blinded, and his ears were stung by the awesome blast of the twelve-gauge in the confined space. Unable to see his target or anything else, he pumped another round into the chamber and fired again in the same direction.

The echoes faded slowly in the three-story-high hangar and were followed by an empty silence. Andy's hearing returned before his vision, and he strained to catch the sound of any movement from the other side of the helo. He squeezed shut his eyes to try to speed the return of his night vision as he continued to listen. There was nothing—no footsteps, no breathing, no sound at all. Andy chambered yet another round, the clack of the slide sounding deafening in the silence.

"Andy . . . ?" Kim's shaken voice was barely audible.

"Stay where you are!" he shouted. "Are you hurt?" His vision was slowly returning.

"No," she said, her voice sounding stronger. "That man with the gun . . . I think you killed him." Her voice trailed off at the end of the sentence.

The lack of any response to their shouted questions told him she was right. With great caution he slowly got to his feet. Now he was able to see as well as before he'd fired. Holding the shotgun in his right hand and feeling his way along the side of the helo with his left, he carefully made his way aft. When he rounded the rotor section and looked down the other side of the aircraft, he saw the body. The sunlight filtering through a joint in the hangar blast door cast a tiny shaft of light onto the fallen man's legs below the knee. The shotgun had been horrifyingly effective.

The riot gun still at the ready, Andy approached the Iranian. When he knelt cautiously beside the man, the light was good enough for Andy to confirm that he was dead. The body was twisted unnaturally, the black uniform shredded by the second blast of buckshot.

"Yeah . . . he's dead all right," Andy said in a voice barely above a whisper. He had never even seen a dead man before, let alone killed anyone himself. The fight on the flight deck had been impersonal, save for Steele's injuries. Not like this. He felt his gorge rise, the acid climbing into his throat. Doubling over, he retched twice, but no vomit came.

Andy stood up straight and shook himself, trying to banish the nausea. After taking several deep breaths he worked his way back to the helo's open door. There was a dim light from within the aircraft. He looked through the doorway and saw Kim, a guttering match in her hand, kneeling beside Steele.

"I'm sorry," she said, "your friend is dead too."

∎

Rafsani heard the shrapnel from the fragmentation grenade carom off the heavy watertight door. The explosion in the armory passageway had been impressive, even with the closed steel door to muffle it. He waited three seconds and then signaled the marine across from him to open the door again. He had a brief impression of smoke and cordite stench from the darkened passageway as the marine pulled the door open a scant four inches. It was enough. With greater force this time, to get the grenade farther forward, he tossed the second lethal orb. With smooth precision the other marine slammed the door and closed the dogging arm as soon as the Sergeant Major's hand was clear.

Even as the second grenade was detonating, Rafsani was pulling a third from his black combat vest. He had left his Sterling with the team that was working on securing the berthing compartments. He appreciated the advantages offered by the silenced weapons, but they were not accurate enough after the first shot to suit him. Additionally, the cramped spaces in the forward part of the ship were an invitation to lethal ricochets. He doubted if the one they were chasing could be brought down by one or two nine-millimeter rounds anyway.

Rafsani pressed himself back against the outboard bulkhead as much as his huge frame would allow. He held a grenade in one hand and an evil-looking dagger in the other. It had been a gift from a Gurkha noncom at the SBS School in Dorset. The man had said, only half in jest, that Rafsani should never unsheath it without drawing blood. Since that faraway moment, the *kukri* had tasted Iraqi blood in the Sergeant Major's hands many times. The marine tightly gripping the door across from Rafsani found nothing unusual in his Sergeant Major's choice of armament; he had seen Rafsani work close in before.

Rafsani was confident they had trapped if not killed their quarry. He and this marine along with two Guards, had methodically worked their way forward from the berthing compartments. The ladders outside the compartments were the last that led upward in this part of the ship, and with their forward progress the group had narrowed their search to this deck. When the port and starboard passageways had converged into one, he had sent the Guards back to augment the other sentries. He no longer needed numbers, he needed effectiveness.

They'd heard the hammering sound long before they reached the watertight door. Rafsani had run through the map of the ship in his mind and determined that it was the *Bulkeley*'s armory that was on the other side of the steel door. With that knowledge the hammering had made sense to him. His swift hand signals had silently directed the marine as to what they would do.

Now the Sergeant Major armed his third grenade and signaled the marine once again to pull open the door. This time Rafsani did not toss the grenade through the opening; instead, he waited, listening. There was no sound, not even the dying echoes of the last grenade. The smoke and the smell of gunpowder were much more powerful this time. He pulled a red-filtered penlight from his belt and slowly scanned the darkened deck. Satisfied that their prey had fled forward, Rafsani motioned the marine to open the door wide enough for him to pass through.

He stepped into the smoky space, turning to present only his side and shoulder and reduce the target he offered. The *kukri* was held straight out from his body, making his arm into a deadly spear. He held the grenade out of view. When he gained the armory door without incident, he signaled for the other marine to join him. The marine carefully secured the door behind him, to slow their quarry if he somehow got by them.

A quick examination of the high-security lock alleviated Rafsani's worst fear; the man had not succeeded in penetrating the armory. He would not have grenades or be otherwise better armed than before. Keeping five meters between them, the Sergeant Major led the other marine forward in the dark ship. His knowledge of the *Bulkeley* told Rafsani that the man they chased was almost at the end of the line. Forward of the armory there were only the anchor chain locker and a few adjoining storage spaces for the Bosun's Mates. He expected the man would make a stand as far forward in the ship as he could get. That would be fine— there was no escaping the screaming steel of Rafsani's grenades in these cramped shipboard rooms.

The next door they reached was marked as a bosun's locker and had a regular aluminum door rather than a heavy watertight one. Rafsani smiled coldly when he noticed the lock and hasp had been ripped clear with brute strength. Once again his hand signals conveyed his intent. By opening the previous door they had given their man a warning and time to escape; this time the Sergeant Major would opt to sacrifice some of his own safety in exchange for total surprise. Following his direction, the other marine backed up ten feet from the door and ducked around a corner: only his head and gun were visible. Rafsani lay back against the bulkhead on the left side of the door, clear of the marine's field of fire. With practiced skill, he laid his *kukri* in one of the bulkhead angle irons beside him and pulled and armed an additional grenade.

Rafsani nodded to the other marine, and the man opened up with the silenced Sterling, stitching a tight pattern into the lightweight door. The first rounds tore at the aluminum and sent fragments flying back at Rafsani; the second burst blew the door off its hinges and back into the space behind it. The marine held his fire as the door gave way and Rafsani stepped briefly into the opening. The Sergeant Major lobbed the two projectiles underhand into the dark space, sending one farther than the other. Even as he speedily pulled back from the opening, he expected to hear the sputter of his quarry's weapon.

There was little separation between the two explosions. The hot gases and blast, seeking an escape, flashed out the open doorway, stunning Rafsani and singeing his skin. He heard a supersonic shrapnel fragment hiss by within an inch of his head. Shaking off the blast, he crashed into the smoke-filled space, the knife once again in his hand. It was a small room, a large closet really, and through the smoke he slashed a deadly arc that would have struck down anyone still standing. His blade did not make contact. Rafsani went into a low crouch to try to get below the rising smoke. There was plenty of light, and no sign of the man he sought. Plenty of light? The rest of the ship had been dark or poorly illuminated—why was this space so bright? He rose and slashed with his *kukri* to speed the clearing of the smoke.

Looking up, Rafsani saw the scuttle. The warm colors of dawn were evident through the open hatch.

7

THE BULKELEY

"You spoke well on the radio," Aziz said, addressing Stewart. He watched the American for his reaction. "I would not have had your captain's death," the Major continued, glancing across the bridge at the bloodstained deck, "but now you can hold no misunderstanding of our seriousness."

Stewart stared back at Aziz in silence, his face maintaining the impassive look it had worn since Donelli's murder. Aziz met the uncompromising gaze for a few moments longer and then turned to head across the bridge. Halfway to the chart table he stopped and turned back to Stewart.

"In your words to the helicopter you mentioned the other aircraft on board. Why?"

Stewart let the Iranian's question hang in the air of the silent bridge for several seconds before answering. Despite the brutal heat outside the skin of the ship, the *Bulkeley*'s air-conditioning plant kept the bridge a comfortable seventy degrees, but the air-conditioning system could not purify the air enough to remove the stench of death.

"They would have expected us to launch the other helicopter if we could, to rescue them if they had to ditch," Stewart said tonelessly. "I was just telling them not to expect help from the other aircraft."

Aziz watched Stewart for a moment as if weighing the truth of his words. "If I direct you to speak on the radio again," he said quietly, "do not go beyond what I instruct you to say." The Major turned and continued across the bridge to join Kalil at the chart table.

Stewart remained beside the captain's chair and the bridge-to-bridge radio, studying Aziz. The Iranian had bought his story about Sealord 26, but just barely. Stewart hoped for another chance to send a signal that the ship was in trouble, and he prayed that Hammond would react to his obviously unnecessary statement. With Aziz watching him, he did not know how many chances he would get.

Stewart had always known command could devolve upon him if the Captain and executive officer were somehow incapacitated, but he never expected anything remotely like this. With Donelli dead and Lawrence's whereabouts and condition unknown, he was the de facto captain. There was no one senior to him to turn to for advice. Stewart hoped Lawrence was alive and in a position to do something to free the ship, but he knew that he now bore the responsibility for the lives of the two hundred sailors on *Bulkeley*. Stewart appreciated the lonely nature of Donelli's position as never before.

He flexed his shoulders and neck, as if to relieve muscle strain in his back, but his real intent was to try to exorcise his own fears and uncertainties. The Iranian leader, the Major, looked up from the chart table at Stewart's movement but quickly resumed his work. The other man, the one whom Stewart had come to think of as the Killer, paced the far side of the bridge restlessly, immersed in his own thoughts.

I'm responsible all right, Stewart thought. And I sure as hell better figure out what it is they're up to if I'm going to save the ship and crew. He had observed that the courses they were steering were taking them away from Iran rather than toward it. Why? Why would the Iranians possibly want to increase the amount of time they were exposed to detection? Aziz was obviously no Prince Henry the Navigator, but the rest of his operation had been too efficient for this to be a navigational error. Stewart was sure that if Hammond had relayed the story about the fire on *Bulkeley* to COM JTF, it would be taken at face value. But the first thing the Admiral would do would be to order other assets to the *Bulkeley*'s location to assist her. The Iranians could hardly benefit by hanging around until another ship arrived and then trying to keep the fire charade going. There was something else to this.

"Colt Sabre, this is Deadline, over." The distinct English words cut through the background chatter on the bridge-to-bridge speaker. Everyone on the bridge turned to look at Stewart. Aziz was beside him in three quick steps.

"Colt Sabre, Colt Sabre, this is Deadline. Deadline, over."

"What is this 'Deadline'?" Aziz asked.

Stewart was not certain if he detected real concern in the Major's voice, but he observed that Aziz scooped up a pair of binoculars and started to scan the horizon. He thinks it's a ship, Stewart realized. "One of our units—an American unit," he replied.

"What kind of 'unit'?" Aziz's tone made it clear he would have little tolerance for word games. The Major continued to check nearby shipping with the binoculars.

"I don't know what kind of unit," Stewart lied. "The code names change. I've never heard of Deadline." Stewart had immediately recognized Deadline as the call sign for the AWACS surveillance aircraft assigned to the southern Gulf. He was gambling that Aziz would not know where to look in the CIC for that information.

"Colt Sabre, Colt Sabre, this is Deadline, over."

"Answer him," Aziz directed. The Iranian had apparently decided that preventing their caller from becoming suspicious was more important than knowing his identity.

Stewart picked up the VHF handset and acknowledged the call. The response was almost immediate, the signal very strong.

"Colt Sabre, this is Deadline. I relay from Blackjack. Interrogative status of your fire? Break; request extent of damage, number of casualties, and impact on your mobility. How copy? Over."

"This is Colt Sabre. Solid copy; wait, out." Stewart noted that they had not asked for the fire's impact on *Bulkeley*'s combat readiness. Knowing everyone in the Gulf could be listening in on this conversation, COM JTF had foregone its desire to know their complete status in order to avoid compromising the *Bulkeley*'s degree of vulnerability.

"Well?" he asked Aziz combatively. "What would you like me to tell them?"

The Major lowered his binoculars, having apparently satisfied himself that there were no U.S. warships in the immediate vicinity. Stewart was surprised when Aziz responded without skipping a beat, as if he had known these questions would be asked all along.

"Tell them that the fire is out, but that you have sustained extensive damage to your Radio Central, helicopter hangars, and control stations." He paused, looking briefly at the dried blood on the deck at their feet. "Tell them that you have no serious personnel casualties and do not require outside medical aid."

"And engineering? What do I say about the fire's effect on our mobility?" Stewart asked. He was surprised at how glib Aziz had been with his responses.

The Major's eyes remained on the horizon. "Tell them that your engineering plant is undamaged and that you are able to make full speed."

Stewart puzzled over the reasoning behind these responses as he recontacted Deadline and relayed what Aziz had said.

"Copy all, Colt Sabre," the AWACS responded at the end of Stewart's transmission. "I relay from Blackjack; what are your intentions? Over."

Again Stewart looked to Aziz. This is it, he thought. The bastard has got to give them some kind of story to cover his true plans for the ship. Stewart did not like the thin, cold smile on the Major's lips.

"Tell them you are under way at twenty-five knots," Aziz said, "and bound for Bahrain, where you will effect repairs to the damage from the fire."

Stewart could not have been more surprised if Aziz had said they were under way for Tahiti.

"And tell them . . . tell them you request permission to come alongside the *Pascagoula* when you arrive. To make use of her repair shops to assist in your work."

Andy and Kim moved slowly forward down the midships passageway that ran between the two helicopter hangars. Although the sun was rising in the sky outside, the passageway was still dark, lit only by the red lamps in the overhead. The crewmen who would have turned the lamps to their daytime white configuration were prisoners in the berthing compartments.

Kim clutched the unfamiliar steel of the silenced gun as she followed Andy's cautious lead down the passageway. He had retrieved the weapon, along with extra magazines, from the man he killed in the hangar. Working with her to determine the mechanics of operating the strange gun had seemed to help him keep his mind off the loss of his friend. She did not like carrying the gun—her professional responsibility was to cover the events on the ship, not to act as a combatant.

After all the shooting—and Steele's death—they had both wanted to leave the hangar as quickly as possible. They had wanted to stay ahead of their pursuers, but also to leave the carnage behind them. Andy had suggested they move to one of the lower deck engineering spaces. He had told her he knew of a hiding place there that the Iranians would be extremely unlikely to find. Still shocked at the violence that had erupted around her, Kim had quickly agreed to go with him.

What they needed most, Kim thought as she trailed behind him, was time to think and a secure place in which to do it. The path he was following would, she knew, take them dangerously close to the occupied wardroom. They were headed for the midship's quarterdeck, from where a ladder descended down one deck and led to the auxiliary machinery space Andy had selected. As they continued forward, she could see over Andy's shoulder that the lights at the quarterdeck, twenty-five yards ahead of them, had been switched from red to white.

Without warning, Andy flashed his right arm out from his side, signaling her to halt. Wordlessly, he dropped to one knee on the steel deck. Kim was not sure what was happening, but she immediately followed suit. Initially she saw nothing as she concentrated on the illuminated quarterdeck ahead of them. Then there was a sound . . . heavy footfalls coming from the obscured starboard side of the quarterdeck. The sound drew closer, and she had a brief glimpse of a man crossing the quarterdeck from right to left. She could immediately tell he was one of the Iranians— their black uniforms were unmistakable—and she could see he was carrying some large object. The Iranian quickly passed from view, and the diminishing sound of his footsteps told her that the man was headed forward. When the sound had faded she moved to rise, assuming the danger had passed. With an urgent jerk of his arm, Andy signaled her to remain where she was.

He must know something I don't, Kim thought as she resumed the uncomfortable position in the darkness. To her it seemed their best bet was to get moving for the ladder now, before someone else came along. She imagined she could hear her heart beating in her chest as they waited in the darkness. A few seconds later she detected the sound of someone else approaching from the same direction; another Iranian crossed the quarterdeck, staying in their field of view longer than his predecessor had. This man was smaller than the first and was struggling with the load he carried. The man's progress was slow enough that she was able to make out the object he was straining to transport: the Iranian carried a large wooden crate, of roughly the size and dimensions of a foot-locker. From his obvious difficulty with the crate, Kim knew it must be quite heavy. The second man passed from view, and she heard him continue his wheezing progress forward in the ship.

She watched Andy for a sign of whether they were staying in place or moving on. He remained motionless for half a minute and then tilted his head sideways, as if straining to hear a distant sound. After another thirty seconds of silence he slowly rose from his crouch. "Let's go," he whispered over his shoulder. Kim stood up, her strained thigh and calf muscles stretching in pleasant relief, and followed Andy as he started off down the passageway.

She was surprised to see him walk right by the ladder trunk they had set out to reach and continue on to the quarterdeck. As she followed him, he cautiously rounded the right-hand corner of the quarterdeck and took up a position beside the open door leading to the outside deck. He signaled her over to stand beside him while he remained hidden from anyone out on the weather deck. With extreme caution, careful to reveal only one eye and a fraction of his face, Andy peered out the open doorway. And then he was gone, through the door with great speed, leaving Kim alone on the quarterdeck.

His sudden move surprised Kim and left her with no direction.

She waited a moment, listening for any sound of danger, and then followed him outside. As she stepped onto the outside deck, Kim was almost knocked over by the staggering combination of dazzling sun and blast furnace heat. She was momentarily blinded as her eyes tried to adjust to the dramatic change in light. In a moment she could see clearly, although soft rainbow coronas appeared around everything until her vision adapted completely. Glancing across the desk, she saw Andy standing at the ship's rail, looking down at something. As she went to join him, Kim noticed she was perspiring freely after less than thirty seconds in the incredible Gulf heat.

When she reached the lifelines, Kim saw what Andy was staring down at. Tied to the side of the *Bulkeley* were five black rubber rafts. They were clustered together with military precision and made fast to each other as well as to the ship. The boats were straining against the *Bulkeley*'s hull as the ship moved through the water at high speed. She noticed that four of the five boats were equipped with outboard motors, and the fifth boat was the only one containing cargo. In the bottom of that boat were two crates, similar to the ones the Iranians had been carrying forward. She looked at Andy, who continued to stare down at the rafts, deep in his own thoughts.

"We could take one of those," she suggested hopefully. "Maybe get away and go for help."

He spoke without looking up. "Yeah . . . but where are we anyway? Where do we *go* for help?" She could hear the sadness in his voice. "I'm afraid I don't know much navigation—knowing we're in the Gulf is about it. Besides," he said, his voice hardening, "they'd see the boat and come around and blast us before we could get clear."

Kim turned and looked back anxiously at the open quarterdeck door. "We better get moving, Andy. They're going to be coming back for those other crates any time now."

"You're right," he said. "And I sure hope what's in those crates is something real important to them."

Kim shifted her attention from the open doorway back to Andy. She saw that he had leaned his shotgun against the lifelines and was reaching behind his back with his right hand. With one fluid motion he drew and snapped open the buck knife that had been holstered at the small of his back.

"Yeah, I hope those crates and these boats are real important to them."

With speed and certainty, he methodically sliced through each of the grapnel ropes that made the Zodiacs fast to the *Bulkeley*. Even before the razor-sharp knife severed the last of the lines, the rubber boats were pulling away from the ship's hull. As Kim and Andy watched, the closely packed group of rafts slipped aft and were left in the *Bulkeley*'s twenty-five-knot wake.

Lawrence carefully eyed the Iranian marine nearest him before continuing to speak. The two marines assigned to watch over the *Bulkeley*'s officers had taken up position beside the wardroom's two doors. They kept their backs pressed against the bulkheads behind them and their weapons leveled at the assembled officers. Satisfied that the closest marine was ignoring their conversation, Lawrence resumed talking. He kept his voice low enough that the others at the table had to strain to hear him.

"Okay, so they've got our ship, taken in the dead of night in a very professional operation." He looked slowly around the table as he continued to speak. "If we buy what they've said, we're under way for Iran as a prize of war. But clearly either their navigation is totally dicked-up or we're headed someplace else."

"There's also the question of Sealord," Nelson added, careful to keep his voice low. "She's long overdue. We should have been at flight quarters for her an hour ago. Do you think they shot the helo down?"

Lawrence's face darkened at this thought. "It's possible. Or Hammond may have gotten wise to what's happened here and gone for help. But we can't count on that."

Bosca, who had been silently following Lawrence's review of the situation, leaned across the table toward him and spoke. "From what you've said, these bastards have every reason to want to reach the safety of their own waters as quickly as possible." He paused as Lawrence nodded in agreement. "So if we rule out navigational incompetence, it would seem that their true intent is something altogether different." He watched Lawrence anxiously, searching for a sign that the naval officer might have a clue as to what that intent might be.

Lawrence remained silent, his eyes fixed on the blank bulkhead above and behind Bosca. The XO unconsciously dabbed with his handkerchief at the now dried wound at his forehead. After a long pause, Lawrence shifted his eyes to meet Bosca's.

"I'd love to know what their real plan is, but what's more important," he said, looking meaningfully toward Nelson, "is that what they're doing is giving us time to act. The key for us is to throw a wrench into the gears and make it as difficult as possible for them to continue with their plan."

Neil Perren had listened quietly at Bosca's side since Lawrence had been brought to the wardroom. "I don't see how getting more of us killed is going to improve the situation," he said now, speaking for the first time. "From what you've told us, all the attempted heroics so far have done nothing but get men killed." There was an element of fear as well as scorn in Perren's voice. "What does it matter what they're doing with the ship, as long as they release us eventually?" He looked directly at Lawrence, his voice rising as he continued. "In case you've forgotten, they have all the guns!"

Lawrence looked at Perren coldly. The man's outburst had drawn the attention of the two marines, the closest of whom now trained his weapon on the corner of the table where Lawrence, Bosca, and Perren were clustered. Lawrence placed his hands palms down on the table and smiled at the marine in an effort to convey that there was no problem. He continued to smile at the marine as he spoke, his words addressed to Perren. "If you compromise us again, Mr. Perren," he said, his tone reflecting the warmth of his smile, and both intended for the marine's benefit, "you'll have more to worry about than the Iranians."

Satisfied that whatever had prompted the rancor among the Americans had subsided, the marine relaxed his stance and returned to his watchful scanning of the entire wardroom. Lawrence swung his gaze from the obviously shaken Perren back to Bosca and Nelson.

"The first thing we need," he said, lowering his voice once more, "is a way out of here."

■

The smooth hum of the *Bulkeley*'s twin gas turbine engines integrated seamlessly with the other sounds of the four-thousand-ton ship as it sped through the Gulf. On the bridge, the sound had the quality of white noise as it rose and fell with the slight port-and-starboard roll the speed brought to the frigate.

Stewart stood behind the ship's control console, splitting his attention between the sand-swept waters ahead of the ship and the actions of the Iranians on the bridge. At this high speed he knew the *Bulkeley* would have almost no time to react if another ship appeared out of the storm ahead of them. He looked across the bridge at Aziz, who had assumed a position beside the captain's chair and the bridge-to-bridge radio. The Major was studying a chart he had brought from the table at the rear of the bridge. Looking to his left, Stewart saw Kalil standing by the port bridge-wing door. The big Iranian was staring aimlessly out to sea. Neither one of them was paying close attention to him or the bridge watch team. But a quick look over his shoulder reminded him why they could be so unconcerned: an Iranian marine stood watch at the rear of the bridge.

As Stewart eyed the sentry, the quiet of the bridge was suddenly shattered by the noisy arrival of another Iranian, who clambered frantically up the ladder trunk and darted onto the bridge. The man searched the bridge, a look of fear in his eyes, until he located Aziz. Screaming urgently in Farsi, he raced to the Major's side. Stewart saw the look of professional calm vanish from Aziz's face as the man continued to speak. Aziz listened for a moment longer and then shoved the man aside and turned to Stewart.

"Turn the ship around!" Aziz yelled, concern evident in his voice. "Bring the ship around at once!"

Scott Septenano turned to Stewart, a questioning look on his face. Stewart studied Aziz in silence, making no move to comply.

"Turn this ship now!" Aziz commanded urgently.

"Right full rudder," Stewart ordered Septenano, his eyes on Aziz all the while. Septenano hesitated briefly, not believing Stewart could want such a turn, until a look from the older officer told him he was serious.

"Right full rudder!" Septenano ordered the helmsman.

Slowly at first, but then with unexpected speed, the *Bulkeley* heeled to starboard in answer to the helmsman's turn of the wheel. The deck of the bridge canted steeply to the right as the high-speed turn took effect. Loose gear on the bridge went flying to the deck as the angle became steeper. With a shout of confusion, the Iranian sentry lost his footing and went crashing into the recently arrived marine, sending both of them sprawling to the deck. Wedged between the captain's chair and ship's control console, the Major struggled to keep from losing his balance as the ship continued its roll.

Stewart and the other *Bulkeley* sailors had braced themselves against the control console, knowing what the turn would bring. Stewart looked across the bridge at Kalil, who was desperately holding on to the operating arm of the port watertight door, a look of confused terror on his face. Stewart turned back to Aziz just as the Major lost control of his Sterling as he fought to keep his balance. The weapon clattered to the deck. Sensing his chance, Stewart released his grip on the console and lunged for Aziz.

The subdued hum of the ship's engines shifted to a low, straining roar as the wardroom heeled violently to starboard. There was shouting from the Iranians struggling to remain upright as the *Bulkeley* took on first a twenty- and then a thirty-degree list to the right. Lawrence and the other officers instinctively grabbed the rims of the wardroom tables to keep themselves from sliding to starboard or being thrown from their chairs. The coffee cups and ashtrays that had been on the tables raced down the Formica surfaces like supercharged hockey pucks, crashing into the unlucky occupants of the seats at the heads of the tables. With a yell of surprise, one of the marines lost his footing and careened across the steeply canted wardroom to collide noisily with the starboard bulkhead.

Looking up from his white-knuckled grip on the table in front of him, Lawrence saw that the marine nearest him had wedged himself against the low wardroom couch. Although braced in an awkward position, the marine maintained his coverage of the officers with his silenced machine gun.

■

Stewart was almost on top of Aziz when he felt steel slam into his stomach. The force of the pistol barrel thrust against his abdomen halted him in his tracks a foot short of the Major. Stewart had seen the recognition in Aziz's eyes when he had lunged toward him; he had not seen the other gun until it was too late.

"Do you wish to die?" Aziz said, pressing the pistol barrel harder into Stewart's stomach. With his free hand he steadied himself against the captain's chair beside him. Stewart took a step back from the pistol before answering.

"That's as fast as she'll turn, Major." Stewart's voice carried a mocking note of professional scorn. Aziz returned Stewart's gaze, hoping he appeared to still be totally in control. But the look on the American's face indicated the man now realized the marines were not completely at home with the dangers and capabilities of his ship.

Slowly, the angle of the ship started to ease as the frigate came out of the turn. The Major longed to commence his search for the missing boats, but he could not divert his attention from the Americans as long as his own men were incapacitated.

"Steady zero-eight-zero," the helmsman called out, as the ship completed the tight starboard turn.

"Hosayn! Nizarem! Get to your feet, quickly!" Aziz yelled to the two marines who had lost their footing. Beyond the console he could see Kalil shakily making his way across the bridge. The Guards Commander's expression conveyed his concern over what wild maneuvers the ship might next make.

"I am beside you, Major." Hosayn appeared at Aziz's elbow, his tone making it obvious he hoped to make up for the disgrace of losing the Zodiacs. Aziz first verified that the marine had the Americans covered with his weapon. Then he brushed by Hosayn, heading for the bridgewing door. He scooped up a pair of binoculars from the chart table before wrenching open the water-tight door and hurrying outside.

The Major ignored the intense early morning heat as he rushed to the forward rail and brought the binoculars to his eyes. The powerful glasses were not so forgiving of the forty-degree shift in temperature from the bridge to the deck outside, and it took a full minute before Aziz could defog them enough to present a usable image. His concern only rose when he discovered the caprice of the sandstorm limited his visibility to roughly two miles. Aziz forced himself to remain calm as he conducted a deliberate scan of the waters ahead of the ship. At twenty-five knots they were covering the visible area too quickly, so he yelled for Stewart to slow the ship to ten knots. The reduced speed would allow him to search more carefully.

"You should kill that one at once!" came Kalil's harsh voice from behind him.

Aziz's concentration was briefly snapped by the knowledge that the Guards Commander had once again come up on him without a sound. He ignored Kalil's demand and refocused his attention on his search.

"Any sign of the boats?" Kalil asked, a note of concern replacing his usual combativeness.

"This cursed sand," Aziz said, frustration evident in his voice. "The boats could be right out there"—he gestured to the dense curtain of grit that was so close to the ship—"and we would never see them."

Kalil joined him at the rail. "From what that idiot Hosayn said, it cannot be more than fifteen minutes since the boats disappeared," he offered. "How far could they go in so short a time?"

Aziz continued his methodical search of the sand-blown waters around the frigate. He spoke without lowering his binoculars. "Under motor power, the Zodiacs could be so far away by now that we would never find them in this storm. But they are not under motor power. I directed Rafsani to temporarily disable all the electric motors once we came aboard."

"Why was I not told this?" A low angry note was clear in Kalil's tone.

"Just a minor military detail, Colonel. A trifle you did not need to be burdened with." Aziz lowered his glasses. "No. I would never even have turned the ship if I thought the boats were under motor power. Now I fear we will not be able to find them at all because of this damnable visibility." He scanned the horizon with his unassisted eye, a look of resignation on his face. "We will search for half an hour. We can spare no more time than that."

"And what of whoever did this?" Kalil asked impatiently. "The boats did not just float away of their own accord!"

"It is up to the Sergeant Major and his search teams to find those responsible. We have no additional men to spare in chasing them down. Rafsani will find and stop them." Aziz brought the binoculars back up to his eyes and continued his search.

"You forget the importance of the lost cargo—and of the Zodiacs themselves," Kalil sneered. "How will we complete our mission if they are lost to us?"

Aziz did not respond immediately. He was determined not to let Kalil know how concerned he actually was. When he did answer, he tried to do so with an air of professional nonchalance.

"Hosayn reported that he had unloaded all but two of the crates. The ones that we have aboard are more than sufficient to accomplish our mission."

"But the boats! What if we cannot find the boats?"

The Major smiled thinly without lowering the binoculars. "Then, as in all things, God will provide."

THE PASCAGOULA

It was near the breakfast hour on board the *Pascagoula*, but it was obvious that the men at the table in the flag mess had more pressing concerns with which to deal. The flag mess was part of a small suite of rooms reserved for the personal use of Rear Admiral Boone. The large rectangular table at the center of the mess had been used for almost as many meetings as it had meals. The Admiral's daily briefings took place in the Tactical Decision Center with the entire staff present. The flag mess was reserved for meetings of a particularly sensitive or potentially explosive nature.

A mess attendant hovered close at hand to see to the needs of the officers at the table. He was kept well occupied, as the men drank cup after cup of coffee following what had been a long night for many of them.

Garmisch sat in silence, as he had since entering the mess ten minutes earlier. There had been only perfunctory conversation since his arrival. The assembled officers were waiting for the Admiral.

Directly across from Garmisch, Captain Lacey was stirring his coffee somewhat absentmindedly. Jim marveled again at the flawless appearance of the man after an almost sleepless night. Next to Lacey and closest to the Admiral's chair at the head of the table sat Captain Vargas, the commanding officer of the *Pascagoula*. Vargas was a spare, balding man with the look of an academic. The image was reinforced by the Navy-issue "Clark Kent" glasses he wore, but it was somewhat confounded by the oil-stained coveralls that he had not had time to change. Vargas had explained to Lacey when he arrived that he had been taking advantage of the early hour and the "cold iron" status of his plant to conduct an inspection of his main engineering spaces. Garmisch, career engineer that he was, had been unable to repress a smile at Vargas's explanation.

Two chairs removed from Garmisch was Commander Kelly, the staff's head "spook." The youthful Kelly appeared far too young to be a full commander, but Garmisch knew the quality of his intelligence work assuaged any concerns Kelly's appearance raised among the more senior officers on the staff. Although Kelly was not on the staff watch bill, it was well known that he put in hours the equal of any staff watch officer. In front of Kelly on the table was his ever present "bubble"; the thick three-ring binder in which he kept all the current intelligence estimates for the Gulf, as well as countless other pertinent messages. Garmisch saw that Kelly was deeply engrossed in whatever he was reading in the bubble. Several times in the span of a few minutes he observed Kelly unconsciously running his hand through the overlong blond hair that was his trademark.

Garmisch was about to motion for another cup of the flag mess coffee, which he did not hold in high esteem but which at least had caffeine in it, when Boone entered the mess. The four officers around the table rose to their feet as the Admiral crossed to his chair. Boone's damp, jet black hair revealed he had just come from the shower.

"Seats, gentlemen, please."

Garmisch studied Boone carefully as he took his seat, searching for an indication of what lay ahead in the meeting. The Admiral looked refreshed, which was a good sign, but beyond that Jim could read nothing.

"I was on the horn to CENTCOM up until a few minutes ago," the Admiral began. "They're about as pleased with this as we are. But they do concur with all the actions we're taking."

"Are they going to fill in the White House, Admiral?" Lacey asked.

Boone gave the Chief of Staff a cold smile. "General Brighton is going to let them know at a low level, more because of likely press interest than anything else. I told him that the Gulf Common conversations pretty much guaranteed that one of the press stringers in the Gulf would pick up on the story." The Admiral paused, looking around the table. "I imagine that the President would prefer to find out one of his ships has had a damaging fire from JCS and CENTCOM rather than from the networks."

"We've already had a query from the AP guy in Bahrain," Lacey said.

"Okay, I've got public affairs people to deal with that side of things." Boone folded his hands together on the table and leaned forward, indicating he wanted to get to the heart of the business at hand. He looked directly at the Chief of Staff. "Where are we at now with the *Bulkeley?*"

"Jim just came in from talking to Deadline," Lacey said as he turned to Garmisch. "What's the latest?"

"Deadline has been out of contact with the ship for over an hour—in fact, since the first conversation on Gulf Common, when we got their status. Our weather guessers say the atmospherics make it likely that Deadline will only have the *Bulkeley* on radio intermittently. The AWACS has to stay above the sandstorm, and the dust is acting like a radio blanket." Garmisch paused, shifting his gaze from Lacey to the Admiral. "Fortunately, Deadline has been able to maintain continuous radar contact on *Bulkeley*. One curious thing, Admiral. Just as I was leaving the TDC, Deadline reported observing *Bulkeley* in a turn back to the east."

"What do you make of that?" Boone asked.

"Hard to say, sir. Maybe they've had a reflash and this has something to do with fighting the fire. Or it could be a steering problem or a man overboard. At least they're still making way."

"How far out are they now?" Captain Vargas interjected.

"About two hundred miles, Captain," Garmisch replied. "At twenty-five knots, assuming they head back to the west, they could be here before dark. Figuring they slow when they enter the channel, they'll make the harbor in ten hours or so."

"What about pulling the hook and heading out to meet them?" Boone directed his question to the *Pascagoula*'s captain.

"I recommend against it, sir," Vargas responded. "We're in a good secure anchorage here in Sitrah. Even assuming we can find a usable anchorage out in the Gulf proper, it would put us in a much more vulnerable position relative to the Iranians and Iraqis."

"I concur, Admiral," Kelly said, speaking for the first time. "Exposing *Pascagoula* at anchor out in the Gulf would give the Iranians a very tempting target. Their previous patterns of operation aside, they seem to be spoiling for a fight right now."

"Which I will be only too happy to give to them," the Admiral said, sitting back in his chair. "But it's going to be on our terms, at a time of our choosing. I agree with you, gentlemen. The *Pascagoula* will remain here and wait for the *Bulkeley*, barring a further deterioration in the situation." He fixed his gaze on Kelly. "What's changed in the threat in the last few hours, Bill? Give it to me with the assumption that *Bulkeley* can't defend herself."

Kelly rapidly turned messages in the bubble until he found the traffic he sought. "Very little change, Admiral. The last hot work was that RevGuard attack in the tanker lanes around zero three hundred. *Abaland* remains on patrol in the eastern Gulf."

"Deadline has maintained continuous contact on the *Abaland*," Garmisch interjected. "They say it's business as usual for her. She's made no move to close with or follow the *Bulkeley*."

"That's the only significant combatant the Iranians have currently deployed," Kelly continued. "Based on the position the AWACS is reporting for her, *Bulkeley* is right on the edge of the max range of the Abu Musa–based RevGuard gunboats."

"What about the air threat?" Lacey asked.

"No unusual activity. There's an F-4 CAP up over Bandar Abbas at the moment, but not much else. We had an Iraqi Badger raid on Kharg Island at zero five hundred, but nothing after that,"

Kelly said. "Things are actually pretty quiet, all in all. I'd say that other than the mines, the only possible threat to her would be some type of go-for-broke air strike out of Bandar. That's assuming the Iranians picked up the Gulf Common transmissions and made a fast decision to go after her."

"*Daniels* is coming into the Gulf behind *Bulkeley* too, Admiral," Lacey added. "In a couple of hours any air strike will have to fly through the *Daniels*'s missile envelope to get to *Bulkeley*."

"But if *Bulkeley* comes about and resumes course for Bahrain, *Daniels* will never overtake her, Captain," Garmisch addressed the Chief of Staff. "I've done the math, and at thirty knots *Daniels* will never catch *Bulkeley*, a hundred miles ahead of her and doing twenty-five." Garmisch could see Lacey was not pleased with this news. The Chief of Staff, who had made the decision to send the other ship after the *Bulkeley*, was about to respond to Garmisch when the Admiral spoke.

"That's not a problem, gentlemen. Right now *Bulkeley*'s headed more in the *Daniels*'s direction than in our own. We'll keep *Daniels* coming as our thirty-knot insurance policy. If *Bulkeley* is having more trouble, then *Daniels* will be there in a few hours to assist." The Admiral rose, signaling that the meeting was at an end.

"We'll meet again in two hours," Boone said. "I'll be splitting my time between the TDC and here." He looked at Vargas. "Have your repair shops cranked up and ready, Ed. We don't know how bad the damage to *Bulkeley* will be."

"My boys will be ready, Admiral," Vargas responded confidently.

Admiral Boone stopped as he was turning to go as if struck by a remembered thought. "Any more word from the crash site, Jim?" he asked Garmisch.

Garmisch stiffened. The news had not been good. "Nothing new to report, sir. The Omani Navy helo is on the scene. They've found some floating wreckage, but no sign of the crew. There's an Omani patrol boat on the way to help in the search." He paused and then added hopefully, "The water's so warm in the Gulf that their survival time is almost unlimited."

Boone gave Garmisch a wistful smile that reflected his years of combat experience. "I've been shot down twice—and almost lost it both times," the Admiral said quietly. "Surviving is a matter of the man, not the water temperature."

THE <u>BULKELEY</u>

Mosopu stopped just short of the quarterdeck to try to catch his breath. Running for his life in the one-hundred-ten–degree heat and direct sunlight was taking a lot out of him. The pain in his left leg had not abated—if anything, it was getting worse. Bent over double, his hands on his knees, he looked back the way he had come to ensure there was no immediate pursuit. He could see all the way forward down the starboard weather deck to the enclosed break. There was no sign of his pursuers. Surprise jolted him upright as he saw that he was leaving a trail of blood down the nonskidded deck.

He had barely gotten up and out of the forward bosun's locker in time. The first grenade had gone off just as he was pulling his legs clear of the scuttle, and he had felt the white-hot pain of several fragments tearing into his left calf. Thankfully, he had been clear of the open scuttle when the second grenade had detonated. Ignoring the pain in his leg, Mosopu had rushed to the starboard break to get clear of the open fo'c'sle. If anyone on the bridge had seen him, they had given no indication. He had reached the entrance to the break just as the ship had gone into a high-speed turn that nearly caused him to lose his footing. Mosopu had had no time to wonder what had happened on the bridge to prompt such a radical maneuver. Once inside the watertight break that separated the fo'c'sle from the weather deck aft, he had sealed the heavy watertight door behind him. He had pulled a four-foot length of fire-hose applicator pipe from the bulkhead inside the break and forced it into the operating guts of the watertight door, jamming the door in place.

The blood trail was going to be a real problem. He looked down at his wounded leg and saw that the shrapnel had shredded his dungarees where it had struck him. Got to stop the bleeding or I'll lead 'em right to me, he thought.

He glanced around the open deck for something to bind his

wound. He was just forward of the quarterdeck, and his eyes quickly locked on to the many severed lines dangling from the life rail stanchions. Mosopu grunted to himself with displeasure, his current situation momentarily forgotten, as he thought of how unseamanlike it was for the bosun's mates who owned the quarterdeck area to leave those small lines adrift. The idea of stemming the flow of blood with raw line held little appeal for him, and he continued to look about for some other alternative.

Looking aft of the quarterdeck doors, his gaze crossed the sealed watertight door of the paint locker.

Rags.

The paint locker was supposed to be clear of that combustible essential to shipboard painting, but Mosopu's knowledge of the bosun responsible for the paint locker told him there would be rags in there. He crossed the deck quickly to the locker door, trying as he went to keep from spattering the deck with his blood. Reaching to his belt, he pulled a massive ring of keys from beside his holstered marlinspike. He rapidly located the proper key and unlocked the steel door.

As always, the stench of the multitude of paints was staggering when the locker was first opened. He flicked on the overhead light and stepped inside, gingerly lifting his injured leg over the hatch coaming. He left the door wide open, as a locker filled with highly flammable paint and fumes was the last place in which he would want to be cornered. The locker was strictly utilitarian, with shelf upon shelf of old and new cans of paint of all colors crowding the bulkheads. There was barely enough room in the cramped locker for a man the size of Mosopu to turn around.

His eyes darted over the shelves and bulkheads, searching for rags. Nothing on the shelves. He found what he needed at the base of one of the racks—BM3 Crocker had not disappointed him. Mosopu picked up the wad of rags from the foot of the rack and quickly sorted through them. He discarded small or heavily paint-soaked rags until he found a dishtowel-size piece of cloth that was relatively clean. The Samoan pulled the leg of his dungarees up until the undamaged cuff covered his wound. As he wrapped the rag around his calf, Mosopu concentrated on his next move.

Getting back to repair locker two and the exothermic cutter was going to be tough. The Iranians had chased him all the way forward, and they were now undoubtedly in control of the armory area, and of the repair locker around the corner from it as well. He knew they had a number of men stationed around the coops, and trying to fight his way in there would probably be suicidal. Mosopu hissed through his teeth at the pain as he tightened the rag over the denim cuff of his dungarees in order to bind his wound. Don't cut off circulation, he told himself, just stop the flow of blood. In a moment he was satisfied with his makeshift battle dressing and ready to move on. But to where?

He considered and then discarded the idea of trying to free the chiefs or the officers. He had no way of knowing for sure where they were being held or how many guards there would be. Looking out the open locker door, he could see the water of the Gulf racing by. He'd felt the ship accelerate shortly after the Iranian officer had come on the public address system. They were obviously in a big hurry to get to Iran before their raid was discovered—which also meant, he realized, that the Iranians were trying to conceal what had happened as long as possible. Then it struck him that there was more than one way to fight the bastards who had taken his ship.

Mosopu cautiously peered out the door, looking both forward and aft for signs of the enemy. Seeing that there was no immediate threat, he turned back to the densely packed shelves and started urgently searching through the stacked cans of paint.

8

THE BULKELEY

Kim longed to get up from her cramped position and be able to stretch and move around. She was wedged in, sitting almost across from Andy in the relatively dry bilges. Directly above them on a heavy steel foundation were numerous compressors, pumps, and other types of auxiliary equipment. Even in her hunched sitting position, the foundation over her head was so low that she had to bend her neck uncomfortably. The equipment above them hummed along, oblivious to their presence and to the hostile forces that had seized the ship.

Andy had assured her that they could not be found here by anyone but a *Bulkeley* engineer who knew exactly where to look. He had told her that someone could be standing literally on top of them and never realize they were there. She believed him, although the secure nature of their hiding place did not make it any less painful. I suppose I should be thankful the bilges are as dry as they are, she thought. Although there were a number of small pools of oily residue in the steel basin, she had been able to crawl to a relatively dry spot between the puddles. Andy had taken up position across from her and directly beside the only true access to the bilges. He had said that the space was not ordinarily manned, but that a roving monitor would make several checks of equipment and take readings here each hour. There had been no sign of the systems monitor in the hour they had been in the space, and Andy had said with glum certainty that the man was undoubtedly in the hands of the Iranians.

She knew they had only been in the engineering space for a little over an hour, but the deafening noise and constant vibration had made it seem much longer. When she thought back to the events of the past few hours, Kim was struck by how readily she had made the transition from objective observer to active participant. She knew she was in on the biggest story of her career, but every time she tried to compose her thoughts, her mind shifted from recording what had happened to trying to find a way out of their predicament. Kim told herself she was being unprofessional —reporters were supposed to report events, not shape them— but her instinct now was to act rather than observe.

Forcing the dilemma from her mind, she looked across at Andy and saw that he was submerged in his own thoughts. He looked so young, she thought, his face so unmarked by experience or pain. She could sense the awesome responsibility he felt, not only to help his shipmates, but to protect her. Despite her assurances and the obvious evidence that she could take care of herself, it was apparent that he felt he must keep her safe. She smiled at the thought of his youthful gallantry in so awful a situation.

Kim knew that Andy felt that responsibility for their safety and for figuring out what they should do next was on his shoulders. But she was concentrating equally hard on their situation. Periodic thoughts of Stewart and what had become of him disrupted her attempts to think a useful plan through. It seemed unreal to her that she and Stewart had been brought back together under these most horrible of circumstances. She was brought out of her reverie when Andy spoke.

"If we're gonna do something, we're gonna have to do it pretty soon. I don't know how far we were from Iran when this whole thing started, but at the speed we're goin', we can't be too far away by now."

"I agree," Kim said. "But what have you got in mind? We both know there's no way you can shoot it out with these people." She almost had to shout to be heard over the sound of the machinery overhead.

Andy's dour countenance remained unchanged. She could see

the effort he was putting into trying to force an idea to come to him.

"Even if we could free some of the crew and get some more guns, it would just be a bigger version of what we're doing now," he said. "Heck, we could still be fightin' these guys when they pull alongside the pier in Iran!"

"What if the ship doesn't get to Iran?" she asked. An idea was taking shape in Kim's mind.

"How do you mean? You mean we grab the ship back and turn it around?"

"No . . . I mean suppose it never reaches Iran at all." Kim paused, observing the interest and the spark of enthusiasm in his eyes. She leaned forward toward Andy. "You're an engineer; can you break this stuff as well as fix it?" She gestured to the foundation supporting the machinery over their heads.

Looking back at him, Kim saw Andy's nascent enthusiasm appear to cool. "I'm not that kind of engineer," he said. "At least, not yet." He saw her quizzical look and continued. "I'm a damage controlman. I know fire fighting, structural work, that sort of thing; not running machinery. Sure, I know enough to secure some of this auxiliary stuff, but the main engines are a lot tougher to disable—and the steering gear room is kept locked."

Kim refused to give up.

"Okay, but let's assume you wanted to stop the ship—and break things, so no one could get it moving again, at least for a while. Isn't there some way you could do that?"

Andy thought hard for a moment, running over all the possibilities. "Main Control," he said. "Whoever owns that space controls the ship. You can start and stop almost anything from there, including the main engines."

"So why don't we go after this Main Control then?" she asked hopefully.

"That's one place the bad guys are sure to be," Andy said quietly. "And even if we took it from 'em, you can be sure they'd show up with every guy they've got to take it back."

Kim leaned even closer to him, so that their faces were less than a foot apart. "We don't have to stay there," she said with a surge of excitement. "What if we shut the engines down and then destroy the equipment in Main Control that lets you start them back up?" She moved back from him and resumed her position against the side of the bilge.

Andy's eyes looked through Kim rather than at her as he considered the idea. "We could do a lot of damage to the propulsion control console," he said almost to himself. She saw him absent-mindedly slide his hand to the pump on his shotgun. He addressed her directly. "If we could fight our way in there, I think we could disable the ship."

"Let's do it then."

"I should do it alone," he said. "You're a civilian—and a woman. It's not right for you to have to risk your life again." He shrugged. "Besides, it's my ship, and you've done enough for us already."

She leaned toward him, her face once again close to his.

"They've got my friends too, Andy," she said forcefully. "And I don't think the Iranians are likely to go any easier on me just because I'm a woman."

He was forced to smile at that. She certainly was unlike any of the girls—women—he had known before.

"Well, I guess keeping you from going would be a lot tougher than taking you with me." He bent low, and scooped his index finger through a pool of oily liquid. On the deck between them he drew an irregular-shaped box using his finger as a marker.

"This is roughly the layout of Main Control," he began.

"That is the end of it," Aziz said resignedly. "We can spare no more time to search." He let the binoculars fall to his chest, but still he continued to scan the sand-shrouded water as if hoping for one last chance. The visibility had grown worse rather than better as they had backtracked along the ship's wake. It was ironic, the Major thought, that the same qualities that had made the Zodiacs so useful in their assault on the ship now conspired to make them unfindable. Even if the boats presented a radar reflection, they would merely be one of a hundred small craft appearing on radar within ten miles of the *Bulkeley*. No, finding them would be difficult under optimum conditions, and they had exhausted all the time available to search.

As he reentered the bridge, Aziz saw that Kalil remained where he had been for the last thirty minutes. The Guards Commander stood directly behind the ship's control console, glowering at the executive officer, who seemed to ignore him. Apparently Kalil felt himself too important a figure to be involved in anything as tedious as a visual search.

"Turn the ship around, Commander," Aziz directed Stewart as he crossed the bridge to join Kalil. "And bring our speed back up to twenty-five knots."

Stewart complied in the surly fashion Aziz had come to expect. He had not expected the Americans to obey willingly; all that mattered was that they obey.

"So," Kalil began in a combative tone, "the search is a failure— one of a growing number of problems with your operation, Major."

Aziz noted that now that problems had arisen, it had become "his" operation, rather than a joint Marine–Revolutionary Guards triumph. He kept his face impassive as he responded.

"There will always be setbacks in an undertaking of this sort. Thus far our successes outnumber our failures."

Kalil was about to reply when a noise at their backs announced the ascent of someone on the ladder that led up to the bridge. Both men turned to look at the ladder well and were surprised to see the heavily bearded face of Sergeant Major Rafsani appear out of the trunk. As he quietly made his way up the stairs, it was apparent to the two men that Rafsani had seen further action. Both his beard and clothing were dusted with a fine gray powder that Aziz recognized as the result of the close-quarters use of grenades. His uniform had several small tears above the breastbone, but there was no blood in evidence. Rafsani's trademark knife was in his fist at his side, the evil-looking blade appearing to have been grafted onto his hand.

"I have an urgent report, Major," the big man rumbled as he gained the bridge. He crossed to join Aziz, ignoring Kalil.

"Go ahead, Sergeant Major," Aziz replied, adding, "Have you seen success, my friend?"

The beard-swathed face grew dark and the giant marine's muscles drew taut beneath his uniform. Then just as quickly, he relaxed his body with a noiseless sigh. The Major knew at once that Rafsani's hunt had been unsuccessful.

"Your forgiveness, Major; the man is still free in the ship. I thought I had him cornered with no chance of escape, but this one is clever, as well as strong."

Aziz nodded his understanding, but he was concerned that Rafsani had halted his pursuit to inform him of his lack of success.

"Our men continue the hunt," the Sergeant Major said, sensing the unasked question. "But I believed I must report to you, as other things have changed as well."

"How so?" Kalil asked. "Make your point, for we have little time to waste."

The Guards Commander could have been a shadow, for all the attention Rafsani paid him. Again, he addressed Aziz directly.

"At first, we had this man trapped in a limited area and the search was easy," Rafsani began. "Now he is abroad in the ship at large, a ship which he knows as we do not. He is wounded, and that will help, but our task is now far more complex." He paused, fixing his eyes on the Major's. "But I would not bother you with that alone. One of our men found me and reported that Sergeant Hoveyda has been killed." Rafsani stopped to let his words register.

"How?" Aziz asked tonelessly. "And where?" He did not appear shaken, but the Sergeant Major recognized the danger in his bloodless voice.

"Hoveyda was found shot to death in one of the helicopter hangars. There was another corpse there as well; one of the Americans, presumably one of the gunners we seek. Hoveyda's gun was gone. It is undoubtedly now in the hands of the Americans who killed him."

"Americans?" Kalil interjected. "Why do you speak in the plural? You said your man found one of the gunners dead!"

This time the Sergeant Major turned to answer Kalil directly. "The deck of this hangar is slick with hydraulic fluid from some repair that was under way. When my marine succeeded in turning on the overhead lights, he found one set of intermittent tracks in this fluid leading from Hoveyda's body to the helicopter—and then two sets of tracks leading to the door out of the hangar."

Aziz was silent. Kalil was slow to grasp the impact, but then he understood.

"So we have lost another man. . . . But the number of Americans on the loose remains the same? How long can this continue?" Kalil demanded.

Rafsani turned back to the Major, who appeared lost in thought.

"I can find and stop them all, Major. But it will take time, and I knew you must know this at once."

"You can find them all?" Kalil asked in an agitated, scornful voice. "At your rate of progress, half the American crew will be free—and all your marines will be dead!"

In a blinding reflex action, Rafsani brought his knife hand up in front of him, the blade leveled at Kalil's chest inches away. In that instant, everyone on the bridge but the Sergeant Major thought the Guards Commander was a dead man. Just as quickly, the *kukri* was back at Rafsani's side. The big marine silently watched Kalil with a look that revealed nothing.

"Stop this," Aziz said angrily, granite in his voice. "These roving Americans are extracting too high a cost." He turned and looked across the bridge at Stewart. "I will no longer fight a war of attrition with your men." With a curt gesture he summoned Stewart to join him at the 1MC control station. Aziz pulled the public address mike from its stand, his eyes remaining on Stewart all the while.

"American sailors." Aziz's voice was carried throughout the ship by the 1MC. "American sailors. We are in control of your ship. We hold your lives and those of your shipmates in our hands. Yet there are some of you who choose to resist us after all hope is gone." Aziz clicked off the mike and waited.

"Major, I can find them," Rafsani said, a note of concern creeping into his deep voice. "All I need is time. This is not necessary."

Aziz gave the Sergeant Major a brief, mirthless smile.

"Time is the commodity we no longer have, old friend. Time and sufficient manpower to do all we must." Aziz returned his gaze to Stewart. He could read nothing in the American officer's face. Depressing the mike switch, the Major resumed his speech.

"I speak to those individuals who still resist us. Surrender now or you will bring about the death of your fellow sailors. I have your executive officer here with me. If you do not surrender at once he will die, and we will continue to kill other sailors until you do surrender." Aziz unkeyed the mike. He had watched Stewart throughout his address and observed no reaction save a curious half smile at the mention of the man's own impending death. The Major did not need to look behind him to know that Kalil's assault rifle was already trained on the American. Aziz shoved the microphone at Stewart.

"Speak. Speak and live. Tell your men to surrender. You know that this is not a bluff."

Stewart did not answer, nor did he acknowledge the Major in any way. He merely reached over and took the microphone. Aziz brought his own Sterling up to high port and watched Stewart bring the mike to his lips.

"All hands, this is Lieutenant Commander Stewart speaking." Stewart paused briefly as the Major studied him intently. "The Captain is dead." He paused again and looked at Aziz. The Major saw a broad, inexplicable smile come across the American's face, and in that instant Aziz knew there would be trouble. Before he could jerk the microphone away, Stewart was speaking, then yelling into it.

"The Captain would want you to keep fighting and so do I. I—" Stewart was silenced by the ugly sound of steel against skin and cartilage as Aziz brought the heavy barrel of his Sterling crashing into the American's face. The Major had clubbed Stewart before Kalil could react and fire. Stewart collapsed to the deck on all fours, his head swinging in a low arc just above the rubber-matted surface.

"Let me finish him!" Kalil was at the Major's side, the barrel of his gun inches from Stewart's head.

"No," Aziz said flatly. He gestured to Rafsani. "Continue with your search. We are running out of time." Rafsani nodded curtly and headed aft to the ladder trunk. As the Sergeant Major started down the ladder, Aziz pulled a Beretta pistol from his belt. Not knowing what to expect, Kalil cowered back from the pistol, but the Major pointed it in the direction of the open bridgewing door and brought the 1MC mike up beside it. The three quick reports were painfully loud in the confined space of the bridge as Aziz fired the automatic, the mike keyed beside it. While the others on the bridge strained to regain their hearing, Aziz spoke into the microphone once more.

"American sailors. Your executive officer is dead. Many more will die until those resisting us surrender."

"Jesus Christ." The whispered expression of horror was loud in the silent wardroom. In the wake of the chilling words over the 1MC, none of the men present seemed certain how to react. Some of the officers looked at each other in shocked disbelief; others avoided the eyes of their shipmates and stared at the table before them to mask their grief and sense of impotence. Bosca watched Lawrence, seated across the table from him, for a reaction. The executive officer registered neither the shock nor the anger of the others, but rather conveyed a sense of bewildered disbelief. The pain from Lawrence's wound had been growing steadily worse, and he was finding it difficult to concentrate.

"The Captain and John both?" Lawrence said quietly. "They're willing to keep on killing until they get precisely what they want."

"Does that come as a big surprise to you?" Perren asked, hoping he sounded properly incredulous.

Lawrence did not respond immediately; after a few moments, fighting through the pain that fogged his thinking, he managed to speak. "It tells me they're serious . . . about not caring whether we get to where we're going with the crew alive or dead."

"Which is all the more reason to cooperate with them!" Perren said. "The sooner those other crewmen give up, the better for all of us."

Lawrence turned to face the reporter. "You don't get it, do you, Perren?" Lawrence's voice was almost a growl, prompting an increase in interest from the nearest marine. "If they didn't need us to run the ship, we'd *all* be dead by now." A wave of pain ran through his forehead. He lowered his voice. "After the killing they've done here, I don't see them just handing us over to the International Red Cross when we reach Iran. Do you?"

Perren sat back in his chair in silence. His expression showed he was contemplating a previously unseen and unpleasant possibility.

"No," Lawrence said, turning once again to Nelson. "We've got more reason to fight them now, not less."

"What do you make of this business of them thinking Stewart was you?"

"No idea. Hope that's not what got him killed. I . . ." Lawrence slumped forward in his chair, his head nodding against his chest.

Bosca and Nelson got up and went to Lawrence as quickly as they could under the watchful scrutiny of the Iranian sentries. They pulled him clear of his chair and laid him on the carpeted deck between the two tables.

"He's breathing," Nelson said, as he elevated Lawrence's head with a hardbound book.

"Maybe a concussion," Bosca said, kneeling beside the stricken officer. The Iranians looked on with interest but made no move to intervene or assist.

"Maybe," Nelson replied. "We've got to get him medical help either way."

Nelson got to his feet to address the Iranian guards. Bosca was about to do the same when he noticed that something had fallen out of Lawrence's pocket. He shifted his gaze from the object to Nelson, who was standing between him and the closest Iranian. As Nelson tried to communicate the need to summon a corpsman, Bosca surreptitiously picked up the small object. He rose to his feet with the lock-back knife concealed in his palm.

Mosopu sat perched on a foot-high scuttle, his broad chin cradled in his hand. The sun's harsh rays assaulted him there on the open deck, but the ship's return to twenty-five-knot speed had created a breeze, which offered some relief from the heat. He was on the O-2 level of the superstructure, two decks above the weather deck. From his position aft of the *Bulkeley*'s lone stack, he was invisible to anyone farther forward. Ten feet aft of where he sat, the superstructure dropped off in a vertical bulkhead down to the flight deck, a thirty-foot drop. The Sterling submachine gun rested across the big man's lap, and from where he sat he could easily cover all the approaches to his position.

But defending himself was the least of Mosopu's concerns now. The chilling voice on the 1MC, audible topside as well as within the skin of the ship, had challenged his whole sense of the correctness of his actions. Had he been doing any good by eluding the Iranians, or was he merely causing the deaths of his shipmates? The painful argument raged in his mind as he agonized over whether or not to surrender. Mr. Stewart had said to keep on fighting—and they had killed him. What good was it to continue to resist if the Iranians would only kill more of his friends?

He was startled out of his thoughts by movement to the left of the massive stack. He quickly brought up his weapon, only to see that his opponent was a small seabird that had landed beside the stack. Mosopu cursed himself for becoming so distracted that he had been surprised. He knew that if the Iranian marines had come upon him deep in his own thoughts, he would be dead. The incident made up his mind for him. Mosopu realized he couldn't wage a successful guerilla war against the Iranians—not with the thought that he was causing the death of more of his shipmates preying on his mind.

With a sigh of resignation, Mosopu pulled himself to his feet. He was about to head forward to the bridge when he stopped in his tracks. It occurred to him if he just showed up without warning, he might be killed before he could give himself up. He pondered the best way to surrender and came to the conclusion that it would be safest to call the bridge on a sound-powered phone. He would tell the Iranians that he was willing to give himself up and let them tell him what to do.

Satisfied with this but still anguishing over the need to surrender, Mosopu headed forward. He stepped around the paint cans he had brought up to the O-2 level, telling himself his original plan might still do some good.

The nearest sound-powered phone he knew of was at the midships quarterdeck, two decks below. He made his way around the stack to a scuttle that held a ladder down to the deck outside the

76-millimeter-gun magazine. From there, he knew, another ladder descended directly to the midships quarterdeck. Lifting open the scuttle, he climbed down into the cool interior of the ship.

When he reached the base of the first ladder, Mosopu was surprised to see that the door to the 76-millimeter magazine was wide open. Usually the massive steel door was kept closed, even when there were men in the magazine. He assumed the Iranians must have grabbed the gunner stationed there and left the door open when they took him out. As he was about to descend the second ladder to the quarterdeck, it occurred to him that he could use one of the sound-powered phones in the magazine rather than risk going down to the quarterdeck.

Mosopu stepped through the open magazine door and headed for the gunner's control room, where he knew there were a number of sound-powered phone lines. He was familiar with the layout of the magazine, having spent many off-watch hours there talking with a gunner's mate who was a close friend. He was halfway across the gun magazine when something unusual caught his eye. He turned and looked at the immense rotary magazine that dominated the center of the space. The rotary magazine held eighty 76-millimeter shells and was designed to feed them mechanically up to the gun mount directly overhead. The shells were stacked on end in the giant ring that made up the rotary magazine.

What caught Mosopu's eye was not the loaded magazine, which he had seen a hundred times before, but what had been added to it. All the way around the rotary magazine, spaced at even intervals of every five shells, brick-shaped objects wrapped in wax paper had been affixed to the magazine ring, alongside individual high explosive rounds. As Mosopu made his way slowly around the ring, he noted that two cords or electric cables ran from each package to the next. When he completed his circuit of the ammunition ring he stopped, staring at the whole deadly device.

Mosopu was no demolitions expert, but he knew he was looking at enough high explosives to cripple or sink the *Bulkeley*.

Common sense told him that explosives of this type were usually rigged to detonate if an attempt was made to disarm them.

The presence of the mammoth bomb made it clear to him what his course of action had to be. Thoughts of surrender now eliminated from his mind, he headed out of the magazine.

THE PASCAGOULA

Ten o'clock arrived far too quickly for Jim Garmisch's liking. It seemed he had just laid down his head on the pillow when he awoke to the sound of his electronic watch alarm. Still, he thought, two hours of sleep was better than nothing. After a fast shower and a change of uniform, he found himself sitting in the same spot at Boone's table in the flag mess, feeling as if he had never left.

The players around the table had shifted in only one regard, Jim noted: the Admiral had apparently excused Captain Vargas to tend to his ship. In his place now sat Commander Barnum, the COM JTF operations officer. Barnum, like Captain Lacey, was a longtime veteran of Gulf duty, both on board ship and on the staff. His crew-cut graying hair coupled with his deeply lined face made him appear older than the Admiral, who was in fact eight years his senior.

Captain Lacey started off the briefing this time. He had directed the staff watch to make up a large portable chart showing the track of the *Bulkeley* and her current position. As he rose to speak, he lifted the chart and stood it on end on the table so all could see it.

"*Bulkeley* resumed course for Bahrain a little under three hours ago. Whatever caused them to head east seems to have ceased to be a concern. Based on the position from the AWACS, at zero nine forty-five she was approximately here." Lacey pointed to a small marker representing the *Bulkeley* on the chart. "That would indicate that she's still able to make almost twenty-five knots good, which would mean that whatever her damage, she's still quite seaworthy."

"Has Deadline had any luck raising her on Gulf Common?" the Admiral asked.

"No sir. Deadline comes up every fifteen minutes with a radio check for her and gets no response. There's been nothing since that first transmission."

"All right," Boone said, "tell Deadline to cease trying to raise her but maintain a guard on Gulf Common in case *Bulkeley* transmits." He turned and looked at Kelly, the intelligence officer. "There's no sense in letting the Iranians or Iraqis get the impression we're too concerned. We don't want to make *Bulkeley* look more vulnerable than she actually is." Kelly nodded in silent agreement.

"Will do, Admiral," Lacey responded as Boone returned his attention to the chart. "As I was saying, that zero nine forty-five position puts them approximately one hundred twenty-five miles east of Bahrain at ten A.M."

"Before you go any further, Bob," the Admiral interrupted, "has Deadline been able to overfly the ship and get a look at her?"

"They've tried several times, sir," Lacey answered. "But the vis is just too bad. The storm is masking everything from sea level up to forty-five hundred feet."

"I see," Boone said, a thoughtful look coming over his face. "Thank you, Bob. Please continue."

"Our estimate, based on her ten A.M. posit, is that she could be here in Sitrah Anchorage as early as seventeen hundred. That's taking into account her need to slow down when she gets into the channel into Bahrain."

"Sunset is at nineteen thirty," Garmisch offered.

"Well, the timing's good anyway," the Admiral said. "If *Bulkeley* is going to come alongside *Pascagoula* at anchor, Donelli will sure as hell want to do it before dark."

"Vince Donelli is a superb ship handler, Admiral; I've known him a long time," Lacey said. "But just in case he doesn't have full maneuvering capability, I've arranged for a couple of tugs to be standing by."

"Good idea." Boone turned back to the intelligence officer. "Any change in the threat level?"

"Nothing we've been able to detect, Admiral. Her current location effectively takes her out of the range of anything but an air strike, and there's no sign of that."

"*Daniels* is just entering the Gulf now from the Straits," Lacey added, "and she's reporting normal levels of activity in the eastern Gulf."

"Good—that's good," Boone said quietly, his concentration obviously somewhere else. "Red," he began, addressing the operations officer without looking directly at him, "what have I got in my 'air force' that could get to *Bulkeley* now and get back if there was no way to land on her?"

The grizzled commander did not answer immediately. Garmisch suspected he was running through the locations, range, and capabilities of all the helicopters assigned to COM JTF.

After a minute of thought, Barnum responded. "You've got two choices, Admiral," he began, speaking slowly and selecting his words carefully. "There's the Blackhawk here on board *Pascagoula*. She's got the legs to make a two-hundred-fifty-mile round trip with gas to spare. But I'm not sure a hundred-mile overwater navigation flight, with nobody they can talk to on the receiving end, is a good mission for our Army pilots." Garmisch recognized that Barnum was referring to the specially equipped UH-60A Blackhawk helicopter embarked on *Pascagoula*. The aircraft was on loan from the Army for the Gulf mission. Garmisch knew the Army pilots were excellent—they had quickly mastered the difficult task of landing on a moving ship—but a lengthy overwater flight in a sandstorm was not something they had trained for.

"The other option is to use the Duck." The Desert Duck was the nickname for the SH-3 Sea King helicopters based out of Bahrain International Airport. The workhorse SH-3, with Navy pilots and crew, was the supply lifeline ferrying vital parts to ships patrolling within the aircraft's range of Bahrain.

"Has the Duck got the legs to get there and back?" Boone asked in mild surprise.

"Not at this range," Barnum responded. "But when *Bulkeley*'s a hundred miles out, then the Duck can get to her, and back if she has to, with a little gas to spare."

Boone sat back in his chair and thought for a moment. "Get on the horn to the cargo detachment at the airport," he said to Barnum. "Tell them I want a Duck on deck—here—fueled and ready to go in one hour. Tell them this takes priority over any other mission they have going."

"Aye, sir," Barnum responded as he got up to head for the TDC.

"Bob," Boone said, turning his attention to the Chief of Staff. "I want our staff doctor, with full kit, on the Duck, as well as the *Pascagoula*'s two top damage controlmen."

As the Admiral paused, Lacey, who was writing down Boone's instructions, looked up. "Do you want their damage control assistant or engineer to go also?" he asked.

"No," Boone answered smiling. "I've got my own engineer to send." He turned to look at Garmisch. "How 'bout it, Jim; you up for a little helo ride?"

Garmisch's momentary surprise was quickly replaced by enthusiasm for the unusual challenge. "My bags are packed, Admiral," he said with a grin.

"Don't bother to take your dress blues," Boone said dryly. Then, more seriously, "You may be able to help the ship from a damage control standpoint, but that's not my purpose in sending you—they've got their own people for that." His voice hardened. "I've got to know what's happened on that ship, the extent of the damage and whether she can still fight. Being out of communications with her—with a war going on around us—is intolerable."

· Boone was interrupted by the distinctive tone of the intercom phone that linked all the COM JTF spaces on the ship. Reaching under the table, he pulled the handset from its bracket on one of the table's legs.

"Admiral; go ahead," he said into the phone. Boone listened in silence for thirty seconds, as the other officers studied his face for signs of the content of the conversation.

"Good," he said, his face brightening into a smile. "That's excellent. I'll have to thank the sultan of Oman myself."

Garmisch and Kelly exchanged puzzled glances.

"Ask them to please continue the search, and have our people in Dubai put the uninjured one on the fastest flight to Bahrain. That's good news. Thank you." Boone put the receiver back under the table. His smile remained in place. "An Omani Navy helicopter just picked up two of our boys from *Bulkeley*'s helicopter."

"That's great news, Admiral," Lacey said. "Any sign of the third crewman?"

"No, but they're continuing to search. One of the two they found, the aircrewman, is busted up pretty bad. The other man, one of the pilots, is cut and bruised but otherwise fine. I told them to get him on the next plane headed our way." He looked at Garmisch. "I want some answers about what's taken place on *Bulkeley*."

Boone got up from his chair, and the others rose with him as a sign of respect.

"Everybody's got their marching orders?" he asked. The officers nodded in agreement. "Don't stray too far from the radio on the Duck," he said to Garmisch. "You're my eyes."

THE BULKELEY

Stewart felt himself being dragged up from the deck. At first he did not think his legs would support him, but when the Iranians raised him up he found he could stand on his own. His eyes did not seem to want to focus properly, and he felt a trail of liquid snaking down the side of his scalp where Aziz had struck him. The pain at the point of impact was not immediate, but he knew that would come later. Before he could fully steady himself, the Iranians were pushing him across the deck toward the captain's chair.

As Stewart approached the chair, his vision cleared enough for him to make out Aziz and Kalil in conversation beside it. He heard the bridge-to-bridge radio crackling in the background, its volume turned down low.

"Colt Sabre, Colt Sabre, this is Deadline. Do you copy, over?"

The Iranians appeared to ignore the radio call from the AWACS, which was just as well, Stewart thought. The unanswered call on the universally monitored channel was almost as good as a distress signal from the *Bulkeley*—or so he hoped.

When Stewart came to a halt before Aziz and Kalil, the two men stopped their conversation in Farsi. The Major met Stewart's still-unsteady gaze and spoke in his precise, accented English.

"You look well for a dead man." There was no humor in his voice.

Stewart forced the fog of pain from his mind. "Did my 'death' cause these crewmen you're so worried about to surrender?" he asked, not really expecting an answer.

"They have not come forward thus far," Aziz said. "But little time has passed. They will surrender—or we will proceed." His emphasis on the last word chilled Stewart in spite of his anger.

"Why didn't you kill me?" he asked quietly.

"This is ridiculous!" Kalil broke in. "We are not here to answer questions!" He turned to Aziz. "Let us finish this one and bring up another who will serve us."

Aziz had kept his eyes fixed on Stewart throughout this exchange. He spoke to him, ignoring the Guards Commander.

"Because, Stew-urt," Aziz said, stumbling over the curious name he had heard Stewart give on the 1MC, "you have shown us you are willing to give your own life to protect your fellow sailors. But I do not believe you will let them die in your place." Aziz turned and looked at Scott Septenano and the other Americans clustered near the ship's control console. They had been following the conversation as well. He returned his gaze to Stewart. "If you fail to carry out our orders precisely or attempt to frustrate our actions, we will kill one of your sailors—and we will keep killing until you do cooperate."

9

THE BULKELEY

G as Turbine Specialist First Class Derek Clay carefully watched the gauges on the propulsion control console while trying to ignore the loaded gun he knew was pointed at his back. Clay was a tall, black sailor in his late twenties whose athletic build showed the results of countless off-duty hours in the ship's weight room. As he monitored the panel he told himself to focus on his job, but his mind kept coming back to the image of the chief engineer, beaten into unconsciousness during the Iranians' initial assault, and still out cold, as far as Clay knew. Following the initial dustup with the Iranians, the gunmen had ordered the engineers to carry the chief engineer into Damage Control Central, which adjoined Main Control. They had singled Clay out to continue to man the propulsion control console, probably because he had been running the console when they attacked.

Clay could not see them, but he knew that just around the corner from his console the six other engineers were seated on the deck around the prostrate chief engineer. The Iranians had left only two men to watch over Main Control. The one behind him and to his left seemed to be the leader. The man leaned easily against the wooden rail running the length of the electrical console but clearly remained alert. Periodically he would say something in their strange language to the other man who guarded the engineers in Damage Control Central. His voice held the tone of authority. The Iranian in DC Central was the one who had assaulted the chief engineer. Seeing the engineer struck down, Clay had leapt onto the Iranian, ignoring the guns of the others. GSE1 Clay smiled ruefully to himself as he reflected that pounding that Iranian had been the only bright spot since the Iranians had hit his ship.

He continued as if on a normal watch, monitoring the parameters of the two main engines and regularly checking the status of the auxiliary and electrical systems at the consoles that surrounded him. The propulsion control console was the electronic brain of the *Bulkeley*'s engineering plant. It ran from deck to overhead and stretched three quarters of the way across Main Control. Tired as he was after nearly eight hours on watch, Clay still pondered how easy it would be to turn the *Bulkeley* hot, dark, and quiet with only the adjustment of a few controls. Clay glanced at the Iranian covering him, to remind himself that he would not live to see the result of such an effort.

He had to force himself to turn back casually from the Iranian to the propulsion console, as he had each time before.

Clay couldn't believe what he had just seen.

Over the Iranian's shoulder and to his left, a few inches of gun barrel protruded from behind another console that obscured the entrance to Main Control. Clay was sure he had seen the gun barrel and seen it move a few inches. It was all he could do not to react and draw the Iranian's attention to it. What the hell was going on?

Before he had any more time to think, Clay heard a sickening crash of metal against bone and a muffled grunt behind him. The engineer wheeled from the console in time to see the Iranian slumping to the deck, a *Bulkeley* sailor standing over him with a shotgun—even more unbelievably, there was a woman with a gun a few steps behind the sailor!

"Get out of the way!" Clay heard the young sailor scream. Instinctively, Clay dived to the deck to his left. As he moved, he saw the second Iranian come charging around the console. There was a wrenching blast that stung Clay's ears as the shotgun fired. He waited for more shots, hoping he was out of the field of fire. The only sound in Main Control was the mechanical slide of the pump shotgun.

Clay looked up and saw the armed sailor—he could see now that it was Andy Barron—in a low crouch, the woman behind him following suit.

"How many more?" Andy asked him in an urgent whisper. Clay noticed he kept his eyes on the open access to DC Central, from which the second Iranian had come.

"You got 'em all, man," Clay said as he struggled up to a sitting position.

Andy relaxed visibly. He and Kim both rose and came forward into the center of the space. Andy offered Clay his hand.

"Thanks," Clay said as he got to his feet. He turned toward DC Central and called out to the other engineers, "It's all clear, guys, the DCs have landed!"

The remaining engineers cautiously made their way into Main Control. A burly engineman picked up the second Iranian's weapon as he stepped over the man's body.

Clay turned to Andy and Kim, the shock of the second assault on his space in six hours wearing off. "Now where the fuck did you two come from?" he asked incredulously. Smiling sheepishly, he quickly added, "Not that I'm complaining, mind."

Andy was filled with the adrenal rush of combat and anxious to tell his fellow engineers all that had happened to them. But before he could answer, Kim spoke.

"We've been on the run since the Iranians grabbed the ship," she said briskly, her eyes straying to the bewildering array of lights on the propulsion console. "What's more important now is . . . can you stop the ship from here?"

"Wait a second," a young-looking chief petty officer interrupted, concern etched on his face. "You two have been sparring with these guys for six hours? Didn't you hear what they said on the 1MC—what happened to Mister Stewart?"

"No," Kim said slowly. "What do you mean?"

"They said if you didn't give yourselves up, they were going to start killing members of the crew." The chief's voice grew somber. "And then they popped him. Mister Stewart. Right then and there on the 1MC."

Andy turned to Kim, a look of horror on his face. She opened her mouth as if to speak, but no words came. Andy saw her go pale and feared she might collapse. GSE1 Clay saw the same thing and rushed to support her. She took his offered arm but said nothing.

"We've been in the bilges in aux two for the last couple of hours." Andy said softly, looking from Kim back to the chief. "We heard something on the 1MC ten or fifteen minutes ago, but there was no way to understand it in the bilges, with all the noise."

"Well, there's a lot more of us on the loose now," growled the engineman, a look of determination in his eyes. "What about it, Chief? We gonna turn ourselves in? I don't think our odds of living through this just got any better." The big man poked the unconscious Iranian with his steel-toed shoe for emphasis.

The chief looked from the engineman to Andy, and finally his eyes settled on Kim. Her color was still not good, but she was watching him intently.

"Do it," she said, an unnatural tone to her voice. "You have to do it."

The chief stared at her for a moment in silence. He thought about the chief engineer, still unconscious in the next room and maybe never coming out of it—and suddenly his decision was an easy one.

"Take throttle control from the bridge, Clay. We're shuttin' this baby down."

Stewart leaned against the ship's control console for support. His vision had returned to normal and the pain in his head was subsiding, but he still felt weakness in his legs. Looking across the bridge, he studied the two Iranian leaders carefully, looking for anything he might be able to use to his advantage. He complied with Aziz's course changes, when the Major's rudimentary navigation required them to adjust the track of the ship. But little else of consequence had occurred since his "execution."

What could they possibly be planning?, he wondered. As best he could determine, the ship was headed in the general direction of Bahrain, and at high speed. It was obvious they had no intention of taking the ship to Iran, as they had earlier stated. But why the deception? And what was their true purpose? If their aim was to hold the ship and its crew hostage, they could do so far more effectively in Iranian waters. If the goal was to humiliate the U.S. Navy and embarrass the American government, they had no need to take the ship to Bahrain to do so. As he considered the various possible aims of the Iranians, he could not think of one that would be advanced by driving the *Bulkeley* right into the lap of COM JTF. There's something missing here, Stewart thought, a piece of the puzzle that I haven't found.

Checking his watch, Stewart determined that it had been almost half an hour since he and Aziz had spoken on the 1MC. As far as he could tell, there had been no indication during that time that any of the *Bulkeley*'s renegade crewmen had given themselves up. He wondered briefly if Kim might still be free. Given the lethal disposition of the Iranians, she might be safer in hiding than as their prisoner. And if she had not been taken, at least that was one lever they could not use against him. Unfortunately, that thought brought him back to the realization that the other members of the bridge team and crew were hostages to his good behavior. Risking his own life for the ship was one thing, but sacrificing others . . . the idea stung him. To banish that image from his mind, he resumed his watch on Major Aziz, who was making small adjustments to the track he had laid out on the chart table.

The Major's movements were very precise; no effort was wasted, and his hands were very steady. If the recent setbacks the marines appeared to have suffered had chastened him, it was in no way apparent. A strong, contained officer, Stewart thought— but what to make of his ongoing feud with the other leader? The arguments between the two men hardly seemed in keeping with the rest of Aziz's temperament. They had not tried to use their public acrimony for the basis of any kind of "good cop, bad cop" badgering as far as Stewart could see.

It was while he was looking back at the chart table, studying Aziz, that Stewart realized the *Bulkeley* was slowing down. There was a subtle change in the vibration of the ship and a gradual easing of the noise from the engines. Stewart glanced to the ship's control console and determined that the other Americans had not yet noticed the change. He looked back at Aziz, who remained

intent on his work. Then the Major seemed to detect the altera-
tion. He looked up, paused as if feeling the reduced motion of the
ship, and spun around toward the ship's control console.

"Why are we reducing speed?" he demanded urgently.

Scott Septenano moved to look over the helmsman's shoulder
and down at the console. The young sailor behind the wheel
located the source of the problem before Septenano could do so.

"Main Control has taken throttle control," the helmsman called
out.

Aziz rushed forward to crowd with the sailors around the control console. He looked confusedly at the complex array of indicators before turning to Stewart.

"What does this mean? How have they taken control of the
engines from us?"

"It means they have control and we can't get it back on the
bridge until they give it to us," Stewart answered coolly, his attention focused on Aziz's reaction to this new problem.

Aziz darted a look at the ship's speed log, which showed seven
knots and then six, as the ship progressively slowed. He punched
the button on the control console intercom marked MAIN CONTROL
and depressed the toggle switch. The Major barked a few swift
sentences in Farsi into the intercom. He released the toggle and
waited. There was no reply.

"But this is ridiculous!" Kalil boomed. He had joined Aziz at
the console. "Our men control this engineering space! What is
happening?"

"Perhaps they control it no longer," Aziz said under his breath
as he darted across the bridge to the 1MC station. Wrenching the
microphone from its holder, he depressed the mike switch and
loosed a rapid stream of Farsi. He paused and then repeated the
same sentences into the microphone.

With a muttered oath of frustration, Rafsani was moving before
the Major had completed his first orders over the 1MC. They had
just followed the trail of the big American's blood to some sort of
storage locker. Leaving one of his men to watch the locker, with
instructions not to try to open it, Rafsani took off at a run, a

marine and a Guard trailing behind him. He halted inside the enclosed quarterdeck area before descending the ladder to the level of Main Control. His gut told him this was going to be a dirty job. Directing the others to wait, Rafsani ran up the passageway to the officer's wardroom. Throwing open the door, he ordered Nefud to accompany him, which would leave Corporal Ali to maintain the watch over the officers and civilians. He did not like reducing the guard force for the American officers, but he was running low on men.

Rejoining the others, he led his small team down the waiting ladder. How could the Americans have regained control of their engineering command space?, he wondered. Aziz's terse orders over the PA system had indicated that it was in enemy hands and must be regained, regardless of the cost. That was all well and good, he reflected, as he eased his large frame down the narrow ladder, but then the last of Aziz's hurried commands had directed that they not damage the engineering control equipment when they retook the space. That would be the difficult part.

The ladder led to the deserted mess decks, a hundred feet forward of Main Control, if Rafsani's memory served him. He went to the nearest small dining table and started to empty the pouches of his vest as the other Iranians gathered around. When he had finished there were seven grenades on the table, three of the flash-bang type and four fragmentation grenades. Rafsani scooped up the fragmentation grenades and returned them to his vest. He handed one of the flash-bangs to Nefud.

"You and Kia will form one team," he said to the two marines. "You," he said, pointing the ever-present *kukri* at the lone Guard across from him, "will accompany me." With practiced ease he drew the big knife across the Formica surface of the dining table. In seconds he had etched out a rough diagram of the target space. God be thanked that I passed through this Main Control when I was first checking the sentries, he thought.

"We will strike from two directions, one team from each entrance." Rafsani pointed to the two entry points he had carved, one in Main Control, the other in Damage Control Central. He looked at Nefud. "When you hear my flash-bang go off, throw yours in your doorway; when you hear my second grenade detonate, that is the time to strike. Stay on your side of this partition," he said, pointing to the propulsion console that divided the two spaces, "until you hear the firing stop from our side of the space."

He studied the three men, his gaze resting on each face in turn as he spoke.

"We cannot know how many we will find in there, or what their disposition will be. If each team stays in their assigned portion of the space, the only thing in our field of fire will be the enemy."

Taking the two remaining flash-bang grenades from the table, Rafsani signaled that it was time to go.

"One final direction," he said, as the other men checked their weapons. "We are not looking for prisoners here. The Americans cannot be allowed to damage the engineering equipment, as they surely will if they have the chance. Cut down everything that moves."

DESERT DUCK 03

Garmisch tried to block the noise and vibration of the helicopter from his mind by concentrating on what he might find on the *Bulkeley*. Like many surface ship officers, riding in a helo was not high on Garmisch's list of favorite activities. The Sea King in which he was embarked was an aging but reliable aircraft that had served the Navy well. Let's hope it's got at least one more mission in it, he thought to himself.

They had left the deck of the *Pascagoula* fifteen minutes ago, after a short briefing for the pilots and passengers by Captain Lacey. The Chief of Staff had provided them with an outline of what was known by COM JTF about the *Bulkeley*'s situation. Garmisch reflected that they really did not know very much about what had happened on board *Bulkeley*. What kept coming back to him, as he reviewed the chronology of events in his mind, was the ship's unwillingness to recover its helicopter. Almost everything made sense and was in line with the actions a normal commanding officer would take—except the abandoning of the helo. Well, we'll see soon enough, he thought. At ninety knots, the trip out to the injured frigate was expected to take just over an hour.

Glancing out the observation port across from him, Garmisch could see a thin finger of land bounded by water on both sides. The Duck was headed north, following the shipping channel out from Bahrain in accordance with Bahraini flight rules. In a moment, the last trace of land disappeared and then the helicopter was banking to the right to head eastward on its course to the *Bulkeley*'s position. Garmisch was about to turn his attention back inside the aircraft when a large object on the water, two to three miles distant, appeared through the port. Garmisch stared at it in puzzlement before realizing he was looking at Barge Apollo. He had never seen Apollo from the air before, he realized.

The large rectangular floating platform was anchored in a hundred feet of water a few miles outside the entrance to the Bahrain Channel. Garmisch could make out the distinctive silver shapes of two Spectre Mark III patrol boats moored to the barge. The Spectres were heavily armed descendants of the World War II motor-torpedo boats, torpedoes having been replaced by lightweight rapid-fire guns on the Spectres. There were a number of other small boats made up to the barge, and Garmisch could see a large crane on Apollo lifting one of the boats free of the water. He could not see the weapons, but he knew the barge was defended by a host of heavy-machine-gun and Stinger missile positions.

As he studied the barge, Jim reflected that being stationed on her must be tough. He knew there were well over a hundred men based on Apollo, including the crews of the small craft and the technicians and support personnel who kept the patrol boats running. The other occupants of the barge kept a very low profile in the Gulf but were equally vital. Garmisch recalled his tour of Apollo with a young SEAL officer who had showed him that a detachment of SEALS, as well as certain special forces experts from the other services, were billeted on the barge.

As the Duck continued on, Barge Apollo faded from view, and Garmisch turned his attention within the helo. Looking around the relatively open interior of the large helicopter, he examined the other members of his rapidly assembled team. The squadron doctor, whom Garmisch knew only slightly, sat strapped in beside him. The physician's expression mirrored Garmisch's own lack of enthusiasm about helicopter rides. The doctor didn't look much more than twenty-five years old, Garmisch thought, as he glanced quickly from the young physician's bespectacled face to the medical bag he clutched tightly in his lap.

Across the aircraft from Garmisch were the two senior damage controlmen from the *Pascagoula*. The older of the two, a senior chief of Filipino origins, appeared relaxed and unflappable. He looked around the aircraft with a practiced professional eye, as if interested in the structural science that held the vibrating collection of moving parts together. Beside him sat a stocky damage controlman first class, who had apparently never flown in a helicopter before; the man's expression of enthusiasm and fascination made that fact apparent to Garmisch.

Garmisch was diverted from his review of the other passengers by the clasp of a strong hand on his left shoulder. Looking up and to his left, he saw the SH-3's lone aircrewman standing beside him. The man was pointing forward toward the cockpit. Garmisch saw that one of the pilots up in the cockpit was turned back toward the cabin, gesturing for Garmisch to come forward. I wonder what's up?, Garmisch thought as he unbuckled his harness and got to his feet. With the aircrewman in the lead, he made his way forward in the aircraft.

When he reached the cockpit, Garmisch was momentarily distracted by the view out the windscreen. The sky appeared unnaturally, incredibly blue, particularly in contrast with the sea of windblown sand that seemed to undulate just below the helicopter. Garmisch forced himself to shift his attention from the beautiful view through the windscreen to the pilot seated below him. Beside the pilot who had signaled him, the left-seat pilot, currently flying the helo, appeared totally focused on his work. The man who had summoned Garmisch had a compact aviation chart spread out on his lap and seemed to be adjusting a track he had laid out on it. Jim leaned down over the pilot's shoulder to increase his odds of hearing whatever the man wanted to pass on to him.

"Just got off the secure circuit with COM JTF," the pilot yelled, his mouth close to Garmisch's helmet in an effort to be heard over the deafening engine noise. "They wanted me to pass some new information direct to you."

"Go ahead," Garmisch shouted back, his own voice barely audible over the background sounds.

"*Bulkeley*'s stopped dead in the water." The pilot paused to make sure Garmisch had heard him. "The AWACS was tracking her at twenty-five knots until a few minutes ago, and then the ship just slowed and stopped." He looked up at Garmisch expectantly for a reaction.

Garmisch did not say anything. His mind raced through the possibilities and the potential impact. Had the fire reflashed or the engineering plant been damaged? Or worse, had the ship struck a mine, or been attacked? Damn the lack of radio communication with them! Looking down at the pilot, Garmisch registered why the man had the aviation chart out.

"Can we still make it to her?" Garmisch shouted. The helo's ability to intercept the *Bulkeley*, with enough gas to make it back, had been based on a closing situation. Now the ship would not be contributing its twenty-five-knot component to the equation.

The pilot looked quickly down at his chart and then back at Garmisch.

"I think so," he yelled, "as long as we don't have to waste any time looking for her. But that shouldn't be a problem as long as AWACS keeps track of her and we have a good TACAN lock."

Garmisch nodded and looked back up at the view out the aircraft's windscreen.

"Thank God they're pretty much out of the range of Iranian attack," he said, too softly for the pilot to hear.

USS DANIELS

The guided-missile destroyer *Daniels* cut like a giant dagger through the flat waters of the Gulf. At flank speed, she was making better than thirty knots, and a six-foot-high rooster tail of spray plumed up from her stern. The dozens of small boats within sight of her remained well clear, their masters wanting nothing to do with the dangerous wake that the eight-thousand-ton warship made at speed.

Lieutenant Chris Booker, officer of the deck on board *Daniels*, stood at centerline on the bridge, his binoculars pressed almost against the bridge windows, his legs widespread to steady him on the slowly rolling deck. Booker had every available pair of eyes in his bridge watch team scanning the waters ahead of the ship. The visibility in the sandstorm ranged from bad to worse, averaging little over two thousand yards. Booker knew that at thirty knots he would have very little time to react to anything that they detected out in front of them. His CIC team, using surface search radar, would alert him to the large ships that could pose a collision threat to the *Daniels*. His real concern, though, was the array of small boats that littered the eastern end of the Gulf. He did not even want to think about mines; at this speed, and with the late detection common to floating mines, it would take a miracle to avoid one. Still, his mine watch was posted in the eyes of the ship, carefully scanning the waters ahead of them.

This was the first time as an OOD that Booker could remember wishing *Daniels*'s helicopter was available and airborne. Right now I'd love to have it searching out in front of us, he thought. Even in this sandstorm, the helicopter could more than double their advance warning on contacts ahead of the ship. But the destroyer's one helicopter had been ferrying a sick sailor down to the *Roosevelt* in the North Arabian Sea when the order into the Gulf had come through. The *Daniels* had headed into the Straits immediately. There had been no time to wait for the aircraft to complete its seventy-five-mile trip and return to the *Daniels*. Booker knew they would not see their helo again until they returned to the Gulf of Oman.

When Booker had first come up on watch an hour ago, the *Daniels*'s mission had seemed destined to be an exercise in futility. With both ships at high speed and a hundred miles separating them, it had seemed implausible that the *Daniels* would ever catch up to the *Bulkeley*. But that had all changed ten minutes ago when the TAO had called up to the bridge to tell Booker that the wounded ship had gone DIW—dead in the water. Booker was cheered by the possibility of catching up to the *Bulkeley* now that the frigate was stationary. He did some fast figuring and determined that if the damaged frigate remained immobile, *Daniels* would join up with her in just over three hours. It would be good to have this tail chase accomplish something, he thought. But his enthusiasm was muted by the knowledge that the *Bulkeley*'s having come to a halt undoubtedly meant things had gotten worse for her—maybe much worse.

Booker was about to lower his binoculars and give his eyes a brief rest from the intense concentration on what lay ahead of *Daniels*, when he caught a faint image of something in front of the ship at the edge of visibility. Straining his eyes to focus, he was just able to make out the small contact dead on the *Daniels*'s bow at about one thousand yards. Booker reacted quickly. He looked to his right and left to make sure there were no other contacts close aboard and then gave his order.

"Right five degrees rudder." It was only necessary to use slight rudder adjustments when at high speed. As the helmsman acknowledged his command, Booker felt the ship start to come around to the right. He would steer around this small boat and then resume course. Booker moved to the centerline gyrorepeater to watch the contact and ensure that it was drifting left and away from the *Daniels*.

Before he could reach the repeater, he heard the voice of his junior officer of the deck yelling in from the starboard bridgewing.

"Contact ten degrees off the starboard bow!"

Booker had his binoculars back up in an instant. There was another small contact to starboard, and he was turning right into it!

"Holy shit! Rudder amidships—steady as she goes!" Booker hurriedly shouted the order.

As the helmsman halted the turn and steadied the ship to drive between the two small craft, Booker heard his boatswain's mate of the watch sing out, "There's another one on the bow, Mr. Booker!"

Booker did not need to bring his glasses up to see this one. It was dead on his bow at less than five hundred yards. The three similar contacts were strung out in front of him, almost like a boom, at intervals of twenty to thirty yards. There was no place for *Daniels* to go.

"All stop!" Booker ordered. "All back full!"

The helmsman pulled back on the throttles and the *Daniels* instantly started to lose speed.

"There's a fourth one to starboard!" the JOOD yelled in from the wing.

As the destroyer's twin screws began to dig in, their blades shifting to astern pitch, the entire ship started to shudder.

"C'mon, baby," Booker said under his breath as the *Daniels* drew closer and closer to the small boats, now less than a hundred yards away. At this range it became clear that two of the seemingly identical black boats were joined together by a length of line.

"What the hell's going on up here?" The voice of the captain of the *Daniels* filled the bridge. Booker turned to answer, but he saw the captain had quickly taken stock of the situation and was headed for the starboard bridgewing. The nearest of the small boats was to starboard.

Booker followed the captain out the bridgewing door, noticing as he went that the ship had almost completely lost headway.

"All stop!" the captain boomed from the bridgewing, as the vibrating hull of the *Daniels* glided to a halt a scant twenty-five yards from the nearest boat. Three of the four boats bobbed within fifty yards of the destroyer, blocking her forward passage.

Booker was surprised to see the boats were Zodiac rafts, similar to those used by Navy SEAL and UDT teams.

THE <u>BULKELEY</u>

"Want me to turn out the lights too, Chief?" GSE1 Clay turned from the propulsion console and eyed the electric systems console behind him.

"Negative on that," the chief replied. "At least not right away." He turned to Kim and Andy. "You two were moving around the ship for a while. Did you see any indication that our people might be in control of Radio or CIC? I don't want to kill the juice and end up cutting off a distress call going out from the ship."

Andy looked briefly at Kim before answering.

"We haven't been in that part of the ship, Chief," he said. "We've pretty much been in the hangar, aux two, and here."

The chief considered a moment before speaking again.

"These guys have already shown us they can get around pretty good in the dark. I don't think it's worth risking screwing up our own people to black the Iranians out."

"Roger that." Clay smiled. "Besides the bad guys aren't going anywhere now."

"Until they take this place back from you, you mean," Kim said, speaking up for the first time since they had taken control of the engines.

The chief looked at the stocky engineman covering the entrance to Main Control before he replied.

"I think they're gonna find it pretty tough to do that with only two ways in here and us covering both of them." His voice did not reflect the confident nature of his words.

"Why don't we just destroy this stuff and get the hell out of here, Chief?" Andy said as he uneasily eyed the various control consoles.

"That's not going to help us too much if we're sitting in Bandar Abbas Harbor, is it?" the chief asked rhetorically. "No. As long as we hold this space, there's a possibility of help getting here and us getting out of this mess under our own power. What if we completely disable the ship and some of our other guys who are loose snatch it back from the Iranians? We'd be hosed!"

"We haven't run across any others, Chief," Kim said fatalistically. "Andy and I may be all the resistance there is, other than yourselves. Besides, you haven't seen the Iranians in action. They—"

Kim was interrupted by a metallic popping sound behind her. As she and the others spun around, they were shocked to see the engineman firing the odd Iranian weapon in the direction of the console-obscured door to the space. She watched in frozen horror as a can-shaped object slid from the doorway across the deck toward the firing engineman. Before she could determine what the object was, she was knocked from her feet as Andy tackled her from the side.

She threw her arms out to cushion the fall and felt the hard collision of her elbows with the deck. There was an overpowering crack that stung her ears and a flash from behind her as the device detonated. She could hear nothing. The flash that had filled the space clouded her vision, but since the explosion had been behind her, she could still see reasonably clearly. There were two subsequent explosions that she felt rather than heard, as she kept her head sheltered in her arms. Kim felt the weight of Andy's body lift from her own, and she turned her head to call out to him, but she could not hear her own voice.

As if in a drugged state, she watched the hazy action unfold.

Andy had moved from her clouded field of view—where had he gone? Through the thinning smoke she made out a terrible grim figure charging—very slowly, it seemed—past the recumbent body of the engineman and into Main Control. The giant apparition appeared to her to have no face, only a dense, all-encompassing beard. He held one of the pistol-grip silenced machine guns in one hand as if it was a revolver. In the other he clasped a sinister-looking knife. She thought his gun must be firing, for spent cartridges were flying from it, but there was no sound, not even the silenced sputtering she had grown to fear. She saw the engineering chief snap backward as if he had been hit in the chest with a brick and then crumple to the deck.

With a shout of rage that she could not hear etched on his face, GSE1 Clay vaulted toward the massive killer. They grappled amid the fallen sailors, and Clay appeared to knock the Iranian off balance. But then she saw the marine wrestle his knife hand free and in an instant the engineer was staggering backwards from him. She watched helplessly as Clay collapsed over the propulsion console, covering it with his blood.

Although it registered on her slowly, Kim realized that the hulking Iranian was firing at someone or something over her shoulder. He seemed to have emptied his gun, for he threw it aside and stepped across her toward the center of the space.

Kim was about to turn to follow the advance of the murderous giant when she felt something cold and hard press against her forehead. Looking up through the worsening fog that fouled her vision, she could barely make out a second Iranian, his weapon pointed into her face. She wanted to say something, tried to form the words of a question, but her mind did not seem to be working correctly. First John and now me, she thought, more with resignation than fear. The gun in her face filled her field of vision, but suddenly a shadow darkened that vision. She looked up to determine what was obscuring her crystal view of the instrument of her death and saw that the monstrous Iranian had returned. No —not the knife! The last image she saw as her vision darkened into unconsciousness was that of the giant—the destroyer— pushing away the other man's weapon.

Mosopu moved cautiously but methodically forward through the quiet ship. He advanced with a singleness of purpose fueled by the knowledge that he might be the only hope of survival for his shipmates.

Minutes earlier he had noticed the winding down of the ship's engines, and the shift in the frigate's motion from the steady, slow roll of high-speed transit to the bobbing motion that signaled the ship was dead in the water. This puzzled him—surely the Iranians had not reached their destination already? If they had, he knew it was doubly important for him to act, and quickly.

Faced with the horrendous fact that the Iranians had turned his ship into a giant seagoing bomb, Mosopu had decided his only course of action must be to immediately free as many of his shipmates as possible. He had to give his fellow sailors a fighting chance of escape from their own ship. The explosives themselves made no sense to the Bosun's Mate. It would have been easy enough for the Iranians to kill the whole crew, if that was their intent, without destroying the ship in the bargain. The only thing Mosopu could figure was that the bombs were intended as a desperation measure if the *Bulkeley* was overtaken by American ships coming to her rescue. Ultimately, he thought, the reason the explosives had been planted didn't matter; what was important was that they proved the Iranians' willingness to sink the ship and murder the entire crew.

Mosopu was headed forward to the berthing compartments. He was certain that the coops and the armory and repair locker forward of them would be heavily guarded. But there was no way around a direct fight now—finding the explosives had made him realize the futility of his cat-and-mouse game with the Iranians.

He advanced carefully down the starboard passageway leading to one of the coop trunks. The two ladder trunks, one on the port side and one on the starboard, held a succession of ladders that led to the entrances of the individual coops. This gave each of the berthing compartments an access on either side. Unfortunately, Mosopu mused, the design of the ladder trunks also made it simple for a single sentry on each trunk to hold all the men in the coops below at bay. Any man wanting to exit the coops had to come up the ladders in one of the trunks.

Mosopu passed the galley serving line and stopped at the watertight door that he knew opened onto the passageway where the starboard coop trunk was located. Moving very cautiously and trying to avoid making any telltale sound, he slowly released the mechanical securing dogs on the door. The big Samoan cracked the door open a couple of inches and looked through the opening. He could see the trunk clearly, bathed in the red night-lighting, which no one had turned to daytime white. The Iranians had apparently lowered the watertight hatch onto the coop trunk and dogged it down. That would make their job of maintaining control even easier, he thought. But there was no sign of a sentry. Mosopu remained where he was, watching and listening for the Iranian he knew must be nearby. A minute passed and still there was nothing. Mosopu decided to move.

The big man was surprisingly light on his feet, and in a few quick steps he was up the passageway and standing at the corner of the athwartships intersection, which, he knew, led across to the port trunk. Keeping out of sight around the corner, he listened for footsteps. Maybe the sentry had gone over to the port trunk to talk to his buddy, he thought. When after a hundred seconds of waiting no sound came from the athwartships passageway, Mosopu risked a quick look around the corner. Nothing.

Well, he thought, I've either gotten real lucky or these guys aren't as smart as I thought. Knowing there was no time to waste, in a matter of seconds he'd crossed the open space and was on his knees, working to pop the scuttle in the center of the trunk hatch. The operating wheel was frozen in place. He was surprised at this roadblock, but he simply redoubled his application of torque, certain that he could move the wheel. But even straining his muscles for all they were worth, he could not budge the wheel. Puzzled at his failure, Mosopu bent down to look under the wheel and see what was fouling its action. He was startled and then angered to see that the threads on the wheel's shaft had been melted, fused into the scuttle. Springing to his feet he examined the large hatch itself. His investigation confirmed the worst: all the way around the hatch, its edge had been fused to the coaming it rested upon. The ladder trunk hatch and its scuttle had been welded closed.

Heedless of his own safety, Mosopu raced across the athwartships passageway to the port side. As he rounded the corner, gun at the ready, he collided with a squat, trash can–shaped object and sent it flying. Lucky for me there's no sentry on this side either, he thought. He turned to look at the thing he had collided with and instantly recognized it as the portable welding rig that the ship's engineers sometimes used. There was a sick feeling in his stomach as he turned back to the ladder trunk. He already knew what he would find: the port hatch had been welded shut as well.

Easy to see why they didn't leave any guards behind, Mosopu thought. But this was worse than encountering armed sentries. Even if those explosives went off but failed to sink the Bulkeley immediately, his shipmates would still drown, trapped in the coops with no hope of escape. He was their only chance. He would have to free them or die in the attempt.

10

THE BULKELEY

Kalil paced back and forth across the bridge, his worry apparent in his every step. Leaning against the chart table, his arms folded in front of him, Aziz watched the Guards Commander punish the deck and hoped his concern was not as obvious as Kalil's. The Major had issued his hurried orders over the 1MC almost thirty minutes earlier and the lack of word from Rafsani was starting to tell on him.

Aziz looked over to where Stewart was standing by the captain's chair, and was met with the same impassive glare as before. The crack to the man's skull and Aziz's threat had apparently failed to cow him. The Major was tempted to tell the American officer the truth—that whether his ship was incapacitated here or continued on, his death and that of all of his shipmates was a certainty. That would quickly erase the man's mocking confidence. But it would not serve the mission or the Major's immediate needs. In one thing Kalil was probably correct: he should have killed this officer and selected another who was more cooperative. But against reason he had let the American live. There was something in his own nature that made him want to deal with a fighter, a man he could respect, rather than one who would meekly do as he was told.

Aziz glanced at his watch and did a rapid equation in his head. The delay so far was not a critical one—not yet. But every minute they were held up gave the Americans, both on board the *Bulkeley* and elsewhere in the Gulf, additional time to unravel what was happening to the ship. He was about to use the 1MC to direct the Sergeant Major to report, when a voice broke the silence of the bridge—a voice speaking in Farsi from the ship's control console intercom.

"Bridge, this is Rafsani in the engineering Main Control."

Aziz could not keep the smile from his face as he rushed to the console to answer his old comrade-in-arms. As he moved to depress the toggle switch and respond, he looked briefly at Stewart, who was now watching him with a far more concerned expression on his face.

"Go ahead, Sergeant Major," Aziz said in Farsi. "Make your report."

"We have retaken the Main Control," the voice boomed metallically from the intercom speaker. "One man wounded, Nefud, but it does not appear to be serious. There is limited damage to two of the consoles down here from stray rounds, but they remain operational, as best I can determine."

"Excellent, my friend. You have done well." Aziz paused and considered the next move. "Can the Americans give us back engine control on the bridge?" he asked.

There was a long empty pause with no response from the intercom. Finally, Rafsani answered, his voice a register lower.

"There are none left able to operate the equipment," the voice said slowly. "All the American sailors here have been killed or severely wounded." The intercom went silent.

Aziz was taken aback. Rafsani has done his work too well, he thought to himself.

"What now, Major?" The voice of Kalil came from behind Aziz. The Guards officer had obviously been following the conversation. The Major turned to answer him.

"There are other engineers on board this ship, Colonel."

"Yes—but we have sealed them all up in their living spaces! Or do you not recall?" Kalil thundered.

Aziz thought for a moment, his eyes straying to Stewart.

"We have isolated some of them, the chief petty officers and other enlisted men, but not all," Aziz said, returning his attention to Kalil. "We still have the officers." Before Kalil could respond, the Major shifted his attention back to the intercom.

"Sergeant Major?"

"Here," the voice echoed back from the steel box.

"I want you to leave the Main Control in the care of your men," Aziz began. "Go up to the officers' wardroom and collect two officers who can run the engineering system." He looked toward Stewart as he continued. "If the officers with this knowledge will not identify themselves or refuse to cooperate, use whatever means of persuasion you require to achieve this end. We must get the ship moving again." Aziz paused to let the order sink in. "Do you understand, Sergeant Major?"

The response was immediate. "Your orders are understood, Major," Rafsani said. "I have one other element of information that may interest you," he continued.

"Go ahead."

"Amongst the Americans in the engineering space there was . . . a woman."

"What?" Aziz said in disbelief. "A woman?" He turned and looked at Stewart, who returned his gaze uncomprehendingly.

"There can be no mistake," Rafsani said humorlessly. "She survived our assault and is relatively unharmed. I do not know what she is doing here, Major—but what do you want me to do with her?" For the first time Aziz heard his old friend sound perplexed.

"Are these Americans without self-respect?" Kalil asked angrily. He was now beside Aziz. "That they would bring a woman into a battle zone?"

Aziz ignored the Guards Commander as he tried to adapt his thinking to this new reality. After a few moments of thought he made up his mind.

"Hold her in the Main Control until you return with the new engineers," he said into the intercom. "Once we have the ship moving forward again, bring the woman to the bridge."

"As you direct," Rafsani responded, and the intercom fell silent.

Aziz looked up from the console and stared at the still-puzzled Stewart.

"Now, Commander," he said, fluidly shifting from Farsi into English, a grim smile on his lips, "explain to me why you have a woman on board."

■

"What do you suppose they're up to?" Bosca directed his question to Jack Nelson at the end of the table.

Nelson briefly eyed the lone marine guard who had been left to watch over them. Then he shifted his gaze to the reporter. "Hard to figure. I can't think of any reason why they'd want to stop in the middle of the Gulf." He lowered his voice. "The way that big bastard stormed in here and grabbed that other marine makes me think they've got a problem somewhere. Hopefully, a real big problem." Nelson looked down at Lawrence, who remained unconscious on the deck. He had tried unsuccessfully through a series of hand signals to convince the Iranian sentry to allow him to cover the XO with a blanket from the cabinet beneath the wardroom couch. Lawrence was breathing regularly, but he was far too pale.

"From what you said earlier, the Iranians are at greatest risk until they get into their own waters," Bosca said. "What reason could they possibly have for stopping and increasing their exposure?"

"That's the point," Nelson responded. "They've got trouble, either in engineering or on the bridge, and whatever's happening has forced them to stop the ship and divert manpower to deal with it." He looked again at the lone Iranian sentry. "If we're going to make a move, we're probably not going to get a better chance than this." Nelson's voice was at its most subdued. The other officers listened attentively, ready to follow his lead.

Unconsciously, Bosca fingered the thin shaft of the knife in his hand. Both hand and knife were out of sight below the table, where he had quietly opened the folding blade.

"What's it going to take to convince you guys?" Perren said, speaking for the first time since Lawrence's collapse. "You want to keep playing at war with them until we're all killed? They've said they're going to turn us over to our own government once they get the ship to Iran; I don't see any reason not to believe that."

"It's obvious you didn't cover the embassy hostage crisis, Neil,"

Bosca said contemptuously, "or you wouldn't be so trusting of our 'friends.' "

Perren was about to reply when the after door to the wardroom was thrown open and the bearish figure of the Iranian Sergeant Major filled the doorway.

"Here's trouble," Bosca said under his breath.

The big marine crossed the space and stopped at the table at which Bosca, Perren, and Nelson were seated. He was followed into the wardroom by the marine sentry he had earlier withdrawn. The Sergeant Major looked down briefly at Lawrence before addressing Nelson, whom he evidently had identified as the most senior American officer present.

"Two engineering officers," the marine rumbled to Nelson in heavily accented English. "I require two of your officers who can operate the engines." The man stared hard at Nelson. He held his weapon at his side, as if confident that his mere presence was enough to enforce his demands.

Nelson did not respond immediately. He returned the massive Iranian's gaze in silence, all the while feeling the eyes of the four engineering officers in the wardroom drilling into him. Nelson briefly considered and then discarded the idea of putting up a principled and heroic resistance. One look at the torn and bloodstained uniform of the big marine and the ruthless cast to the man's features told him that refusal to cooperate would mean certain death, for him and many others. No, there was a time to fight back, and this wasn't it.

"Morris; Irwin," Nelson said slowly, as if it pained him to speak the words, "go with him. Cooperate until you hear different."

Two officers at the other table got to their feet a bit uncertainly. They looked first at Nelson and then at the towering Iranian. Nelson looked away, a mixture of anger and humiliation bubbling within him.

The Iranian gestured to the wardroom door, and the two young officers headed toward it, with one last look back at Nelson and their seated comrades. When the door had closed behind the three men, Bosca turned back to face Nelson.

"You really didn't have any choice, Lieutenant," he said sympathetically.

Nelson was silent for a long moment. When he spoke there was ice in his voice. "This fight is a long ways from being over."

DESERT DUCK 03

Garmisch waited with growing anticipation as the Desert Duck drew ever nearer to the *Bulkeley's* position. In what was a technical violation of safety rules, he crouched directly behind the pilots in the cockpit, with no harness to restrain him. It was the only way they could hook him into their communications system so he could both send and receive radio transmissions. Admiral Boone had been quite explicit in his desire to have Garmisch be his link to the stricken ship.

Garmisch had swapped his cranial helmet for one that could connect directly with the helo's communications system, and he now had the luxury of being able to talk to the pilots without screaming. They were about twenty minutes away from the *Bulkeley*, by Garmisch's estimate, when the pilot who was navigating the aircraft addressed him.

"I'm going to start trying to raise them on Gulf Common," the pilot said. "They should be able to read our IFF sqwawk, but to be on the safe side I'll start identifying us now. The last thing we need is to suck up one of their missiles if they think we're a hostile."

Garmisch nodded in agreement, and the pilot began trying to raise the *Bulkeley* on the VHF circuit. Garmisch mentally kicked himself for not being the one to think of calling up the ship as a precaution. Under normal circumstances the *Bulkeley's* IFF identification system would interrogate the aircraft's IFF transponder, and the returning friendly signal, the "sqwawk," would tell the ship that the incoming aircraft was friendly. But now, with who knew what extent of damage to the frigate, she might be operating on radar alone or perhaps even be completely electronically blind. It was his job to foresee those possibilities. That's the sort of thing you're along for, he told himself.

That line of reasoning brought other questions into his mind. Just what would they find when they reached the ship? Why had they lost radio comms with the *Bulkeley*, and what had happened to immobilize her? When the ship had reported the fire and headed back to port, he had discarded his idea that she was targeted for an attack. But the report from the AWACS that the frigate had gone dead in the water had brought the possibility of an Iranian attack rushing back into his thoughts. Whatever had forced the *Bulkeley* onto the clear VHF net, for all the Gulf to hear, might ultimately have resulted in the ship's being hit. The Iranians would find it difficult to pass up the wounded target the ship presented. He was certain the Admiral was having similar misgivings and would be pacing the Tactical Decision Center on the *Pascagoula*, waiting for his report.

Alone with his concerns, Garmisch listened as the pilot tried to raise the *Bulkeley*.

THE BULKELEY

Stewart stared out the bridge windows at the flat seas around the becalmed frigate. Lucky for all of us that there are no seas to speak of, he thought, or we'd be rolling like a drunken pig. He stood leaning against the shelf below the bridge windows, which the crew referred to as the dashboard, his arms folded on the narrow ledge.

Stewart scrutinized the billowing sandstorm that surrounded the *Bulkeley* and tried to estimate the current range of visibility. He had observed a supertanker passing down their starboard beam a few minutes ago, and from its size and relative visibility, he figured the current visual range was about two miles. If they passed another warship within that range and the visibility held, there was a good chance the other ship would try to raise them on bridge-to-bridge or by flashing light. He knew from the U.S. force disposition that there were likely no American ships in the *Bulkeley*'s vicinity, but that did not rule out encountering the British and French warships that also patrolled the Gulf. If another ship actually observed the *Bulkeley*, perhaps they would be able to determine that something was wrong and inform COM JTF. At worst, Stewart hoped for another situation where the Iranians used him to talk on the radio. Give me another chance to set you up, you bastards, he thought, staring across the bridge at Aziz and Kalil.

Stewart looked at the clock over the ship's control console and confirmed that they had been stopped for close to an hour. Whoever had gummed things up for the Iranians in Main Control deserves all our gratitude, he thought. Apparently Kim had been involved in the action somehow. How in hell had she ended up in Main Control? Even Kim would not go to that length to cover a story, he told himself. Silently he wished she had stayed in hiding. Thank God she wasn't hurt, or at least she was well enough off that they were worried about what to do with her. If the situation was not so grim, he would have laughed at Aziz's obvious consternation at word that there was a woman on board. That had taken some explaining, and Stewart had elected to tell him the truth and play up her importance as an internationally known media figure, in the hope of buying her some protection.

He was jarred from his thoughts by the quiet but still distinct voice that came from the bridge-to-bridge radio beside him.

"Colt Sabre, Colt Sabre, this is Duck Three. Am inbound to your position from two-six-zero at twenty miles."

What on earth was the Desert Duck doing out here? Stewart wondered. He was surprised when Aziz rushed across the bridge and turned up the volume on the VHF radio. The Major and the other leader had been ignoring all of Deadline's attempts to raise the *Bulkeley*. What had gotten Aziz's attention now? As the helicopter broadcast its identity and position once again, the Iranian officer turned to Stewart.

"That will be one of your transport helicopters out of Bahrain, yes?" The Major's tone indicated he knew the answer already. Stewart remained silent. The bastards knew about the Duck, he thought. Not that the existence of the small group of logistic helicopters was any great secret, but Stewart was still startled by the depth of the Iranians' knowledge of U.S. operations. The Major pulled the microphone from the radio set and pushed it at Stewart.

"Find out what they want," he directed.

Stewart hesitated for a moment before accepting the microphone. Lifting it to his mouth, he turned from Aziz to look out the bridge windows.

"Duck Three, this is Colt Sabre. Say again your location, over."

The response from the helicopter was almost immediate.

"Roger, Colt Sabre. We are on your two-six-zero at fifteen miles, currently at angels three and descending to your position, over."

Stewart concealed his own surprise at the imminent arrival of the aircraft and keyed the microphone again.

"We copy, Duck Three. What is your mission? Over."

This time there was a brief pause in response and then a different voice answered for the helicopter.

"Colt Sabre, this is COM JTF rep embarked in Duck Three. We are inbound to you with medical and damage control assistance party, over."

Stewart turned to Aziz, who had a look of concern on his face. "Looks like our headquarters decided to send us some help. What do I tell them?"

Aziz appeared to think for a moment before answering. "They cannot land here," he said. "You must send them away."

"Exactly how am I supposed to sell that?" Stewart countered.

"As before. Tell them that the fire has reignited and it is unsafe to land on the ship." Aziz's voice hardened. "For your survival and that of your comrades, *convince them.*"

Stewart stared back at Aziz. After pausing to consider how to deal with the situation, he addressed the helicopter again.

"Duck Three, this is Colt Sabre. We are unable to recover you —landing conditions are unsafe, over."

"This is COM JTF rep," the voice from the aircraft responded. "My orders are to put down on your deck and provide assistance. We do not require a flight quarters team if one is not available. Over."

Stewart looked at Aziz, whose cold expression remained unchanged. "Convince them," the Major repeated softly.

Stewart had the chance he had been waiting for. He rapidly searched his mind for a story that would both deflect the helicopter and signal the men on board it that there was trouble on the *Bulkeley*. After a moment, he spoke again.

"Duck Three, this is Colt Sabre. Negative on landing. Fire on board is out of control." He paused, forcing himself not to look at Aziz, and then added, "Fire in auxiliary one space is threatening flight deck fueling system. Flight deck is unsafe, over."

Aziz spun from the radio. "Hosayn!" he yelled across the bridge to one of the marines. "The smudge pots! Get back to the helicopter hangars and ignite the smudge pots!" The marine nodded his understanding and took off down the bridge ladder at high speed. Aziz returned his attention to Stewart and the radio just as the voice from the Desert Duck resumed.

"COM JTF rep copies: negative on landing. Request current status of your fire, over."

"Tell him the fire is severe, but you have hopes of containing it and moving forward," Aziz directed Stewart.

"Fire remains out of control in several engineering and comm spaces," Stewart said into the mike. "We hope to be able to control it and resume transit under our own power."

"Copy, Colt Sabre," the voice from the aircraft came back. "There are other units en route to your position to provide assistance. Request status of your personnel casualties, over."

"That is enough conversation for now," Aziz said, pulling the microphone from Stewart's grasp.

Stewart stared at Aziz in silence as the helicopter continued to try to contact the *Bulkeley*. He scanned the sand-obscured skies ahead of the ship for any sign of the aircraft.

DESERT DUCK 03

"Keep trying to raise them," Garmisch directed the copilot. When the *Bulkeley* failed to respond, Garmisch had turned the VHF radio over to the flyer so that he could call COM JTF on the separate secure HF frequency. The Admiral had not been very happy with the news from the frigate—particularly the ship's unwillingness to let the Desert Duck land. He had directed Garmisch to stay in the area as long as the helo could and to get as much information from the ship as possible.

Now the aircraft was continuing its descent through the sandstorm, its radar holding contact on the *Bulkeley*, for a look at the stricken ship. As they passed through the densest part of the storm at about one thousand feet, the airborne sand closed visibility down to almost nothing. Garmisch had been in aircraft descending through thick clouds before, but this was a different sensation, almost like being underwater in a muddy pool.

"If they won't let us use their deck, we can't hang around for very long," the copilot said, looking up from his calculations. "We're only going to have about ten minutes of on-station time before we have to turn around and head for the barn."

Garmisch nodded his understanding. That would be enough time, he thought, for a comprehensive look at the ship. Lacking radio contact, he would have to determine as much as he could about the extent of damage to the ship from her appearance.

The occupants of the cockpit breathed a collective sigh of relief as the aircraft broke out of the storm at an altitude of three hundred feet. And there was the *Bulkeley*, bow on to the helo's nose at just over two miles. The four-thousand-ton frigate sat all but motionlessly on the flat seas, its superstructure silhouetted by a dense cloud of oily black smoke that rose from the ship's stern. Garmisch leaned forward in the cockpit, straining to make out details on the ship.

"Take us in as close as you can and orbit her," he instructed the pilot. "I need a complete three-sixty look at her."

The Desert Duck nosed down to one hundred fifty feet and headed straight for the stationary warship. When they had closed to within a hundred yards of the bow of the ship, Garmisch could see that the billowing smoke was coming from the vicinity of the flight deck. Observing that the wind was carrying the smoke away to port, the pilot headed the Desert Duck down the *Bulkeley*'s starboard side. As they passed down the ship's starboard bow, the aircraft descended almost to the height of the bridge. Garmisch was sure he could make out figures on the bridge, but there was no sign of any personnel topside. The pilot gave the smoke-enveloped flight deck a wide berth as he brought the helo down the side of the frigate, but he came close enough for Garmisch to confirm that the dense smoke was coming from the two hangars.

The aircraft's orbit took them down the port side, well clear of the smoke, while the copilot tried once again to contact the ship on Gulf Common. His radio call was met by silence. As they rounded the bow, Garmisch addressed the pilot.

"Go ahead and elevate so we can get an overview of the ship."

The pilot complied, bringing the aircraft slowly up as they made their second pass down the ship's starboard side. As they passed aft of the ship, the aircraft crested at two hundred feet, a good fifty feet above the cloud of black smoke. At low speed, almost approaching a hover, the pilot brought the helo forward over the stern of the ship and the flight deck. The Duck crossed over the pillar of oily black smoke, and the top of the after superstructure came slowly into view.

"What in the hell does that mean?" the copilot said, echoing the question in the minds of all the men in the cockpit. Below them, on the broad expanse of deck aft of the stack on the superstructure, someone had painted in six-foot-high letters of red lead primer:

S O S

I R A N

THE BULKELEY

Aziz watched the departing helicopter, along with every other man on the *Bulkeley*'s bridge. He turned to look at Stewart and saw that the American officer was following the flight of the aircraft with an almost superhuman intensity, as if he thought he could bring it back through the force of his own will. Aziz returned his focus to the helicopter in time to see it disappear into the sandstorm at a range of two to three miles still climbing as it went.

Aziz had more than one reason to be glad the aircraft was gone. When the helicopter had made its close flyby inspection of the ship, Kalil had become so concerned that he had wanted to try to shoot the helo down. Aziz had had to restrain him from running out on the bridgewing with their lone rocket-propelled grenade launcher. Now the RPG and its satchel of rockets were once again safely stacked beside the chart table.

The Major went to the ship's control console and was about to call Main Control to check on the status of the engineering plant when Kalil's voice jarred him from across the bridge.

"Do you think that feeble lie has convinced the Americans?" he demanded angrily in Farsi.

Aziz was slow to answer. Dealing with Kalil was sapping his attention from more important things, he knew, but there was little choice.

"There is no need for them to believe the story completely," Aziz said. "They only have to be confused and uncertain. Besides, why should they question the story when it comes from the lips of one of their own officers?"

"Would you be taken in by such a ploy?" Kalil asked indignantly.

Aziz paused thoughtfully before answering. For once the Guards officer had asked a relevant question.

"I do not know if I would or would not. Many strange things happen in the Gulf; the Americans know this. They will believe what their own ship tells them, until they have reason to do otherwise."

Kalil crossed the bridge to join Aziz. He lowered his voice so the other Iranians on the bridge could not hear him.

"And what of the other 'units' on their way here that the man in the helicopter spoke of? What if we are still adrift when other American ships appear?"

Aziz's reply was drowned by Rafsani's booming metallic voice coming from the intercom speaker.

"Bridge, this is Rafsani. We are ready to give you control of the engines once more."

Aziz gave Kalil a mildly satisfied smile and depressed the toggle switch to reply.

"Excellent work, Sergeant Major, and not a moment too soon. Proceed with the transfer."

"The American engineers say your engine controls must match those in this room. Bring your engine controls to all stop."

"Engines all stop," Aziz said, looking at Stewart as he spoke.

Scott Septenano watched Stewart for a sign to comply and was rewarded with a curt nod. Septenano gave the required order, and the helmsman brought the *Bulkeley*'s aircraftlike throttle down to the all stop position.

"Our controls are at all stop," Aziz said into the intercom.

"Stand by," Rafsani answered.

Almost immediately a light began to flash on the ship's control console. The light was in a grouping headed *Station in Control*, and as it flashed, the word *Pilot House* was visible on its bulb.

"Go ahead and take control," Stewart said flatly.

Septenano complied by turning a switch below the flashing indicator, which stopped flashing but remained illuminated.

"The bridge has throttle control," Septenano said.

Aziz turned again to Kalil. "You see, Colonel, it is as God wills." Before the Guards Commander could reply, Aziz looked at Stewart.

"Make our speed twenty-five knots."

DESERT DUCK 03

"They had *what* painted on their superstructure?" Boone's incredulousness was unmistakable on the secure radio circuit.

" 'SOS Iran,' Admiral," Garmisch answered through his helmet microphone. "It was on the oh-two level deck, aft of the stack, painted as if it was intended for an aircraft to be able to make out from above."

"Did you ask them what the hell it was doing there?"

"We weren't able to raise them after our initial conversation, Admiral. We kept trying to talk to them until we had to go off station, but there was no response." Garmisch unconsciously looked over at the Desert Duck's fuel gauge, which now showed less than half a tank. "I'm not sure what it means, although I've got a hunch there's more wrong on that ship than just a fire."

"A fire as widespread as they described would be bad enough," Boone responded. "Did you notice anything else out of the ordinary besides this strange SOS?"

"Just what I described to you before, sir: plenty of black smoke coming from the hangars, enough to indicate a major oil fire, but no topside fire parties visible. What bothers me most is something else I didn't see." Garmisch paused, waiting for the Admiral's response. The helicopter was back in the thickest part of the storm, climbing to free itself from the curtain of sand.

"Well, go ahead," came Boone's impatient-sounding voice in Garmisch's ear.

"The overboard discharges, Admiral," Garmisch said slowly. "There was no sign of a heavy flow of water from her overboard discharges. If they're fighting a fire as large as all that smoke would indicate, they should be pumping thousands of gallons of spent firefighting water over the side. I didn't see anything beyond the normal discharges."

"That is unusual." Boone sounded more circumspect now. "But it's possible they have a problem with fire main or another reason for not pumping the water over the side."

"There's one more thing, sir. The man I talked to on the radio said we couldn't land because an out-of-control fire in their aux one space was threatening to blow the helo refueling station."

"So what's so bizarre about that?" the Admiral demanded, his patience obviously drawing thin. "Sounds fairly prudent to me."

Garmisch steeled himself and then replied. "I've served on this class of ship, Admiral. The space he mentioned, aux one, is nowhere near the flight deck or the refueling station. Hell, it's two hundred feet forward of either of them."

"So the man made a mistake," Boone said after a short silence. "I'm sure they've got plenty else to worry about. Who was this you talked to, anyway?"

"Our conversation didn't last long enough for me to find out. But Admiral, this guy—an officer, I assume—didn't sound excited or confused. He didn't sound like the kind of man who would make that kind of mistake."

This time it was almost a full minute before Boone came back on the circuit. "I don't know what your hunch is, Jim, but my gut tells me there's something very wrong on that ship—and I don't mean the fire. Shit, we've got more questions now than we had when you left to fly out there!" Garmisch could hear a conversation in the background as Boone talked to someone with the mike still keyed. Then the Admiral returned to Garmisch.

"Based on how far away you are in the Duck, you should be on deck here in less than forty-five minutes," Boone said. "That pilot from the *Bulkeley* will be here any time now too. I want a complete debrief from both of you as soon as you arrive."

"Roger, Admiral. I'll be ready."

"But as long as you've got no place to go for forty-five minutes," Boone said ironically, "how about giving me a rundown of this hunch of yours."

THE BULKELEY

"Damn those clever bastards!" Senior Chief Gunner's Mate Lanier cursed as he struggled with the scuttle. His tall wiry frame was contorted in an unnatural position on the top four steps of the coop one access ladder, where he fought for leverage on the frozen scuttle. Clenching his teeth, he wrenched the length of safety-rail pipe he had jammed through the scuttle wheel for all he was worth. But the wheel showed no sign of giving.

"Any luck, Gunner?"

Lanier looked down from his cramped stance at the top of the ladder into the broad, weathered face of Command Master Chief Rimes. The master chief was almost swallowed up by the sea of anxious sailors surrounding him in the crew compartment. The volume of sailors in coop one had swelled to fill the entire berthing compartment, as worried men had made their way up from the lower coops.

"No. Sorry, Master Chief," Lanier answered. "This fucker is frozen just as solid as the one on the starboard side."

Leaving the section of pipe jammed in the scuttle wheel, Lanier climbed back down off the ladder to stand on the deck of the crowded coop. "We're gonna have to look for another way out, Master," he said, stretching to work out his screaming shoulder muscles. "Those assholes know their way around a welding rig."

The master chief nodded in somber agreement. He turned and made his way to the center of the space, a corridor opening for him through the mass of sailors. When he came to a halt in the center of the coop, Rimes reached an oil-stained hand up to the ventilation diffuser.

"Still plenty of air coming in," he said, affecting a confident tone. He eyed the duct leading to the diffuser. "Too bad this isn't a movie, or the vent duct would be big enough for us to send a man through."

There was a murmur from the assembled sailors and chiefs, an uneasy mixture of laughter and resignation.

"Think they're really gonna let us go, Master Chief?" a nervous voice asked from behind Rimes.

Turning, the master chief found that his questioner was a young electrician's mate, recently assigned to *Bulkeley*, who was easily thirty years his junior. The young sailor looked at him with anxious expectation. Rimes recognized that the sailor's question reflected the growing concern and helplessness the men felt as the announcements on the 1MC had become ever worse. It was something he would not allow to continue.

"Forget that crap, Givens!" The master chief's roaring response caused the young sailor and those closest to him to back away from Rimes. "Listen up, all of you," Rimes boomed, swinging around to address the bulk of the men in the coop. "This is our ship! Nobody 'lets us go' on our own ship! We're going to find a way out of here and clean the bastards' clocks!" From the look in the assembled men's eyes, the master chief knew he had their attention.

"Coop petty officers, take ten of the guys from your compartment and start tearing it apart!" he rumbled. "Pull out all the false bulkheads and overheads and find us an access that doesn't lead into a fuel tank—find us a way out of here."

As the coop petty officers raced to comply, Rimes turned back to Senior Chief Lanier. "Gunner, take however many men you need and go over all the coops for potential weapons. I know we've got enough folding knives in here to open a camping store, but I want pieces of pipe, swab handles—anything you can find."

"On my way, Master Blaster," Lanier said with an enthusiastic grin. He selected several combat systems department petty officers and headed down the ladder toward coop two.

The master chief turned back toward the young petty officer who had spoken up. The sailor was engulfed in a tide of his shipmates rushing to their assigned tasks.

"I haven't forgotten you, Givens!" Rimes barked with mock anger. "Get together with the other men from your shop." He turned and pointed to the coop access ladder. "I want a way for us to electrify that ladder!"

Givens was moving before the master chief had completed the order.

Mosopu headed forward in the dimly lit ship. He moved quickly, almost recklessly, through the silent passageways, the image of the sealed coops burned into his mind. He was careful, however, not to let that sense of urgency blind him to the dangers that could be anywhere around him. He knew that if he was killed or captured by the Iranians, his imprisoned friends wouldn't stand a chance.

His silenced weapon in front of him, the Bosun's Mate picked his way cautiously forward in the direction of the repair locker. The exothermic cutter was the key to his thinking now. It could slice through the door to the armory or cut through the welded hatches of the coops with equal ease. Mosopu expected to find an Iranian standing watch in the vicinity of the co-located armory and repair locker. They would leave a man there, he thought, because of his own earlier attempts to break into the armory— unless they had welded the armory shut too. But that would present little difficulty once he got his hands on the cutter. Mosopu forced himself to think positively, to believe the cutter would be in the repair locker. Please don't let the damage control assistant have moved it, he thought.

Mosopu slowed his pace as he reached the next to the last watertight door between him and the repair locker. On the other side of this door was, he knew, the large athwartships space where the vast bulk of the missile magazine penetrated this deck and continued down several decks below. There was a small peephole in the watertight door, and Mosopu peered through it. When his check confirmed there were no Iranians present, at least not within his field of view, he quietly opened the door and stepped inside.

The immense girth of the cylindrical missile magazine all but filled the space. Sailors had to turn sideways to get past the tubular wall of the magazine at the narrow point where the magazine and the space's bulkhead came closest together. Mosopu had always had a tough time squeezing his broad form through the confined opening. As he reached the narrow junction, he was shocked to find that even an uncomfortable passage between magazine and bulkhead was now impossible.

The missile magazine had been wired with explosives in the same fashion as the rotary magazine for the 76-millimeter gun. Mosopu stepped back from the massive steel magazine structure and verified that the same brick-shaped charges had been wired around its cylinder. One charge had been placed, intentionally or haphazardly, at the narrow junction that led forward to the repair locker. Mosopu considered trying to squeeze past the ugly lump of explosives but decided against it. Three feet off the deck, the charge was placed so as to make it equally dangerous to try to go either over or under it. After considering his options, the Bosun's Mate decided to circle back around and come up the starboard side of the magazine, hoping that there wasn't an identical charge on the far side of the magazine cylinder.

As he opened the watertight door through which he had come, Mosopu reflected on just how much explosive power had been located in the guts of the ship. The *Bulkeley* might survive the detonation of the 76-millimeter ammunition, but never the explosion of the missile magazine. He knew the magazine contained close to forty anti-aircraft and antiship missiles. The warhead of just one of the Harpoon antiship missiles detonating this far forward in the ship would surely sink her—but it would not be just one missile. Sympathetic detonation of all forty-odd missiles and their rocket motors would send the *Bulkeley* up like a small nuclear weapon.

Mosopu tried to erase that image from his mind as he stepped through the watertight door. He didn't see the figure with the gun trained on him until it was too late.

11

THE PASCAGOULA

C ommander Kelly hurried through the relatively wide passageways of the flagship on his way to the admiral's mess. He had not expected to return there until the next scheduled meeting at 1400. Boone's summons had come moments ago, as Kelly was working his way through the latest intelligence traffic with two enlisted intel specialists. The Admiral had said he wanted to see him—now—and there had been no further discussion.

Kelly reached the door to the mess and knocked hard twice before entering. Boone was seated at the head of the table, his fingers steepled under his chin, a look of intensity on his face. Kelly knew immediately that something very serious had occurred.

"Sit down, Bill," the Admiral said, his powerful gaze now fixed on Kelly.

Wordlessly, the intelligence officer went to the table and took a seat one chair removed from the Admiral. Boone kept his eyes on him all the while.

"I know I've pulled you out of your twice-daily message marathon, but I think we have a real problem on *Bulkeley*."

Boone was never one to skirt around an issue, Kelly thought. "You mean beyond the fire, Admiral?" he asked.

Boone nodded; his look remained almost inhumanly intense. "I've just finished talking to Jim Garmisch out there in the Duck.

He's had more of the same from the *Bulkeley:* won't let him land, lost comms, and, most critically, there's evidence that there may not be a major fire on the ship. To put it another way, we appear to have smoke but no fire."

Kelly sat back in his chair to consider what Boone had said. "What makes you doubt the validity of the fire, Admiral?"

"Principally because of an observation made by Garmisch. He pointed out that if there's a mass conflagration on *Bulkeley*, there should be excess fire-fighting water pouring out of her overboard discharges. There's no sign of that, nor any other indication of fire-fighting activity." Boone shook his head. "This whole fire story feels wrong." The Admiral paused, and Kelly waited, fascinated, for him to continue.

"But I wouldn't have called you up here just because of that. I don't believe there is a major fire on board that ship, but there might be some other reasonable explanation for what her captain's doing. At least, I'd think so if . . . if not for something else Garmisch found out there."

Boone looked down at the table while Kelly waited, unconsciously pushing his hair back from his forehead.

"Garmisch described to me," the Admiral began, speaking slowly, "that someone's painted a message, in red lead paint, on the after superstructure of the ship. A message that reads 'SOS Iran.' "

Boone looked up from the table at Kelly, as the other officer's face registered his surprise.

"SOS Iran?" Kelly said, his voice just above a whisper. "Did Garmisch ask the ship what it's supposed to mean?"

"He tried. *Bulkeley* is now, conveniently, radio silent again."

Kelly looked away from the Admiral as he mentally sorted through possible explanations that fit all that had happened. In a few seconds he had culled one frightening possibility that loomed large over the others. He turned back to Boone and was met by the other man's grim smile.

"I believe we're thinking the same thing, Commander." The smile faded from Boone's face. "I want to see everything you have on the potential for Iranian seizure of one of our ships—every estimate, rumor, and wild-ass guess that we have on file."

"Aye, sir." Kelly understood with crystal clarity what Boone was thinking. He rose to depart.

"And, Bill," the Admiral said quietly. "Needless to say, I need that information yesterday. I'm getting on the satellite to CENTCOM right now, and I'm sure I'll be talking to the NSC right after that." Boone looked away from Kelly. "I'd rather be known as an alarmist than get Pearl Harbored by one of my own ships."

THE <u>BULKELEY</u>

Kim returned to consciousness slowly, as if wakening from a deep sleep. As her vision gradually cleared, she noticed that her hearing had returned, although her ears retained some residual pain from the grenade blasts. Her head throbbed with a dull ache, but she was able to focus her thoughts. She became aware that someone had placed her in a chair beside the electrical console. The pain in her wrists drew her eyes to them first, and looking down she found that her arms had been bound together with a pair of the plastic carseals used to secure items around the ship. She struggled briefly against the thin white restraints, quickly realizing that they were immovable.

The clouds left her vision and Kim was able to clearly make out the situation in Main Control. She was surprised to see that there were no bodies surrounding her chair on the deck. The bloodstains and expended cartridges that littered the deck made it clear, however, that the nightmare battle she recalled was no dream. But where were the bodies—and where was Andy? She hoped he had survived the swift, brutal fight, but what she remembered of it did not fill her with confidence. For a brief moment she almost wished she had died in the battle. With Stewart dead, and probably Andy and the others as well, she felt a sense of pervasive hopelessness.

There were two new engineers at the propulsion console, their backs to her. From the khaki uniforms they wore, she knew they had to be officers or chief petty officers. They were working under the careful scrutiny of one of the Iranians. The sentry stood in the opening between Main Control and Damage Control Central. He shifted his eyes every few seconds from one space to the other, apparently charged with watching them both. He briefly looked at her and, realizing she had come to, let his eyes linger on her for a moment. Kim thought she recognized him as the Iranian whom Andy had clubbed when they first entered Main Control. The marine stared at her without emotion for a moment and then resumed his watchful monitoring of the engineers and whoever was in DC Central.

Kim did not understand the engineering workings of the *Bulkeley*, but she had been on the ship long enough to know that the renewed machinery sounds and the gentle rocking of the hull meant that the frigate was moving once again. She wondered how long the ship had been immobilized. Please let it be long enough to have had some effect, she thought to herself. It would be horrible if the engineers—and Andy, too—had died for nothing.

Kim struggled in the hard metal chair to try to get into a more comfortable position. She noticed that the Iranian sentry was distracted from his guard duties by her movement. But the guard practically snapped to attention as the immense figure of the Sergeant Major came into Main Control from DC Central. The giant Iranian ignored the respectful reaction of the other marine as he crossed to stand in front of her. The man's size and intimidating appearance were magnified by Kim's defenselessness as she sat bound in the chair. Staring straight ahead into the mass of the man's body, Kim saw the terrible knife the marine carried, sheathed at his waist. Determined not to show fear, she looked up into the eyes of the towering figure.

"It is good you have awakened," the Iranian rumbled in heavily accented English. "Now we will go to the bridge."

Before Kim could say anything in response, the marine had lifted her out of the chair by her shoulders and set her on the deck.

"As your hands are bound, I will lead the way," the Iranian said, his tone indicating it was an order. He turned and headed for the door to Main Control.

Kim took one last look around before following the big marine to the door. As she stepped forward, her movement feeling unnatural because of the restraints at her wrists, she noticed that one

of the engineers had turned from the propulsion console to watch
her go. The officer gave her a look that she knew he meant to be
one of encouragement, to raise her spirits. But the man's face
communicated more helplessness than confidence.

Mosopu knew he was dead.

He waited for the crash of gunfire in the narrow passageway
and was surprised when it did not come. He could make out only
an outline of the figure with the gun. The man was standing in
the shadows at the opposite end of the red-lit passageway, his
weapon leveled on the Bosun's Mate. After several seconds of
waiting and no bullets or words from his opponent, Mosopu was
ready to bring his own gun up and take his chances.

Then the man with the gun collapsed noisily to the deck.

Mosopu was initially too startled to react. But after a moment of
confusion, he trotted down the passageway to the fallen man, his
gun at the ready. When he reached the crumpled figure, Mosopu
first searched the adjacent bulkhead for a light switch. Finding
what he sought, he turned the passageway's lights from red to
white; to his astonishment, the white light revealed the fallen man
to be a *Bulkeley* sailor. Although the sailor's face had an unhealthy
pallor, Mosopu recognized the man as Andy Barron, a young
petty officer from the engineering department.

The Bosun's Mate knelt beside the injured sailor, who was lying
on his side and breathing shallowly, clearly injured. He picked up
the petty officer's weapon, which proved to be one of the ship's
riot shotguns, and leaned it against the bulkhead. Putting one
beefy arm under Andy's shoulders, Mosopu rolled him over onto
his back, careful to keep the man's head elevated. When he got
him turned over, the nature of the sailor's injuries became dread-
fully apparent. The man's dungaree shirt had been laid open in a
diagonal slash running from his right shoulder across to just
below his rib cage on his left side. Mosopu could not tell how
deep the underlying wound was, but the sailor's shirtfront was
soaked through with blood. He had seen a similar wound inflicted
on a merchant sailor in a knife fight in Pusan. That man had not
survived.

As Mosopu held the badly wounded sailor, he wondered what to do. If the man was to have any chance at all, Mosopu knew he would have to stop the bleeding. Running possible options through his mind, the Bosun's Mate remembered that the repair locker he had been headed for would contain a sizable first-aid kit. The battle dressings included in the kit might give him a chance of slowing the man's loss of blood. But he would never get to the first-aid kit, he realized, if the starboard-side passageway around the missile magazine was blocked by explosives as the port side had been. Well, he thought, if it's blocked, it's blocked —and we'll have to find another way through. He was about to hoist the sailor up and carry him around to the access to the starboard passageway, when the sailor murmured something. Mosopu put his head closer to the seemingly unconscious sailor's face and listened.

"Kim . . . Kim, I . . ." The man's voice was barely a whisper, but still distinct.

"Relax, buddy," Mosopu said softly. "You gonna be okay. Don't worry 'bout talking. Save your strength."

Andy's eyes opened briefly, fixed on Mosopu, and then fluttered closed.

"It hurts bad, Boats," Andy said, pain evident in his voice.

That's something, Mosopu thought. The guy recognized me. He's not out of his head from the pain. Mosopu thought for a moment. It would be better not to strain the sailor further, but he had to know if there were others like him loose in the ship. He had to have all the information he could get. The more than two hundred of his shipmates trapped in the coops had to be his priority.

"Where did this happen to you, kid? How did it happen?"

The sailor's eyes opened again, meeting Mosopu's. He coughed a brief, rasping cough and then, strangely, a little smile formed on his bloodless lips.

"We took Main Control back from 'em," he croaked. "Kim and I. We stopped the ship—at least for a while." His eyes closed once more.

They took Main Control? Jesus, Mary! Mosopu thought, I'm not the only one still fighting the bastards! He could not think who this Kim might be, but that did not really matter.

"But what happened to you? How did this happen?" he asked again quietly, pressing Andy to tell him all he could.

This time the wounded man responded without opening his eyes, his voice even lower. "They hit us . . . hit us back, in the same way we grabbed the space. Big guy cut me with this . . . machete, before we knew what was happening."

"Did anybody else get away?"

Andy paused, trying to catch his breath before answering. "Don't think so. Too much blood." He coughed again. "Big guy cut me and went right on past. Other guy saw so much blood, must have thought my throat was cut and left me. I stumbled out the door while the shooting was still going on." He screwed up his eyes as if trying to hold back tears. "I don't think anybody else got out alive."

Mosopu had his answers. They were not the ones he would have preferred, but at least he knew the truth. He and the badly wounded sailor were likely the only resistance there was left.

"You just stay quiet now, buddy," he whispered. "This is gonna hurt some, but we gotta go. Now."

Slinging his submachine gun over his shoulder, Mosopu slid his free arm under Andy's knees and lifted him gingerly from the deck. Traveling this way would be clumsy and also taxing on the injured man, but there was no choice. If the starboard passageway was not blocked, they would only have to move forty more feet forward to reach the repair locker. Stooping at an angle while maintaining his load, Mosopu grabbed the barrel of the man's shotgun. As he crossed the hatch coaming to circle around to starboard, he whispered in the sailor's ear.

"Don't you die on me, buddy. We got some scores to settle."

Aziz kept his eyes on the ship's densely instrumented control console. For the last twenty minutes, since the return of engine control to the bridge, he had scrutinized the console, shifting his gaze only occasionally to take in the view through the bridge windows. It was ridiculous, he knew; this superstitious feeling that if he just watched over it, the ship would not betray him again. But realizing that did not stop him from continuing to lavish the console with his attention. He was about to force himself to transfer his focus to the chart table and his track, when Kalil called out to him from across the bridge.

"Major, please join me on the bridgewing."

Aziz looked up to find the Guards Commander standing by the starboard watertight door, his hand on its operating arm. What now? Aziz wondered as he crossed the bridge in silence to follow Kalil outside. It was better, he realized, for both his own men and the Americans to see no more of Kalil and him in conflict. Before he stepped through the hatch, the Major eyed Stewart carefully. He believed he had read the man correctly and that his threat of harm to Stewart's shipmates would ensure his cooperation. Still, Aziz was uneasy going out of sight of him. He saw that Stewart was staring silently out the windows at the sea ahead. Verifying that his two men were alert and watchful, Aziz stepped onto the wing, closing the door behind him.

Kalil was leaning against the life rail with his back to the water, his elbows resting on the rail. As Aziz approached him, the Guards Commander took a deep, luxuriant breath and smiled. He is overplaying the role, Aziz thought, and would be far more comfortable in the air-conditioned bridge, as would I.

"Why do you have such a pained look upon your face, Major?" Kalil asked. "Is it not good to be out in the golden sun and clean air of our beloved Gulf?"

In silent answer, Aziz scanned the dirty-white sand clouds that hung over the sea all the way to the murky horizon. He swept his eyes over Kalil.

"What do you wish to discuss, Colonel?"

The smile left Kalil's face. He was offended that his one attempt to display collegial goodwill had been rejected.

"When are you going to contact the Council and tell them of the various compromises of our mission?" Kalil demanded.

Aziz's hand reflexively went to the large walkie-talkie on his belt and just as quickly moved away. "I do not believe there is reason to risk communication."

"But this is precisely the type of information the radio link was established to convey!" Kalil thundered. "Now is the time to contact them and let the Council decide whether we should continue!"

Aziz's reading of the Guards Commander had been correct. He had anticipated Kalil would become more nervous as they came closer to the point of maximum risk in their mission, and so he was. The powerful VHF radio at Aziz's side was set to transmit on a special frequency that was being monitored by military listening posts on Iranian oil platforms scattered throughout the Gulf. As soon as any of them picked up a transmission from Aziz, they would relay it via HF radio to the Supreme Defense Council in Tehran. Aziz had no intention of using the radio unless he was certain that their mission was going down to defeat.

"The authority to use the radio was left in my hands," he said coolly to Kalil. "And I do not believe our situation merits its use."

"But what of the helicopter? They saw us! Do you think they believe there has been a fire on board this ship?"

Aziz chose his words carefully. "If you recall our briefing, it was always assumed that we would come in contact with other American units before reaching Bahrain." He paused and looked past Kalil out into the Gulf. "The key to our mission remains that although the Americans may be confused, suspicious even, they do not understand what has occurred. And nothing has happened so far to change that."

The primary objective of their plan had always been to use the *Bulkeley* to destroy the *Pascagoula*. The Supreme Defense Council was certain that the loss of the Americans' key command and control facility in the Gulf would cripple their ability to function. It was also believed that the loss of almost a thousand sailors with the destruction of the two ships would drive the United States from the region. The men of the Defense Council were well aware of the Americans' timid inability to accept large numbers of casualties.

Kalil's anger was etched in his face as well as his voice. "And what if you are wrong? What if they do suspect, and they let us travel to Bahrain only to seize or destroy the ship at their convenience?"

Aziz had weighed this possibility, but he still felt the odds were in their favor. Besides, he thought, the end result would be almost the same.

"Then we succeed only partly, but succeed nonetheless. There will be no successful counterseizure of the *Bulkeley!*" He raised his voice to convey to Kalil how adamant he was on this point. "We will destroy the ship—with the hope of destroying the American flagship in the process—but we will destroy this ship regardless."

In the event the *Bulkeley* could not reach the *Pascagoula* to deliver the death blow, the backup plan called for sinking the ship in the narrow channel leading to Bahrain. Blocking the channel would bottle up the American warships and allied merchantmen in Bahrain Harbor for weeks, perhaps months, as well as choke the commercial lifeline to the Americans' Bahraini allies.

"But . . ." The fire had gone out of Kalil's voice as he realized that what had been an unpleasant element of their plan, casually acknowledged at their briefing, stood a real chance of becoming a reality. Destroying the ship if the Americans tried to recover her would mean the death of all the Iranians, as well. "But if we are fully successful, our raiding party will escape."

Reality has finally penetrated, Aziz thought. "That is to be hoped for," Aziz said. "But we must be prepared for the other possibility if we are to deal this lethal blow to the American interference in our Gulf."

Aziz turned toward the bridgewing door to reenter the pilothouse. He could not keep himself from taking a parting shot at the now shaken Guards Commander. As he torqued the door open he turned to Kalil, who had a far from superior expression on his face.

"Remember, Zade Kalil. The warrior who does God's will has the most honored place in paradise."

THE PASCAGOULA

Desert Duck 03 touched down on the flagship just after two P.M. The Duck was coated with a fine layer of sand and dust, which gave it the appearance of having been painted over in desert camouflage.

Garmisch stepped out of the aircraft while its rotors were still spinning and was led off the flight deck by an officer in full flight quarters garb. Once they were inside the superstructure of the ship and away from the helo's noise, the officer removed his cranial helmet and Garmisch did the same.

"No time to clean up, I'm afraid," the officer said, as he turned to lead the way forward into the heart of the ship. "They want to see you immediately."

Garmisch understood. He had figured there would be no time to waste. Still clad in his inflatable life vest and with the cranial under one arm, he followed the officer down the passageway.

When they entered the flag mess, Garmisch was surprised to see that it was crowded with officers. The Admiral's table was full, save for one seat apparently reserved for him. Both Captain Vargas and the operations officer were present, along with Kelly and the Chief of Staff. Next to the Admiral, in the seat usually occupied by the Chief of Staff, sat a pilot, a lieutenant commander with a large bandage across his forehead. A surface warfare lieutenant commander, who Garmisch vaguely remembered as Fraser, the officer in charge of Barge Apollo, sat in one of two extra chairs that had been set up beside the table. Beside him was Lieutenant Beach, who headed the small SEAL detachment assigned to COM JTF. Conversation stopped as Garmisch entered the mess, and all eyes turned toward him.

"Ah, right on time," Boone said. He gestured to the chair beside him. "Grab a seat, Jim. We'll get to your report in a moment." The Admiral turned his attention back to the injured pilot. "Go ahead, Lieutenant Commander Hammond. Finish what you were saying."

The pilot was slow to respond. It appeared to Garmisch that he was feeling pain unrelated to his wounds.

"That's about it, Admiral. After she rolled over, the SENSO got out his escape hatch, and my copilot and I went out the door on my side; his was jammed." The pilot's eyes left the Admiral's and he looked down at the table in front of him. "I know he got out, but we didn't see him anywhere on the water's surface. We tried diving back to the aircraft in case he had gotten snagged on something, but the wreckage sank too fast."

"Damn shame," Boone said sympathetically. He allowed the man a few seconds of silence and then continued. "Think back for me now, to when you first returned to the *Bulkeley*. Was there anything unusual other than their refusing to let you land?"

Hammond thought for a moment before answering. "Telling us to bingo was unusual enough. But I was surprised to be talking to the weapons officer and not the CO or XO under those circumstances."

"You said he told you the Captain was involved in fighting the fire?" Captain Lacey interjected.

"Yes sir. But the order not to land was supposed to have come from him. What bothers me—what stayed with me—was something else the weapons officer, Lieutenant Commander Stewart, said."

"What was that?" Boone asked.

"He told me the ship wouldn't be able to recover us or launch Two-Six, our other bird." Hammond paused before continuing as Boone waited in silence. "Admiral, Stewart knew full well that Sealord Two-Six was hard down and there was no way she could fly off the ship. I know this officer well, and I can't understand why he'd waste valuable time on some nonsense statement in a situation like that."

Boone considered this for a moment before asking, "Did you see any physical signs of a fire? Any flames, smoke, or obvious fire-fighting activity?"

"None, Admiral, although dark as it was, flames would have been the only thing we would really have been able to see."

Boone turned to Garmisch. "That conforms to your description, Jim. You said that smoke was the only visible sign of a mass conflag."

Garmisch nodded in agreement. "That's correct, sir. There was none of what you'd expect to see with a major fire. No sign of dewatering, no hoses on deck, or topside fire parties. In fact . . ." Garmisch's voice trailed off for a moment, and then he added, "In fact there was no sign of topside personnel anywhere—not even the Stinger and fifty-cal gunners."

Boone looked across the table at Commander Kelly, the intelligence officer, who returned his gaze with a look that said their suspicions had just been further confirmed.

"And this business about the location of the fire," Boone said, returning his attention to Garmisch. "You told me over the radio that it didn't make sense to you."

"That's correct, sir. I don't know if I spoke to the same officer as Lieutenant Commander Hammond did, but if the fire's where they said it was, in aux one, then it would pose no threat to the flight deck or JP-five refueling station."

"You've already told me you think that report on the fire's location was intentionally incorrect." Boone's voice hardened. "Why do you think they told us something patently inaccurate?"

Garmisch did not answer immediately. When he did speak, he chose his words carefully. "I think it, along with the bizarre statement they made to the helo, are a way of telling us that something has gone wrong on that ship, something they're not free to talk about."

"You think the officer you talked to on the radio was under duress?" Lacey asked.

'I'm not sure, sir. But there are too many things going on out there that don't make sense. I've seen major shipboard fires before, and if there's one on the *Bulkeley* it's cleaner and more convenient than any I've ever encountered."

"What do you mean by 'convenient'?" The captain of the *Pascagoula* asked.

"Just this, Captain. This fire has severed every means of contact we'd ordinarily have with the ship. It's so severe that they lose all comms and tell their helo to ditch, yet they're able to make twenty-five knots good through the water, or they were until recently."

"They're back up to speed," Commander Barnum interjected. "Deadline reported they started making way again about twenty minutes ago."

Vargas shook his head in amazement. "It doesn't make any sense."

"It may," the Admiral said, a determined note entering his voice. "Tell them what we just got from the *Daniels*, Bob."

The Chief of Staff turned in his seat so that everyone in the mess could hear him.

"Fifteen minutes ago I had a conversation with the CO of the *Daniels* on the Command Net. He's in the eastern Gulf, going hell-bent-for-leather to catch up to the *Bulkeley*. It seems that at about thirteen thirty, he literally ran into a swarm of Zodiac rubber boats, similar to the ones we have on Apollo for special operations." He looked over at the two officers in the extra chairs. Their added interest was obvious in their faces. "Thing is, these boats were unmanned, apparently abandoned. When the *Daniels* recovered them with grapnels, they found they were equipped with special silenced electric motors." Lacey paused to let the information sink in. "All that would be bizarre," he continued, "but not overly disturbing, except for what they found in one of the boats." He paused again for dramatic effect. "One boat had two crates stacked in it. The crates were each packed with one hundred pounds of C-four or some similar plastique."

The SEAL officer let out a low whistle. "That is one helluva lot of bang," he said.

"Agreed," Boone said. "But what's most disturbing about this is these boats were found right along the track of the *Bulkeley*, in waters she had earlier passed through." The Admiral looked across at Kelly and gave him an almost imperceptible nod. They had agreed to talk the other officers through all the evidence and let them convince themselves of its validity.

"Ship seizure," Kelly said flatly. All the officers turned to look at the youthful commander. "You've got a ship seizure."

"I think so," the Admiral said softly.

The flag mess grew very quiet.

Boone turned to Garmisch. "You've been pushing the idea of the *Bulkeley*'s vulnerability all along, Jim. But I don't think I would have bought this without the last piece of evidence you found on your trip out there." He gestured to the assembled officers. "Go ahead; tell them."

As the staff officers listened with rapt attention, Garmisch described the distress signal he had seen painted on the *Bulkeley*. He repeated his belief that all the evidence pointed to the frigate's having been seized by the Iranians.

"But this doesn't make any sense," Barnum said, breaking the silence following Garmisch's remarks. "Why would someone snatch the *Bulkeley* and then drive her back to Bahrain, right into our hands? Besides, where are the ransom demands, the trumpeting to the press?"

"You're right, it doesn't conform to the scenarios we envisioned for this sort of thing," Kelly said. "But if you put all the evidence together, from the lost comms to the painted distress signal and the abandoned Zodiacs, it matches up with what we've feared could happen, and with the tactics we believed they would use."

"But what's their motive?" Lacey asked. "They've already got the means to humiliate us royally. Why on earth would they be bringing the ship here?"

"I'm not certain," the Admiral said, satisfied that the assembled officers had accepted the *Bulkeley*'s seizure as a fact. "My job— our job—is to get her back. We'll let the other elephants and the intel types puzzle out the Iranians' motivation," he said, using the popular slang for his fellow flag officers and high-ranking politicians. "What's important to us at the tactical level is the fact that, for whatever reason, they're driving the ship right into our own backyard. I've just been on the Command Circuit to CENT-COM and JCS, and they're going to brief the President and the National Security Council within the hour. I've got the go ahead form CENTCOM to plan a rescue mission—but not to go any further forward until we get confirmation from the White House."

"I hope they move relatively quickly," Lacey said. "At twenty-five knots, *Bulkeley* will be here in about six hours."

"After dark," the SEAL officer said quietly. "That's good. It will make things a lot easier."

"In some respects," the Admiral said. He looked first at Kelly and then at Lieutenant Commander Fraser, seated beside the SEAL. Fraser had remained silent thus far. "I know we've planned for this contingency, and your people have practiced for it, Paul. What exactly will you need for a counterstrike?"

Fraser, his face lined and deeply tanned from months of service on the exposed deck of Barge Apollo, thought carefully before answering. He had been considering just that question ever since the Admiral had directed him and Lieutenant Beach to get to the flagship on the double.

"The main thing I'll need, Admiral, is the use of the Blackhawk. We've trained with the Army aircrew, and they know what the SEALs require. I've got the boats and the equipment at Apollo to handle the rest."

"Where will you intercept them?" Captain Vargas asked.

Fraser looked over at Lieutenant Beach before responding. "We'll hit them in the channel, Captain. They'll have to slow down on their way in because of the traffic and small boats."

"What if they don't slow down?" Lacey asked.

Fraser shrugged. "Then it becomes a little tougher, but not impossible." He looked down at his watch. "We can be back on Apollo and start briefing our people in thirty minutes. When we're set, no later than seventeen hundred, I'll need the Blackhawk on deck on Apollo to coordinate with Lieutenant Beach and the SEAL det."

"Without appearing too negative," Captain Vargas interrupted, "and with all due respect to the SEALs and Spec Boat boys—what if there's a problem and they aren't able to retake the ship?" Vargas looked directly at the Admiral. "I feel pretty exposed sitting here at anchor, Admiral."

"I understand that, Ben. And you raise an issue we haven't resolved." Boone looked at Kelly. "What were all those explosives doing in that Zodiac boat?"

"Some of our projections show that the Iranians might try to sink one of our ships outright, if they ever seized one," Commander Kelly answered grimly. "That could explain all the plastique."

"But why would they abandon the boats?" Lacey asked, growing frustrated by all the questions for which they lacked answers.

Kelly paused to consider his answer. Before he could respond, Garmisch spoke up.

"From the description that the Daniels gave, it sounds like the Zodiacs were probably lost to the Iranians by accident. You wouldn't think they'd want the boats drifting around to provide us with any clues. Maybe they didn't intend to leave the explosives in the boat."

"We've no way of knowing for sure," the Admiral said. "But losing the boats and the explosives doesn't seem to have derailed them from their intent to bring the ship here."

Captain Vargas had been listening to the theoretical discussion and growing more concerned with each passing minute. Finally, he decided to speak his mind.

"Admiral," he began, trying to keep the concern out of his

voice, "from what Commander Kelly says, it's not unlikely that the Iranians would want to blow up the *Bulkeley*."

Boone nodded in agreement.

"But if that's their intent," Vargas continued, "why would they bring her all the way here, running the risk of being stopped?" Vargas paused and then spoke again before the Admiral could respond. "Admiral, what if they intend to use the *Bulkeley* as some kind of . . . seagoing car bomb?"

The question was met with silence from Boone, who stared hard at the *Pascagoula*'s captain as he considered the man's lethal hypothesis. The Admiral turned to Kelly; his tone was grave.

"What about it, Bill? Have we ever had any indication they might try something like that?"

"There's no intelligence to support it, Admiral. But then we never anticipated they would seize a ship and drive it to Bahrain, either. Most suicide-commando–type actions are carried out by individuals acting alone. It's hard to imagine they could recruit the number of men sufficient to seize and hold a ship who were all willing to die."

Boone pondered Kelly's answer for a moment before he spoke again.

"It's a fantastic scenario, but as you've said, we're already dealing with a situation we never imagined would happen. All right, Ed," he said, turning to Captain Vargas, "be ready to get under way in two hours. I'm not willing to risk sending you out into the channel, where you might encounter *Bulkeley* in an even more confined position. But we won't leave you as a sitting duck, either." He turned to the Chief of Staff. "Get ahold of *Manchester* at pierside, and tell them I want them under way no later than eighteen hundred. If need be, they can screen *Pascagoula* from the *Bulkeley*."

"It may be tight, Admiral. I'm not sure where they're at in their repairs."

"*Manchester*—under way by eighteen hundred," Boone said to Lacey in a voice that brooked no argument. The Admiral turned to Beach and Fraser, who appeared anxious to be on their way back to Barge Apollo.

"Before you go, gentlemen, I'll need a detailed brief of your assault plan." Boone looked off into the middle distance. "I'll probably be briefing the President in the next couple of hours," he mused.

"Yes sir," Lieutenant Beach responded for both officers. "And, Admiral," he added, "the SEALS won't fail you."

Boone responded with a grim smile.

"You'd better not, son, because I may have to have the *Manchester* blow that ship out of the water if you do."

THE BULKELEY

Stewart watched the flat surface of the Gulf as the *Bulkeley* followed the track of the sun across it. West; they were still headed west to Bahrain—but why? He was certain that the destination held the key to the Iranians' plan. Whatever their goal was in seizing the *Bulkeley*, it seemed it could only be completed in Bahrain. Accepting that as a fact, Stewart decided that he did not need to know precisely why the Iranians wanted to take the *Bulkeley* to Bahrain. What mattered was that to defeat their purpose he would have to stop the ship before it reached Bahrain Harbor. The crewmen who had briefly immobilized the ship from Main Control had had the right idea, he thought. Their only mistake had been in not irreparably damaging the engineering control systems. To stop the Iranians, he knew he would have to find a way to permanently cripple the mobility of the ship. But how to do that without his actions resulting in the death of more of the crew?

Stewart wished he could have been a fly on the bulkhead—a fly that spoke Farsi—and listened in to Aziz and Kalil's recent conversation on the bridgewing. Whatever they had discussed was apparently so critical that speaking in Farsi was not safeguard enough. No, Stewart thought, whatever the topic had been, the two men did not even dare to speak of it in front of their own people. He was still puzzling over this when he saw the big marine, the one Aziz called the Sergeant Major, appear out of the ladder trunk. Stewart was taken aback when Kim emerged, following the marine up the ladder. He could see her wrists had been bound with plastic carseals; with her arms tied in front of her, she had to move carefully to work her way up the ladder. She looked pale but appeared otherwise unharmed.

Rafsani waited for her to reach the bridge and then led the way to where Aziz and Kalil waited at the chart table. As she crossed the bridge, squinting from the transition from the ship's dim internal lighting, her eyes found Stewart. She gasped when she saw him and froze in her tracks. Kim tried to move toward him, a smile breaking over her face, but Rafsani stepped between them. He took her arm and steered her toward Aziz's position at the chart table. Kim looked back at Stewart and was about to speak when she caught the short urgent shake of his head urging her not to address him. Stewart followed her with his eyes; he tried to keep an expression of recognition or sympathy from his face, but he knew Aziz would not have missed her reaction. It was already bad enough without the Iranians realizing he and Kim had a special relationship. As Kim reached the chart table, still in Rafsani's grasp, Aziz turned and beckoned Stewart to join them. Reluctantly, he moved to the chart table.

Aziz said something in Farsi to Rafsani, who nodded in acknowledgment and left the bridge. The Major turned his attention to Kim, who stood facing Kalil and himself across the narrow chart table. Stewart stood at the corner of the table, between them. Stewart saw Aziz muster a faint smile as he addressed Kim.

"So, Miss Mitchell, Stew-urt tells us you are a journalist?"

Kim looked at Stewart briefly before answering. Don't give them anything to use, Stewart groaned inwardly.

"Yes," she answered carefully. "With World Network News."

Aziz looked at Kalil before continuing. The other Iranian had a look of discomfort on his face, as if he felt the conversation was a waste of time.

"I understood the presence of the other journalists. That is a caprice of God's will. But you being on board—a woman—that is most extraordinary."

Kim remained silent. It was difficult for her to keep her eyes on the Iranian and not turn to Stewart. He was alive—thank God! She was not sure if she was supposed to respond to the Major or where this was all leading.

Aziz continued, speaking to her but looking at Stewart. "Why did you not surrender when I called for an end to resistance over the public address system?" His smile remained in place, but his tone was dangerous. "You are not a soldier, yet you have resisted us," Aziz continued when Kim did not answer immediately. "I believe the noncombatant status normally granted journalists has been invalidated by your actions." Aziz leaned across the table toward her. "You took part in the attack on the Main Control, yes?"

Kim did not look at Stewart this time. She could see no point in trying to avoid facts that were already known to the Iranians.

"Yes. I took part." She met the Major's gaze evenly.

"And many men died," Aziz said immediately on the heels of her answer. "Many Americans, and one of my men. And you accomplished nothing! Nothing but more death."

"I—"

But Aziz did not let her continue. "What has become of the big sailor, the one who killed my man near the berthing compartments?" he demanded. Stewart noted that Kalil's interest seemed to sharpen at this question.

"I don't know what you mean," Kim answered defensively. "There were only the two of us; just Andy and me."

Aziz looked at Kalil. Rafsani had been right! The review of the dead and wounded in Main Control had not turned up anyone who matched the man he had been tracking. The only one strong enough to fit the profile of the renegade sailor was the black, whom Rafsani had killed. But that sailor had been in Main Control all along. The Sergeant Major had been correct to want to resume his search immediately.

"Then you claim to know nothing of this other American sailor?" Aziz continued.

"There were only the two of us," Kim repeated. Then she went on the offensive herself. "The sailor who was with me—did you kill him?" she asked Aziz.

The Major did not respond immediately. He looked briefly at Stewart before returning his eyes to Kim. "I do not know if your friend lives," Aziz said quietly. "Everyone in that place, save you, is either dead or terribly wounded."

Kim looked down at the table.

Aziz turned again to Stewart. "So, Stew-urt, what would you have us do with Miss Mitchell?"

Stewart kept his eyes fixed on Aziz, forcing himself to remain impassive. His fear that Aziz had picked up on Kim's reaction had been confirmed.

"You said this was a military operation," Stewart responded coldly. "This woman is protected under the Geneva Convention provisions regarding journalists as neutrals."

"Ah, yes," Aziz countered, cutting Stewart off. "But she has freely confessed to taking part in a combat action against our forces." The Major paused for emphasis. "Clearly not the action of a neutral party."

Aziz kept his eyes locked on Stewart's. The man showed, or tried to show, no emotion for the woman or her fate. Perhaps he tried a little too hard, Aziz thought.

"I think we will keep Miss Mitchell with us on the bridge," the Major said finally. "And if Stew-urt pursues any thoughts of being uncooperative, the woman's life will be immediately forfeit."

12

THE <u>BULKELEY</u>

Mosopu was pleased with Andy's more regular breathing. He shifted in his position on the bench in the repair locker so as to be better able to watch both Andy and the watertight door to the locker. He winced as he stretched his leg out from the bench, a stab of pain reminding him that the young engineer was not the only one who was wounded.

Mosopu could see that Andy was either unconscious or dozing. He had nodded off after the Bosun's Mate had finished bandaging his wound. Mosopu had been glad to find that the first-aid kit was as well stocked as he had remembered. Propping Andy up against a pile of fire-fighting coveralls, he had cut off the young sailor's shirt with his knife. The wound that was revealed looked terrible, but Mosopu did not think it was too deep. Andy was no longer bleeding very much, and Mosopu had spread an antiseptic cream over the wound before wrapping the sailor's chest in a large athletic-bandage–type of battle dressing. It was the best he could do.

They had reached the repair locker without event. Mosopu had been tremendously relieved to find that the starboard passageway around the missile magazine had not been blocked by explosives. Still, it had taken a fair amount of contortion for him to get through the narrow opening with Andy in his arms. Mosopu had stopped just short of the door leading to the repair locker and set Andy down on the deck. Then he had cautiously moved forward, expecting that he would encounter an Iranian near the locker or the armory. Mosopu had been surprised to find both spaces unguarded; he had been particularly baffled by the absence of a sentry at the armory. Didn't they know he had been trying to break into it? Puzzled but not displeased by the lack of enemy presence in the area, he had returned to Andy and carried him inside the repair locker.

As Andy lay on the deck, his back propped up by the coveralls, Mosopu stared at him and contemplated what to do next. It was obvious to the Bosun's Mate that Andy would be unable to move anytime soon. Whatever Mosopu did, he would have to do on his own. He stared at the exothermic cutter on its rack at the back of the locker. That had been the first thing he had looked for upon entering the locker, even before trying to find the first-aid kit.

Carrying and operating the device by himself would be no easy task. The oxygen bottle alone appeared to weigh over a hundred pounds. The cutter itself was remarkably simple in operation. A hose ran from the oxygen bottle to a five-foot rod of rolled mild steel, which was the core of the cutter; a sleeve blew oxygen down the length of the one-inch rod to its very end. By turning on the oxygen and sparking the separate igniter at the end of the rod, the tip of the cutter would burst into superhot flame. As long as the oxygen kept coming and the rod did not burn all the way down, the cutter could burn through just about anything on the ship. Mosopu remembered the demonstration he had seen where the chief hull technician had sliced through an eight-inch beam with the cutter as if it were damp cardboard.

Mosopu knew that once he got the cutter going he would have no trouble cutting into either the coops or the armory—but which one to break into first? His heart told him to go free his shipmates immediately; the last thing he wanted was to have the means of saving them and not use it in time. But then he considered what would happen if he freed them and the Iranians found him out before he could get back to the armory and provide his shipmates with arms. The coops were also in a more open, heavily traveled part of the ship; discovery there would be more likely than at the relatively remote armory. Having weighed the two options carefully, he made up his mind. He would cut into the armory first and take as many weapons aft to the coops as he could carry. It would mean a second trip back for the cutter, but this way he could immediately arm some of the crew when he freed them.

He also wanted to get his hands on another shotgun. He thought he understood how the strange Iranian gun worked, but he would be far more happy with a weapon he knew.

Mosopu rose from the bench, looking down at Andy. Deciding not to try to wake him, he slung the Sterling over his shoulder and moved to the cutter rack. Fortunately, the cutter's oxygen bottle had been placed in a carrying harness. With a low grunt, Mosopu hefted it onto his back. He stuffed the igniter into his belt and picked up the rolled steel rod, which was surprisingly light. Lastly, the Bosun's Mate picked up the shotgun from where he'd leaned it against an equipment rack.

With one last look at Andy, resting near the rear of the space, Mosopu headed for the door. As he was about to set down the shotgun to open the watertight door, Mosopu stopped and reflected on something he had not previously considered. Turning, he crossed the locker back to where Andy slept. As gently as he could, the big Samoan lay the twelve-gauge across the wounded sailor's lap. Andy stirred uneasily but did not wake up.

The large search party that Rafsani commanded had made its way from the stern of the ship forward to Main Control, with no sign of its quarry.

Having reached Main Control and methodically searched all the area aft, the Sergeant Major detached one of the Revolutionary Guards from the search team to double the manpower guarding the critical space. That meant there were now two men in the officers' wardroom, two on the bridge with the Major and Kalil, and two in Main Control. Rafsani had lost so much time with his assault on Main Control that he had felt the only possible way of finding the missing American would be to take every available man and search the ship from end to end, space by space.

He had sent Nefud to gather the other marines, who were not really needed outside the welded-up berthing compartments, and bring them to him on the flight deck. The Americans from Radio Central and the Combat Information Center had been placed in the berthing compartments an hour ago, before the compartments had been sealed, to eliminate the need for sentries in those spaces. Rafsani had even pulled his sentry from the armory, having seen how impossible its lock was to penetrate without explosives.

With a series of simple directions, he outlined the next phase of the search to his remaining men. They would operate in three teams, as before, with sergeants Nefud and Eslam each leading a team and Rafsani taking the third. Rafsani elected to take the bulk of the Guards with him on his team. He directed Eslam to proceed into the superstructure and search, moving steadily forward. Nefud would search the belowdecks engineering spaces and the dining and galley areas. Rafsani would have preferred to search the engineering spaces himself; there were too many good places to hide, but he knew he should cover the main and weather deck areas so that he was effectively in the middle of the search. If something went wrong, or the American was discovered, it would be far easier for his men to find Rafsani if he was searching just one deck above or below them.

Rafsani's orders, should they encounter the American, were brutal and precise. "Do not wait to notify me," he told them, "hit him immediately with guns, grenades—everything you have." He reminded them that the American had killed Harare as if snapping a branch. He could see in the faces of his men that his last statement had provided the motivation he desired in them.

Deciding to strike a medium between thoroughness and speed, Rafsani directed his men to take no more than thirty minutes in this next leg of the search. They would rendezvous at the starboard ladder trunk into the berthing compartments at 1600.

Stewart looked across the bridge to where Aziz and Kalil stood talking at the chart table before he continued to speak. Kim stood beside him on the port side of the bridge. Aziz had cut off the restraints, and she was slowly rubbing her wrists to speed the return of circulation.

"They don't seem to care if we talk to each other," Stewart said, turning away from the chart table to minimize the distance his low voice carried.

Kim looked at the Iranian officers, who continued to ignore

them, and at the other two gunmen posted in opposite rear corners of the bridge, before responding.

"I guess they don't consider us to be much of a threat," she
said, under her breath.

"That, or they figure the best way to ensure my cooperation is
to keep me reminded of you," he paused. "And what they're
willing to do to you."

She turned to find him staring at her. Stewart quickly looked
away, out the bridge windows.

"I can't believe you took part in the fighting." His voice held a
mixture of surprise and disbelief. He turned back to her. "What
happened to your famous objectivity? Taking a side isn't really
your style, is it?" He was sorry for the words before he had finished saying them.

Kim watched him in silence for a moment. Stewart knew that
he had hurt her and found that he was ashamed.

"Sorry you think so little of me," she said quietly. "I know it's
not what you expected, but I had to do something. Watching
things happen wasn't enough." She glanced briefly toward Aziz
and Kalil. "What are you going to do, John?"

"You heard what Aziz said," Stewart replied, his voice a harsh
whisper. "I try anything, and they'll kill you."

"Now I'm surprised." Her tone held a faint edge of sarcasm. "I
thought you put the welfare of your ship ahead of everything."
Kim's tone softened. "You've got to do what's best for the ship.
After what we've seen so far, I'm not sure any of us is going to
survive this unless we keep fighting back."

Stewart continued to look straight ahead.

"Do you know who the other sailor is they were asking me
about?" she asked.

"Not for certain. I have a hunch it might be one of our Bosun's
Mates. He's missing from this watch team, and he definitely fits
the description of the kind of guy they're searching for."

Kim looked down at the deck. "I hope I didn't compromise him
when I told them he wasn't with us at Main Control. He may be
our only chance."

"You just confirmed something they seemed to know already."

Stewart turned to look back at the chart table. Aziz was watching them. After a few seconds of staring at Stewart, he shifted his

attention back to the chart before him and resumed his conversation with Kalil. Stewart continued to look at the two men, but his
focus was now on the chart they were studying.

Stewart turned back to the bridge windows. "Mosopu's not our
only chance," he said to Kim. "Listen carefully to what I say. If I
get the opportunity I'm looking for, you're going to have to react
quickly. There won't be any time for questions."

THE PASCAGOULA

The Tactical Decision Center on board the flagship was a maze of
activity. The normal staff watch had been almost tripled to deal
with tactical control of the operation at hand. Operations specialists maintained a running update on the tactical plot of the positions of *Bulkeley, Daniels,* and every other American unit that could
possibly be employed in the current situation. Every table and
console in the TDC was occupied by COM JTF staff members planning or coordinating some phase of the operation. Garmisch and
two other staff officers spoke animatedly on separate radio circuits. Every few minutes petty officers would hustle into the space
with fresh message traffic concerning the *Bulkeley.*

Garmisch finished his radio conversation and replaced the
handset in its cradle. He stopped for a brief moment and marveled
at the furious activity around him. They had just received the go-
ahead from the President, via the Joint Chiefs, to execute the
rescue mission on the *Bulkeley.* Not a lot of time to put this one
together, he mused. As he walked across the TDC through the
organized chaos of the staff, Garmisch was secretly proud that
they were responding so well with so little time to plan and execute their mission. We've got to get this right the first time, he
thought to himself.

Admiral Boone sat quietly in the center of the front row of
ready-room chairs that were set back and slightly above the deck
of the TDC. Seated beside Boone, the Chief of Staff was plowing
through an inch-thick stack of messages. As Garmisch reached
the Admiral's side, he saw Lacey stop shuffling the papers, apparently having come upon the one he sought.

"I knew I kept this," he said turning to Boone. "This is the background message, Admiral. We got this in about three months ago. I've highlighted the pertinent parts." He handed the message to Boone.

Boone read the marked paragraph aloud, raising his voice slightly to be heard above the din around him.

" 'Resumption of Tanker War makes it likely that Iran will employ ship-boarding-and-seizure teams against Iraqi-Allied merchant shipping. Last use of this tactic observed in eighty-seven–eighty-eight Tanker War.' " Boone skipped several lines giving the dates of the seizures and the names of the ships involved. " 'Boarding-search-and-seizure teams were composed of Iranian Marine commando forces assigned to Southern Command. Boarding-seizures were carried out by both helicopter and small-boat delivery of IRMC teams. This capability is presumed to remain operational.' " Boone handed the message back to Lacey. "Well, that gives us a pretty good idea of who we're up against."

The Chief of Staff nodded in agreement.

Boone thought for a moment and then turned again to Lacey. "Get on the secure circuit to Apollo, Bob. I don't know if this will have any impact on Fraser and Beach's tactics, but we better let them know who the likely opposition is."

"Roger, Admiral." Lacey got up and headed to the nearby bank of radios.

Garmisch addressed the Admiral as the Chief of Staff departed.

"I just got off the horn with Captain Walker on the *Manchester*, Admiral. He's been able to re-call most of the portion of his crew that was on liberty. He says he'll be under way at seventeen thirty at about ninety percent manning."

"All right," Boone said. "That'll have to do."

Garmisch was preparing to speak again when the sounds of the TDC were drowned by the loud, foghornlike blast of the *Pascagoula*'s whistle.

Boone smiled. "Sounds like we're under way."

"Where's Captain Vargas headed with the ship, Admiral?"

"He's going to alternate between trying to hover, maintaining position as much as possible, and making a low-speed crisscross of the harbor." Boone shifted his gaze from Garmisch to a large-scale chart of Bahrain Harbor and its approach channel that had been posted on a nearby bulkhead. "The harbor is plenty big, and the Bahrainis tell us there's not much traffic due in or out of here today. My only specific guidance to Captain Vargas is to stay well clear of the tanker anchorage in the eastern corner of the harbor. We don't want *Pascagoula* getting wedged in against the tankers by *Bulkeley.*"

"That's what I need to ask you about, Admiral. The *Manchester's* CO understands that you want him to try to stay between *Pascagoula* and the *Bulkeley*, but he wants to know under what circumstances he's supposed to actually engage her."

Boone's face took on a somber appearance. He looked up at Garmisch.

"Tell Captain Walker that he is not to let the *Bulkeley* get closer to his own ship or to *Pascagoula* than two thousand yards. If *Bulkeley* gets that far into the harbor, it means the counterstrike has failed. I may direct him to engage sooner than that, but under no circumstances is he to allow them to come within two thousand yards."

"Aye, sir. His only other question was how far you want him to go in stopping her—if it comes to that."

Boone looked back across the TDC to the tactical plot showing the *Bulkeley's* current position.

"If . . . it comes to that," he said carefully, "a mission kill against her weapons and antennas won't be enough. We have to assume the ship is a floating bomb. Tell him he's to use force adequate to stop the ship—dead in the water."

USS MANCHESTER

The captain's cabin on board the *Manchester* was a mirror image of the one on the *Bulkeley*, but for the recently plugged hole in the starboard bulkhead where an Iranian bullet had caromed harmlessly into the stateroom when the frigate had been attacked. The *Manchester's* captain stared absently at the plugged hole from his seat at his desk as he waited for the last of his department heads to arrive.

Captain Walker, the commanding officer of the *Manchester*, was senior to the average frigate CO and had in fact been recently promoted to full captain. His round face and nearly constant smile gave him the fatherly appearance much beloved by his crew. But as his officers and chief petty officers knew only too well, underneath that warm exterior was a man ruthless in his determination that his ship and crew be the best in the Navy.

Manchester's executive officer, seated in a chair near the captain, shifted his eyes nervously from the two officers on the adjacent couch to the door into the captain's cabin. Come on, Cheng, he thought to himself, get your ass up here before the old man blows. The XO stole a quick look at the captain, who wore his perennial, unreadable smile.

There was a sharp knock at the captain's door, followed almost immediately by the entrance into the room of the chief engineer.

"Sorry I'm late, Captain," the engineer said, as he crossed the deck to join the other two department heads on the couch. "We hadn't expected to have to reassemble that lube oil pump on such short notice. We're op-testing it now."

Walker made no acknowledgment of the chief engineer's remarks. He waited until the last officer was seated and then spun in his chair to face the assembled men directly. The smile remained rigidly fixed on his face.

"You all know we've been directed by COM JTF to be under way within the hour," he began. "But what you don't know is why. What I'm going to tell you does not leave this room." He paused, knowing he had their complete attention. "Our sister ship, the *Bulkeley*," he said, drawing the sentence out for effect, "has been seized by the Iranians."

During the silence that followed his announcement, Walker looked quickly from face to face and saw that each of the men was equally dumbfounded.

"Captain . . . how could that happen?" the operations officer asked disbelievingly.

"COM JTF is not sure of all the facts. But they believe Iranian military forces boarded her covertly in the eastern Gulf. Even more amazing is that the Iranians appear to be bringing her to Bahrain." Walker sank back into his chair to let this sink in.

"But that's crazy, Captain," the executive officer said cautiously. "They grabbed the ship to bring it to Bahrain? That makes no sense at all."

"It makes plenty of sense—if their objective is to blow up the *Bulkeley* and take *Pascagoula* and COM JTF with her," Walker said flatly. Seeing in their faces the dozens of questions forming in his officers' minds, Walker decided to proceed to the core of the situation.

"There are a great many unknowns about this whole thing, but what we do know for certain are our orders. We're to get under way and screen the flagship from the *Bulkeley*." He paused again, as the other officers watched him expectantly. "There will be an attempt by the SEALS and the Special Boat forces to recapture the *Bulkeley*. Failing that, we are to engage her before she can get close enough to damage either *Pascagoula* or ourselves."

"COM JTF thinks the ship is wired to explode?" the chief engineer asked.

"That's the supposition, yes."

"But what if it isn't, Captain? What if the Iranians are bringing *Bulkeley* here in a hostage situation to humiliate us . . . or for some unknown reason?"

"I don't see how that matters one way or the other," the captain replied, his smile dimming slightly.

The chief engineer looked at the other officers before continuing.

"My point, sir, is that if the rescue fails and we open up on the *Bulkeley*, we may be killing plenty of our own people who wouldn't otherwise die."

Every man in the room knew personally a number of the *Bulkeley*'s crew. Walker could see the chief engineer's statement had brought the thought of those men home to his officers.

"That cannot be our concern," the captain said briskly. "We have our orders from COM JTF, made on the best information available to the staff. I will not try to second-guess the Admiral." He scanned the seated men before continuing. "*Manchester* has her mission—and *Manchester* will carry out that mission." Before another question could be asked, Walker turned to the combat systems officer.

"You'll be tactical action officer, Joe, with the XO taking my spot in CIC. I'm going to be on the bridge. This is one situation where what I can see visually will be more important than what the radars tell me."

The combat systems officer nodded slowly. "How do you want to take her out—if we have to, Captain?" he asked.

Walker thought for a moment; a distant look came into his eyes. "Our orders are to disable her so she can't get close enough to *Pascagoula* or ourselves to take us with her if she blows. We're likely to be pretty close to her when we get the order." He looked directly at the combat systems officer. "If we're told to engage her at a range beyond five miles, we'll use Standard missiles, backed up by the gun. If she's closer than that and we can choose our target more precisely, I want to use the seventy-six-millimeter on her engineering spaces and rudder. And one more thing; if she gets that close, I want the chain gun to sweep her bridge."

THE <u>BULKELEY</u>

Mosopu held the tip of the cutter away from him as the steel rod ignited with a *whoosh*. Once he had turned on the flow of oxygen it had taken only one jolt from the igniter to spark the cutter into operation. Lowering into place the protective goggles he had brought from the locker, he advanced on the armory door, the burning rod held at arm's length.

At first Mosopu had trouble making out the location of the high-security lock through the intense white-blue flame and billowing exhaust of the torch. He was forced to direct the cutter away from the door so he could get a clear view of the lock. The flame at the end of the rod was not much greater in diameter than the rod itself. It stood out from the end of the cutter approximately twelve inches, looking like the exhaust from a jet fighter on afterburner. When he was satisfied that he could locate the lock through the cutter's fiery brightness, Mosopu swung the rod back into position over the hasp.

He moved the cutter slowly down the length of the lock, an inch at a time, as he had seen done at the demonstration. He hoped the fumes given off by the burning metal were not toxic, as they were slowly filling the space. His vision was obscured enough by the cutter's light so that he could barely see the outline of the lock, and he was surprised when he had almost reached the bottom of the bulky lock and nothing had happened.

With a grinding screech like the sound of a train putting on its brakes, the lock seemed to shiver and then explode into pieces. Mosopu reached down and turned off the oxygen supply. The exothermic cutter extinguished almost immediately, its tip glowing red in the haze of the passageway. Fanning the air to clear the fumes, the Bosun's Mate lifted his goggles to verify that the lock was destroyed. Fragments of the lock and hasp lay smoking on the deck.

Mosopu moved quickly. He set the still-cooling torch down on an adjacent scuttle to keep it off the deck. Looking around him, he was relieved to see that the ship's internal ventilation system was making short work of the cutter's exhaust gases, and the passageway's atmosphere was rapidly returning to normal. Stepping across the remnants of the fractured lock, Mosopu grasped what was left of the handle on the heavy steel door and wrenched the door open. The armory light was always left on, and as he stepped into the confined room, the Bosun's Mate's eyes quickly searched out what he sought.

Mosopu had been on enough drills as a shipboard security force member to know what weapons were kept in the armory and how much ready-service ammunition was stored there as well. On his left, a stand-up rack held five twelve-gauge shotguns and three M-14 rifles. Then he remembered the locking bar. As a means of secondary security, the weapons in the rack—in fact, all the weapons in the armory—were kept under separate lock. There was a steel bar running across the top of the rack holding the long guns in place; a heavy brass padlock secured the bar to the rack. Mosopu looked back out the armory door at the still-glowing cutter. But using the superheated rod in a space filled with ammunition could be suicidal, he knew. Besides, his aim with the cutter was relatively crude, and he feared he might damage the guns in the process of freeing them. Then he remembered the axe.

Stepping out of the armory, he rapidly scanned the deck until he found it. The fire axe was where he had discarded it after his fruitless earlier attempt to open the lock on the armory door. Mosopu scooped up the broad-bladed axe and went back inside the armory. The fire axe had failed to work on the outer high-security lock, but the rifle rack lock was a toy by comparison. Although he was not able to get in a full swing in the cramped space of the armory, his first blow dented and gouged the lock; his second and third crashing swings sent the battered padlock flying.

Mosopu had known before he broke into the armory what he would take. He pulled four shotguns and one M-14 from the rack. Inside the skin of the ship there was no more lethal weapon than the shotgun, he knew, and the rifle would give them flexibility until he could lead his shipmates back to the armory. He stacked the long guns outside on the deck and reentered the small space. The ready-service ammunition was where it always was, in racks next to the armory door. The shotgun rounds were kept in cloth bags of fifteen, each bag having a shoulder strap that allowed it to be worn like a bandolier. Mosopu swathed himself in more than a dozen of these bags and stuffed four M-14 magazines into his belt.

He stepped back out into the passageway and slung the M-14 over his shoulder, rearranging the ammo bags to make room for it. Then he put the Sterling over his opposite shoulder and stooped to gather two shotguns under each burly arm. Mosopu was not completely happy when he had hefted all the weapons. He knew he had optimized himself for transport, but severely limited himself if he encountered any of the Iranians before he could unburden himself of his load.

Deciding there was no other way, Mosopu headed off awkwardly toward the coops, leaving the exothermic cutter in the armory passageway behind him.

BARGE APOLLO

"That's it. Anybody have any questions?"

Fraser stood at the front of the medium-size aluminum shed that passed for a briefing space and classroom on Barge Apollo.

Behind him on the bulkhead were two large-scale charts, one of Bahrain Harbor and its approaches, and a second showing a detailed schematic of the *Bulkeley*. Lieutenant Beach sat at a small table beside Fraser. The remainder of the shed was densely packed with personnel from the different highly specialized units that were stationed on the barge. All the extra bodies had brought the room temperature up to ninety degrees, and two large window air conditioners worked futilely to try to cool the space.

One of those present, a senior petty officer clad in oil-stained green coveralls, rose from his folding chair.

"I've got a question, Skipper. When do you want our boats to break off?"

Fraser turned to the chart of Bahrain Harbor.

"That'll happen on my command—but no later than here." He pointed to a spot near the anchorage area. *Pascagoula* was represented by a marker close to the location Fraser had pointed out. "By the time she's reached this point, either the SEALs will have her, or it becomes a problem for the *Manchester*."

"And for the SEALs," interjected a youngish petty officer wearing a black SEAL warfare device on his camouflage shirt. The assembled men broke into laughter.

Beach rose from his chair, smiling darkly. He joined Fraser beside the charts.

"We don't plan for failure," the SEAL officer said. "But we do plan a way to fight our way out of anything we fight our way into." The smile left his face. "As Lieutenant Commander Fraser said, he and I will be in continuous radio contact. If for any reason we can't complete the mission prior to this drop-dead point," he said, gesturing to the point Fraser had established, "we'll get off her, with all the crew we can take with us." He scanned the crowd of sailors. "But that's only a fallback—we will complete this mission."

"That brings up another point," Fraser said. "If there's any problem with the Blackhawk, we'll have to shift to the SeaFoxes to do the insertion."

A number of the young petty officers in the group looked at each other, their faces showing a mixture of apprehension and excitement.

"Not that I expect any problem," he continued. "But that helo's the only one available that can do the job. If she craps out, we have to have a backup."

"Vertical insertion or by boat; either way is fine for us," Beach said, scanning the group to make eye contact with each of his seven SEALS. "We've practiced it both ways."

"Right," Fraser echoed. "But let's hope the Blackhawk stays healthy. The aircraft increases our element of surprise." He looked down at his watch. "The helo should be on deck here by seventeen hundred."

A chief quartermaster clad in a short-sleeved camouflage shirt stood up in the back.

"What about ammo, sir? Do we go with our usual patrol mix of AP and tracer rounds?"

"I'm glad you asked that, Chief Raye." Fraser addressed his response to the whole room. "Download your armor-piercing rounds. I want your fifty-cal crews to load a conventional solid-slug and tracer mix. Mark nineteen grenade launchers are to be loaded with fléchette rounds exclusively. Boat captains, ensure you go out with the right load."

"What about the chain guns, Skipper?" another chief, also a boat captain, asked. The Spectre Mark III patrol boats had 25-millimeter cannons as their main armament. The chain gun had a rate of fire of hundreds of rounds a minute, and its high-explosive tracer ammunition could punch holes in the armor of a medium tank.

"Negative on the chain guns, Chief." He spoke again to the entire group. "No boat is to employ its twenty-five-millimeter without hearing the order to do so direct from me, over the radio. What we're out to do here is clear the decks of bad guys, not shoot up the ship. Remember when you're making your run in that there are two hundred of our own people on that ship."

"Do you think the crew is still alive, Skipper?" another petty officer asked.

"I hope so. Someone's keeping the ship going." Fraser turned to Beach. "There's no telling what you and your boys are going to find on board her."

Beach nodded in grim agreement and picked up his small sheaf of papers from the table.

Fraser turned back to the seated men. "That's all. Boat captains, report when you're ready for sea, and no later than eighteen hundred."

As the sailors rose to leave, Beach called out over the screeching chairs and subdued voices, "SEAL det, stand fast. We've got a few additional details to go over."

13

BAHRAIN HARBOR

The tiny island kingdom of Bahrain lies nestled in the cleft formed between the peninsula of Qatar and the mainland of Saudi Arabia, in the western Persian Gulf. The only means of approach to Bahrain by sea is through a narrow channel that begins approximately forty-five miles to the northeast of the island state. The Bahrain Channel is not bounded by land but rather it is a deep-water highway in the Gulf, marked only by an intermittent series of buoys. Shallow-draft fishing and commercial vessels can easily skirt the channel and take more expeditious routes into Bahrain Harbor, but larger ships do so only at their peril. The waters outside the channel are a maze of charted and uncharted shoals, oil rigs, sunken ships, and other obstructions.

The *Pascagoula* steamed slowly across Bahrain Harbor. Her captain kept the ship at bare steerageway, ordering a speed just sufficient to overcome the wind, currents, and pull of tide within the harbor. The flagship's speed of advance was scarcely three knots, and at that speed she had a full hour before having to come about and reverse her track in the harbor. Bahrain Harbor was broad and fairly deep, giving the *Pascagoula* roughly a three-mile-long track she could steam before having to reverse course. Topside on the ship, every weapons station was manned by sailors in flak vests and full battle gear. The flagship's two chain guns were ready for action, as well as her numerous .50-caliber machine guns and lighter weapons. The chain gun, although only a 25-millimeter cannon, was the heaviest armament on board *Pascagoula*. The flagship had been built for command and control and amphibious operations, not for self-defense against other warships.

THE PASCAGOULA

Deep in the heart of the flagship, in the Tactical Decision Center, Garmisch continued his radio conversation with the destroyer *Daniels*.

"Affirmative, *Daniels*. Continue in pursuit of *Bulkeley*. We anticipate she will reduce speed upon entering Bahrain Channel, and you may be able to overtake her then."

The voice of the *Daniels's* commanding officer came back almost immediately through Garmisch's handset and a nearby speaker.

"Roger, COM JTF. I understand we are to close her to within effective gun range but not to engage until directed by you. Is that correct? Over."

Garmisch could detect the incredulous tone of the captain of the *Daniels* over the secure circuit. I still don't really believe it either, Captain, he thought to himself before continuing.

"This is COM JTF. That is correct. Our estimate here is that if *Bulkeley* slows to ten to fifteen knots to navigate the channel, you will close to within five miles of her by nineteen hundred. Over."

"This is *Daniels*. You're basing that on my maintaining thirty knots in the channel? Over." The chaptain's chagrin at having to maintain flank speed in the narrow, often crowded channel was evident in his voice.

"Affirmative, *Daniels*. Bahrain Port Control has directed all incoming merchant traffic to wait out in the Gulf and all outbound shipping to remain at anchor or pierside. You should have the channel to yourself, Captain."

There was a pause, and then the voice from the *Daniels* came back.

"This is *Daniels*. Orders understood. Will report when we have visual on *Bulkeley*. Over."

"This is COM JTF. Roger, out." Garmisch replaced the radio

handset and turned to look across the TDC just as Admiral Boone entered. Garmisch moved to intercept him at the ready-room chairs at the back of the crowded TDC. He reached Boone just as the Admiral was sinking into one of the leather chairs. Boone spoke before Garmisch could make his report, a mischievous smile on his face.

"Just came from the bridge," the Admiral began. "Ed Vargas is none too happy about having to maneuver in such close quarters. I don't think I've seen anybody give as many orders or move from one side of a bridge to the other so quick since the last time the *Nimitz* went through the Malacca Straits."

"Who was the *Nimitz*'s Captain then, Admiral?"

Boone looked up at Garmisch, still smiling. "Me." He chuckled. "Okay, Jim, what's the latest?" he asked, turning serious.

"I just got off the Command Net with *Daniels*, sir. They've rogered your orders, although I don't think the CO's too wild about the idea of transiting the channel at thirty knots."

Boone's smile returned faintly. "That's all right. There's going to have to be a lot of unusual seamanship before the night's over. If it's any comfort to him, I don't think Captain Vargas or Captain Walker are any happier about their situations."

"Yes sir. Speaking of Captain Walker, the *Manchester* just reported themselves at sea detail. They should be under way shortly."

Boone nodded, shifting his attention from Garmisch to the tactical plot board. Petty Officer Fisher had just hurried over to the plot with a list of coordinates in his hand and had begun updating the positions of the various units. Garmisch turned to watch the changes along with the Admiral.

As he moved the last marker, the one representing the *Bulkeley*, Fisher turned and called out to Boone, "Admiral! *Bulkeley*'s just now entering the channel, sir!"

BARGE APOLLO

Fraser kept his waterproof binoculars trained on the frigate as it cut its path through the Gulf. He had watched from his radar shack on Apollo until the radar return showed the *Bulkeley* to be ten miles away. Then he had left the shack and moved to the northeastern corner of the barge to wait for the ship to become visible through the sand.

Barge Apollo's anchored position, four miles south of the entrance to the Bahrain Channel, ensured that the frigate would have to pass by the barge on its way into Bahrain. *Bulkeley* had first become visible at what Fraser judged to be a range of about five miles. That was not so good, he realized. Visibility was improving, and with it the chances that the Iranians would spot his assault force as it approached. But it would be dark then, he knew, or rather twilight. Twilight was the time of poorest visibility at sea. The setting sun and the rising darkness would combine with the haze and the wind-blown sand to create the worst visibility of the day. That was when the assault force would strike.

Fraser watched the *Bulkeley* continue on toward the mouth of the channel. Her closest point of approach to the barge was around four miles, and he wondered if the Iranians on the ship could make out the low, flat silhouette of Apollo through the storm.

The ship gave no sign of reducing speed, and that concerned him. There was always the possibility that *Bulkeley* would careen recklessly down the channel at high speed, the Iranians hoping to minimize their exposure and maximize their element of surprise. If Fraser's radar showed them to be maintaining twenty-five knots, he would have to get his boats under way earlier than he desired. The Mark III patrol boats had a twenty-knot speed advantage on the *Bulkeley*, but he could not allow the gap to grow too wide. The thing he feared most about the *Bulkeley* maintaining high speed was not the need to get his boats under way early; he had prepared for that. But if he was forced to move up the time of the assault, the SEALs would have to attack in the late afternoon light.

If the frigate had taken notice of Barge Apollo, there was no indication. Fraser saw the ship bisect the first pair of channel buoys and continue ahead. He knew that even at twenty-five knots the *Bulkeley* would not reach Bahrain Harbor for close to two hours. Fraser watched *Bulkeley* for another few minutes as the ship passed by and began to recede in the dirty haze of the sand-storm, and then he turned to head back to the radar shack.

As he strode across the steel deck, its reflected heat warming the soles of his combat boots, Fraser looked across at his boats. The three Mark III boats and the three smaller SeaFox patrol boats were covered with sweating sailors, rushing to complete their work. The crews were distinguishable by their open flak jackets and the occasional helmet, but more than half the men on the boats were technicians from the barge making last-minute checks of critical equipment. Enginemen gunned and adjusted the boats' high-performance engines, while electronic technicians verified radio and radar operation and gunner's mates hurried to ensure the correct ammunition loadout. A stranger looking at the fren-zied preparations would have to believe the boats couldn't possi-bly be combat-ready in half an hour—but Fraser knew better.

THE BULKELEY

"This is Lieutenant Commander Stewart. I have the deck and the conn! Right five degrees rudder!"

Aziz and Kalil were still trying to react to Stewart's sudden action—taking over direct control of maneuvering the ship from the officer of the deck—when he turned to yell at them.

"We've got to slow the ship down!"

After entering the channel, *Bulkeley* had narrowly missed strik-ing a radar reflector that Scott Septenano had not seen until it was almost too late. Stewart had realized that the strain of driving the ship for eighteen hours straight had burned out the young officer. The three enlisted watch standers had been able to rotate through the helmsman job and keep some degree of freshness, but there had been no one to relieve the OOD. Stewart knew that in Septen-ano's exhausted state, he was not up to the immediate decisions and precise maneuvers called for at high speed in the narrow channel.

"I'm telling you, we've got to slow her down if you want to make it to Bahrain!" Stewart said harshly. He shifted his gaze from Aziz to look quickly out ahead of the ship and then back at the Major.

"Maintain speed," Aziz said quietly. "You are to maintain speed."

Stewart was about to respond when Septenano's voice called out from behind him.

"You've got a dhow at zero-one-zero relative!"

Stewart spun around to see the small fishing craft appear out of the sand a hundred yards off his starboard bow.

"Left ten degrees rudder!" he ordered. At the *Bulkeley*'s high speed, even the relatively small amount of rudder ordered caused the ship to heel over to port. The Iranians, now a great deal wiser to this sort of thing, immediately clutched at the nearest stationary object. Almost as quickly as the turn was begun, Stewart ordered the rudder back amidships, and the ship steadied up. Aziz and Kalil watched in silence as the wooden dhow passed down the frigate's starboard side, a scant thirty feet away.

Stewart looked at Kim, who had taken up his old spot between the captain's chair and the console, to ensure she had not been knocked off balance by the turn. She had braced herself with her hands flat on the console. Kim gave him a quick smile to reassure him she was all right. Seeing that the water ahead of them was clear for the moment, Stewart turned once again to Aziz.

"I'm not going to tell you again. We've got to slow the ship! There's no one to navigate up here, no bearing takers, nothing. What we're having to do is buoy-hop from one set of channel markers to another. If I miss a buoy because of this shitty visibility, or we make a late turn, this high speed just about guarantees we go out of the channel and run aground!"

Aziz listened to Stewart's tirade in silence. When Stewart finished, the Major glanced briefly at Kalil, who was still clutching the chart table with white knuckles, and then back at Stewart.

"Why should you care if we run aground?" The question was asked in a flat tone, but the suspicion in Aziz's voice was palpable.

Stewart glanced back out the bridge windows before responding.

"Look, Major—or whatever the fuck you are—I don't know what your master plan is, what you're hoping to accomplish, but I do know what'll happen if this ship runs aground or collides with another ship. You've got most of our crew trapped below-decks with no way out. If the ship is holed below the waterline, a lot of my sailors stand to drown." He paused, just long enough to check the channel ahead of the speeding frigate. "Right now, I'm a helluva lot more concerned with keeping this ship afloat and saving the crewmen you haven't butchered yet than I am with what you want in Bahrain." *I hope this is convincing,* he thought to himself.

Aziz stared back at Stewart's angry face, his own an expressionless mask. After a seemingly endless delay, he spoke. "Slow the ship to twenty knots. But we will maintain that speed all the way into Bahrain."

As Stewart was about to give the order, Aziz interrupted him.

"Now it is in your hands whether we run aground and your crew dies or we reach Bahrain Harbor and they live."

Stewart ordered the reduced speed and stalked past Aziz to the chart table. He appeared to study the layout of the channel into Bahrain, but his true focus was on other features of the chart. After a few moments scrutinizing the chart under the watchful eye of Aziz, Stewart turned back to the bridge windows.

He had found the sandbar on the chart—right where he remembered it. The shoal water was just beyond the left side of the channel, a mile short of the entrance to Bahrain Harbor. All it would take would be one hard turn at the speed they were moving. He had the conn, and he would make enough radical maneuvers on the way down the channel to accustom the Iranians to sudden turns. It was a risky plan, with the bulk of the crew trapped belowdecks, but Stewart was willing to gamble that grounding in the soft sand would not hole the ship. The grounding might be perceived as an accident by the Iranians, or the impact might stagger them, enabling himself and the other Americans on the bridge to strike at their captors. Either way, the *Bulkeley* would not enter Bahrain Harbor.

Ignoring the others on the bridge, Stewart searched the water ahead of the ship for the next set of channel markers.

Mosopu struggled forward with the exothermic cutter. The weight of the oxygen bottle was heavy on his shoulders, and he knew his strength was ebbing. His wound and the nearly continuous action of the last fourteen hours were taking their toll on him.

Heading aft on the starboard side of the missile magazine, he reached the narrow point where the magazine trunk almost joined the outer bulkhead. Removing the oxygen bottle, he squeezed his muscular frame through the tight opening and then dragged the bottle through behind him. After reseating his load, he hefted the cutter rod and proceeded aft, sweat running from his forehead.

On his previous trip, he had carried the weapons and ammunition aft from the armory to the starboard-side coop trunk. Once he had reached the trunk and unburdened himself of the taxing load, he had looked around for a place to conceal the guns until he returned with the cutter. Mosopu had decided to stash the weapons and ammo inside the higher of the angle irons that ran down the starboard bulkhead. The exposed steel beams ran parallel to the deck the length of the bulkhead, like the strakes of a wooden boat. When one of the long guns was layed flat in the angle iron, the three-inch lip of the beam effectively concealed the weapon. He had hidden all the arms and ammunition in this fashion, except for the one shotgun and two bags of shells he retained, and then gone back to the armory to retrieve the cutter.

When he reached the watertight door that opened out onto the coop trunk passageway, he stopped and lowered his load to the deck. Shotgun at the ready, he slowly cracked open the watertight door a few inches to check out the passageway. Mosopu could see no evidence of the Iranians, so he opened the door and padded quietly to the trunk. A quick check of the guns in the angle irons showed they had not been disturbed. For added security, before beginning his work with the torch, he jammed the next aft-leading watertight door shut, obstructing its operating arm with an applicator nozzle, so that he could not be approached from that direction. Lastly, he cautiously made his way across the athwartships passageway that led from the starboard coop trunk to the one on the port side. There was no sign of the enemy there, either.

Returning to where he had left the cutter, Mosopu picked up the bottle and rod combination and wrestled it into the coop trunk passageway. In a few moments he had positioned the bottle properly, donned his goggles, and was ready to spark the cutter. Thank God, he thought. At last I'm able to get them out.

At the second spark from the igniter, the rod burst into flame with its characteristic *whoosh* of gases. Mosopu stared at the ladder trunk for a second before deciding to cut open the entire hatch rather than the small scuttle in its center. It would never be possible to bring a large number of men out quickly through the scuttle. He knew there was no telling how long they'd have before they were discovered, and he had to free the maximum number of shipmates in that time. Cutting open the big hatch was the best way to do that. Bending low to the hatch coaming, he brought the rod's flame to bear on the welded seam that had sealed the hatch. Because of the length of the weld and the difficult angle, the work was slower than it had been on the armory lock, but he cut through almost two feet of the weld in only a minute.

The sound of the torch ripping through the weld echoed in the passageway, and the exhaust gases billowed around him. But then he heard a distant sound, not connected with the cutter. Mosopu stopped and listened, the cutter hissing in his hands. There was definitely another metallic sound, unrelated to the torch, but he could not make out what it was. He bent down and shut off the cutter's oxygen flow, and the torch extinguished almost immediately. Pushing his goggles up onto his forehead, Mosopu strained to locate the source of the sound. With the noise of the cutter gone, the direction of the sound was apparent: the sound was coming from the watertight door behind him, the one he had jammed.

Dropping the cutter on the hatch, Mosopu whirled to face the aft-leading door. Someone was struggling to force open the jammed hatch. The operating rod on the door was moving a few inches back and forth, working against the applicator nozzle with which he had jammed the door's action.

Mosopu bent to get his shotgun and the bags of ammunition from the deck, but then he straightened. He was so close! Should he continue trying to cut the hatch open, hoping the door would hold until he could complete his work? If he fled now, he was not likely to get another crack at cutting into the coops; the Iranians would see his handiwork and undoubtedly post multiple sentries at the ladder trunks. He was racked by uncertainty as he watched the hardware of the watertight door flex as if it were a thing alive.

He was shocked out of his deliberations by other sounds—

sounds from the port trunk area. Mosopu stood stock still and listened. He had not imagined it: the sound of footsteps, moving carefully down the athwartships passageway toward him. He stood beside the trunk, around a blind corner from the passageway that led across to the port side. They were coming—how many? He could not tell from the footsteps.

Mosopu crossed the six feet between his position and the corner bulkhead that turned onto the passageway as quietly as he could. He hoped the metallic rattling from the jammed door would mask the sound of his movements. His back to the corner bulkhead, he listened as the quiet footfalls drew closer.

Without bothering to look down the passageway, he thrust the twelve-gauge around the corner and fired, revealing only his arms and the shotgun. Intent on staying out of sight, he awkwardly pumped the exposed shotgun. The second blast from the twelve-gauge came as he saw the first grenade roll to a stop beside the ladder trunk.

Sergeant Nefud threw himself face down on the deck as the grenade exploded. The ear-wrenching blast was followed immediately by the whistling sound of shrapnel streaking past above his prone body. Looking up from the deck, he could not make out any movement in the smoky cloud from the explosion near the starboard trunk. His opponent might still be alive, he knew, and hiding around the blind corner near the trunk. At least he was no longer firing the shotgun.

Nefud crawled forward to the stricken form of Corporal Arrani. Arrani had been stealthily leading the way down the athwartships passageway when the barrel of the shotgun had appeared from around the corner. Nefud had immediately gone into a crouch, but Arrani had not reacted quickly enough. As Nefud had watched in horror, the first blast from the shotgun had caught Arrani full in the chest, sending him staggering backward to crash to the deck in front of Nefud. Nefud had tossed his ready grenade at the same instant the shotgun boomed another blast down the passageway. He had caught a couple of pellets in his right thigh as he dived to the deck, but he was otherwise unharmed. Now as he listened in the stillness, Arrani's motionless form before him, Nefud realized he could just as easily have been in the lead rather than the corporal.

After listening in silence for thirty seconds, Nefud reached out from his position flat on the deck and grabbed the neck of Arrani's shirt. Moving slowly of necessity, he backed down the passageway, dragging the other marine. Nefud kept one hand free to hold an armed grenade, his eyes fixed on the starboard trunk area ahead as he laboriously dragged Arrani to safety. He had to stop every couple of feet to catch his breath: sliding backward on all fours on the cool deck while dragging Arrani's immobile form was grueling work. Finally, with his vision still locked on the starboard side, Nefud realized he had reached the port ladder trunk. He hauled himself up from the deck, wincing at the pain in his thigh, and ducked behind the blind corner near the trunk. His back to the corner bulkhead, he paused a moment to gather his strength before reaching out into the exposed passageway to drag Arrani in with him.

As Nefud sat back against the wall, he got his first good look at Corporal Arrani. It was clear from his lifeless eyes that the man was dead. Why didn't I wait for Rafsani? The sergeant cursed himself silently, the grenade still clutched in his hand.

When his search team had reached the jammed watertight door, it had taken Nefud only seconds to realize they had found their prey. He had known the berthing compartments were on the other side of the door, and as his men struggled to open it, Nefud had heard strange, unidentifiable sounds coming from the other side. He had immediately dispatched one of his men to summon Rafsani. Then, leaving a marine to work on the door and cover that route of escape, he and Arrani had circled around to come in from the port side. He had hesitated briefly, undecided about whether to wait for the Sergeant Major, before electing to go after the American. He had remembered Rafsani's words about striking swiftly once they found the renegade sailor and not waiting for the Sergeant Major to reach the scene.

He had followed his orders—and now Arrani was dead. But had he killed or wounded the American? The lack of sound from the starboard side indicated the former. Nefud looked down at the broken body of Arrani. There was no sign of the Sergeant Major as yet, and the American could still be alive.

Nefud reached down and closed the vacant eyes of Corporal Arrani. Taking a deep breath, he leaned out into the passageway and sent his second grenade skittering down the deck toward the starboard trunk.

BARGE APOLLO

Fraser stood next to the small bank of radios and watched his six boat captains hurriedly leave the radar shack. He turned from the door and put his hand on the shoulder of the seated operator who was watching the surface search radar.

"Any change, Porter?"

The lone operator spoke without looking up. "Negative, Skipper. She's still tracking at the same speed. She's definitely holding to the channel, though."

Fraser silently watched the green dot that represented the *Bulkeley* pulse every several seconds as the radar sweep returned. The sweep also clearly defined the landmarks of the channel, and what land was visible to the radar at the set range of twenty-five miles. Fraser took his hand from the operator's shoulder and moved to the bank of radios. He keyed the separate, secure mission net that had been established for the operation, and in seconds he had the flagship on the line.

"COM JTF, this is Apollo; Fraser speaking. I need the Admiral."

There was a half-minute delay, and then Boone's distinctive baritone resonated in the radar shack. "Apollo, this is COM JTF. Go ahead."

"This is Fraser, Admiral. *Bulkeley* is maintaining twenty to twenty-five knots, even in the channel. I need permission to move now. We're going to have to go early or we'll never catch them."

Lieutenant Beach silently entered the radar shack and came to join Fraser.

"I understand, Apollo," the Admiral's voice came back. "We've been tracking the same thing. This will mean you'll have to approach and do the insertion before twilight, correct?"

"I'm afraid so, Admiral. But it doesn't look like we have any choice. I'm moving the strike time up to nineteen fifteen, if you concur. At the ship's current speed that will still let us get on board her ten miles, or roughly half an hour short of the harbor."

There was a short pause before the Admiral responded. "Permission granted, Apollo. We will adjust our timetables accordingly."

Fraser looked at Beach before he spoke again. The SEAL officer was silently watching the sweep of the radar, but Fraser knew he was listening intently to the radio conversation.

"Roger, Admiral. I will be switching strike command to the boats immediately."

"This is COM JTF, I copy. Good luck. Out."

Fraser set down the microphone and turned to Beach. "Showtime's moved up, Ned."

"So I heard."

Beach followed Fraser to the door of the shack, where the officer in charge scooped up his flak jacket from a folding chair. They left the shack and crossed the deck in silence. As they made their way to the waiting boats, Fraser looked over at the barge's crude helo pad where the large Blackhawk helicopter was parked. A number of SEALS, distinctive in their all-black combat uniforms, were loading various pieces of equipment into the Blackhawk.

"You have all the details worked out with the Army crew?" Fraser asked as they continued across the steel deck.

"Just like we've practiced it in the past. They're ready."

Fraser swung his gaze from the aircraft to the three SeaFox fast boats moored astern of the Spectre Mark IIIs, alongside the barge.

"Let's hope the Blackhawk is mechanically one hundred percent. At the speed *Bulkeley*'s doing, using the SeaFoxes for insertion is no longer an option. I'm going to take them with me. They won't be able to keep up with the Mark Threes, but they should catch up once you slow the ship."

Beach smiled and turned to his friend. "Stop the ship, you mean."

"Right. Stop the ship." Fraser returned the other man's smile. They came to a halt at the edge of the barge, beside the lead Spectre boat. The engines of all six of the boats were rumbling softly at idle. Each boat was fully manned, with a gunner at every weapons station.

"I'll radio-check with you again as soon as we're away from the barge," Fraser said.

Beach nodded and reached up to flip on the small radio that was fixed on his equipment vest. The two men shook hands and Fraser stepped off the barge onto the Mark III. He signaled the boat captain to cast off and then turned back to Beach, standing on the pier.

"Remember, Ned, you've got the final word. When you get over the deck, if you don't like it—abort."

Beach gave Fraser a grim smile. "I'll remember," Beach said quietly. "But we'll like it."

Fraser nodded in silent understanding and turned to enter the patrol boat's pilothouse.

As Beach watched, the boats pulled away from the barge with practiced precision, each following on the heels of the boat before it. When all were clear of the barge, Fraser's lead boat started to accelerate and head for the channel. Without signal, the other two Mark III boats took up station on the wings of the lead boat, forming a wedge of high-speed firepower. The slower Sea-Foxes duplicated this maneuver and followed in the wake of the lead formation. Beach watched the boats until they faded from sight in the sandstorm, and then he turned and started for the Blackhawk.

THE BULKELEY

"You heard me, Major! I want one of the detonators!"

Aziz stared back at Kalil, a slow rage building in him. He had not wanted to join the Guards Commander on the bridgewing again—especially not with the ship making high speed in the confined channel. He had no doubt of Stewart's seamanship skills or of his cooperation, now that the woman's life was at stake, but one navigational mistake at this point would render their mission at least a partial failure. But Kalil had been particularly insistent, and Aziz had decided it was better to comply than to have another noisy argument in front of the Americans and their men. Now the Major could not believe what he was hearing.

"Listen to me carefully, Colonel," Aziz began, trying to contain his anger. "The detonators will remain in my possession. That was the plan and that is how it shall be."

"But that is preposterous! There are two of them—why must you hold both? What if something—God grant that it does not— but what if something were to happen to you?" Kalil's tone was insistent.

"As you well know, there are two detonators for purposes of reliability—not to split the authority to detonate the charges!" Aziz could contain himself no longer. Kalil could not possibly have forgotten the explanation at the briefing. There were two detonators for the same reason they had mined both the gun and the missile magazines: redundancy. It would hardly do to have come this far and not to succeed because of the failure of a single mechanical or explosive device. Although the radio detonators were the best of their type, they were also vulnerable to the intrusion of sand or water into the mechanism. Aziz had no intention of removing one of the sensitive devices from its secure waterproof pouch until it was needed. He also did not care for Kalil's reference to something happening to him. Surely the oaf wasn't trying to threaten him?

"That may have been the original plan," Kalil all but shouted. "But much has not gone in way of the original plan. For the good of our mission and to ensure its eventual success, you must give one of the detonators to me!"

Is this it? Aziz wondered. Is this the moment I've dreaded but also expected, where Kalil endangers the mission? Innocently, the Major let his right hand drift down to rest on his belt. His fingers were inches away from the waterproof pouch containing the detonators, but also inches away from his holstered Beretta. Kalil followed the motion of Aziz's hand, his eyes burning with intensity.

When Kalil looked back up into Aziz's face, he saw that the Major's attention had shifted from him to the waters ahead of the ship. The Guards Commander followed his gaze but could see nothing out of the ordinary—in fact, there was little to see at all. Kalil was about to speak again when Aziz bolted from the bridgewing. Puzzled by the Major's sudden action, Kalil followed him inside the bridge. Aziz was standing next to Stewart at the center of the bridge. The Major stared at the American, whose face was set in concentration on his task of piloting the ship.

"Where are the other ships?" Aziz demanded of Stewart.

Stewart did not take his eyes from the seas ahead of the *Bulkeley* as he replied, "I don't know what you mean."

"Where are the ships! We have seen tanker traffic all the way across the Gulf, and now nothing. Bahrain Harbor is one of the busiest in the Gulf, and we have not seen a single ship in the channel, only small boats. Where are the ships?"

Stewart glanced over at Aziz. He had noticed the lack of shipping traffic when the *Bulkeley* had first entered the channel. The change in the flow of shipping clearly indicated something was up, but what it was he had no way of knowing. He had hoped that the Iranians would be too preoccupied to notice the change. Now that they have, he thought, there's no reason not to capitalize on it.

"Maybe it's some kind of holiday," he offered, "or maybe a lot of ships have decided to wait out the sandstorm in the harbor." He paused. "Of course, it's also possible that seeing a ship racing down the channel at twenty-five knots has attracted a little attention."

"What do you mean?" Kalil broke in. Aziz studied Stewart carefully.

"Just that maybe there's a reception waiting for us—for you—in the harbor. Maybe somebody's figured out what's happened on this ship and they're anticipating our arrival." Stewart looked back out at the narrow channel.

"That is not possible," Aziz said flatly.

"Why is it not possible, Major?" Kalil asked angrily. "Enough mistakes have been made. What if the Americans are waiting for us? Perhaps we should proceed no farther."

"Be silent," Aziz said to Kalil coldly.

"I will not be silent! Let us stop the ship and act now, while there is still time to escape!"

Stewart felt his gut turn to ice at the Guards Commander's words. They were barely out of Kalil's mouth when Stewart heard the flat crack of skin on skin. Spinning around from his spot behind the gyrorepeater, Stewart saw Kalil stagger back from what must have been an openhanded slap from Aziz. The Major's hand still hung in the air where he had made contact. Kalil moved to unsling his gun, but the marine on the port side of the bridge had already brought his own gun up to cover both Kalil and the Guard who stood on the starboard side. The venom in Kalil's face radiated through the bridge.

"Enough foolishness," Aziz said, dropping his hand and adopting a tone that spoke of a return to normalcy. "We are only an hour away from our objective. Let us not ruin everything now." He turned and moved to the chart table. Kalil watched him go and then looked at the other marine. The marine kept his weapon trained on Kalil and the other Guard. Aziz had given no sign for the man to change his protective stance.

Kalil relaxed, or tried to give the impression he had relaxed, and moved casually to the port side of the bridge. He stopped a few paces from the marine, turned his back to the man, and stared out the windows to sea. The time had come, he knew, to take control of the mission.

USS MANCHESTER

The *Manchester* appeared to hover in place at the eastern side of Bahrain Harbor. The ship was positioned in relatively open water near where the approach channel emptied out into the broad expanse of the harbor. The *Pascagoula* moved slowly along her track to the west of the *Manchester*, using most of the good water in the harbor to carry out her low-speed track. To the east of the *Manchester* lay the tanker anchorage, densely packed with giant merchant ships, some of whose masters were growing more irate by the hour at the mysterious delay in underway time that the Bahrainis had imposed on them.

On the bridge of the frigate, Captain Walker shifted his attention from the slow-moving *Pascagoula* back to the two objects on the harbor shoreline that he was using as a reference to tell him if his ship was changing position significantly.

Behind him on the bridge, his navigation team worked steadily at a more precise version of the task he was using his seaman's eye to accomplish. Every minute, the navigator would call out how far removed the ship was from the position Walker had selected to maintain while waiting for the *Bulkeley*, and the OOD would adjust the ship accordingly. With most ships, the only way to maintain a relatively stationary position would be by dropping anchor, and that would not allow the frigate to move again quickly, which Walker had to be able to do. He had an option other than anchoring, however, because his class of ship was equipped with underwater bowthrusters known as auxiliary propulsion units. The twin APUs were essentially extraordinarily powerful outboard motors that could be lowered from the center of the ship. Either one of the APUs could train a full three hundred sixty degrees, and by using them properly the OOD or conning officer could hold the ship in position remarkably well.

Captain Walker was pleased with the spot he had chosen to wait for the *Bulkeley*. Positioned as *Manchester* was, at the point where the channel opened out into the harbor, she could block *Bulkeley*'s access. Walker was confident there was no way the captured frigate could get to the *Pascagoula* without going through him.

Manchester's tactical action officer had just reported that the *Bulkeley* was less than thirty miles distant, and Walker could feel the excitement level of his crew start to rise as the drama they were a part of drew closer to its climax. Two minutes on the 1MC, once they had gotten away from the pier, had been enough time for him to explain to his crew what was going on. The stunned looks on the faces of his bridge team had undoubtedly reflected the reaction of every man on board.

Walker moved to the starboard side of the bridge and brought up his binoculars to study the mass of anchored merchantmen to the east of him. That was the only thing he did not like about the spot he had chosen; the anchored ships were less than a mile to the east and would limit his ability to move in that direction if he needed to. He trained his glasses from ship to ship and finally came to a halt on the tanker nearest him. This one was less than half a mile away and was anchored a good distance from the forest of other ships. He'll be the biggest problem if I need to move that way, Walker thought. Straining his eyes, he was just able to make out the tanker's name: it read *Andes Commerce*.

14

BLACKHAWK 44

The UH-60A Blackhawk helicopter flew low over the water, not quite wave-skimming, but only a hundred feet above the channel's surface. In silhouette, the Blackhawk appeared nearly identical to the SH-60B Seahawk helicopters that operated off the frigates and destroyers in the Gulf. The Navy aircraft had, in fact, evolved from the Blackhawk's design. But the black-painted helicopter was designed for something far different.

Beach adjusted the noise suppressor over his lightweight radio headset before speaking into the microphone. The uncomfortable suppressor was the only way for him to hear incoming radio transmissions on the mission circuit over the noise of the Black-hawk's engines. They had just lifted off from Barge Apollo and, as planned, he was calling Fraser to let him know.

"Strike Command, this is Team One. Over," he said into the hands-free mike.

Fraser's response came back immediately, crystal clear even over the muffled noise of the helicopter.

"This is Strike. Roger, over."

"Team One is airborne and proceeding down channel. Over."

"Roger, Team One. Report when you have suppression force in sight. Strike Command, out."

Beach sat back against one of the bench seats that lined the Blackhawk's internal bay. So far, so good, he thought.

Directly across from him, sitting on the port side of the aircraft's bay, were Chief Austen and three of the SEALS. The other three SEALS sat beside Beach on the starboard side. Forward of the bench seats, an Army aircrewman stood at the open bay door, manning a gimbal-mounted M-60 machine gun. Beach looked above the open door and saw the four coiled lines, spaced at two-foot intervals, which were attached by steel rings to the helo's internal frame. He knew without having to ask that Chief Austen had already checked out the drop lines.

Looking from the bay door back at Chief Austen, Beach was struck by how little the chief resembled the public image of the SEALS. A small man, not much over five foot seven, Austen displayed neither the bulging muscles nor the granite chin of popular imagination. The thirty-four-year-old chief was of average physique and had a tanned, expressionless face that appeared to be that of a man ten years older. The only clue to the man's vocation was the absence of eyebrows from his face: pencil-thin lines of hair were all that remained after Austen had gotten too close to a high-explosive blast on a mission that he did not talk about.

Beach knew he could not have a better man to be his second-in-command on the detachment. In fact, the entire group had coalesced extremely well, he thought. They had worked together long enough, both before deploying and in their two and a half months in the Gulf, so that each man could anticipate what the other would do. They had achieved that integration of understanding and purpose that reduced the need for verbal orders to a bare minimum.

Beach's eyes moved from Austen to each man on his team. They were all preparing themselves in a different way. Some were checking weapons, others just staring at the deck of the helo, their faces rigid with concentration. The men were all clothed in identical black uniforms, and everything from their equipment vests to their boots matched the uniforms in color. They had greased their hands and faces with black camo paint and most wore a black cloth headband or watch cap. They made do without bulky flak vests in favor of greater mobility.

When Beach returned his attention to Austen, he saw the chief shift the large Stoner M63 5.56-millimeter machine gun he carried in his lap. The Stoner was the only large weapon Beach had authorized for the assault. It held one hundred fifty rounds in its drum magazine and could deliver tremendous firepower. With the exception of Austen, every other man on the team carried an identical Colt Commando, the carbine version of the M-16 rifle, and a silenced 9-millimeter pistol. Getting down the rope and moving through the ship quickly required that they be unencumbered by heavy equipment.

Beach knew that speed and surprise would be everything when they hit the ship, especially since they were uncertain how many Iranians were on board. The four rafts the *Daniels* had found meant there could be as few as a dozen or as many as thirty of the enemy. There was not a lot of information on how good these Iranian marines were. Not too good, let's hope, he thought. It was critical that they strike swiftly, before the Iranians could react and harm the ship or the crew. Beach dreaded the thought that the *Pascagoula*'s CO might be correct and they would find the ship wired with explosives. Well, he thought, that was all the more reason for taking the Iranians out as quickly as they could.

The SEAL det had rehearsed this type of operation many times, and Beach was confident they would succeed. Once they were on deck he would take his three men and proceed immediately to the ship's bridge. At the same time, Austen would move with his three SEALs to Main Control. With the surprise and confusion their assault would create, as well as the ruthless approach they would employ, Beach expected to have control of the two vital spaces in less than three minutes. Then they could stop the ship and proceed to mop up any remaining Iranians.

Beach shifted his attention from Chief Austen to the open bay door. The light outside was growing a little dimmer as it grew later in the day. He looked down at his watch. 1900. Too early for twilight, he knew. But they would have to live with that.

THE BULKELEY

Mosopu cursed aloud as he wedged himself through the narrow gap in the missile magazine. He cursed not from the pain in his back and ribs, where the grenade fragments had caught him, but from the knowledge that his chances of freeing his shipmates were now practically nonexistent.

He had been able to flatten himself against the bulkhead when he saw the grenade roll down the deck, and the hatch coaming he stood on had fortunately diverted most of the blast away from him. Mosopu had felt the hot gases on his skin and the shrapnel ripping into his back and ribs as the grenade went off. But that pain was nothing to what he felt when he turned and saw the cutter. The grenade had punctured the oxygen bottle in several places, venting the gas and rendering the exothermic cutter useless. His rage and frustration had been so great that he had almost charged down the athwartships passageway in a suicidal lunge for the Iranians. But, swiftly facing up to the reality of his situation, Mosopu had realized he was finished at the coops and had to save himself to have another chance of rescuing the others. He had closed the watertight door behind him just as the second grenade went off.

Now he was headed forward, back toward the repair locker that held the wounded sailor. He wanted to punch the bulkhead in frustration, but he continued on. As he opened the watertight door leading to the repair locker passageway, Mosopu heard the door behind him on the aft bulkhead of the missile magazine passageway start to open. He turned, bringing the shotgun up, but he quickly realized he could only fire through the small opening beside the magazine ring. And, more critically, loose rounds fired in the passageway might set off the mass of explosives the Iranians had rigged around the missile magazine.

Mosopu stepped through the doorway and closed the hatch behind him. Where to now? He could try to make a stand in the repair locker with Andy—but the grenades the Iranians possessed would turn the locker into a deadly trap. He knew there was no way he could carry the wounded sailor and have any chance at all. He had to move swiftly—the Iranians certainly had. Mosopu decided to try to draw the marines forward, away from the locker and after him. He had no idea where he would end up, but he had to keep moving—his pursuers were too close.

He levered open the repair locker door and stuck his head inside. His searching eyes rapidly found the wounded sailor, asleep where he had left him. "Buddy—hey, kid! Wake up!" he shouted.

Andy stirred restlessly, his head bobbing as if he were trying to fight his way through to consciousness.

"Wake up, man! There's no time, you gotta come out of it!" Mosopu yelled. He turned to make sure the watertight door leading to the magazine passageway remained closed.

Andy's eyes opened slowly. Looking confused, he tried to register his surroundings. Finally his sleepy gaze found Mosopu.

The Bosun's Mate was relieved to see the sailor come to. "Okay, buddy, listen to me," he said. "Those fuckas are comin' right behind me. I'm gonna lead 'em off from here. Anybody opens this door, it's a bad guy. You got it?"

Andy looked at Mosopu dazedly, at first seeming not to comprehend. Then he nodded his head slowly in acknowledgment. Mosopu was glad that he seemed to understand.

"Okay. I'm gonna shut off the lights too. Maybe make it more likely they pass you by."

Mosopu found the wall switch and shifted the locker's lights from white to off. Andy was now hidden by the darkness.

With a fast motion, Mosopu closed the locker door and levered down the operating arm. He stopped in the middle of the passageway, listening for sounds of his approaching pursuers. Hearing none, he headed across the athwartships passageway that led from the repair locker to the armory. When he reached the port side, he rounded the corner leading to the armory and came to a halt. He stopped there to listen once again.

It was not long before the sound came—the sound of the door to the repair locker passageway being slowly opened. Mosopu waited until he heard the door open fully and then ticked off ten seconds. He figured that would be enough time for the Iranians to cross cautiously into the passageway outside the repair locker.

With a horrifying war cry, he lunged from around the corner, firing before he had a target. He exposed himself just long enough to get off two rounds down the passageway. Then he was diving back toward the armory. In that brief moment, he had seen one Iranian outside the repair locker and the head of a second peering through the open door from the missile magazine passageway.

He was certain his first blast had gone high, over the head of the startled, crouching Iranian. He wasn't sure if his second shot had made contact; he had already been darting back out of the Iranian's field of fire when he fired.

Mosopu picked himself up off the deck, the burning pain in his back returning. Speed is life, he told himself, as he scrambled up the armory passageway heading forward. He tried to block out the pain from the wounds in his back as well as the renewed pain in his calf while he hustled forward. Not allowing himself a look back, he pulled shotgun cartridges from the bag at his hip, reloading on the run.

Andy snapped awake in the darkness at the sound of the shotgun blasts. At first he was disoriented, uncertain of where he was in the ship. But the searing pain in his gut and the weight of the shotgun on his lap quickly brought awareness back to him.

He listened intently, but there was no sound from outside the repair locker. As he listened in the darkness, waiting for the sound of more gunfire to echo through the bulkhead, Andy felt himself starting to drift back into sleep. The warmth of approaching sleep washed over him, his body urging him to accept refuge from the pain. He fought the impulse to surrender to the warmth, but his eyes slowly drew closed.

The sound at the door did not immediately pull him back from the edge of sleep. Andy lifted his head groggily, in annoyance at whatever sought to deprive him of his rest. The metallic grinding of the opening dogs was a familiar sound, familiar enough so that he almost did not look up toward the watertight door. Just Boats coming back for me, he thought, as the first crack of light penetrated the dark locker. But as he watched the watertight door slowly open, a voice filled his head. *Anybody opens this door, it's a bad guy*, he heard Mosopu saying from a long way off.

Andy battled through the cloud of sleep to focus on the now open door. He commanded his arms to raise the shotgun, but the weapon seemed to weigh a thousand pounds. As the sleep left him the pain returned like a knife blow to his stomach. The silhouette of a man's head appeared in the doorway. *Pick up the gun!* he screamed to himself. The head turned slowly, as if searching in the blackness of the repair locker. Andy had one hand under the slide of the shotgun, the stock resting against his thigh. He couldn't seem to find the trigger. The head had turned toward him, and now a weapon was visible too.

The blast from the gun illuminated the darkened repair locker like an exploding sun.

THE PASCAGOULA

"There's the Blackhawk," Garmisch said as the helicopter symbol appeared in amber video on the console.

Garmisch, along with Admiral Boone, the Chief of Staff, and Commander Kelly, was standing behind the operator of the largest of the three tactical data consoles in the TDC. The four men maneuvered for the best view over the operator's shoulders. The console displayed symbols for the *Pascagoula* and the *Manchester* in the harbor, as well as Barge Apollo and the Mark III patrol boats to the northeast. All of the men could clearly see the symbol representing the *Bulkeley* making its way down the channel at high speed. Admiral Boone had ordered the AWACS, Deadline, repositioned almost directly over Bahrain Harbor, and now its radar picture combined with those of the surface ships to provide a precise depiction of the unfolding action.

Boone spoke without looking up from the console.

"We've got the President's approval, and in another fifteen minutes we're irrevocably committed. If any of you see anything I'm missing here, now is definitely the time to speak up."

Garmisch looked at Captain Lacey, who kept his eyes riveted on the console along with the Admiral. Jim shifted to look at Kelly, who met his gaze with a humorless smile that conveyed that he had nothing more to say.

Boone waited a minute and then said, almost as if speaking to himself, "Well, I don't see any other way than this. However it goes, we're going to have control of our ship back within the hour."

"Admiral," Lacey said, pulling himself away from his fascination with the scene that the console displayed, "did General Brighton or the chairman say anything about what our next move is to be once the immediate situation with the *Bulkeley* is resolved?"

Boone smiled grimly before answering the Chief of Staff.

"They're considering a wide range of retaliatory 'options.' Apparently State hasn't said a word about this to the Iranians yet; they don't want to tip our hand before we try to recover the ship."

"Thank God for that," Lacey sighed, relieved.

"But they plan to go before the UN, and the President will inform the nation," the Admiral continued, "as soon as we know how this comes out."

"*Roosevelt* has been moved into the northernmost part of the North Arabian Sea," Kelly said flatly. "And the *Wisconsin* battle group is on its way up from the Indian Ocean."

"First things first," Boone said. "Until one of our people actually sees an Iranian on board the *Bulkeley*, all we have is a potential crisis, not a confirmed one."

"COM JTF, this is Strike Command." Fraser's voice carried throughout the TDC. The Admiral had ordered all the other circuits turned down and the mission net put on the main speaker for the duration of the operation.

Garmisch donned a radio headset and keyed the microphone, acknowledging Fraser's call.

"This is COM JTF. Roger, over."

"This is Strike. I have a visual on the target. Still appears to be maintaining high speed. We will be in position to commence strike in five minutes. Over."

Boone looked at Garmisch. "Find out what they've got for visibility," he directed.

"Strike, this is COM JTF. Copy five minutes to strike. What is your current visibility? Over."

There was a pause, and then Fraser's voice came back clearly on the circuit. "Estimated visibility, four to five miles. If they're looking for us, they're going to find us. It's still not dark enough. Over."

Boone bent down to speak to the seated console operator. "Current range to *Bulkeley*?" he asked.

The operator moved his rolling ball tab from the *Pascagoula*'s symbol to the *Bulkeley* and depressed a button.

"Fourteen miles, Admiral."

Boone straightened up. "Okay," he growled. "We've got no more time to play with. Tell Fraser we're going on schedule."

"Strike, this is COM JTF. Proceed with strike as planned."

PATROL BOAT 600

Fraser replaced the radio handset in the console in the lead boat's pilothouse and raised his binoculars. *Bulkeley* was becoming more and more visible as they slowly gained on her. The boats were closing on the frigate from astern at thirty knots, a speed just sufficient to let them catch the ship without overtaking her too soon. Ten minutes ago, when they had first been able to make out the *Bulkeley* through the sand and haze, Fraser had ordered his three boats to break the wedge they had been traveling in and form a column. The column would minimize what anyone looking at them from the *Bulkeley* would see: one patrol boat would appear far less threatening than three.

Fraser turned and looked aft with his binoculars. There, faintly visible five miles back, were the SeaFoxes. The smaller boats were speeding ahead for all they were worth, but Fraser knew they would probably not catch the *Bulkeley* until the action was over. That was all right, though; the small patrol boats would provide invaluable security for the ship once it was stopped. Shifting his gaze from the SeaFoxes to the Mark IIIs directly astern of his lead boat, Fraser could see that every weapon except the prohibited chain gun was manned on each of the boats. The Mark IIIs carried a dual .50-caliber–grenade launcher mount, as well as an independent .50-caliber and a MK-19 automatic grenade launcher. Additionally, he could see the crewmen who normally manned the chain guns were armed with M-60 machine guns and positioned behind the 25-millimeter cannons.

Fraser turned and refocused his attention on the *Bulkeley*. She was less than three miles away now, he judged, and details on her flight deck and superstructure were becoming visible. Don't let them have stationed an aft lookout, he prayed silently.

The sweep second hand of his chronograph was fifteen seconds short of 1915 when Fraser picked up the radio handset once again. As the second hand completed its arc, he spoke into the handset.

"Team One, this is Strike. Execute. I say again, execute."

While Fraser was talking on the strike net, the chief, who was the lead Mark III's boat captain, was talking into another radio.

"PB Seven-Eight-Eight, PB Seven-Two-Five, this is PB Six Hundred. Execute. Over."

Even as the boat captains on the trailing patrol boats acknowledged the command over the radio, their engines roared with increased speed. The lead boat accelerated as well, but at a speed less than the trailing boats. With a flash of spray, the second boat heeled over to the right and the third boat pulled out of the column to the left. As Fraser's boat steadied at thirty-five knots, the other two patrol boats rocketed down her port and starboard side at close to forty-five knots.

With the two faster-moving boats in the lead and Fraser's boat now at the rear, the horseshoe-shaped formation descended on the *Bulkeley* from astern.

THE BULKELEY

Rafsani went up the ladder steps two at a time, oblivious to whether the three Revolutionary Guards followed him or not.

The Sergeant Major had arrived at the coops moments after Nefud had thrown his second grenade, and within seconds the third search team had been on the scene as well. Rafsani had wasted no time in making his decision. He had sent Nefud and his men, with the addition of the marines from the third team, forward into the missile magazine passageway. He had taken the Guards and headed for the nearest ladder that would take him to the weather deck. There would be no escape for the dangerous American this time, he thought. The Sergeant Major was headed for the fo'c'sle and the still-open scuttle to the bosun's locker, through which the American had escaped the first time. Nefud's team would drive the sailor forward into Rafsani's grasp.

Gaining the top of the ladder, he rushed down the passageway to the nearest watertight hatch leading to the weather deck. Heedless of his own safety, Rafsani shoved open the door and leapt over the coaming onto the exposed deck. He ignored the blast of hot air that greeted him along with the relative brightness of the outside light. The Sergeant Major raced down the open deck of the port side, headed toward the break. He threw aside his Sterling while on the run and pulled his *kukri* and a grenade from his belt. He could hear the excited Guards running behind him, struggling to keep up.

When the Sergeant Major reached the watertight door inside the port break that led to the fo'c'sle, he halted. Now was the time for caution. Opening the door a few inches, he carefully verified that the fo'c'sle was clear. Satisfied that the American had not yet reached the open deck, Rafsani threw open the hatch and darted out onto the fo'c'sle. He approached the open scuttle in a wide circle, signaling the Guards to stay back near the superstructure and cover him. When he was behind the scuttle, his back to the bow of the ship, he crept forward to the lip of the open hatch. Rafsani looked up, intending to signal the Guards to approach, but what he saw when he raised his head chilled his blood. Just visible as he looked aft toward the break and the open sea was some type of fast patrol boat, approaching from astern of the ship at tremendous speed.

Rafsani hesitated only a second. Thoughts of the lone American banished from his mind, he raced for the break.

"Cover!" he shouted to the Guards. "Get back within the break, behind the steel bulkheads!"

The Guards looked at him uncomprehendingly, but when Rafsani raced by them and into the port break, they followed. Rafsani ran back to where the exterior of the break tapered down to a four-foot-high bulkhead that faced out to sea. Crouching, only his eyes and the top of his head visible above the rail of the low partition, he watched the approaching patrol boat. It was only a hundred yards shy of the ship's stern. Spinning around, Rafsani grabbed the closest of the Guards and pulled him down beside him.

"Look!" He pointed to the rapidly gaining boat.

The Guard's eyes grew wide when he finally picked out the inbound craft.

"Keep the others under cover here until the boat draws even with you—then open fire!"

Before the Guard could mouth a question, Rafsani was up and gone. As the kneeling Iranian watched, the Sergeant Major vaulted down the deck and ducked back into the open hatch to reenter the skin of the ship.

PATROL BOAT 600

Fraser watched his two lead boats draw even with the stern of the *Bulkeley*, one on the port and the other on the starboard quarter; each boat was roughly one hundred yards from the frigate. His own Mark III was two hundred yards dead on the stern.

"All boats commence fire," he said to the boat captain, who raced to repeat the order over the boats' tactical circuit. Fraser had the microphone for the mission circuit in his hand.

"Team One, this is Strike. Executing suppression fire. Over."

Beach's reply was almost drowned out by the thunderous roar of the guns on Fraser's boat opening up.

"Team One copies. We are inbound."

Fraser looked over his shoulder and was able to make out the Blackhawk, down low over the water at a distance of about three miles and closing fast.

Returning his attention to his boats, Fraser saw the lead boats had already advanced fifty feet forward along the hull of the *Bulkeley*. Their combined weapons were pouring a lethal fire onto the open decks of the *Bulkeley* to clear them of any topside Iranians. Fraser knew the Mark IIIs were low enough in the water that there was no danger of them hitting each other as they sped down the port and starboard side of the frigate's flight deck. He could not hear their weapons firing over the pounding sound of the guns on board his own boat, but the smoke and muzzle flashes from the lead boats confirmed their action.

Fraser's command boat kept the flight deck and fantail under a withering hail of machine-gun and grenade rounds. They would continue to saturate the flight deck until the Blackhawk passed overhead on its way in. The sparks and flying splinters of steel visible on the flight deck told him that nothing on the deck would remain alive to meet the helicopter's arrival.

The sun was low over the horizon as the light continued to fade.

THE <u>BULKELEY</u>

Bosca heard the sound begin, like a chain saw starting up in the distance; then it drew closer. He looked over at Jack Nelson, who was listening, trying to discern what was happening.

The roar kept growing, and Bosca saw the marine sentries grow uneasy. The one closest to Bosca's table said something in Farsi to the other, who darted out the wardroom door heading aft. Seconds later the oncoming sound had become distinct; there was a steady pounding sound mixed with small explosions.

"Down! Everybody hit the deck!" Nelson screamed.

Bosca still was not sure what was going on, but he followed the example of the officers who were kicking back their chairs and diving under the tables. As Bosca got down on the deck next to Lawrence's pale form, he saw that the Iranian marine was uncertain how to react. He held his weapon as if he was confused by whatever was happening.

The gunfire arrived suddenly, shredding the starboard bulkhead of the wardroom like cloth. Bosca saw the Iranian go down on one knee beside the table, just as the wardroom was hit. A number of rounds rocketed into the wall behind the Iranian. The roar of the guns was deafening. The marine crouched down further, trying to escape the blast and bringing his shoulders level with the table Bosca hid beneath.

Amid all the explosions, Bosca realized the open knife was still in his hand. The Iranian's chest and bent legs were exposed under the table, only two feet distant from him. There was another volley and then the blast of the gunfire seemed to move forward, away from the wardroom. The Iranian shifted position as if he was preparing to rise.

You must do it! Bosca told himself. Grimacing with the effort, he threw himself on the deck toward the marine. Bosca thrust his knife hand forward, burying the blade in the Iranian's chest.

"What in God's name is that?" Kalil cried out, as the roar of the patrol boats' guns was heard on the bridge.

Aziz rushed by the Guards Commander and threw open the port-side watertight door. Once on the bridgewing, he saw the patrol boat moving steadily forward down the side of the ship, its guns blasting a six-foot swath from the weather deck up. A round caromed off the bridge superstructure from dead aft, and Aziz spun around to see a second boat firing on the ship from astern. Turning back to the first boat, he saw it was almost even with amidships and moving forward. He ducked back into the bridge, yelling as he ran.

"Get down! Everyone down on the deck!"

The Americans and his own men looked at him in puzzlement at first, and then Stewart echoed his order.

"Do as he says! Everyone on the deck!" Stewart turned to the helmsman. "All stop!"

Before the helmsman could respond, Aziz had his pistol out and pointed at Stewart.

"No!" he ordered. "The ship remains at speed! You and the man at the wheel continue as before."

Stewart was prevented from answering by the crash of the first bullets ripping into the bridge.

Kalil and the two other Iranians hit the deck along with Kim, Scott Septenano, and the two other enlisted watch standers.

Aziz stood frozen in place, ignoring the steel projectiles ripping through the bridge. Fragments and pieces of shrapnel erupted from various fixtures on the bridge as the high-caliber rounds made contact. The helmsman ducked as low over the ship's wheel as he could. Stewart and Aziz were the only ones still standing in the deadly hail of fire. The two men faced each other across the bridge in surreal disregard of the increasing danger.

Not yet, Stewart thought, looking into Aziz's determined eyes.

"Maintain speed, Turner, " he said, as he turned and crouched behind the helmsman.

A grenade round detonated outside the port bridge windows, showering Kalil and the nearby prone marine with glass. Stewart watched over his shoulder as Aziz coolly walked across the bridge to the 1MC panel. Pulling the mike from its holder he spoke forcefully into the PA system.

"Take defensive stations—the ship is under attack!"

As he was repeating the phrase, Aziz saw the Sergeant Major's head appear in the ladder well as he came up into the bridge. Aziz turned back to the 1MC station, but before he could finish his orders he was suddenly knocked to the deck from behind. Rafsani had tackled him at the instant that a lattice of concentrated fire stitched the bridge from the starboard side. All the starboard windows exploded inward and bullets streaked through the bridge from two feet off the deck upward. The sailor on the deck closest to the starboard side was literally spun around where he lay as a bullet ripped into his leg. His scream went unheard in the maelstrom of sound on the bridge.

Then the fusilade moved forward, and only the occasional round hit the bridge. Aziz felt Rafsani's weight lift from him, and when he looked up, he saw the big marine spring to the chart table. Rafsani scooped up the loaded rocket launcher and the bag of grenades and vaulted over the bodies on the deck as he headed for the port-side watertight door.

Before Aziz could scream at him to stop, the Sergeant Major was out the door to the port bridgewing.

BLACKHAWK 44

"Everybody up!" Chief Austen yelled, trying to be heard above the noise of the Blackhawk's rotors. He echoed the command with a hand signal to ensure that it was understood.

The SEALS rose as one from the bench seats and turned toward the open bay door. Beach was already there, beside the door gunner, looking down at the water below.

As they passed over the trailing patrol boat, Fraser's boat, Beach saw rather than heard the boat's guns go silent. He strained to see ahead of the helicopter to the flight deck. From what he could see, the deck was clear.

The Blackhawk was losing altitude as it closed to within a hundred yards of the stern of the ship. The Army pilots would shoot for a drop height of as close to thirty feet as they could get. As the large helicopter passed over the stern of the ship, Beach yelled into his headset radio.

"Team One drop commencing!"

Chief Austen and the Army crewman kicked the drop lines out the bay door as the helo slowed its advance over the flight deck. The lines had weights at their ends to keep them from being sucked back up into the engines or rotors by the helicopter's prop wash. The big aircraft nosed up in a sliding stop to achieve its hover position. As soon as they had reached a moderately stable hover, the Blackhawk just keeping pace with the ship's forward speed, the aircrewman gave Beach the go sign.

Beach, Chief Austen, and two other SEALs were immediately on the drop lines and on their way down to the deck.

THE BULKELEY

Rafsani saw the patrol boat moving down the port side, its progress slightly behind the one that had raked them from starboard. He hefted the RPG to his shoulder as the boat moved steadily forward. Suddenly, the Guards on the deck below him opened up on the boat.

God be praised, they're good for something! Rafsani thought. The gunfire from the Guards seemed to divert the attention of the gunners on the boat, who had been steadily working their way to the bridge. They shifted their fire to the deck to counter the Guards. Rafsani was thankful for the extra seconds he would gain to aim at the difficult, high-speed target. Satisfied with his lead on the patrol boat, the Sergeant Major was about to trigger the rocket when something caught his eye from aft of the bridge. Even as he cursed himself for allowing whatever it was to distract him from shooting at the boat in his sights, he turned aft to see a large helicopter rapidly approaching the ship.

Rafsani understood the significance immediately. The patrol boat forgotten, he raced aft from the bridgewing. He was twenty feet aft of the bridge when a bullet pierced his right leg below the knee. His leg gave out, and he crashed to the deck, still clutching the grenade launcher. Grinding his teeth as he tried to withstand the excruciating pain, he looked up from the deck to see the helicopter coming to a halt over the flight deck and dropping down out of sight behind the ship's superstructure.

Uttering every oath he could remember, Rafsani forced himself to his feet. Using the RPG for support, he dragged his wounded leg along as he headed back toward the rear of the superstructure.

Within seconds of hitting the deck, Beach, Austen, and the other two SEALS set up a defensive perimeter forward of the drop zone. Beach was pleased to see there was no sign of the opposition on the flight deck. The boats had done their work well. He could still hear their guns working over the forward part of the ship.

Crouching low on one knee, Beach turned to check the progress of the other half of the team. He was glad to see them all on their drop lines and descending.

Then there was a sound, a whooshing noise he vaguely recognized, coming from somewhere forward in the ship.

He was about to turn to look forward for the source of the noise, when he saw a bright orange exploding flower bloom on the nose of the hovering Blackhawk. The sound of the blast was not great, and at first he could not believe what had happened. In the second it took him to register the event, Chief Austen had grabbed him by the shoulder and thrown him forward toward the hangar. But Beach could not tear his eyes from the awful vision over the flight deck.

The Blackhawk hung in its hover for seconds after the rocket strike and then canted to port and slowly descended toward the deck. Beach thought at first that the aircraft might survive the drop. But, as it continued to fall, the twist to port became more pronounced.

He heard Austen screaming something about the rotor blades, and he launched himself forward, face down onto the deck. The impact of the Blackhawk caused the entire ship to shudder as it crashed with a second, more powerful explosion.

15

PATROL BOAT 600

"Jesus Christ."

Fraser looked on in horror as the Blackhawk crashed to the deck, erupting in a flaming explosion as it impacted. Watching from the patrol boat, he had seen the first small explosion, somewhere up forward on the aircraft, as the helo was maintaining its hover over the descending SEALS. Then the Blackhawk had rolled lazily to port before plummeting to the deck.

"Team One, Team One! This is Strike; do you copy? Over."

There was nothing but static on the mission circuit.

"Team One, this is Strike Command. Acknowledge this transmission!"

Still, there was no response from Beach. From Fraser's vantage point in the command boat, the entire flight deck of the *Bulkeley* appeared to be awash in flames.

"COM JTF, this is Strike. The Blackhawk has gone down—it's crashed on the flight deck of the *Bulkeley*!" he said urgently into the radio.

There was a ten-second delay, and then the deep voice of Admiral Boone came on the circuit.

"Say again, Fraser. You say the helo has crashed? What about the SEALS?" Boone's voice was controlled, but his concern was evident.

"Affirmative, COM JTF. Aircraft has impacted the flight deck with large secondary explosion. There was some kind of blast on board the helo that brought her down." Fraser paused and then rekeyed the microphone. "Status of Team One is uncertain. I've lost comms with them. I'm going in for a closer look."

The boat captain, who had been monitoring Fraser's conversation, ordered his helmsman to increase speed to forty knots and close the *Bulkeley*.

"Roger, Strike," Boone's voice came back. "We have to know their status as soon as you can determine anything. Is the ship still making way?"

"She hasn't slowed at all, Admiral. The crash doesn't seem to have affected the ship."

"Roger. Report as soon as you have anything. COM JTF, out."

Fraser watched the rapidly nearing stern of the *Bulkeley*. The prevailing wind was blowing the flames and smoke from the fire across the flight deck to starboard.

"Bring us in on the port side, Chief," he directed the boat captain. As the Mark III sped toward the frigate, the tactical circuit crackled in the pilothouse.

"PB Six Hundred, this is PB Seven-Eight-Eight. Have suppressed enemy fire on port weather deck below ship's bridge. I am taking new fire from amidships area. Will circle back to engage."

Fraser grabbed the handset for the other circuit.

"Roger, Seven-Eight-Eight. Restrict your counterfire to weather decks only," he ordered. In the original plan, some of the SEALs were intended to move up the vertical ladder on the helo hangar to reach the top of the superstructure. From there they were supposed to come up on the bridge from behind. Fraser wanted to ensure that his boats kept their fire below that level of the superstructure.

"PB Six Hundred, this is PB Seven-Two-Five. Have completed sweep of starboard side. I have reversed course and am receiving fire from the starboard break. I am reengaging. Over."

Fraser acknowledged the second boat's message. The Iranians were apparently fighting back—going into some sort of defensive posture.

As Fraser's patrol boat pulled even with the *Bulkeley*'s stern, a scant twenty-five yards away, he could see the extent of the devastation. The Blackhawk was engulfed in flame and was already skeletal, its fuselage burning and breaking away in large sections. The aircraft's fuel had spread to cover most of the flight deck and was burning furiously. Dense waves of black smoke billowed up from the corpse of the helicopter and the fiery deck. If there was anyone alive on the flight deck, Fraser could not see them.

THE PASCAGOULA

The atmosphere in the TDC on board the flagship was funereal. The circuits, other than the mission net, continued their transmissions, and their subdued buzz was the only sound in the space. The Admiral, Lacey, and Kelly stared disconsolately at the console below them, where the symbol for the *Bulkeley* continued on as before.

Garmisch completed a time and distance calculation at a nearby chart table and hurried back over to the Admiral with his information.

"Twenty minutes, Admiral," Garmisch said. "In twenty minutes, at her current speed, *Bulkeley* will enter the harbor proper."

Boone turned from Garmisch to look down at the video symbols on the console below him. His focus was the *Manchester*, guarding the entrance to the harbor. The symbol representing the *Bulkeley* was headed right for the *Manchester*.

"Okay," the Admiral began quietly. "If Beach and his boys survived that crash, that's how much time they've got to stop her —or get off her."

"They knew about the drop-dead point going in, Admiral," the Chief of Staff interposed.

Boone nodded, his gaze remaining on the tactical data console. "Raise *Manchester*," the Admiral directed Garmisch. "Tell them previous orders remain in effect. If *Bulkeley* reaches the harbor entrance, they are to take her under fire."

THE BULKELEY

Stewart raised his head above the level of the ship's control console and looked around the bridge.

The bridge had vibrated with the shock from the powerful explosion back aft. Stewart did not know what the cause of the blast was, but he felt certain it was related to the Iranian Sergeant Major's heading out of the bridge with the rocket launcher. The direct gunfire targeted on the bridge seemed to have stopped, although he could still hear the distinctive pounding of the patrol boats' guns. There was a new sound mixed in with the attackers' guns; the sound of small-arms fire directed from the ship outward.

He looked for Kim first. She had crawled over the deck to the wounded sailor and was crouched over him, trying to stop the bleeding from his wound. Feeling his eyes on her, she looked up and met his gaze. He saw the fear and confusion in her face, but also a great deal of strength. She watched him for a moment and then returned to caring for the injured sailor. Continuing to scan the bridge, Stewart saw that Kalil and the two Iranian gunmen were just rising from their defensive positions on the deck. Aziz was already back at the 1MC station. He was speaking into the public address system, giving a series of quick orders in Farsi. Stewart figured he was directing whatever defense his men were putting up against the boats.

And what about the boats? Stewart wondered. This attack on the ship meant that COM JTF knew what had happened on the *Bulkeley*. But why attack the ship? And why without any warning, and without giving the Iranians an opportunity to surrender? Stewart realized that if he carried out his own plan without knowing COM JTF's intentions, he stood a real chance of ruining the apparent rescue. The strafing attacks by the patrol boats had confused the issue, and he had only seconds to decide whether to go ahead with his plan or place the ship's fate in the hands of COM JTF.

Footsteps from the port bridgewing caught Stewart's attention and he turned to locate their source. Leaning in the doorway unsteadily was the Sergeant Major, his right leg soaked in blood from the knee down. He braced himself in the hatchway for support, the spent rocket launcher held like a cane in his right hand.

"A helicopter!" he barked across the bridge to Aziz. "The Americans were trying to land a helicopter on the ship's flight deck!"

Aziz looked from Rafsani's shattered leg up to the man's face.

"That explosion . . ." The Major's voice trailed away.

"I destroyed the aircraft," Rafsani growled, as he limped into the bridge. Stewart watched the big man, obviously in great pain, cross the bridge to join Aziz. Kalil moved to his side as well.

"Major," the Sergeant Major croaked out in English. "It is time to go."

Aziz met Rafsani's determined gaze with one of his own. Stewart looked back and forth between the two men, trying to read the significance of the remark. Aziz stared at the Sergeant Major for a long ten seconds as the sounds of gunfire continued to reverberate through the ship. Finally he responded to Rafsani.

"I agree. Make your preparations, Sergeant Major."

Rafsani nodded and headed for the ladder. Then he stopped in midstride and wheeled to address Aziz.

"Your forgiveness. But with this leg," he said, gesturing to his blood-soaked calf as if it were an inconvenience, "I shall need another man to assist me."

Aziz understood immediately. He turned to the other Guard on the bridge and gestured toward Rafsani. "Accompany the Sergeant Major," he ordered.

Kalil was about to protest, but a look at Aziz told him it would be futile.

Stewart watched the two of them leave the bridge, Rafsani moving quickly despite his injury. A bullet ricocheted off the starboard bridgewing, but Aziz ignored it as he crossed to where Stewart stood.

"We leave your ship now," he said, and then turned from Stewart to look out the bridge windows at the rapidly approaching darkness.

"For our departure to be successful, the ship must continue on as before. Your comrades on the boats and the other ships must not know we have left the ship." Aziz fixed his gaze on the *Manchester* growing larger and more distinct as the *Bulkeley* drew closer.

"You will continue on into the harbor at this speed. Once you reach the harbor entrance, you may do what you like. We will be away by then."

Stewart stared at Aziz, uncertain whether the man was mad or diabolically clever. However you leave the ship, Stewart told himself, I'm going to bring her back around and smash you to kindling.

Aziz turned from Stewart and looked down at Kim. He gestured to the remaining marine and then pointed to her.

"Take the woman."

The marine hustled over to Kim and grabbed her arm to pull her to her feet. She resisted, trying to stay with the wounded sailor, but the marine yanked her up from the deck.

"No, God damn it!" Stewart growled to Aziz. He started across the deck toward the Major, who quickly brought his weapon up and trained it on Stewart. The American halted a step short of Aziz. "Take me, if you want a hostage. You don't need her!"

Before Aziz could answer, Kim spoke up, still in the grip of the Iranian marine. "It's all right, John," she said, a look of grim determination on her face. "You stay with your ship."

"Enough!" Aziz barked, cutting off Kim. He returned his attention to Stewart. "You will continue on into the harbor. The woman will come with us. If you deviate from my instructions, we will kill her."

Bosca pulled his hand quickly back from the knife's handle like it was a thing on fire. The Iranian marine grunted once and then collapsed into a sitting position on the carpeted deck of the wardroom. The marine's face wore an expression of puzzled confusion as he looked down at the knife protruding from his chest. Bosca stared at the man from his position under the table, appalled at what he had done.

Jack Nelson was the first of the others to see what had happened. He sprang up from his spot under the head of the table and hurried over to the Iranian. Nelson picked up the marine's submachine gun from where it had fallen. As the other officers and the reporters began to get up from the deck, Nelson kept the marine covered with his own weapon. The Iranian looked up at Nelson, as if to speak, and then his head tumbled forward to rest on his chest.

Bosca, now on his feet, continued to stare at the marine in

horror. As Nelson was about to say something to him, there was a renewed sound of heavy-caliber gunfire from beyond the starboard bulkhead of the wardroom. A stray bullet ripped through the wardroom, passing over all their heads.

"Everybody down!" Nelson ordered, as he quickly knelt beside the table. The others in the wardroom followed his example.

Almost immediately, the heavy-caliber fire from off the ship was answered by gunshots, which sounded to Bosca as if they were coming from the quarterdeck area, just aft of the wardroom. This new gunfire had a flat cracking sound and was all but drowned out by the heavy pounding of the other guns.

"Well, that cinches it—we're not heading aft," Nelson yelled out over the dueling gunshots. Several more rounds could be heard striking the ship near and aft of the wardroom. Nelson scanned the remaining officers and directed his remarks to them.

"Whoever's shooting up the ship is presumably on our side. We can help them, and help ourselves, if we take back the bridge." He looked across the deck to the officers closest to the inert body of Lawrence. "Wiley, you and Chuck move the XO out of here. Put him in the forwardmost stateroom in officers' country." The two officers hurried to comply. They raised Lawrence up as quickly as they could and carried him forward out of the wardroom.

Half a dozen stray rounds ripped through the already shredded bulkhead, sending everyone in the wardroom diving for the deck.

Nelson looked around at the men under the tables. "Hanging around here looks like a great way to get killed. Let's go for the bridge," he said.

Without waiting for a response, he darted in a low crouch across the wardroom to the door that opened on the passageway to the staterooms and the forward part of the ship.

"What about us?" Bosca called out to Nelson as the officer opened the door to the passageway. Nelson turned to Bosca, who was now kneeling beside Perren and Mack.

"You're welcome to come along. We can use all the help we can get. But it's your choice; you've all been exposed to enough already."

Bosca looked over at Tim Mack, who gave him a goofy smile

that Bosca knew meant agreement. He did not bother to look at Perren.

The four remaining officers hustled out after Nelson, and Bosca and Mack quickly followed.

Perren, still on all fours beside the table, called after them, "You're not really going with those lunatics, are you, Bob?"

Bosca let the door close behind him without looking back.

Beach slammed the heavy steel hatch, sealing the intense flames outside the hangar. He had had to take one last look before accepting what had happened. The heat on the flight deck had been incredible. The fire was still spreading as the fuel from the Blackhawk's ruptured tanks continued to pour over the deck. Beach had gotten twenty-five feet from the burning fuselage, as close as he could get, and he had known they were all gone. Neither the aircrew nor his men under the helicopter on the drop lines could have survived.

He crossed the hangar deck to where Chief Austen kneeled over one of their men. He was hurriedly wrapping the burned man's hands in a battle dressing; they had no burn cream. The only other surviving member of the team was laid out a few feet from where Austen worked. The man was unconscious, having been struck by some fragment of metal when the Blackhawk exploded on the flight deck. Beach feared a concussion, but at least the man was breathing. Reflecting on it, Beach realized they would probably all have been killed if they had not been in their defensive perimeter forward of the drop zone. And, he reminded himself, if Austen had not pulled him clear . . . it was remarkable any of them had survived to seek refuge from the fire in the hangar.

Beach dropped down on one knee beside Austen. The chief had been burned as well, his shirt seared clean through around his lower back, but not as badly burned as the man on the deck. The injured SEAL's hands and left arm had been burned massively, and while he tried not to cry out, the pain was written on his face.

"That was a rocket—took the helo out," Austen said while he continued to wrap the man's hands.

"You sure, Chief?"

"Yeah. Not that it really matters." He finished his work and placed the first-aid pouch under the burned SEAL's neck, to keep his head slightly elevated.

"Just lay back and think of something better, Duffy," Austen said softly. "We'll get you real help as quick as we can."

At Austen's words, Beach looked down at the now useless radio still strapped to his chest. He yanked the radio, which had been smashed when he dived to the flight deck, off of his equipment harness and discarded it. Austen got to his feet and went to the nearby SH-60B helo, with Beach following behind. When they were out of earshot of the injured man, Beach looked at his watch and spoke.

"We're going to have to move fast, Chief. We've got less than ten minutes before the ship drivers think we've failed and open up on the *Bulkeley*."

Austen nodded in understanding. He looked back toward the two injured SEALs.

"I'd say hitting both spaces is no longer an option," the chief said. "Splitting up would just reduce our chances."

"Agreed. And if we're going to only one location, it's got to be the bridge. That's where their command and control will be."

Austen did not say anything else. He went over to the hangar door and picked up the Stoner machine gun from where he had left it. Looking out the tiny observation port in the door, he confirmed that with the fire still raging there was no way they could use the outside ladder to scale the superstructure and approach the bridge. He turned and went past Beach to the forward door of the hangar.

"The bridge is on the same deck that rocket came from, too," Austen said over his shoulder.

"You don't have to take her," Stewart said, trying to keep any trace of emotion out of his voice. "I'll keep the ship inbound for Bahrain—why wouldn't I?"

The two men stared at each other while the sound of gunfire continued unabated outside the bridge. Aziz gave Stewart a knowing smile.

"Because you would do what I would under the circumstances: you would do anything in your power to stop us. No, the woman goes with us. She will be released when we are well clear."

Aziz turned to the marine who had Kim by the arm and gave him an order in Farsi. The man headed for the port bridgewing door, with Kim in tow behind him. Stewart watched her go, his only impulse to choke the life out of Aziz. But he maintained his composure—he would not be the cause of her death. His eyes made contact with hers just before the marine escorted her off the bridge. There was real fear in her face now, belying her earlier confidence. Stewart knew her brave words had been for his benefit. He forced himself to turn away and face Aziz.

The Major had crossed to the bridge-to-bridge VHF radio. Without warning, he pulled his pistol and fired three rounds into the radio set, blasting it to shards. Then in a few quick steps he was at the 1MC station.

"I will tell the men to break off the fight and proceed to the boat deck," he said to Kalil, who had been standing at the back of the bridge ever since the patrol boat attack. Aziz turned to grab the 1MC mike.

Kalil had listened to Aziz, but his eyes had been on the marine as he passed from view through the port windows, pulling Kim behind him. His face remained impassive. He turned to Aziz.

"Put it down," Aziz heard Kalil say in a commanding tone.

Aziz spun back toward the Guards officer—but he already knew he was too late. Before Aziz could bring up his pistol, Kalil had his assault rifle trained on the Major's chest.

"Put the microphone down," Kalil repeated.

The Americans on the bridge stood frozen, uncertain of what was happening. Stewart watched the confrontation with more than just morbid interest; this might be the opportunity he had waited for.

Aziz coolly replaced the microphone and continued to stare at Kalil.

"Now the detonators, *Major*." Kalil pronounced Aziz's title as if it were a curse.

"Is that the point of this, Kalil?" The time for formalities had long since passed.

"That has always been the point, you idiot," Kalil sneered.

"The man who accomplishes this mission will reap the rewards of success. There is not enough glory for two. Now—the detonators!"

Stewart wished he understood Farsi. He turned from the conversation long enough to see that they had closed to within five miles of the *Manchester*, which seemed to be anchored or hovering near the harbor mouth. It was rapidly growing dark, and the *Manchester* had already turned on her running lights. As he turned back to the Iranians, he saw one of the patrol boats reverse course and head in for another run on the ship. The volume of gunfire increased.

"At least let me summon the men to the boat deck," Aziz said flatly. "You do not need to kill the remainder of our men to achieve your purpose."

Kalil's face brightened in a sinister grin. "Their lives will not be wasted, Aziz. Their resistance to the Americans will cover our departure. Now, for the last time—give me the detonators."

Aziz saw his own death more clearly than he saw Kalil. There was no way the Guards Commander would let him survive. His free hand moved unthreateningly to his belt, to the pouch that held the twin detonators. And then he was diving to his right, swinging the Beretta up to fire.

To Aziz's surprise, he had almost brought his gun to bear before Kalil opened fire.

Stewart saw the short burst from the Guards Commander's rifle drive Aziz down to the deck, as if nailing him into the tile. Aziz came to rest face down, the Beretta still clutched in his outstretched hand. Kalil kept his weapon trained on the prone figure, evidently fearing some trick. He circled behind Aziz so he could cover the Americans as he rolled the Major over. When Kalil flipped Aziz over on the deck, Stewart saw from the movement of the Major's chest that he was still alive.

Kalil went right to what he sought, pulling the waterproof pouch from Aziz's belt. The Iranian lifted the flap, and pulled and quickly inspected each of the two small radio detonators, searching for any sign that they had been damaged when Aziz had fallen to the deck. When he had satisfied himself as to their condition, Kalil reholstered the detonators and then fastened the pouch onto his own belt. Seeing the electronic devices increased Stewart's concern. Lastly, Kalil yanked the Beretta from Aziz's hand and shoved it into his own belt.

With his prizes in hand, Kalil rose from Aziz's now motionless form. He swung his rifle in a wide, slow arc, covering all the Americans. Kalil took a step toward the port bridgewing and then halted and returned to where Aziz lay.

The Guards Commander spat once onto the inert figure of the marine officer. Then he headed for the port wing.

He stopped before stepping out the door and addressed Stewart, but his words were intended for all on the bridge.

"Remember the woman!" he hissed.

Mosopu waited in silence, listening for signs of pursuit.

He had been certain the Iranians were dead on his ass when he had fled down the armory passageway with bullets careening after him. But, for the last few minutes he had neither heard nor seen his pursuers. He had moved steadily forward in the ship until he was just outside the bosun's locker that had been the scene of his earlier escape.

Mosopu concentrated hard in the dim light of the passageway, listening for any sound that would signal the arrival of the Iranians. All he heard was the distant sound of gunfire and the occasional sound of something impacting the ship. What was going on? he wondered.

Satisfied that his pursuers had given up or slowed substantially for the moment, he made his way into the bosun's locker. The door had been blown off its hinges, and grenade fragments still littered the deck. He looked up and saw that the scuttle leading out to the fo'c'sle was still standing open, as he had left it. The black-purple sky of twilight was visible through the open hatch.

Mosopu mounted the ladder below the scuttle and cautiously started up it. He climbed just far enough to be able to poke his head up through the scuttle with a minimum of exposure. The sounds of gunfire, both on board the ship and from across the water, echoed distinctly in the bosun's locker. Raising his head above the level of the scuttle, the Bosun's Mate was amazed at what met his eyes.

It took several seconds for his vision to adjust to the growing darkness, but he was immediately aware that the *Bulkeley* was in some sort of harbor: the blinking buoys and anchored ships clearly visible in the middle distance made that apparent. We're in Bahrain Harbor!, he realized with a start as his eyes adjusted. As sea detail boatswain's mate of the watch, he had been on the bridge during trips in and out of Bahrain well over a dozen times, and the harbor was very familiar to him.

Mosopu was jolted from his surprised survey by the sound of bullets striking the fo'c'sle near the scuttle. He ducked out of sight until the pounding of bullets on steel moved away. Looking warily out to port, he found the source of the gunfire: some kind of gunboat was blazing away at the *Bulkeley*, its hull illuminated in the gathering darkness by the flashes from its guns. He realized that somebody, presumably the U.S. Navy, was attacking the ship. But why? To help free them, or to stop the ship? In an instant he remembered the high explosives placed in the magazines. Mosopu was not sure what the *Bulkeley* was doing in Bahrain Harbor, but it confirmed to him that the Iranians intended to sink the frigate with all hands on board. He had to get to the bridge and let someone know.

Oblivious of the rounds that were striking the fo'c'sle around him, Mosopu squeezed out of the scuttle and hit the deck running. He recalled having obstructed the starboard break, so he headed for the break on the port side. He was just about to step through the entrance to the break when he heard the sound of an automatic weapon going off from just inside. He hesitated for a moment, trying to think of another way to reach the bridge. But there was none—and time was running out. Steeling himself, he ducked inside the break, the shotgun held in front of him.

Mosopu immediately took in the scene. In the fading light, one Iranian was firing out to sea, using the edge of the break bulkhead for cover; on the deck on either side of him were two of his comrades, apparently felled by the gunfire from the patrol boat. Mosopu did not give the Iranian time to realize he was there; he fired the shotgun twice in rapid succession, catching him in the side and the back. The man was almost thrown overboard by the blast.

Then Mosopu was running again, sidestepping the fallen Iranian to head for the route up to the bridge.

PATROL BOAT 600

A secondary explosion erupted from amid the Blackhawk's wreckage, with enough force to send a shock wave through Fraser's boat. He had directed the boat captain to draw within twenty feet of the burning flight deck in an effort to confirm whether anyone had survived the crash. They had seen no one; only the deadly fuel fire, which showed no signs of abating.

Fraser signaled the boat captain to take the Mark III out to a hundred yards as he keyed the mission circuit.

"COM JTF, this is Strike. There is no sign of survivors on the flight deck. Over." His grim tone reflected the feeling of all the men on the patrol boat.

"This is COM JTF. Roger. Any joy on the radio circuit?"

"Negative," Fraser answered. "No comms since before the drop —break—there is no sign of the ship slowing. Over." As he spoke, Fraser watched the gunfire from PB 788 continue to rake the port side of the *Bulkeley*. Return fire sputtered back for a few seconds and then ceased. There was no response from COM JTF for several seconds.

"We copy, Strike." It was Boone's voice. "Break off your attack. Repeat, break off your attack and clear the immediate area. Once you are clear, *Manchester* will engage. Over." The sadness in the Admiral's voice was obvious.

"This is Strike. Wilco. Out."

Fraser put down the handset and picked up the one for the tactical circuit.

"PB Seven-Eight-Eight, PB Seven-Two-Five, this is Strike. Break off attack. Repeat, break off attack. Clear the target at max speed, in whatever direction will open the fastest. Report when clear by two thousand yards."

THE BULKELEY

With the assistance of the other marine, Rafsani had succeeded in putting the *Bulkeley*'s motor whaleboat at the rail. They had been able to lower the boat on its large davit crane to a position along-side the boat deck. This enabled them to load the boat with pas-sengers before setting it in the water. Once the boat was loaded, a lone man remaining on board could operate the davit to drop the boat into the water. That man would then shinny down the monkey lines from the davit to the boat.

Rafsani and the marines had trained with a number of small boats and related davits against just such a need. The Sergeant Major had been insistent that if something went wrong, they be able to improvise with what was available on the ship.

A great deal had gone wrong, Rafsani thought to himself, as he forced his mind away from the incredible pain in his leg. But they still had the time and the means to carry out their secondary mission. With the Americans obviously alerted, Rafsani knew there was no way they would let the *Bulkeley* approach their flag-ship. It was still possible to flee the ship by boat, however, and sink the *Bulkeley* in the harbor channel. Thankfully, the American boats had stopped firing only moments ago and were moving away. Rafsani was uncertain of the significance of that move; he only knew that it would serve to aid them in their escape.

He hissed through his teeth in pain as he and the other marine passed the woman from the boat deck into the arms of the Guard waiting in the boat. He remarked to himself that, even now, the woman maintained her composure and treated them coolly. Battle was hardly the place for a woman, yet this one had fought well. Rafsani hoped she would live through it, but he did not believe it would be so.

As the woman and the Guard settled in the boat, Rafsani heard the sound of the hatch opening behind them on the boat deck. He and the marine spun around in a defensive posture, Rafsani with the *kukri* instantly in his hand, the marine with his Sterling. Kalil stepped through the open hatch and out onto the boat deck. He looked briefly at Rafsani and then turned and dogged down the hatch behind him.

"Where is the Major?" Rafsani demanded curtly.

Kalil gave him a strange look, hard to discern in the late twi-light, almost as if he were trying to suppress a smile.

"Dead," the Guards Commander said harshly. "Killed on the bridge by the fire from the American boats."

Rafsani stared emotionlessly at Kalil for a moment, and then down at the deck. Finally he looked back up at Kalil.

"You did not bring him?" he asked softly.

"Bring him?" Kalil said in agitated surprise. "Do not be ridiculous! The man is dead! Besides"—Kalil patted a pouch at his belt—"I have the detonators."

"I will not leave him." Rafsani's voice was frightening in its unearthly determination.

Before Kalil could respond, the Sergeant Major had brushed by him and was opening the closed hatch. Kim watched their conversation from the motor whaleboat in baffled silence.

"This is insane!" Kalil cried, turning after Rafsani. "The man is dead. There is nothing for him!" He paused and then added, "Leave us now and we will abandon you here to die!"

Halfway through the hatch Rafsani turned back to the Guards Commander. "Do what you will," he rumbled, his voice low and controlled. "He was my friend, and my leader. I will not leave him."

And then he was gone, down the dark passageway, before Kalil could say anything further to stop him. The Guards Commander could barely contain his rage, almost firing his weapon after the departing man. But in a moment he regained control and turned to the remaining marine.

"You can operate this machine?" He gestured to the boat at the rail. "And this boat?"

"Yes, Colonel," the marine stammered out. "But, the Sergeant Major, the—"

"He has made his choice," Kalil snapped. "There is no time to wait." He clambered over the rail and into the motor whaleboat. Kalil pointed his assault rifle at the marine on the boat deck.

"Now lower us into the water and join us in this craft."

MV ANDES COMMERCE

Rolf Hauser, master of the *Andes Commerce*, paced his bridge in a high state of agitation. It was not supposed to happen like this, he thought. Not like this at all!

From their position on the periphery of the commercial anchorage, the men on the bridge of the *Andes Commerce* had an excellent view of the unfolding action. Too good a view, Hauser thought. First he had seen the American warships get under way, one moving to less than a mile from his ship, apparently to block the channel. Then the Bahrainis had sent harbor police from ship to ship in the large anchorage, directing the merchantmen's masters that no ship was to get under way until further notice. That was fine—he had intended to wait at anchor anyway, departing only after making the pickup. But now, even if the Iranians were successful, he could not get under way without the permission of the damn Bahrainis!

If the Iranians were successful. He would have laughed out loud at how ludicrous that idea seemed at the moment, had his own skin not been on the line as well. He had seen the small boats start their attack in the distance, and then the massive explosion somewhere back on the *Bulkeley*'s fantail. Could anything else go wrong? Whatever element of surprise the Iranians had hoped to achieve was obviously gone.

The only good thing about all of this was that if the Iranians failed in their primary mission but continued on in pursuit of their beloved martyrdom—either blowing up the ship and themselves with it, or dying in battle with the Americans—he stood a good chance to getting away clean. And payment was not contingent on the success or failure of the Iranians' mission. That gave him a little comfort, but not much.

Had the plan gone like clockwork, he knew the Iranians had intended to abandon the *Bulkeley* when she was in close to the *Pascagoula* and make their way to the *Andes Commerce* under cover of darkness. The confusion that would be caused by the warship's explosion was to have ensured they would make good their escape. With the massive explosion and the danger of fire in the harbor, the most logical thing in the world would have been for conscientious masters like himself to get their ships under way and take them out to sea. That was how it was supposed to have worked, he thought grimly.

"There is a boat moving away from the *Bulkeley*!"

The voice came from the Saudi first officer, stationed on the starboard bridgewing with a night vision scope. Hauser looked over at the officer and tried to follow his angle of view out to where the boat would be. It did not work, nor could he see the boat through the darkness with his binoculars.

"Captain, they are headed toward us!" the first officer called out excitedly.

Hauser let his useless binoculars fall to his chest as he stared into the darkness. He let loose a colorful Bavarian oath, incomprehensible to the Shias, who made up his bridge team. Turning, Hauser headed aft to his cabin.

The situation called for additional liquid fortification.

USS MANCHESTER

"Eight thousand yards and closing!" The tactical action officer's voice echoed in the *Manchester*'s bridge. Captain Walker had directed that the sound-powered phone line from his CIC be placed on the bridge speaker, so he could monitor his fire control solution. He stepped out onto the starboard bridgewing, the better to watch the oncoming *Bulkeley*. She did not have her running lights on, but the fire still burning on board illuminated the distinctive outline of the warship.

Moments ago he had copied Fraser's conversation with the Admiral, and he was only waiting for Boone's order or for the *Bulkeley* to close to within a mile to open fire. As he studied the onrushing frigate, its flight deck like a burning jet-engine exhaust, he could hear the sound of the drive motors of his 76-millimeter cannon periodically moving the turret to follow the track of the *Bulkeley*. Looking down to his starboard midships area, he saw the 25-millimeter chain gun, fully manned and tracking the flaming ship. Walker had positioned the *Manchester* so that she presented a beam aspect to the charging *Bulkeley*; this allowed the maximum number of his own weapons to be brought to bear. His topside machine gun and grenade launcher gunners were in place, but he did not think the *Bulkeley* would get close enough for them to get into action.

He watched the Mark III patrol boats sprinting away from the captured frigate at flank speed, to clear *Manchester*'s field of fire.

"Target is at five thousand yards," the TAO's voice carried out from the bridge.

"All weapons systems are tracking. Target will be at two thousand yards, engagement range, in just under five minutes."

Walker smiled to himself. He'd be damned if he was going to let her get that close.

16

THE BULKELEY

Beach hugged the deck as a stream of bullets ripped over his head. It had not taken them long to find the Iranians.

He and Austen had left the hangar, moving down the amidships passageway that ran between the two hangars. As soon as they had entered the passageway, they had heard the distinctive sound of assault rifles firing from the quarterdeck area where the passageway terminated. The two SEALs had moved cautiously down the passageway toward its terminus, but had seen no sign of the men doing the firing. It was then that Beach had realized that the Iranians were firing out at the patrol boats from the cover of the midships area. He had figured they were just out of sight around the corners, firing through the quarterdeck doors.

Following silent hand signals, Austen had copied Beach's actions as he got down on the deck twenty feet aft of the quarterdeck. They had then simultaneously rolled grenades down the poorly lit passageway and flattened to the deck as the explosives detonated in the quarterdeck area. The flat blasts of the grenades had been followed by screams and curses from the quarterdeck and now gunfire directed their way.

The surviving marines at the quarterdeck were exposing themselves just long enough to get off a burst of fire, then ducking back behind the protective bulkheads. Beach did not think the marines knew exactly where he and Austen were. To complicate the Iranians' problem, he fired a short burst into the overhead light fixture nearest their position on the deck, extinguishing the red illumination and throwing them into darkness. As two of the Iranians showed themselves to shoot, Austen fired a lengthy burst from the Stoner that drove them back out of sight.

Beach looked across the deck and saw Austen's signal. Silently they rose from the deck and braced their backs against the opposing bulkheads of the passageway. When the next marine revealed himself to try to get a shot off, Austen opened up with withering fire from his machine gun. He kept firing, breaking off the bursts for an instant every half dozen rounds to prevent jamming, as Beach raced down the passageway, hugging the starboard bulkhead. Austen's practiced aim tore up every corner of the quarterdeck except for the point Beach was headed for.

Without slowing his breakneck run beside the hail of bullets from the Stoner, Beach reached the entrance to the quarterdeck. Looking across to port, he saw only one standing marine. Beach took the startled Iranian down with two quick rounds from his assault rifle, at the same time diving for the deck and rolling to his right. A burst of fire went over his head as the marine on the starboard side of the quarterdeck opened fire. You're too late, Beach thought, blasting the man back through the open quarterdeck door with a three-round burst from his own weapon.

Austen was at his side immediately. They took a second to survey the scene before heading forward. The grenades had killed one marine and severely wounded another. The two Iranians that Beach had killed brought the total to four.

How many others? he wondered, as he and Austen silently continued forward toward the bridge.

Stewart knelt beside the fallen Iranian Major. He had passed the conn back to Septenano while he tried to rouse Aziz. They had propped up Aziz's head with one of the bridge flak jackets. It was clear to Stewart from the man's wounds that nothing could be done for him.

"Aziz," Stewart said loudly to the prone marine, trying to bring him around.

There was no response. The Iranian's breathing was growing ever more labored, the bleeding from his chest continued.

"Aziz, can you hear me?"

Aziz's eyes flickered open briefly and then closed. "Leave me, Stew-urt," he croaked. "It is over."

Not for us—not yet, Stewart thought as he bent closer to the dying man.

"What was the plan, Aziz?" Stewart's voice was quiet but insistent. "You've failed, but what was your reason for bringing us here?"

The Major's eyes flickered open again.

"The woman—she is your woman?" he whispered, looking for a reaction from Stewart.

Stewart nodded. There was no sense in trying to pretend now, he thought.

Aziz managed a grim, fading smile. "She may survive. . . . There is little honor in killing a woman." Aziz's eyes closed again. "But your ship will die."

As Stewart was about to press the Iranian further, he was startled to see first a gun barrel and then a pair of eyes appear over the rim of the bridge ladder trunk.

"Jesus . . . Stewart—you're alive!" came a distinctly American voice from out of the trunk.

Gun still at the ready, Jack Nelson moved up the ladder. He stared at Stewart for a long moment and then shifted his gaze to scan the bridge. "What's happened up here?" Nelson's tone expressed his shock at the carnage that greeted him. He was followed onto the bridge by half a dozen officers and two of the reporters.

"It's been bad up here," Stewart said. "And it could still get worse." While the newcomers were still absorbing the destruction on the bridge, he took charge. "Jack, take the conn." As Nelson began giving the necessary orders, Stewart addressed the next most senior officer. "Wiley, take the rest of the guys and head for the coops. See if you can free the crew. The Iranians said something about having sealed them in—whatever that means."

The pilot acknowledged the order and headed back down the

ladder. Nelson gave his submachine gun to one of the officers who followed Wiley.

"What can we do, Commander?" Bosca asked. He and Tim Mack had remained on the bridge.

Stewart looked across the bridge to the sailor wounded in the boat attack. "If you know any first aid, you can try to help that man," he told him.

Bosca nodded, his face darkening in concern as he looked around the bridge. "Has there been any word of Miss Mitchell?" he asked.

Stewart looked from Bosca across the bridge and out at the port bridgewing.

"The Iranians have her," he said quietly. "They've taken her off the ship."

Before Bosca could say anything else, Stewart was moving across the bridge toward the port wing. He stopped at an equipment rack near the door and picked up a night vision device. As he opened the hatch, he turned back to Bosca.

"See if you can do anything for that Iranian officer," Stewart said. And then he was gone, out onto the dark wing of the bridge.

Mack went to the wounded sailor and Bosca knelt beside Aziz. After a moment, Bosca got to his feet.

"This man is dead," he said softly.

Mosopu headed up the steel ladder. One more to go and I'm on the bridge, he thought to himself. He climbed slowly, having to favor his injured leg. When he reached the top, he headed down the passageway to the next ladder.

With a cry of surprise, he collided with a black-clad figure, moving in the same direction in the dark passageway.

The figure wheeled on him with a terrifying yell and sent him crashing into the port bulkhead. Mosopu held the shotgun across the front of his body like a quarterstaff as the man's body slammed into his own. The Bosun's Mate pushed himself off the wall, trying to force the man off him, and was amazed at the strength facing him. His opponent held him pressed against the bulkhead, his hands gripping the shotgun, as did Mosopu's.

For an instant, Mosopu looked into the coal black eyes in the bearded face inches from his own. There was a glint of something like recognition in the Iranian's eyes, and then some of the pressure on the shotgun against Mosopu's chest seemed to ease. He rushed to exploit the opening, putting all his force into throwing the big marine off him. With a powerful grunt, he shoved the shotgun away from his body, and the marine gave ground. Suddenly he realized the Iranian had released the shotgun, breaking their clinch. The marine had stepped back a full two feet from him, and Mosopu raced to bring the shotgun down to fire.

And then his right hand was radiating a white-hot pain, as if scalding water had been poured over it. He lost control of the hand and saw the shotgun falling away from his grasp, as if in slow motion. His gaze took in his ruptured hand, the tendons slashed across the top, and the large, lethal knife that the fearsome Iranian held. Mosopu knew immediately that this was the man who had savaged Andy.

For a few seconds the Iranian stared at Mosopu without making a move to attack. The marine held his hands in front of him, his elbows bent. Then his left hand flashed out from his side, and even as Mosopu's eyes reactively followed it, he knew it was the other hand that held the knife. The Bosun's Mate pushed off from the bulkhead and ducked low just as the blade came flying in from his right. He cried out in pain as a glancing blow from the blade scissored across his shoulder. Then he was on the marine, moving under his guard in a low, driving tackle. Mosopu slammed the Iranian back into the opposite bulkhead with an impact that drove the air from the man's lungs. He threw his right forearm against the inside of the marine's knife arm, pinning it against the bulkhead. Mosopu was rushing to bring his left hand up to the Iranian's throat when he felt a wedge of pointed fingers slam into his left kidney. The pain was excruciating, and he collapsed backward onto the deck.

Mosopu looked up from the deck, his vision clouded by incredible pain. The marine remained against the bulkhead, bent over double and gasping for breath. After a few seconds, the Iranian looked up from his stooped position. The man held the immense knife at his side as he slowly crossed the space between himself and the Bosun's Mate. Summoning all his remaining strength, Mosopu forced himself up from the deck onto one knee. His right hand was useless now, and the pain and unsteadiness from his host of wounds combined to make him weave slightly from side to side as the Iranian approached.

The big marine stopped just out of reach from Mosopu and bent over, resting his hands on his knees. The Iranian continued to breathe laboriously, as he looked down into Mosopu's eyes. The Bosun's Mate was amazed to see what appeared to be a smile form on the man's ferocious face. The Iranian held the smile for a moment, and then, raising himself to his full height, he tossed the giant knife down the passageway, sending it clattering into the darkness.

God damn! Mosopu thought, I've had enough of this shit! With a bloodcurdling yell, he launched himself up from the deck just as the giant marine leapt upon him.

Stewart watched the motor whaleboat as it headed toward the tanker. An accommodation ladder was being lowered on the merchant's starboard side to receive the small craft. The boat was far too distant for him to make out Kim or any of the figures on board. At least I know where they're going, he thought, as he noted the position of the tanker, anchored away from the rest of the merchantmen. Apparently the merchantman had been intended as the Iranians' means of escape, and the *Bulkeley*'s continued progress into the harbor was supposed to divert attention from that escape. But what about their reason for bringing the ship there in the first place? Aziz had said the *Bulkeley* would die, but unless the Iranians had planned to use her to ram the *Pascagoula* or some other ship, Stewart could not see how.

Still puzzling over the Iranians' plan, Stewart was about to lower the night vision device and return to the bridge when he felt cold, hard steel pressed into the back of his neck.

"Don't move if you want to live," he heard an American voice whisper from behind him.

After a moment the pressure was gone. "All right, go ahead and turn around slowly," the voice said.

Stewart did as he was directed and was astonished to find himself confronting a blackened-faced commando who was clearly not Iranian. The man took one look at Stewart and lowered his weapon from its ready position.

"Sorry," the man said carefully. "SEALs," he added as an afterthought. Seeing the understanding dawn in Stewart's eyes he continued, "We expected to find some of the bad guys up here."

"They've all left the ship," Stewart said, still confused over what was going on. "Or at least their leaders have."

Before Stewart had finished his sentence, the man had turned from him and was darting inside the bridge.

"C'mon," the man called over his shoulder. "Hurry!"

Stewart quickly followed the SEAL into the bridge, only to find that there was another one standing by the open starboard bridge-wing door. He held a large, menacing machine gun, and it was unclear to Stewart whether he was covering the *Bulkeley* sailors or was just exceptionally cautious.

"One KIA," the man with the machine gun said, gesturing towards the prostrate body of Aziz.

"No sign of any others in the immediate area," the first SEAL replied.

Reaching the center of the bridge, the first man turned to Stewart. "Looks like you're the senior man here."

"The Captain is dead."

"Sorry to hear that. But you've got to stop the ship—now!" the SEAL said forcefully.

"What's so important about stopping the ship?" Nelson interjected from his conning station behind the control console. "The Iranians are gone—besides, they've got the woman."

The SEAL leader turned back to Stewart. "The reporter?" he asked.

Stewart nodded slowly. He could feel his heart thumping in his chest. "They took her as a hostage," he said. "To ensure we wouldn't come after them."

"That's too bad," the SEAL said with a mixture of sympathy and urgency. "But you're going to have to forget about her." He turned and pointed out the bridge windows toward the ever larger silhouette of the *Manchester*. Still pointing at the other frigate, he addressed Stewart.

"In just under two minutes that ship is going to open up on us with everything she's got. They have orders not to let you enter the harbor."

"Can't you call them off?" Nelson asked from across the bridge.

The SEAL answered Nelson while continuing to study Stewart. "If I could, it would've been done already. No radio."

Stewart understood their situation only too clearly. He looked out the windows at the rapidly closing *Manchester*.

Stewart spun from the windows to hurriedly address the bridge team's quartermaster.

"Brooks, you can send light. Get on the flashing light and tell the *Manchester* that we've regained control of the ship! Move!"

The signalman nodded and ducked out the starboard hatch, heading for the signal light.

"You've got to stop this ship," the SEAL repeated quietly.

BAHRAIN HARBOR

From her position near the bow of the motor whaleboat and facing aft, Kim could clearly see the silhouette of the *Bulkeley*. The ship continued on toward the harbor at high speed.

Kalil sat directly across from Kim, keeping a watchful eye on her but occasionally turning to look back toward the frigate. The marine was at the wheel of the boat, the other Guard beside him. The tiny motor whaleboat bumped across the low waves of the channel, and Kim had to hold tightly to the gunwales as the marine squeezed every ounce of speed he could out of the craft.

What had been the point? she wondered, watching the *Bulkeley* move farther and farther away. All those men killed—both American and Iranian—and all they had succeeded in doing was bringing the ship to Bahrain. Now it appeared that the three men in the boat with her would be the only survivors of their useless mission.

Kim switched her attention from the *Bulkeley* to Kalil, who was looking at something over her shoulder. She turned to follow his gaze and saw that they were rapidly closing in on a large tanker. The tanker appeared to be showing the usual lights of a ship at anchor and looked no different than a dozen others anchored nearby.

When she turned back around she saw that Kalil's eyes were on her. The man was smiling unpleasantly as he watched her.

"You should thank me for saving you," he said over the sound of the boat's motor.

Kim was silent.

"You are far better off in this craft than back upon the ship," he added when she did not respond.

She regarded him, puzzled by Kalil's obvious desire to boast of what seemed to be a failure. "What are you talking about?" she asked.

"The warship." He gestured back towards the *Bulkeley*. "I will let it reach the entrance to the channel, where it can do maximum damage—and then destroy it!" He laughed at this, as if it was a great joke.

An uneasy feeling settled over Kim. What could he mean?

"All I see is the four of us in this boat," she said. "And a bloody plan that failed."

Kalil stopped laughing, but his smile remained in place. "Our plan—our mission—will be a success!" he said forcefully.

As Kim stared at him, the Guards Commander's hand went to the waterproof pouch at his belt and pulled out one of the detonators. She saw that he was careful to hold the electronic device close against his body to shield it from the spray when the boat splashed across the *Bulkeley*'s low wake.

"With this I will complete the mission. And you will be able to observe its success."

USS MANCHESTER

"Range, thirty-five hundred and closing."

The *Bulkeley*'s bow-on silhouette filled Walker's binoculars, looking even closer than the stated range. He let the glasses fall to his chest. The frigate was so close now that he no longer needed them. He bent down to the intercom on the *Manchester*'s starboard bridgewing.

"Stand by to fire."

"TAO; aye," the response came back through the steel box. "All fire control systems are locked on and tracking."

Walker turned toward the open bridgewing door and called out to his officer of the deck, "Any word from the flagship?"

"Nothing, Captain."

"Very well," Walker said, returning his attention to the *Bulkeley*. Well, here goes, he thought to himself.

"Flashing light from the *Bulkeley!*" the OOD suddenly called out from inside the bridge. Walker saw the signal light start up, and his own signalman raced to answer it.

"It's too late for that type of trick," Walker said under his breath.

"Captain; TAO. The closing rate is dropping!"

"But they're still closing, correct?" Walker boomed into the intercom to the CIC. He could damn well see with his own eyes that the *Bulkeley* was continuing to close!

"Still closing, Captain." The tactical action officer's tone was urgent. "Range three thousand. But they're slowing down—they've reduced speed to almost nothing!"

"I'm not going to bet my ship that this isn't some kind of deception!" Walker stormed back. "Open fire on my command!"

Then, through the open door, he heard the radio.

"*Manchester*, this is COM JTF. Hold fire—I say again, hold fire! Do not engage. Over." It was clearly the Admiral's voice.

"Batteries tight! Batteries tight!" Walker screamed into the intercom. He turned and yelled into the bridge. "Get us out of here! Move away from the *Bulkeley* and toward the *Pascagoula!*"

THE <u>BULKELEY</u>

"So what now?" Stewart did a poor job of keeping the anger out of his voice. He knew that he had just killed Kim by stopping the ship. The fact that it was her life against the lives of everyone on board the *Bulkeley* did not comfort him.

Beach stared back at him in silence. The whole bridge was quiet, and the ship itself seemed to have grown still after the helmsman had executed Stewart's order to come to all stop. Finally Beach spoke.

"Our best bet is to remain stationary, look as harmless as we can, until they decide to send the patrol boats back in to investigate."

"*Manchester*'s moving away," Scott Septenano said. Following his gaze, the men on the *Bulkeley*'s bridge could see the other frigate headed into the inner harbor.

"So we wait till they check us out," Stewart continued. "How long after that until you can go after the rest of those bastards on that tanker?" He pointed out to port at the *Andes Commerce.*

"They won't get away," the SEAL said flatly. "I guarantee you that."

There was a loud crash in the ladder trunk leading to the bridge, and the other SEAL was over the trunk in seconds, his gun trained down the ladder. He turned to Stewart.

"Is this one of yours?"

Stewart crossed quickly to the trunk and looked down it past the man's weapon. Collapsed across the bottom of the ladder was the bloodied and all but unrecognizable figure of BM2 Mosopu. Stewart elbowed the SEAL aside and hurried down the ladder.

"Christ," Stewart said softly. "He's one of our men all right. Give me a hand with him," he called over his shoulder.

The SEAL backed up from the trunk, maintaining his weapon in a defensive stance, and let Bosca move by him. Together, with considerable strain, Stewart and Bosca lifted the heavy Bosun's Mate the rest of the way up the ladder.

When they reached the bridge, they laid Mosopu out on the deck. Bosca propped up his head with another of the flak vests and dragged the first-aid kit over to the big man's side. He did not know where to begin. There seemed to be hardly an inch of the Samoan's body that was not bruised or bleeding. Mosopu had lost part of one ear and suffered numerous stab wounds, the depth of which Bosca had no way of gauging. His right hand was a bloody shambles and the left side of his face was black and blue, the eye swollen shut. But his other eye was half open and looking at Stewart, who knelt beside him.

"Mister Stewart . . ." he gasped out in a hoarse whisper.

"Don't waste your strength on talk, Boats," Stewart said quietly. He tried to put on an optimistic front. "Just let us take care of you. It's going to be okay."

"No . . ." Mosopu responded, trying to ignore his great pain. "*Gotta* talk . . . the bombs."

Beach moved across to kneel with Stewart.

"What's this about bombs?" Stewart asked, his compassion for the wounded man now displaced by his greater concern for the ship.

Mosopu arched his back in an agonized spasm of coughing. When his breathing returned to normal, he rolled his head back toward Stewart.

"I found bombs . . . inna gun mag," he croaked out. "And around the missile mag." Seeing the comprehension in Stewart's face, the Bosun's Mate sank back against the flak vest, closing his one good eye.

Stewart got to his feet. "That explains the little radios they were so concerned about."

Beach also rose. "What did these radios look like?" he asked Stewart.

"Like what you'd use to operate a toy, or like a remote control." He looked from Beach out the port-side windows toward the tanker. "They took them with them."

"But what's stopping them from blowing up the ship?" Jack Nelson interjected.

Beach shrugged. "Who knows what their plan is. But our stopping the ship short of the harbor may push up their timetable to pull the trigger."

Stewart looked first at Beach and then at the other SEAL. "Can either of you disarm explosives?"

Beach shook his head. "We could try, but we're not EOD. I'm afraid if they've rigged them right, there's just as good a chance that we'd sink the ship as disarm them." Beach's tone became far more forceful. "You've got to abandon ship—now," he said to Stewart.

"We can't," Stewart responded flatly, looking again toward the *Andes Commerce*. "A group of our officers went down to the berthing compartments and found that the Iranians have welded most of the crew in down there. We don't have the tools to get them out."

"Then you've got to save who you can!" The SEAL officer was insistent.

Stewart stared at Beach in silence. He knew that by stopping the ship he might have already killed Kim; he had no way of knowing for certain. The one certainty was that the presence of the bombs on board threatened the survival of both his ship and crew. Stewart looked down at Mosopu's horribly mangled body, and that made up his mind for him. One life had to be of less value than many.

Brushing Beach aside, he headed for the port wing. He stopped at the open hatchway and turned to look back across the bridge. Every eye on the bridge was on him. Stewart looked like a man who had stared into his own grave. The cold, dead eyes settled on Scott Septenano.

"Scott, get down to CIC and switch control of the gun to the port target designation tracker."

"But Mosi said the gun magazine is wired with explosives!" Septenano said in surprise.

"That's a risk we have to take," Stewart said harshly. "Do it. Now."

Before the gunnery officer could respond, Stewart had wheeled and headed out of the bridge. After a second's delay, Beach followed him onto the wing and aft to the ladder that led to the 0-3 level over the bridge.

Septenano stepped over the prostrate form of the Bosun's Mate and hurried down the ladder to the CIC.

BAHRAIN HARBOR

Kim shifted her attention from Kalil to the tanker as the motor whaleboat prepared to pull alongside the large ship. She could see that a large accommodation ladder had been lowered from the weather deck amidships. The platform at the base of the ladder rose a few feet above the water, and an armed man was waiting on it in the darkness. The marine at the helm of the motor whaleboat made a horseshoe turn and skillfully brought the boat alongside the platform. The Guard in the boat threw a line across to the man waiting on the platform as the boat settled out beside the tanker.

Kalil stepped up from the boat and onto the platform and ges-

tured to Kim that she was to get out next. She turned toward the
tanker, and, with the assistance of the man on the platform,
climbed up out of the boat.

As the crewman on the platform reached down to help the
remaining two men up, the relative silence of the night was
ripped by a cracking boom that rolled over the harbor. The occupants of the boat and those standing on the platform spun to seek
out the source of the noise. Kim saw a bright orange flash emerge
from the center of the *Bulkeley*, followed by another boom. She
looked from the flash to Kalil, who was standing at the base of the
accommodation ladder, staring back at the frigate.

Suddenly the water a hundred yards off the beam of the tanker
erupted in a noisy explosion, sending a geyser of saltwater rocketing skyward. A second shell landed even closer to the *Andes
Commerce*, its impact causing the men in the unsteady boat to lose
their footing. Kalil remained frozen, apparently stunned by the
appearance of the advancing shells.

Kim saw her chance. She dived off the lip of the platform,
catching Kalil and the crewman by surprise. Her dive carried her
into the water astern of the motor whaleboat, and she fought
desperately to get as deep as she could, the warm black waters
shielding her from view.

THE <u>BULKELEY</u>

Stewart forced himself to focus totally on the task at hand. He
stood stooped over the target designation tracker's binocular
sight, his face pressed against the eyepieces, one hand on each of
the grips on the TDT's yoke as if holding the handlebars of a large
motorcycle. He willed himself to think of nothing but the gun and
the target, but he could not drive Kim from his mind. Beach stood
beside him in silence on the TDT platform on the deck above the
bridge. The intense blast of the 76-millimeter gun going off was
painful to the unprotected ears of both men, but Stewart welcomed the pain as another way of blocking from his thoughts the
inevitable result of what he was doing.

Stewart was having a hard time seeing the splashes from his

falling rounds in the darkness. The whole purpose of the target designation tracker was to allow the gunner to visually correct for the fall of shot, until one hit the target. The *Andes Commerce* was not far away, less than a mile in fact, and he could just make out the motor whaleboat made up against the tanker's hull. With each round he closed in on his target, but the splashes were still hard to judge against the black night sky.

MV ANDES COMMERCE

"That hell-spawned, unclean American bitch!" Kalil cursed furiously as he brought his rifle to bear on the spot at which Kim had entered the water. Before he could fire, another cannon shell ruptured the surface less than fifty yards from the tanker. Kalil staggered backward on the platform, his back slamming into the massive hull of the tanker. As the Guards Commander attempted to regain his footing, the merchant crewman elbowed past him and scampered frantically up the accommodation ladder.

Idiot! Kalil thought, looking after the man. There is no chance for your ship unless I save it! He had hoped to wait to sink the *Bulkeley* until it had drawn closer to the other American vessels. But now the madmen were trying to kill him! Aziz had overestimated their concern for the woman. A cruel smile appeared on Kalil's face as his hand went to the waterproof pouch at his belt. He pulled one of the detonators free just as a massive explosion erupted a scant twenty-five yards from the platform. The concussion sent Kalil tumbling to the steel-grated deck of the platform, the detonator slipping from his hand. No! his mind screamed. I cannot fail—it is God's will that I succeed! He grabbed for the detonator, reaching it just as the mass of seawater sent skyward by the shell's detonation rained down on the platform. The curtain of water descended on Kalil like an angry cloudburst, soaking him to the skin and dousing the sensitive detonator.

The Guards Commander staggered to his feet, the detonator clasped firmly in his right hand. As he pulled out the device's antenna and pointed it toward the *Bulkeley*, a trickle of water bled from its plastic casing onto his hand. Flicking on the detonator's power switch, Kalil was rewarded by the amber light that indi-cated the device had power. Kalil allowed himself a small smile. He aimed the detonator like a gun at the center of the frigate and depressed the detonate switch.

Nothing.

Kalil pushed the button over and over, but still there was no evidence of any effect on the *Bulkeley*.

"This cannot happen!" he yelled aloud as he continued to push the switch impotently.

In a panic, he discarded the ruined detonator, and his hand went to the pouch at his belt to extract the other one. Before he could pull up the pouch's flap, another shell struck close aboard the tanker. Kalil clung to the ladder rail for support as the shock waves from the blast struck the *Andes Commerce*. He doubled over and shielded the pouch with his body as the remnants of the geyser from the explosion cascaded down on the platform. Real-izing he had to escape the watery fallout from the *Bulkeley*'s deto-nating shells, Kalil turned and raced up the accommodation ladder.

THE <u>BULKELEY</u>

Stewart saw another of his rounds splash abeam the tanker's star-board side. Using his shoulders to torque the TDT yoke slightly to the right, he corrected for the last round. The *Bulkeley*'s 76-milli-meter gun mount followed every move he made with the TDT, whether up or down, right or left. Satisfied with the correction, he closed his index finger over the trigger in the right-hand grip. A shell boomed out from the cannon, and Stewart saw the water plume up from the port side of the tanker.

He had them bracketed.

MV <u>ANDES COMMERCE</u>

The tanker's bridge was a scene of chaos as terrified crewmen rushed to the ladders and the illusory safety of belowdecks. Their yelling was periodically drowned out by the sound of the *Bulke-*

ley's gunfire and the resultant explosions drawing ever closer to their ship.

Hauser was standing near the center of the bridge when the next shell impacted near them. This one fell just beyond the port bridgewing, mirroring the placement of the shell that had just showered water and bits of steel on the tanker's starboard wing. The terrible significance struck Hauser as he watched the plume of water douse the port wing.

"Holy God . . ." Hauser's voice trailed off. He slowly crossed his now-all-but-deserted bridge, walking as if in a trance.

Kalil vaulted from the ladder trunk onto the bridge, almost colliding with Hauser in his haste. "I will destroy them!" he screamed as he raced past Hauser toward the starboard bridgewing.

Ignoring Kalil, the master of the *Andes Commerce* hoisted himself mechanically into his captain's chair—to wait.

THE BULKELEY

Stewart corrected back carefully to his left, splitting the distance between the aim point of the last two rounds. He pulled the trigger again, and this time he was rewarded by the sight of a puff of smoke erupting from the tanker's fo'c'sle. The sound of the high-explosive round detonating echoed back to him from across the water.

The gun was on target.

Stewart knew there was no turning back. If he held the trigger down now, the gun would commence firing at its preset rate of forty rounds a minute. At first his body seemed to battle him, his right hand frozen on the grip. But in the end, he forced the thought of Kim from his mind and his index finger closed on the trigger.

MV ANDES COMMERCE

The first two shells struck the tanker's bridge superstructure. Kalil barely managed to maintain his balance on the bridgewing as the first round impacted the bridge behind him. He braced himself against the rail as the second, closer explosion sent a shudder through the bridge, raining glass and bits of metal onto his back. Pulling the second detonator from its pouch, Kalil suddenly noticed the change in the sound of the *Bulkeley*'s cannon: the gun now sounded more like a machine gun. The Guards Commander forced himself to ignore the change in the gun's tempo and the deadly blasts that were practically on top of him. He yanked out the detonator's antenna, flicked on the power switch, and pointed the lethal device toward the *Bulkeley*.

"God is great!" Kalil yelled out over the chaos around him.

The third round struck a flammables locker adjacent to the bridge. The ensuing explosion seemed to wash over him from behind. The red hot wave of gases and molten steel grew hotter and more furious, igniting him with it.

THE **BULKELEY**

Stewart saw the tanker's bridge erupt into a volcanic pyre. As successive rounds crashed into the helpless merchantman, the devastation grew worse. Explosion built upon explosion, as the deadly shells ripped into fuel and machinery spaces. Finally, close to the end of the thirty rounds that Stewart had triggered, a detonation sent a geyser of flame shooting hundreds of feet into the air.

Stewart released the trigger and stepped back from the TDT. He wanted to look away—to look at anything else—but the stark, awful beauty of the sight was mesmerizing. The *Andes Commerce* was on fire from stem to stern, the great flames lighting up half of Bahrain Harbor.

Beach turned to Stewart and was about to speak when he caught himself. The dampness around Stewart's black-ringed eyes might have been caused by his intense concentration while his face was pressed against the black rubber eyepieces of the TDT.

Then again, Beach reflected, they might not.

BAHRAIN HARBOR

The steaming morning heat pressed down on the crowded harbor, offering no mercy to those on the water. The *Bulkeley* stood at anchor near the center of the harbor.

Stewart ignored the heat on the bridgewing as he continued to stare across the expanse of the harbor at the still-smoking hulk of the *Andes Commerce*. He had been on the bridge for over twenty hours, and the exhaustion did nothing to take Kim from his thoughts. Stewart looked down and saw the stream of personnel boats continuing back and forth between *Bulkeley* and the *Pascagoula*. Boone had insisted that the frigate anchor well clear of the flagship—in fact, away from all other shipping—until the EOD team had disarmed her still-lethal explosive payload.

Watching the boats, Stewart thought back to the night before. It had been some time after his shelling of the tanker before the patrol boats had ventured close enough to find out what had happened on the ship. He had explained their situation to an officer on one of the boats, shouting across the water through a megaphone. His statements and the presence of Beach beside him on the bridge had finally convinced them that it was safe to approach.

The patrol boats had provided them with a portable secure radio, and they had quickly gotten in touch with COM JTF. It was then that Stewart was told how close the other Navy ships had come to taking *Bulkeley* under fire when he had opened up on the tanker. That was one thing he had not thought of. But there had been no alternative—or so he kept trying to convince himself. Boone had believed their flashing light message in the end, and that had saved them.

Once the *Bulkeley* had anchored, the first boats had been alongside in minutes. They had brought the explosive ordnance disposal team, as well as additional security forces to help the SEALS scour the ship for any remaining Iranians. A boatload of medical personnel had arrived after them to care for the wounded.

Stewart watched another boat head back to the *Pascagoula*. He knew that all the wounded, including the XO, had been transported to the flagship. But the dead remained on the *Bulkeley*. The Captain, Chief Marquez, and many others were gone; the courageous young damage controlman, Andy Barron, who had apparently done much to disrupt the Iranians, had been found dead in repair locker two. The medical officer had told Stewart that Mosopu might make it; he was apparently too tough to kill. The same had not been true of his opponent. The SEALS had found the twisted, broken body of the giant Iranian Sergeant Major in the passageway outside Radio Central.

Follow-on boats had delivered a party of damage controlmen. They had ensured that the smoldering fire on the flight deck was permanently extinguished and had quickly cut through the welds that had trapped most of the crew in the coops. The damage controlmen had been taken aback to find the *Bulkeley*'s crew, led by Master Chief Rimes and heavily armed with makeshift weapons, spoiling for a fight. It had taken them some time to convince the crew that the Iranians really were gone and that the threat was past.

"John, you better catch one of these next couple of boats if you want to make that meeting on the flagship."

Jack Nelson's voice came from behind Stewart on the bridge, snapping him out of his bleak reverie. He turned slowly to face the other officer. Nelson had a look of deep concern on his face.

Stewart knew he had a detailed debriefing scheduled with Admiral Boone on the *Pascagoula* at 0900. But it meant nothing to him.

"Thanks, Jack," he said emotionlessly. Stewart walked past Nelson, without looking at him, and into the bridge. He had his foot on the top rung of the ladder, when he heard the bridge-to-bridge radio that the *Pascagoula*'s technicians had jury-rigged crackle to life.

"Colt Sabre, this is PB Six Hundred. Over."

Stewart recognized the voice of Fraser, the patrol boat officer who had been so helpful to them the night before. As Nelson crossed the bridge to the radio, Stewart waved him off.

"I'll talk to him, Jack," he said flatly. He went to the radio and picked up the handset. "PB Six Hundred, this is Colt Sabre. Roger. Over."

"This is PB Six Hundred. Is Lieutenant Commander Stewart available? Over."

"Speaking. Go ahead."

"Stewart, this is Fraser. I'm inbound on your port beam. Can you come out on the wing?"

Puzzled by the request but too exhausted to be inquisitive, Stewart decided to comply.

"I'm on my way. Out."

Stewart put down the microphone and picked up the megaphone he had used the night before. He had done most of his talking with Fraser from the port wing. He wondered what was so serious that Fraser did not want to use the clear VHF circuit. Stewart crossed the bridge and stepped out on the wing. He saw Fraser's Mark III patrol boat a hundred yards off and approaching at high speed.

Whatever this is, Stewart thought, it's got Fraser pretty worked up.

As he watched from the rail, the patrol boat cut its engines and slewed into an expert turn that brought it to a stop just below the *Bulkeley*'s port wing. Stewart leaned out over the rail, looking down, waiting for Fraser to come out of the pilothouse.

The figure that stepped out of the pilothouse would never have been mistaken for Fraser. The navy blanket draped over her did not conceal the woman's reddish-brown hair. Kim looked up at him and smiled, and Stewart had to grip the life rail for support as the surprise of seeing her shook his already exhausted body. She waved to him and said something he could not hear over the noise of the boat's engines.

Pulling away from the rail, Stewart set a new *Bulkeley* record for going from the bridgewing to the weather deck.

THE <u>PASCAGOULA</u>

"That's the goddamnedest story I've ever heard," Boone said, a note of awe in his voice.

"That's the way it happened, Admiral. I'm not sure I believe it either."

Stewart sat across from Admiral Boone in the packed flag mess, trying to stay awake in the too comfortable chair. The silence in the space reflected the attention the assembled officers had given to his recitation of the events on the *Bulkeley*.

"And they never told you their ultimate goal?" the Admiral asked.

"Not until the very end, sir. When the Iranian major was dying." Stewart straightened up in his chair, battling the exhaustion that threatened to overcome him. "Of course, they had every reason for not wanting us to know. Men who are guaranteed of dying lose even the slightest motivation to cooperate."

"We don't know how the Iranians will react when they learn they failed to destroy the flagship," Commander Kelly interjected from across the table.

"I'll leave that to you intel boys to predict," Boone said gruffly. "What matters to us right now is that they seized an American ship and killed American sailors."

"Were any of the reporters killed or injured?" Lacey asked.

Stewart grew more alert at this question. "Fortunately no, Captain. They made it through all right. The woman reporter, Kim Mitchell, had a scary night clinging to a piece of floating wreckage in the harbor, but the water was warm enough so she came through it okay."

"I've got my people debriefing the journalists," Kelly said. "Their principal interest now that the shock is wearing off seems to be in filing their stories."

"Well, they've got a helluva scoop," Boone said, returning his attention to Stewart. "From what you've told us, it appears we owe that young woman a considerable debt of gratitude."

"She did as much as any of us to save the ship, Admiral," Stewart said quietly.

The distinctive tone of the Admiral's private interphone rang out in the flag mess, and Boone reached under the table for the handset.

"Admiral." He listened for a moment. "I understand. Tell them I'll have an answer for them in two hours." He replaced the phone.

"Another operation to plan," he said, directing the statement to everyone in the space.

"Admiral," Stewart said, "if you don't require my presence any longer, I'd like to get back to *Bulkeley* and assess the extent of damage."

Boone smiled. "We can take it from here, son. You head back and take care of your ship."

"Aye, sir."

Boone turned to Garmisch, who had been listening to the briefing in silence. "Jim, how 'bout escorting Lieutenant Commander Stewart to the quarterdeck and seeing that he gets on the next boat out."

"Will do, Admiral."

As the two officers rose to leave, Boone addressed Stewart again. "Are you command-qualified, Lieutenant Commander Stewart?"

"Yes sir, as of six months ago."

Boone gave the Chief of Staff a quick glance and then returned his gaze to Stewart.

"Consider yourself acting commanding officer of *Bulkeley* until we assign a replacement for Captain Donelli."

Stewart straightened up almost to attention. This was not the way he had wanted to achieve command, but there it was.

"Aye-aye, Admiral."

"Oh, and Stewart," Boone added, "the operation we're about to plan will pay those bastards back in part for your ship and shipmates."

Stewart nodded his understanding and headed out of the mess, following Garmisch. The staff set to work before the two men were out the door.

Stewart followed Garmisch through the unfamiliar passageways of the *Pascagoula* in silence. When they stepped through a watertight door and into the noonday sunlight, Stewart was glad to see a personnel boat alongside, preparing to ferry a group of hull technicians over to the *Bulkeley*. Garmisch stopped just short of the accommodation ladder and turned to Stewart. "There you go. Have a safe trip back."

"Thanks," Stewart replied. As he crossed in front of Garmisch to reach the ladder, the other officer spoke again.

"Stewart . . . I'm sorry about your captain, sorry about your ship. I wish we could have done something to prevent this."

Stewart turned to study Garmisch. The staff officer's troubled look reflected his sincerity.

"It was our ship," Stewart said quietly. "We let them get on board her—nobody else." He offered his hand to Garmisch. "You guys did your job. Thanks again."

Stewart turned and headed down the accommodation ladder. He took a seat in the after part of the boat just as the small craft got under way. There was a light breeze, and for some reason the Gulf heat did not feel quite so oppressive to him as it had before.

The personnel boat passed out of the shadow of the massive flagship and headed across the harbor toward the *Bulkeley*. Stewart's eyes were fixed upon the wounded frigate from the moment she came into view. The scars of the patrol boat's gunfire and of the battles that had taken place on board became ever more evident as the boat drew closer to the ship.

Stewart catalogued the various points of damage in his mind, making up a prioritized list of which spaces he should visit first. He saw the davit was still deployed over the side from its lowering of the motor whaleboat the night before. That sight immediately reminded Stewart of Kim. They had agreed to meet again once their respective debriefings were completed and the attendant commotion had subsided. He was not sure what the future held for them, but he knew the bitterness of their past was now ancient history.

Alone with his thoughts, Stewart relished the sea breeze and occasional rain of spray as he returned to his ship.

EPILOGUE

A t 0600 on the following day, approximately fifty hours after
the *Bulkeley* was originally seized, Operation Swift Sword
was initiated.

At that hour the first of four Tomahawk land-attack cruise
missiles was launched from the battleship *Wisconsin*, operating in
the North Arabian Sea. The four conventional-warhead cruise
missiles tracked north at subsonic speed, making landfall along
the southern coast of Iran. The terrain-matching radar guidance
system of the lead Tomahawk correlated physical landmarks on
the Iranian coast with its computer memory and automatically
adjusted course toward its target. At 0615, the first Tomahawk
arrived over its target, the military airfield at Bandar Abbas. Flying at an altitude of two hundred feet, the Tomahawk released
a shower of explosive bomblets over the hardened runways.
A hundred small explosions reduced the runways to useless,
pockmarked asphalt. The second Tomahawk released a similar
cloud of bomblets over the exposed jet park holding ready-action
F-4 and F-14 fighters. The last two Tomahawks struck at the con-
crete-reinforced hangar revetment that housed the bulk of the
Iranian military aircraft at Bandar Abbas. The high-explosive
thousand-pound Bullpup warheads of the two missiles detonated, collapsing the hangar structure.

Simultaneous with the strike on Bandar Abbas, A-6 Intruder
and F/A-18 Hornet attack aircraft from the carrier *Theodore Roose-*

velt struck the Iranian navy base on Abu Musa Island. Although the Iranians were anticipating retaliation, their defenses were not sufficient against the strike. Laser-guided bombs devastated the warehouses, shops, and barracks of the base. A combination of laser-guided and cluster-bombs shredded the base's two large piers, along with numerous small craft tied up alongside them. After-action photos by one of the A-6s would confirm that a number of Boghammer gunboats had been among the craft destroyed.

At 0630 the destroyer *Daniels* and the frigate *Manchester* conducted a coordinated Harpoon missile strike on the Saam frigate *Abaland*, which was operating in the Straits of Hormuz. The first three Harpoons struck the *Abaland*; the fourth impacted on its sinking wreckage.

In reaction to the attack on the *Abaland*, a force of twenty Revolutionary Guard gunboats headed out into the Straits from the port of Bandar Abbas. When the gunboat flotilla closed to within five miles of the *Daniels* and the *Manchester*, the warships opened fire with their guns. A second strike group of aircraft, airborne over the Gulf of Oman in a ready status, was called in by the ships. Naval gunfire from the ships, combined with bombs and cannon fire from the ready-strike aircraft, sunk or damaged fifteen of the RevGuard boats.

No subsequent attempt was made to seize an American ship.